In Earth's Service

Also by Stephen Renneberg

THE MAPPED SPACE UNIVERSE

The Mothership
The Mothersea

The Antaran Codex
The Riven Stars

SF/TECHNOLOGICAL THRILLERS

The Siren Project
The Kremlin Phoenix

In Earth's Service

Stephen Renneberg

Author website
www.StephenRenneberg.com

ISBN: 978-0-9941840-0-9

Illustration © Tom Edwards
www.TomEdwardsDesign.com

For Elenor, with love

Mapped Space Chronology

3.4 Million Years Ago to 6000 BC
Earth's Stone Age (GCC 0).

6000 BC to 1750 AD
Pre-Industrial Civilization (GCC 1).

1750 - 2130
The rise of Planetary Industrial Civilization (GCC 2).
The First Intruder War – unknown to mankind.
   The Mothership
Start of the Blockade.
   The Mothersea

2130 - 2643
The spread of Interplanetary Civilization (GCC 3) throughout the Solar System.

2629
Marineris Institute of Mars (MIM) perfects the first stable Spacetime Distortion Field (the superluminal bubble).
The MIM discovery leads to the dawn of Inceptive Interstellar Civilization (GCC 4).

2615
The Solar Constitution ratified, establishing Earth Council (15 June 2615).

2644
First human ship reaches Proxima Centauri and is met by a Tau Cetin Observer.

2645
Earth Council signs the Access Treaty with the Galactic Forum.
First Probationary Period begins.

Tau Cetins provide astrographic data out to 1,200 light years from Earth (*Mapped Space*) and 100 kilograms of novarium (Nv, Element 147) to power human starships.

2646 - 3020

Human Civilization expands rapidly throughout Mapped Space.

Continual Access Treaty infringements delay mankind's acceptance into the Galactic Forum.

3021

Dr. Anton Krenholtz discovers Spacetime Field Modulation.

Krenholtz Breakthrough enables transition to Incipient Interstellar Civilization (GCC 5).

3021 - 3154

Mass migration dramatically increases human colonial populations.

3154

Human religious fanatics, opposed to interstellar expansion, attack the Mataron Homeworld.

Tau Cetin Observers prevent the Mataron Fleet from destroying Earth.

3155

Galactic Forum suspends human interstellar access rights for 1,000 years (the Embargo).

3155 - 3158

Tau Cetin ships convert human supplies of novarium held in Earth stockpiles and within ship energy plants to inert matter (as human ships landed at habitable planets).

3155 - 4155

Human contact with other interstellar civilizations ends.
Many human outposts beyond the Solar System collapse.

4126

Earth Navy established by the Democratic Union to police mankind when Embargo is lifted.
Earth Council assumes control of Earth Navy.

4138

Earth Intelligence Service (EIS) established by the Earth Council.

4155

The Embargo ends.
The Access Treaty is reactivated, permitting human interstellar travel to resume.
The second 500 year Probationary Period begins.

4155 - 4267

Earth re-establishes contact with its surviving colonies.

4281

Earth Council issues Sanctioned Worlds Decree, protecting collapsed human societies.

4310

The Beneficial Society of Traders established to manage interstellar trade.

4498

Quantum Instability Neutralization discovered (much earlier than galactic powers expected).
Mankind becomes Emergent Civilization (GCC 6).
The golden age of human interstellar trade begins.

4605

    The Vintari Incident.
       The Antaran Codex

4606

    The Battle of Tresik Prime.
    End of the Blockade.
       In Earth's Service

4607

    The Nan Chen Disaster.
    The Xil Asseveration.
       The Riven Stars

Notes:

    GCC: Galactic Civilization Classification system.
    Asseveration: A solemn or emphatic declaration.

Chapter One : Krailo-Nis

Nisk colony world
Nisk Draconis System, Outer Draco
0.94 Earth Normal Gravity
918 light years from Sol
112 Billion Coleopterans

Krailo-Nis was just as I remembered: bleak gray skies, distant dark mountains, mud and fungus as far as the eye could see and the kind of gloom only giant cave-dwelling bugs could love.

It was a depressing sight from the elevated platform that a pair of semi-intelligent Nisk drones had pushed up to the port airlock as soon as the *Silver Lining* had landed. Now, with a light breeze blowing drizzling rain onto my face, the two drones watched me from the ground, oblivious to the water beading on their outer shells or the mud sloshing around their six long black legs.

Beyond the drones was a drab, rain soaked landing

ground occupied by dozens of alien ships – none of them Nisk. Their ships didn't land here, partly because they were too big, mostly because they didn't like mixing with bipeds. That's why they landed outside the security barrier and never within sight of the spaceport. They didn't build many ships, but the ones they did were behemoths. Just one nestship would have taken up the entire landing ground by itself, or so the Beneficial Society's briefing notes said. It had something to do with Nisk mentality: if they went anywhere, it was in enormous numbers packed inside single ships.

I guess they liked the company.

Not that you would know it from Nisport. It wasn't a bug town. It was an enclave set aside exclusively for alien visitors. At the edge of the landing field was a rundown, one level, rectangular terminal, utilitarian to the point of ugliness. Beyond the terminal was a collection of dilapidated, dirty buildings, all non-Nisk design. If you wanted to trade with the Nisk, you had to bring your own buildings. That's why most structures were self erecting prefabs, functional with minimal visible comforts. Only a few were lavish structures designed to impress, an effort wasted on giant beetles with no appreciation of architectural aesthetics.

The force barrier surrounding the enclave wasn't for our protection, but to ensure we didn't go poking around where we weren't wanted. Not that the Nisk were xenophobes. They didn't fear or hate aliens, they simply preferred to keep interactions with other species to a minimum. Considering the instinctive human revulsion for bugs of any sort – let alone giant creepy crawlies – I was happy to respect their wishes.

Even if I wanted to explore, there wasn't much to

see. Nisport was the only settlement on the surface of a seemingly primitive world shrouded in endless gray cloud. On every continent, forbidding mountains rose from quagmire plains and murky rivers emptied into dark oceans – all tectonically engineered by the industrious Nisk. From orbit, Krailo-Nis appeared to be a damp wasteland rather than home to more than a hundred *billion* sentient beings, none of whom lived on the surface.

They inhabited an enormous subterranean world-city that honeycombed the planet's crust while the surface had been engineered to provide an ideal habitat for the fungus and blue green algae that covered Krailo-Nis. The genetically engineered surface life clung to every rock, choked every waterway and saturated every ocean, producing the vast quantities of food and oxygen required by its inhabitants. It was why Krailo-Nis's atmosphere contained more oxygen than Earth's, produced by a fraction of the biomass and why I wore a respirator over my nose and mouth to avoid oxygen toxicity.

A few human ambassadors had been permitted down into the subterranean galleries to present their credentials, but generally visitors weren't allowed below ground. We were free to land at Nisport, providing we completed our business and were gone in three days. The restrictions were partly due to the demand for landing rights by so many races and partly because the Nisk weren't that interested in trade. They were, after all, one of the most self sufficient species in the galaxy.

Fortunately for us, they had a sweet tooth.

They loved sugar and honey, the only products the human race had which held any interest for the giant beetles. It was why the *Silver Lining's* cargo hold and the three vacuum-radiation-sealed containers we towed were packed full of brown sugar. In return, we'd get ten kilograms of niskgel, a gelatinous solution secreted by royals, their highest caste. It was gram for gram one of the most expensive luxury products in Mapped Space. Human pharmaceutical companies turned it into anti-aging creams with seemingly miraculous powers, yet try as we might, we couldn't synthesize the stuff ourselves. We suspected it had something to do with the super fungus they ate, but they wouldn't sell us a sample at any price, so we couldn't be sure. They said it was for our own protection because their mega-fungi could double as an invincible bioweapon able to turn habitable worlds into fungal swamps in the blink of an eye. Likewise for the blue-green super algae, which could raise any world's oxygen content to toxic levels. Maybe it was true or maybe they just wanted to protect their monopoly. Either way, guys like me lugged tons of sugar to what the Nisk considered a remote outpost for a few kilos of gooey gold – only I wasn't really here for niskgel.

Jase Logan, my copilot, would handle the cargo drop. Nisk drones would check its quality and weight, then load a precisely measured quantity of niskgel in return. Normally we'd boost and bubble in twelve hours, only I'd punctured the vacuum seals on some of the sugar containers, deliberately contaminating their contents to slow down the dimwitted drones. Anything out of the ordinary and they'd call for an attendant to assess the situation. I hoped the ensuing argument would keep us on the ground for our allotted three days, just in case my contact was late.

At least that was the plan.

A mechanical whine sounded as the *Silver Lining's* belly door opened down to form a ramp to the ground and the three VRS containers astern were lowered by their supporting gantries. Five drones immediately scuttled forward, mindlessly tramping mud through our internal hold as they began unloading the cargo.

The Nisk were, by all accounts, a respected and peaceful member of the Galactic Forum, the only sentient coleopterans in Mapped Space, yet the sight of them made my skin crawl. It was all those legs scuttling beneath dead black eyes. Perhaps that's why they kept their mostly bipedal visitors in a walled enclosure, because they knew how we felt. Or maybe they felt the same way about us?

They didn't use bots of any kind. They'd rather breed drones than waste resources on machines. It wasn't a technological limitation, but a cultural preference. Ninety percent of the planet's population were drones. The rest were mostly attendants whose primary purpose was to supervise the workforce and see to the safety and comfort of a few million royals. No human ambassador had ever laid eyes on a royal and probably never would. We dealt with attendants who were the organizers of their society, the arbiters of law, the engineers and scientists and when required, the commanders of the mighty Nisk military. Attendants and royals were both highly intelligent, well above human norms, while the drones were about a third below. The aesthetic royals did the breeding and created endless geometric artworks that made no sense to humans, but were highly regarded by the diligent attendants. There was no system of government as we understood it, just biologically determined roles and duties according to physical caste.

Krailo-Nis alone contained more than three times as many Nisk as there were humans in all of Mapped

5

Space and as best as we could determine, its industrial capacity dwarfed Human Civilization's total output. Yet to the Nisk, Krailo-Nis was a remote, relatively unimportant backwater, the only one of its kind in the Orion Arm. We didn't know where their homeworld was or how many colonies they had scattered across the galaxy, only that they were somewhat detached from galactic life. One could only wonder what the galaxy's fate might have been if they'd been an aggressive species, or what would happen to anyone who unwisely provoked them, Access Treaty or not. If ever there was a sleeping giant in our midst, it was the industrious, unassuming Nisk.

Leaving the russet colored drones to their work, I rode the elevated platform's gravity slide down to the mud then hurried across to the terminal for processing. Before landing, I'd been required to transmit profiles of everyone aboard: me, Jase and Izin. I didn't know if the Nisk had been attacked during the Intruder War and carried a grudge against Izin's race, but if they did, they showed no sign of it.

I stepped inside a doorless arch high and wide enough for two Nisk, then a drone scanned me, confirming my identity. It was a meter taller than me with six multi-jointed legs and two slender antenna-manipulator arms. Its thick mandible turned in my direction and spoke through a vocalizer. "Sirius Kade Human of Silver Lining ship, why bring you weapon projectile into Nisk zone open?" it asked in an oddly composed version of Unionspeak.

I glanced at the MAK P-50 holstered at my hip. I'd strapped it on out of habit, not because I expected trouble, although doing pick-ups for Lena Voss – my Earth Intelligence Service controller – always carried risk. "It's for self defense only."

"Sirius Kade Human of Silver Lining ship, weapons firing in Nisk zone open prohibited."

I looked up at the drone, waiting for more, but it just stood staring at me. I shifted uncomfortably, feeling as if the massive coleopteran was considering eating me whole. "I understand."

The drone turned back to its console, making no attempt to confiscate my weapon. After a moment, it handed me a small gray disk inlaid with symmetrical intersecting lines. "Sirius Kade Human to retain identifier locator at times all." It fixed its impenetrable eyes upon me, waiting.

"Will do," I said, realizing the drone not only lacked conversation, but was operating at the limit of its ability.

"Sirius Kade Human, entry temporary to Nisk zone open approved," it said, then promptly ceased to recognize my existence.

Free to proceed, I started across a floor tramped with the muddy footprints of a thousand alien species, suspecting the concept of cleaning had been omitted from the simpleton drone's training. The terminal was a picture of Nisk minimalism with none of the amenities found in human spaceports, just bare walls and a roof over our heads.

Dozens of nonhumans milled around in small groups inside the terminal, casting furtive glances at each other and at the drizzle and mud outside. None wanted to be here a second longer than necessary and by the way some glanced at the big drones, they were as uncomfortable trading with giant beetles as I was. My implanted DNA sniffer area-scanned them all, confirming they were mostly Orion Arm species mixed with a few unknowns from further afield. A couple wore full environment suits preventing line of sight

DNA scanning, although none paid me any attention.

Outside the terminal, two armed sentry drones and a handful of aliens sheltered from the drizzle under a wide awning, more interested in the town than a solitary human passing through. Their lack of curiosity reassured me that this was going to be another routine data pick-up.

I'd received Lena's request nine days ago. She'd said it was a simple retrieve and run, nothing more than a minor detour. I only needed brief physical contact with her agent – a handshake would be enough – then I'd be gone. Nothing I hadn't done a dozen times before, barely worth my fee as a freelancer, especially considering the extra credits the niskgel would bring in. For all the Nisk knew or cared, I was just another biped seeking to profit off the vanity of my species. Even Jase and Izin had no inkling of my true motives for visiting bug central. It had been tricky at times, but I'd managed to keep my EIS sideline hidden from them for a year now. I didn't like lying to them, but it wasn't called deep cover for nothing.

This far from Sol, the only human law was an Earth Navy frigate, and they were rare. There were plenty of alien ships of course and alien worlds, even some big ones, but most were off limits to humans for at least another forty nine years. Once we earned Forum Membership, becoming formally recognized Galactic Citizens, a lot of closed doors would open for humanity providing we didn't screw up. It was all on our shoulders, our responsibility, to prove we could respect galactic law as enshrined in the Access Treaty. That was no small task considering the horde of bottom feeders looking for fast credits far from Earth. And while there was no one to help us, there were plenty watching, waiting for us to fail – again. While most alien governments would report any breach, none would lift a finger to help or take any part in policing mankind.

Nor should they. That was Lena's job – and mine.

Summoning an image of Nisport's grid-like layout into my mind's eye from my threaded memory, I crossed the mud splattered metal grating that passed for a road and headed south toward a small cluster of human prefabs a kilometer away. They contained the Earth Council embassy, a tiny Beneficial Society of Traders office that managed our barter deals with the Nisk and sleeping quarters and stores for both. There were no support facilities typical of human trade bases – no repair docks, bars, merchants, stim dealers or brothels. The Nisk refused to allow anyone to establish permanent bases in the Nisk Draconis System because with such a large population concentrated in one place, a single planet busting attack could have devastated their civilization in this part of the galaxy.

Mankind were the opposite of the Nisk. We spread through Mapped Space like an expanding cloud while they scattered their seed across the galaxy in a handful of super dense pebbles. They might have been the insects, but we acted more like a swarm. Our population was scattered so thinly across approximately two thousand four hundred light years of space that we could have lost a hundred colonies without any impact on our civilization – except for Earth itself. If anything happened to mankind's ancient birth world, all the rest would wither and many would die. It would be that way for thousands of years to come. The Human Exodus might well be in full swing, but Earth would remain preeminent and irreplaceable for a long time to come.

It was the speed with which humanity – the

youngest, least technologically advanced interstellar civilization in the galaxy – was spreading that irritated some. We were driven by a restless, energetic need to expand, to seek opportunity, protected by incomprehensibly ancient galactic law. It was why we were everywhere we could reach, constrained only by the extent of the astrographic charts the Tau Cetins had gifted us, charts that revealed billions of navigational hazards whose gravitational influences could destroy superluminal ships in a nanosecond. Beyond those charts, navigation was so hazardous that the risks of interstellar travel far outweighed the benefits. In half a century, that would change. As full members of the Forum, we'd have access to so much more, allowing the human swarm to flood out toward the limits of a new, redefined Mapped Space – not the entire galaxy, but a larger fraction of it.

It was why I did what I did, why I was here now, hurrying through Nisport's grubby side streets. They were almost deserted, except for a few alien travelers wrapped against the misty rain and the occasional mud splattered surface vehicle that splashed sidewalks without regard for pedestrians. A discordant jumble of grimy, alien buildings lined the streets: towers, domes, squat windowless boxes and a variety of metallic structures reflecting alien designs from across the Orion Arm and beyond, all affixed with sensors and communications gear. The inhabitants of Krailo-Nis's alien enclave might not have been able to make themselves comfortable, but they all spied on each other and the Nisk with equal enthusiasm.

When I was almost halfway there, my listener flashed a yellow marker into my mind's eye, warning of a persistent sound behind me. My DNA sniffer hadn't detected any biomarkers, but the highly sensitive bionetics pervading my auditory senses had picked up footsteps on the road's metal grating. They mimicked my movements, speeding up and slowing down as I did. It was unlikely anyone could have been waiting for me in Nisport, considering even I hadn't known I was coming here ten days ago, yet I didn't believe in coincidences.

I stopped at the next corner, looking around as if lost. The listener's contact marker stopped too, then my shadow vanished behind a building and waited. I didn't look back, not wanting to alert my tail he'd been spotted, but continued on toward the rendezvous point.

Lena's agent was scheduled to visit the Beneficial Society's office on the hour, to pick-up any personal messages they were holding for him and review available work hire contracts on offer at the Exchange. It gave us a reason to cross paths without drawing suspicion, to unexpectedly meet as old friends. Now I had to decide whether to abort or risk exposing her agent. A tail meant someone had penetrated the mission, but who? It could only be someone from Lena's side, but she was mega-psi. No one could lie to her and live.

Or could they?

I turned down a side street, hoping to throw off my tail, but the listener's yellow marker appeared again showing he was still with me, even though he couldn't see me directly. He had to be tracking me with tech, something no street corner thug would do. With the rendezvous only minutes away and a teched-up tracker on my tail, I knew I'd risk exposing Lena's agent if I made contact. To protect his identity, I'd have to abandon him – not something I wanted to do if I could possibly avoid it.

At the next corner, the human prefabs came into

view, a collection of white towers five stories high banded by dark strip windows. They were cleaner and newer than any of the alien buildings, some of which had stood in Nisport gathering grime for millennia. No attempt had been made to hide the eavesdropping sensors atop the towers because such efforts were pointless. Even so, while our tech was bottom rung, we listened in on everyone else with as much vigor as the best of them. The embassy housed an EIS intercept team, all techs, not threaded field agents like me, which was why Lena couldn't use them for data retrieval. No bionetics meant no handshake transfers, and besides, embassy attachés were far more noticeable than shabby Society traders.

I was about to turn away when my listener surprised me. It had been crunching numbers on the sonic data, analyzing the ring of metallic boots on the road's grating, measuring the time delay between footfalls to determine stride length and height and calculating the intensity of the sound to estimate body mass. It now flashed a message into my mind's eye.

WARNING: SONIC CONTACT BIO SIGNATURE UNCERTAIN. HUMAN UPPER LIMITS MARGINAL.

Clarify, I thought, stopping in my tracks.

HUMAN PROBABILITY 16%, NONHUMAN 84%.

If there'd been any chance I was going up against a nonhuman, Lena would have warned me, unless she hadn't known! I spun around, looking back down the street, hoping to verify what my listener was telling me. Two blocks away, a large man wearing a dark gray metallic body suit and a full face helmet darted behind a building with impressive speed. Whatever he was, he was fast for a big man, almost certainly genetically engineered if human. And his suit looked too heavy to be a pressure suit, too light to be human-tech body armor. Whatever it was, it was heavier than the synthweave I was wearing.

A hundred meters away, across a rectangular square, the stylized star chart insignia of the Beneficial Society glowed above a ground floor security door. I could have made it before my tail caught me, but that would have led him straight to Lena's agent. I wondered if I tried to eliminate my shadow, how long it would be before the place was crawling with security drones. They might be simpletons, but properly armed with bug-tech, Nisk drones would make formidable warriors. Definitely not critters I wanted to mess with.

That's when I decided the mission was a washout. Even the backup opportunity in twenty four hours was now impossible. I was simply too hot to risk a second attempt. There was nothing for it but to go back to the *Lining*, get out of Nisport fast and give Lena the bad news. Her agent was on his own, but at least he'd be alive.

I started east, intending to lead the large humanoid away from the rendezvous point. Before I'd gone ten paces, I heard footsteps running toward me from the direction of the human prefabs. A single heavy slug whistled by, striking a building behind me. For a moment I thought someone was shooting at me, then I saw a man dressed as a common spacer running from the Society's Exchange. Two men and a woman appeared further down the street from where they'd been hiding, waiting for the spacer to appear. All three carried JAG-40's, a military grade light assault weapon that fired heavy caliber slugs. They were special forces weapons, hard to control for the novice, deadly in the hands of experts.

In spite of the respirators the humans wore, my sniffer found enough flesh on their faces to get DNA reads on all of them. A red targeting reticule appeared around the face of the man at the center of the three pursuers, the only one listed on my threading's catalogue of cosmic criminals. He was Domar Trask, a stolid looking brute my height, with shoulders as wide as a heavy lifter and a military style buzz-cut. He was wanted by the Union Regular Army for capital crimes, but I didn't have time to study his record as he came charging up the street.

Trask lifted his JAG-40 to eye height and fired an expertly aimed shot that took the fleeing man in the shoulder, knocking him forward. The wounded man tucked and rolled fluidly back to his feet, continuing on with one arm hanging uselessly by his side. That recovery told me everything I needed to know. He was my EIS contact, engineered to survive, confirmed by my sniffer which projected a green targeting reticule around the agent's face. A moment later, white indicators appeared around the faces of Trask's two flankers, indicating they were clean skins on nobody's wanted list.

The fleeing agent's eyes locked onto mine with instant recognition. Neither of us had ever seen the other, but our sniffers knew our DNA codes in a heartbeat. My name flashed into his mind as his flashed into mine.

TIAGO SORVINO, OUTER-ZERO-SIXTY.

The Oh-Zero-Sixty Group was Lena's team, my team, responsible for a vast region from zero north to sixty degrees on the celestial sphere, beyond five hundred light years from Earth. It was an immense region where two deep cover agents rarely met, and never like this.

My contact feigned a stumble, telling his pursuers he was weakening even though his face was flushed and alert. It was a look I knew well. His bionetic implants were overriding his bodily functions, pumping adrenalin through his system, giving him a surge of strength and speed that allowed him to drive through the pain. The tell tale whine of a JAG-40 charging filled the street, then the wounded agent rolled expertly to the side as the woman fired. Her slug whistled past as my contact came to his feet and sprinted again, lining up to pass close by me. Dodging and running like that, with a slug in his shoulder, told me he was ultra-reflexed – the same genetic engineering specialty I had.

I knew he was unarmed, otherwise he'd be shooting back. My hand dropped to my P-50 as I calculated distances and angles. His three pursuers were spread across the street in a skirmish line, firing like experts, advancing together, demonstrating a mastery of close quarters combat that told me they weren't common criminals. With surprise on my side, I could kill one, but the other two would switch to me fast. I'd have to shoot and roll and shoot again and hope they weren't as sharp as they looked.

The fleeing agent saw my hand go to my gun and guessed my intentions. He gave me an imperceptible shake of the head, ordering me not to shoot, demanding I not reveal myself. It went against my instincts, but he was the agent on the ground. He knew the score. I knew nothing. I followed his command and moved my hand away from my gun, slipping into the guise of a confused bystander.

He nodded slightly, approving my move.

Two more tracer shots flashed past the agent's head. Each time he dodged, warned of the danger by his listener. He pretended to stagger as he neared me while I feigned surprise, standing awkwardly in his path. The agent tripped – on purpose – and stumbled into me, knocking me back as he raised his hand, reaching for my ear and the bionetic listener within it. I moved my head as if flinching, turning the side of my face toward him, then his hand slammed against my ear. He hung on for a vital second as the bionetic filaments in his palm linked with those beneath my skin. In that moment, he passed an encrypted data block into my system, then immediately deleted it from his own.

"Don't help me!" he whispered. "They'll kill you! Aleph-null!"

Aleph-null?

He pushed my head away roughly, knocking me aside as he continued running. I feigned a clumsy stumble and fell backwards onto the road as the agent drew his attackers away. In that moment, we both knew, my life and what I carried was more valuable than his.

Another slug caught him in the thigh, spinning him around. His ultra-reflexes took over again, allowing him to regain his balance and continue in a limping gait, barely slowed. His bionetic pain suppressers overrode muscles close to collapse, giving him time to lead the hit squad away.

I sat up slowly, holding my shoulder as if I'd been injured in the fall, watching him stagger away, resisting the temptation to turn and face the three killers running up behind me.

Domar Trask threw me a careless glance as he passed, unaware he was now chasing the wrong target. The female, tall and muscular, with close cropped blonde hair fired at the crippled agent without looking my way, then she was past me too keeping formation with Trask. A moment later, the stocky square-jawed grunt on the right, shorter than the other two, veered toward me and slammed the butt of his gun into the back of my head. I crashed face first onto the road's metal grid as threading alerts flashed into my unconscious mind, warning of critical bone damage.

Left for dead, I lay in the mud and rain, blood draining from a crushed skull, while two blocks away an unarmed EIS agent was gunned down for a secret he no longer carried, an encrypted message now locked deep inside my threaded memory.

* * * *

A muted cacophony of buzzing drowned out the ringing in my ears as consciousness slowly returned. I had a vague sense of floating, immobilized. When I opened my eyes, I found myself face down in the center of a cone of stark white light so bright I was forced to squint. I was suspended two meters from a stone floor in a chamber of rough hewn rock walls with openings to passageways filled with the chatter of billions of Nisk. Armed drones stood in the shadows watching while another smaller bug close to me worked on my shattered skull. My head was numb all the way to the base of my jaw and threading alerts flashed warnings of alien-tech intrusions I couldn't move a finger to stop.

The Nisk close to me touched my forehead with cold metal, a surprisingly delicate, precise touch that caused the last of the throbbing pain to fade away. It emitted a soft hissing sound, then moved toward one of the exits. I was no expert, but the smaller Nisk's shell was a lighter chestnut color indicating it belonged to one of the attendant castes. It carried metallic devices I didn't recognize in its manipulator arms and wore a telescopic instrument over one of its empty black eyes.

After the small Nisk had moved out of sight, an artificial voice sounded from the shadows. "Sirius Kade Human, your damage bone parietal is repaired."

I wanted to turn my head toward the voice, but the field holding me allowed only my eyes to move as another chestnut colored beetle ambled into view. It wore a vocalizer strapped to its mandible and slender strip-like devices on its antenna-manipulator arms. It moved in front of me, then the field rotated my body from the horizontal to the vertical, leaving my feet a meter off the floor and my face level with the attendant's bulging compound eyes. I suppressed my instinctive revulsion at the sight of it, reminding myself attendants were highly intelligent and – more importantly – in charge.

"I Katinuuk am, zone open controller. Report occurrence at five-intersect-twenty-one."

"Someone hit me," I replied, determined not to let the bugs catch and dissect the grunt who'd bashed in my skull. That was my job. "I didn't see who it was."

"Angular analysis indicates Sirius Kade Human struck from above-behind. Explain," it said, confirming the Nisk had not only fixed my cracked skull, but also conducted a forensic analysis of it.

"I was knocked down."

"By what?"

"Another man. It was an accident. He'd been shot and ran into me."

"Is Tiago Sorvino Human known to you?"

"Is that someone you arrested?" I said, feigning ignorance.

"Tiago Sorvino Human is dead. Killer unknown."

"I'm sorry to hear that," I said softly, meaning it. "I'd never seen him before today." According to my EIS deception training, the best way to conceal the truth was with the truth. I hoped it would be enough to hide the anger I felt that a good man was dead. The moment he'd ordered me not to shoot, we both knew he was going to die. He'd only made such a choice because he'd believed the information I now carried was worth more than his life.

Aleph-null!

"Describe Tiago Sorvino Human attackers."

"There were three of them. I didn't get a good look." I assumed I was only confirming what the Nisk already knew.

"Sirius Kade Human equipped with weapon primitive kinetic. Weapon not fired. Explain."

I glanced down at my holster. My MAK P-50 was missing. "That's right. I was told weapons couldn't be fired here. It happened so fast, I never got a chance to use it."

"Sirius Kade Human compliance with Nisk zone open directives noted," the Nisk investigator said, then it emitted a short popping sound.

A drone moved forward holding a metal tray which it slid into the suspension field surrounding me. It left it floating in front of me and backed away.

"Identify objects," Katinuuk ordered.

On the tray was a row of ten millimeter, polysteel jacketed, armor piercing slugs, one of the loads JAG-40 light assault guns were designed for. There were at least twenty of them, all twisted and bent out of shape. Those slugs could punch through two centimeters of durillium armor, not what I'd have selected for assassinating an unarmed spacer in street clothes, yet they'd hit something hard to be damaged like that.

"They're big ass slugs," I replied unhelpfully. "Too big for my gun."

"Projectiles kinetic are military human origin."

"I wouldn't know. I'm not in the military. Never was."

"Projectiles kinetic killed two drones security."

I tried to hide the sinking feeling in the pit of my stomach. The last thing mankind needed was to make the mighty galaxy spanning Nisk mad at us. We had enough trouble with the Matarons constantly plotting our destruction. It explained why Trask and his two clean skins were using armor piercing slugs, not to kill Sorvino but to eliminate any bugs that got in their way. Considering how many billions of Nisk were scurrying around just below the surface, ripping a few security drones apart took crazy guts, and they'd gotten away with it!

"Are you sure they're military?"

"Analysis doubt none."

"We sell those things to anyone, human or not."

"Non humans have use none for weapons kinetic."

Maybe not, but our primitive kinetic weapons had taken down two of their combat drones before they even knew what was happening. "Can you prove humans fired those slugs?"

"Knowledge none. Proof none. Sensors disrupted. Field interference active at five-intersect-twenty-one."

A cold chill ran down my spine. "What kind of interference field?"

"Counter-harmonic resonance."

It wasn't anything I'd ever heard of, which made it my ticket out of here.

"Do humans have such technology?" I asked, knowing the answer but wanting Katinuuk to acknowledge the obvious.

"No. Sirius Kade Human to identify weapon users."

"They were humanoid, maybe human. That's all I know."

Katinuuk studied me a moment, then made a short strumming sound. A drone retrieved the tray displaying the JAG-40 slugs, then I was lowered to the rock floor and freed from the suspension field.

"This drone security to guide Sirius Kade Human to surface. Landing rights revoked."

The attendant headed off into a tunnel as one of the drones near the rock wall approached me carrying my gun in one of its antenna-manipulators and a dull gray circular device in the other which it unceremoniously aimed at me. I holstered my P-50, then it motioned its weapon toward a tunnel to the right. The combat drone was not fitted with a vocalizer, so expecting no conversation, I moved in the direction indicated.

The tunnel was wide enough for two drones to pass each other comfortably and was lit by dull gray illuminator panels. Several times, the tunnel opened onto ramps leading down into vast galleries filled with multilayered metal frameworks linked by single arch bridges. They swarmed with tens of thousands of worker drones operating machines and carrying raw materials, parts and finished products. The industrial galleries were crowded and chaotic, yet frighteningly efficient. Each time I tried stopping to take in the frenetic activity, the security drone would motion for me to move, giving me no time to loiter.

Soon we were on a ramp leading up to a circular door which rose on four telescoping pylons. The drone stopped, sending me up toward the gray light. I emerged in the center of Nisport at an intersection of metal grill covered roads. The door lowered back in place behind me, melding into the center of the intersection as four men approached. They'd obviously been waiting for me to appear. The leader was well dressed and unarmed, while his companions wore dark clothes and aimed pistols at me.

"Captain Kade," the leader said. He was a swarthy, silver haired Indo with a short manicured beard and a diplomat's polite bearing. "I'm Ambassador Singh and you sir, are under arrest."

One of the Ambassador's security men reached down and retrieved my gun, unaware that the Nisk had unloaded it before returning it to me.

"While the Nisk normally do not allow weapons fire on their planet," Ambassador Singh informed me, "my security men are exempted from that law providing they shoot only humans. I trust that exemption will not need to be exercised in your case."

I smiled grimly and raised my hands in surrender.

* * * *

There were no holding cells in Nisport's tiny Earth Council embassy so with restraints on my wrists, I was ushered into the ambassador's well appointed office for questioning. Two guards stood watch while Ambassador Singh took his seat behind a modest simwood desk and activated a holofield displaying several official looking data forms.

"The Nisk proxy has advised me," Singh began, "that they have no direct evidence against you, however, they have lodged a formal complaint with Earth Council stating that human citizens have violated the terms of our concession. Do you know what that means?"

"No more niskgel anti-aging cream for the super rich?"

The Ambassador gave me a dark look. "It could cost us our landing rights. At worst, they may declare humans to have murdered two of their citizens. It would be up to the Forum to decide if that qualified as an Access Treaty violation which could very well extend our probationary period."

I was well aware of the consequences, although the lack of evidence would save us from any sanction and I suspected the royals cared more for our sugar than for the lives of two insignificant drones. Even so, any complaint to the Forum could complicate mankind's forthcoming admission to the Galaxy's big table.

"One of our citizens was also killed," I added.

"By Union Regular Army ammunition! Humans killing humans is our problem, no one else's, but humans killing nonhumans is another matter entirely!"

"They can't prove humans did the shooting."

"The charges pending against you are carrying a weapon in a prohibited nonhuman jurisdiction, being implicated in the deaths of one human and two nonhumans and damaging relations with a major nonhuman power. Should the Nisk lodge a protest with the Forum, additional charges related to initiating an Access Treaty infringement will be laid." He gave me a stern look. "These are serious charges, Captain Kade, charges that come with heavy penalties."

It could have been worse. Infringements bought mostly jail time. Only genuine violations were punishable by death.

"I'm an innocent victim in all this."

"You're a smuggler and a trouble maker," Singh said, unconvinced. "You'll be held here pending transportation to Draconis Station where a formal court of inquiry will be conducted by the appropriate authorities. Do you have anything to say?"

I considered telling him UniPol civil law orbitals were a little dull for my tastes and Draconis Station was no exception, but decided a more direct approach was needed. "I'd like to make a private statement." I glanced at the two guards meaningfully.

The Ambassador looked surprised. "My security team are fully apprised of the circumstances of this case and have full diplomatic clearance."

"I'm bashful," I said, making it clear I would not utter another word until the guards were gone.

Singh gave me an irritated look, then nodded for the guards to leave. When we were alone he touched a control on his desk, activating his holorecorder. "OK, what do you have to say?"

"No recorder."

Singh looked surprised. "I thought you wanted to make a statement?"

"I do, to you. Not to that," I said nodding to his recorder.

"This is highly irregular," he said, switching it off.

"Do you have an eidetic implant?"

Singh arched his brow curiously. "Of course."

Eidetic implants were standard equipment for senior diplomats. It allowed them to retain every document they read and every word of every conversation they heard with perfect accuracy for both diplomatic and intelligence gathering purposes.

"Good. Listen carefully." I retrieved a highly classified, fifty character recognition code stored deep within my bionetic memory and repeated it to the Earth Ambassador. The astonished look that appeared on his face was hardly surprising, considering he would never have received such a code in his life and never would again. "Check that against your diplomatic ciphers. Save yourself some time and start at the highest level." I leaned back, relaxing into the padded chair. "I'll wait."

He was gone less than ten minutes, returning with one of the guards. "Release him." When the guard gave the Ambassador a puzzled look, Singh added impatiently, "And give him back his weapon."

The guard removed my restraints and returned my P-50, then Singh nodded for him to leave. "I'm sorry, sir," he said, once the door closed. "I wasn't advised you were coming."

I sometimes took a perverse pleasure in pulling rank on self important bureaucrats, but the Ambassador had only been doing his duty as he understood it. "Nothing to apologize for. You weren't advised because of the sensitivity of my mission."

"Is there anything you require from me?"

"Yes. Recover Tiago Sorvino's body immediately." If we froze it and shipped it to Lena Voss, the regional EIS commander, her people could tap Sorvino's bionic memory and reconstruct his movements.

"I can't," Singh said uncomfortably. "The Nisk have already processed it."

"Processed?"

"When the Nisk die, they are rendered down into elementary biomatter for dispersal on the surface." He shrugged. "The Nisk are a remarkable species, but they have no regard for the customs of other races."

So the only clue as to what Tiago Sorvino had been doing was the encrypted data block locked in my bionetic memory. "Do you have an identity register?"

"Yes sir, updated monthly."

"How secure is this facility?"

"The entire embassy is protected by quantum suppression fields."

"No guarantee the Nisk can't penetrate that."

"Scrambling quantum signatures is the best we can do. If they can read through that…" he shrugged helplessly.

He was right and I was in a hurry. "I have three DNA scans I want checked. Your eyes only. Don't use any of your staff. Once the search is complete, give me the results and destroy all record of it. The name of one of the subjects is Domar Trask. I have nothing on the other two." If the Nisk saw what he was reading, it would do them no good. Trask's hit squad would already be long gone.

"I'll do it at once, sir." He gave me a curious look, clearly wondering if they were the three who'd killed Sorvino, but he had enough sense not to ask.

"And I need to send two messages."

"We get a fortnightly data sync. The update ship is due in four days. I could send them out with our diplomatic traffic."

"Good. And not a word of my visit, even to your superiors."

"What if the Nisk protest to the Forum?"

"That's no longer your problem."

"Yes sir," he said with a hint of relief. "Are you ready to record your messages?"

I nodded. "Switch off your eidetic implant."

"It's off," Singh confirmed, then activated his holorecorder.

"First message begins. To Marie Dulon, cargo ship Heureux, Jarris System. I've been delayed. Sorry. I'll make it up to you at our next scheduled meet. Try to keep out of trouble. Sirius." I'd been looking forward to seeing Marie for three months, but with a dead EIS agent on my hands and an encrypted data block in my bionetic memory, that was now impossible. She'd make me pay for standing her up, but I had no choice. "Message ends."

Singh closed the data recorder. "Is Marie Dulon also an EIS officer?"

"Definitely not," I replied with a smile. "Second message begins. To Lena Voss, care of Earth Navy, Paraxos System. I regret to inform you that Tiago Sorvino is dead." He'd whispered aleph-null into my ear. It was enough to prevent me sending a copy of the encrypted data block to Lena, not without knowing what was in it. With two dead drones on their hands, the Nisk would be reading our diplomatic traffic no matter how cleverly encrypted it was. Their tech was so far ahead of ours, I had to assume no secret was safe, except perhaps for what my bionetics hid within my body's own cell structure. My greatest fear was the Nisk would realize Sorvino was anything but an innocent victim and decide to prevent me leaving. It was a risk I couldn't take, why I couldn't tell Singh that Sorvino was EIS. For all I knew, the Nisk were listening in right now, even through the Embassy's suppression field. Just giving my recognition code to Singh was a gamble, one I couldn't avoid, but perhaps not enough to trigger a Nisk response. "Wait for me in Paraxos. Aleph-null to you and your family. Message ends."

When the Nisk read that message, as I was sure they would, they'd have a hard time figuring out what it really meant. Lena would not. She'd know the mission was blown, that I had something too hot to risk in diplomatic traffic and no matter what happened, she had to stay in the Paraxos System where I could find her in a hurry.

With aleph-null in the message, the entire galaxy could go to war and she wouldn't budge.

* * * *

After finishing with Ambassador Singh, I ventured back into the drizzle and headed for the spaceport. Almost immediately, my listener detected footsteps behind me, confirming the stride pattern matched the large humanoid who'd tailed me earlier. I'd assumed he'd been connected with Trask's hit squad, perhaps responsible for suppressing the Nisk sensors.

So why was he still here?

On the image of Nisport's street grid floating in my mind's eye, a flashing sonic marker indicated he was closing fast, and me with an empty gun and the Nisk already suspicious. He appeared several blocks away, lumbering toward me like a freight loader in a hurry, making no effort to hide his presence. I broke into a run, trying to put distance between us but soon realized he was faster, not by much, but enough to catch me before I reached the terminal.

I cut into a side street, sprinted one block then turned and drew my P-50, taking aim as he came charging around the corner. He took one look at my gun, not realizing it was empty, and leapt high into the air. A soft blue glow appeared beneath his boots, carrying him across the street to the roof of an octagonal structure, then a moment later, he launched himself in another tech-assisted jump across the rooftops.

He might have looked like a large human, but his speed and tech told me he was anything but. The humanoid was bigger and faster than me and tech assisted in ways I wasn't. Tangling with him with an empty gun was likely to be a one way ticket to the wrong end of a beating. Not wanting to be flanked, I started running toward the spaceport. Each time he landed on the roof of a building a sonic marker flashed, warning he was racing to cut me off.

When he started to pull ahead, I slipped into a side street, hiding under an awning extending around a long, U-shaped building. The script on the grimy walls was faded Cor Carolian, a local Orion power. It looked deserted, then a short rectangular device emerged from above the sealed door, shimmering from a micro acceleration field enveloping it. It floated down, scanning me with a laser thin green light.

"Not now," I whispered, trying to swat it with the butt of my gun. The alien scanner dodged and continued drifting toward the ground, completing its scan as a heavy thud sounded from the roof.

The alien was directly above me!

My listener tracked him as he walked to the edge of the building, searching the street for me. Most alien buildings in Nisport were sensor hardened to block all the eavesdroppers. I hoped the Carolian structure was no exception. I hardly dared breath as I realized he didn't know I was below him. My listener amplified the click of his metal boots as he prowled the side of the building while the Carolian scanner approached the ground beside me. I lifted one foot out of its beam, then as it scanned my other ankle, placed the heel of my boot on top of it and silently pushed it into the ground, hiding its green glow. Above, the humanoid waited for me to show myself, then he tech-jumped across the street. I remained with my back pressed into the entrance alcove as he searched the road, then thinking I'd eluded him, he leapt away toward the spaceport.

The Carolian scanner pushed up against my boot, trying to free itself. I lifted my heel, letting it shoot back up to its home above the door. In my mind's eye, the sonic marker winked out as the humanoid moved out of range. I waited several minutes, but it didn't reappear, then I crept down a side street and circled around the spaceport so I could approach from the opposite direction.

When the terminal came into view, I searched for any sign of my pursuer. Finding none, I ran to the two Nisk security drones stationed at the entrance. It was the first time since landing I was glad to stand beside a giant beetle. To the southeast, the silhouette of the barrel chested humanoid stood on a roof watching. I glanced at my two stoic guardians then gave him a triumphal wave. He made no response, but turned and jumped out of sight.

Filled with a great desire to get off this bug infested quagmire, I hurried through the terminal back to the *Silver Lining* wondering who the humanoid was and why was he tracking me?

Whoever he was, I suspected I hadn't seen the last of him.

* * * *

"Those thieving, six legged bandits!" Jase declared angrily as I visited the flight deck on the way to my stateroom. My blonde copilot sat on his acceleration couch seething as he watched a live feed from the cargo hold. "They're saying five containers were contaminated."

"Accept their count."

"No way, Skipper! I supervised that load. Those

containers were sealed tight. They must have damaged them."

Ories were known for their stubborn combative natures and I couldn't alleviate his anger by telling him I'd sabotaged the containers myself.

"Tell them to load whatever gel they owe us. I want to get off this rock."

Jase glanced in my direction, then furrowed his brow in confusion as he saw the dark stains on my flight jacket. "Is that blood?"

"Yeah," I said sourly, feeling the back of my head. The Nisk doctor had shaved it to the scalp, but the skin and bone showed no sign of the injury thanks to Nisk regenerative tech. "Long story."

Before he could start probing, I headed for my stateroom. After shedding my jacket and mud covered boots, I flopped onto my bunk, feigning sleep. Since Lena had brought me back into the EIS as a freelance asset a year ago, I'd added countermeasures to my cabin to disrupt eavesdropping. I could rely on it to jam human snoopers, but had to assume it was ineffective against alien-tech, which was why I couldn't use the ship's datanet, not with bug eyes on me.

I relaxed, regulated my breathing, then summoned Sorvino's data block and the required encryption key from my bionetic memory. When I put the two together, the data block transformed from meaningless fractals into legible characters. It was a surprisingly simple message: a set of astrographic coordinates to a planet I'd never heard of, a latitude and longitude, and a date. If there was more, Sorvino hadn't had time to transfer it. At the end of the data block was the same security classification he'd whispered in my ear, a rating so high I'd never before encountered it in the field – *aleph-null!*

Derived from mathematics, aleph-null was an infinite cardinal number used by the EIS to describe the highest possible threat. The data block gave no indication what the threat was, but Sorvino had sacrificed his life for it, leaving me in no doubt it was the real deal. All Lena had told me was that Sorvino had been in deep cover for two years. Whatever he'd found was important enough for her to be waiting with Earth Navy in the Paraxos System, squarely in the middle of Outer Draco. From there, they could hit any target in the region. The problem was, Paraxos was three weeks away at maximum bubble. The date in Sorvino's message was just six days from now. If we launched immediately, we could make Sorvino's rendezvous, but Lena would have to wait. Once she received my message, saw the aleph-null reference, that's exactly what she'd do – until Breega froze over.

I wanted to review Ambassador Singh's report on the three man hit squad, but I didn't dare put it in my reader with the Nisk watching. Instead, I rolled over and activated my bunk-side intercom. "Jase, is that niskgel loaded yet?"

"They're bringing it aboard now."

"We're leaving as soon as the last Nisk is off the ship. We've got an errand to run."

"A profitable errand I hope."

"Definitely not."

"Got anything to do with the blood on your jacket?"

"Absolutely."

He chuckled. "And you said this trip would be boring! I'll start preflight."

If I made the reason for the trip a payback for an unprovoked assault, Jase wouldn't ask questions, he'd just want a part of it. Ories were funny that way.

They'd cross the Orion Arm to repay a personal slight without a second thought. Not people you want as enemies. Izin would simply assume I was satisfying a basic human need for revenge. Neither would wonder what the real reason for our detour was – at least not for a while.

I was about to switch off the intercom, when a thought struck me. "Have you been keeping an eye on ship movements out of here?"

"Always." Watching who took off ahead of you was a good way to spot potential ambushes as you boosted to orbit.

"Who launched while I was away?"

"One Ascellan, a Minkaran, two high tech numbers I couldn't identify and a human freighter."

"When did the human ship launch?"

"Two hours ago."

Time enough for Trask's team to get back to the spaceport after eliminating Sorvino. If they hid their weapons, they could have walked past the dim witted drones in the terminal without suspicion. "You get its registry?"

"Sure did. It was the Merak Star, but I didn't get that from her transponder. It was off the whole time. I read it off her hull."

No transponder meant the Society office wouldn't have even known she was here. "What type was she?"

"Gaur class." They were medium transports, four times the size of the *Silver Lining* with good carrying capacity, but slow.

"Any other human ships in or out of here since we arrived?"

"Only one, a small transport. She landed next to the Merak Star while you were away. Same deal, no transponder. She was on the ground twenty minutes, just long enough to pick up a passenger from the Merak Star. I didn't get the transport's name. Her hull had been scrubbed clean."

"Did the Merak Star drop any cargo?" I asked.

"I saw one drone carry off a half tonne container. That's it. And three people got on, just before she launched."

It was enough sugar for the Nisk to grant landing rights and permit a crew transfer, but not nearly enough to justify sending a ship that size here. So the freighter had come to drop off a passenger where no one would see, except the Nisk, who wouldn't care. It was the same ship Trask's hit squad and Sorvino had come in on, but something had happened to blow Sorvino's cover, after he'd gone dirt side. If it had been before, Trask would never have let him off the ship alive. And Jase had seen Trask's team reboard her about the time the Nisk were reconstructing my skull.

I accessed the astrographics database, spent time looking at a dozen worlds I had no intention of visiting – just to keep any nosy Nisk guessing – then I called up the planet at the data block's coordinates. It was a primeval world in a remote system. The only human presence was a tiny corporate trading post I'd never heard of. From what limited data there was, I could see no reason why such a planet would rate an aleph-null security classification.

Yet, that was exactly what Tiago Sorvino had given it.

* * * *

Two minutes after we bubbled and were safely beyond the reach of Nisk spy-tech, I slid Ambassador Singh's data chip into the reader on my desk. Singh's search of the DNA codes had produced dossiers on all three who, no surprise, were ex-military.

And all were from Jase's homeworld – Oresund, mercenary capital of Mapped Space.

Virtually every Orie child, male or female, went to military school. They could shoot before they were six, operate heavy weapons by ten and were piloting combat vehicles and fighting suits by fifteen. Most joined one of the four Earth militaries while some, the reckless types, turned merc for the money and adventure. That's where Jase had been headed before I convinced him otherwise. And then there were the stark raving mad, hard core types – the elite – who stayed on Oresund and joined the planet's own professional military, the Oresund Force. O-Force was widely regarded as the best special forces unit ever produced in human history, the result of a stern culture that valued martial virtues above all else. They worked closely with Earth's four major ground forces, particularly the Union Regular Army with whom they had ancient historical links.

Now I understood why Sorvino had ordered me not to shoot. Trask's hit squad were all O-Force veterans. At the first sign of a weapon, they'd have cut me to pieces without breaking stride.

Domar Trask, the only one of the three on my EIS wanted list, had been a Battle Force Commander, court martialled for killing a URA superior officer in a bar fight on New Liberty. He'd done it in the heart of Washington Base, the URA's largest training facility outside the Solar System, in front of an army of witnesses and the base's surveillance system. The court martial had been a formality, but it had taken four military police, two assault troopers, and an angry barman with a gee-bat to subdue him. Two of the MP's woke up in hospital for their trouble. Showing no remorse, Trask got twenty to life in a military prison. He escaped nine months later, killing one guard and maiming another in the process. Wanted by the URA, O-Force and two ex-wives, he'd turned merc – definitely not the kind of man we wanted having anything to do with alien cultures, not unless we wanted Access Treaty problems.

Trask's two companions had less colorful histories. Stina Kron and Julkka Olen were both O-Force vets, honorably discharged. No trouble with the law, but long associations with Trask before his fall from grace. After leaving their planet's service, both had disappeared from sight.

Olen, the stocky former master sergeant who'd shattered my skull, was a heavy weapons specialist who'd served alongside Trask for more than a decade. Before teaming up with the O-Force Commander, he'd done several stints in the brig for minor infractions. He had a hot temper and a mean streak, but after coming under Trask's influence, his record had been clean, even commendable. He'd even received a commendation for bravery for putting down a bloody insurrection on Yalis.

Stina Kron was a fighting suit expert. She'd served as a specialist instructor with both Indian Republic and People's Federation of Asia forces and had more than sixty orbital training jumps to her credit, most from Earth Navy ships. Unlike her two companions, her record was exemplary. The PFA had tried to recruit her and O-Force had even offered her a commission, both of which she refused.

When I'd finished studying their dossiers, I had more questions than answers. Foremost among them was why three former Orie spec forces types had murdered an EIS deep cover agent on an alien planet, popped off two of the locals who'd got in their way and managed to escape under the noses of technologically superior local law enforcement. Trask was a bad seed, but his two accomplices had solid records, even if Olen required a short leash. Was it personal loyalty to Trask that had dragged them down, or something else?

Whatever the reason, I hoped to find it in the swamps of Novo Pantanal in six days.

Chapter Two : Novo Pantanal

Permian world
Qesari System, Outer Draco
1.09 Earth Normal Gravity
937 light years from Sol
124 Humans

The *Silver Lining* unbubbled at minimum safe distance from Novo Pantanal's gravity well a day before the date in Sorvino's data block. In the time it took Jase to deploy our sensors, a yellow hulled ship with a triangular engine configuration jumped in on top of us. Her transponder was broadcasting and her weapons were hot, although it took them a few seconds to get a lock on us.

"Gutsy move," I said, "jumping in on us blind."

We could have fired before they got their sensors out, if we'd been looking for a fight and if our single cannon had been charged. The sentry ship had thick armor and four medium range weapons, not nearly enough to take on a navy frigate, but a serious threat to any raider and more firepower than we carried.

"She's a merc escort," Jase said, studying the transponder data, "licensed to the Rafha Corporation."

Rafha was one of the thousands of small Second Caliphate operated trade companies proliferating Mapped Space and according to the Society Register, the owner of the trading post down on Novo Pantanal. Tradeco's were a step up from solitary free traders. They tended to stick to the major long haul trade lanes, often hiring armed ships to protect their cargo vessels and occasionally attack their competitors, but Novo Pantanal was a long way from the nearest trunk route.

"They want to talk," Jase said, accepting their hail.

A middle aged man with an elaborate moustache and a red satin turban appeared on screen. "Identify yourself."

I nodded to Jase, who activated our transponder.

When he saw who we were, he said, "State your business Union trader."

My mind raced. Novo Pantanal was a nowhere planet with only a tiny trading post stuck in the middle of a swamp world at a primitive stage of evolution. If that was all it was, it didn't rate a merc escort ship for protection.

Beside me, Jase quietly pointed to his sensor console. He was tracking more than two hundred ships on the ground, clustered close together on the planet's surface. That told me everything I needed to know.

"We're here for the floating souk," I said.

It was a guess, but if I was right, this escort was working for the Rashidun, the Rightly Guided, a secretive Second Caliphate syndicate that operated a notorious black market, the Rashidun Souk. The souk moved from one remote planet to another, always staying one jump ahead of UniPol and Earth Navy. There were many souks scattered across Mapped Space, all elusive, all appearing at certain times and places, then vanishing after a few weeks only to reappear at a later date somewhere else. Catching them was like grasping at smoke, but as they tended to deal only in smuggled goods, the EIS paid them little attention.

"What do you have to trade?"

"Nine thousand five hundred grams of niskgel." It was the only cargo of value we carried, not exactly contraband, but a good swap for an illegal load.

"What do you seek?"

It was a trick question. If I named a cargo, it would prove I didn't know how this game was played and he'd open fire. "Right guidance and privacy." It told him I knew this was the Rashidun floating black market and I reserved my right to conceal what I was looking for.

The escort commander nodded. "The Rashidun Souk welcomes you. After landing, deliver two percent of your niskgel to our factor." It was their cut for running a market where anything could be bought and sold without questions.

"Two percent?" I said. Prices had gone up since my last visit to a Souk.

"UniPol activity has been increasing," he said. "Extra sentries cost money. Keep a constant comms watch. We will broadcast one general warning should Earth Council forces arrive, then our escorts will abandon the system. Disable your transponder after landing and do not reactivate it in this system if the Souk is terminated."

The Rashidun wanted everyone to run, hiding their identity, making it harder for Earth Navy or UniPol to track down the participants.

"A sensible precaution."

The escort commander closed the channel, then his brightly painted ship turned away. By now we had detected four more merc escorts patrolling beyond Novo Pantanal's gravity well, ensuring only genuine black market traders were allowed to approach the surface. Much further out were picket ships, ready to jump in and warn the Souk of the arrival of Earth Navy or UniPol ships at the edge of the system.

"Will those escorts fight if the Brotherhood show up?" Jase asked.

"Depends what the Rashidun are paying them." Trade company escorts would attack Brotherhood ships on sight – that was their job – but Rashidun gunships would only risk battle if they'd been hired for a stand up fight. These mercs looked like they were only on traffic control and picket duty.

While the escort moved off, we headed for Novo Pantanal, a dark green world with low mountain ranges, shallow oceans, thousands of lakes and endless white clouds. It was a hot and steamy world, where the highest life forms were insects and reptiles and while the plant life was abundant, the soils and water were uncomfortably acidic for human needs. On the sunward facing side, a continent sized shimmer reflected off a vast expanse of shallow water lying beneath the greenery, hinting at the great swamp dominating much of the planet's surface.

Small footsteps sounded behind us as Izin entered the flight deck. He climbed up onto the acceleration couch behind mine and Jase's and focused his bulging blue-green amphibian eyes on the screen. My tamph engineer normally stayed in engineering tracking the ship's vitals, especially during atmospheric insertion, but Novo Pantanal had piqued his curiosity.

"Told you there was lots of water down there," I said.

"Just because I'm amphibian, Captain, doesn't mean I have any particular fascination for watery planets," Izin replied through the triangular vocalizer over his small mouth.

"Doesn't remind you of home?" Jase asked.

"Earth is not a swamp," Izin declared, "nor is my people's birth world."

Izin had never seen the Intruder Homeworld and Earth had no contact with the Intruder Civilization, but the Tau Cetins had given us enough information to understand tamph origins. There were risks allowing the tamphs to stay, but the decision had been made millennia ago after a wrecked Intruder ship had crashed on Earth. The tamphs were the descendants of the survivors and they'd been on Earth long enough that we weren't about to kick them off now.

"It is Earth," I said, "as it was three hundred million years ago."

"Its biosphere is comparable to the Permian Era," Izin conceded, "although both Earth and my ancestor's homeworld had more varied topography and more complex life forms at this stage of their evolution."

"So, no swimming?" I asked.

"The astrographics register indicates the sea life, while primitive, is highly aggressive."

Jase turned to him genuinely surprised. "You're not going to let a few angry fish frighten you, are you?"

"I doubt the creatures down there have evolved the capacity for anger," Izin said. "I simply have no desire to exterminate primitive aquatic life forms in order to get wet."

Jase and I exchange amused looks, imagining Izin wading naked through Novo Pantanal's sprawling wetlands with a gun in each hand, blasting every ripple, then the *Silver Lining* slid onto the guide beam and nosed into the atmosphere.

We followed the beam down through white clouds toward a tropical jungle teeming with primitive life. The only cleared dry land was located on a low island close to the equator. When we dropped below the clouds, a squalid collection of buildings came into view. They were closely packed, separated by narrow alley ways and dotted with photon collectors and communication arrays. According to the astrographics database the town, if you could call it that, was named Kedira. The Rafha Corp owned trading post most likely harvested biomatter from the surrounding wetlands, but the real source of its profits would be its periodic hosting of the Rashidun Souk.

Surrounding the town in all directions were several kilometers of cleared land where the ships we'd detected from space were parked. It was unusual to see a spaceport encircling a town. Normally they were located a safe distance away, but this was no standard spaceport. Surrounding the ships were tents and marquees where black marketeers offered their goods for sale or barter. There were so many tents that they had merged together, creating a ring around Kedira Town, a sure sign the Rashidun Souk had been going for some weeks and was almost full to capacity.

"If you want to sell your neutron rifle, Izin," I said, "this is the place."

"Only if I could find something better, Captain."

"Better than a flesh melter?" Jase said. "Good luck!"

There were several landing areas at the edges of

43

the Souk large enough for the *Silver Lining*. Wanting to avoid attention, I picked the smallest one on the southern side, where we could squeeze in between several large ships and the edge of the forest. I circled wide and came in over the trees so I could put her down without knocking over our neighbor's tent stalls.

"Jase," I said as soon as we landed, "Drop our belly door, set up an awning and offer a kilogram of niskgel."

"What do you want for it?"

"Anything we can offload in a legitimate port without getting arrested."

Jase scowled, certain anything he could pick up in a Rashidun Souk would get us thrown in jail. "You're not joining me?"

"No, Izin and I are going to separate out the signatures of every ship here. See if there's anyone we know."

Considering there were several hundred ships to choose from and no transponders active, it would be no easy task.

* * * *

Mapping each ship's neutrino signature proved more difficult than I expected because the ships were so close together and many had similar energy plants. All were idling in prelaunch modes, ready to run should the merc escorts give the word, but even with strong signals, we couldn't identify half of them because they were full time smugglers not listed in the Society's recognition catalogue.

"The men you're looking for could be on any of those ships," Izin said as he stared at his six screens, each filled with rows of white boxes containing wavy green energy signatures.

"Or none of them. We are a day early."

"It's three hours to midnight."

I stood, stretching my legs. "I'm going to get some sleep. I'll deliver the niskgel to the Rashidun factor tomorrow. Maybe I can get something out of him."

"The Rashidun are known for their discretion, Captain."

"And for their corruption."

When I got to my stateroom, I used my threading to trigger instant sleep. Whatever was happening tomorrow, I wanted to be fully rested. After what seemed like only a moment, a side effect of threading induced sleep, the intercom sounded.

"Captain," Izin said, "another ship has just landed. The same ship that left Nisport ahead of us, the Merak Star."

It was almost dawn.

* * * *

With three hundred grams of niskgel in my pocket, I walked down the belly door-ramp into cloyingly thick air. The tropical heat and humidity was made more oppressive by the harsh orange sunlight. Jase had strung several photon sheets from the gantries astern where we normally towed three VRS shipping containers. He'd set up a folding table in the shade with a sign offering niskgel and informing prospective buyers that he'd be open for business at eight.

I hurried past our stall into the tent city. The maze of narrow alleys and multicolored pavilions that had grown up around the grounded ships were just coming to life with vendors laying out their rare and beautiful items for sale. Some were stolen, some were banned because of their intoxicating, sexual, violent or depraved natures, but all would deliver tremendous rewards to any who could sneak them onto a human populated world. The Rashidun Souk was a gold mine for smugglers, collectors and UniPol agents alike, although one had to be well connected to know when and where it would next appear.

Some vendors held up items as I passed, hoping to tempt me to buy, showing only the merest disappointment when I ignored them. Several of the shadier types watched me, wondering what treasure I might be carrying, but with my P-50 in plain sight, none tried their luck. After passing seven ships and the makeshift stalls surrounding them, I reached the dirty prefab walls of the trading post. It comprised a cluster of mostly two story warehouses and sleeping quarters for the sales agents who would stay after the Souk moved on, picking up what local intersystem trade they could while they waited for the floating black market to return.

The factor lived and worked in an imposing white building with an ornate façade in the center of town. When I entered, a well dressed young man offered to accept my exaction, but I insisted on speaking with the factor himself. Without any sign of irritation, he politely showed me through to the inner sanctum, a surprisingly plush office decorated with marble and thickly woven carpet.

"Captain Sirius Kade? I am Jasim Hajjar," he said, extending his hand in greeting. He had a full beard with flecks of gray and wore purple silk robes with a curved thermal-dagger protruding from his sash. "You wished to see me?"

"I did," I said, placing the niskgel on the table as we took our seats.

He quickly calculated the quantity before him, then said, "One hundred and ninety grams is the required amount."

I reached forward and separated the ten gram cylinders into two groups. "For the Rashidun," I said, motioning to the larger group. When his eyes settled on the smaller group, I added, "For the factor."

Hajjar looked intrigued, as I knew he would. "And the service required for such generosity?"

"I'm interested in a ship, the Merak Star. It landed a few hours ago."

The factor nodded slowly. "The Rashidun Souk is fabled for its discretion, Captain Kade."

"I merely seek information. Anything you might know that is worthy of such a gift," I said, motioning to the containers that would more than double his annual income.

Jasim Hajjar's eyes settled thoughtfully on the niskgel. "Why would you seek such information?"

"It is a personal matter. A matter of honor."

"Indeed?" he said suspiciously. "Forgive me, Captain, but what honor is there among thieves and smugglers?"

I smiled sourly. "None, but a sister with child requires a husband, even if he is a two timing, bed hopping, scum sucking, purge rat."

Jasim looked sympathetic, relieved that the matter was something he could help me with. "The Merak Star is an infrequent participant in our market. When she comes, it is always to conduct a private trade, always with the same partner."

"I see. How long have these trades been taking place?"

He shrugged. "Two, maybe three years."

"And who is the partner?"

Jasim winced. "A rather dangerous man by the name of Rix. He will be landing later today."

I nodded appreciatively, then pushed the smaller collection of niskgel containers toward him. "Jasim Hajjar, my sister thanks you."

We shook hands, then I headed out of the trading post, through the tent market, toward the *Merak Star*. It didn't take long before I saw her bulk rising above the tents ahead, parked in an area cordoned off from the rest of the Souk by a high tent wall. It hid what she was unloading and was patrolled by four armed guards who allowed no one to approach. It was not exactly in the spirit of unfettered trade that had made the Rashidun Souks famous, but it left me in no doubt the Rightly Guided were being well paid for their services.

Knowing I couldn't get to the tent blind, I worked my way back through the market, then out into the shallow swamp. The partially submerged proto-forest was teeming with insects and lizards while the trees were packed closely enough that I could sneak past the edge of the tent blind unseen by the guards. Once past the tent blind, I crept back to dry land for my first unobstructed view of the *Merak Star*.

She stood on six stubby landing struts close to the tree line. Her two stern mounted engines pointed toward the forest while her topside sensor array was fully deployed watching the sky. If she had weapons, they were well hidden, but all four of her port side cargo doors were down, providing ramp access to her internal holds. Cargobots were busily unloading her, stacking sealed metal containers in rows between the ship and the vacant half of the private landing area.

I zoomed my short, cylindrical monoscope onto the growing stack, finding they ranged in size from small lockers to large vacuum-radiation-sealed containers requiring two bots to handle. Most were unmarked, some had had their labeling painted over while others had been left untouched, although nothing could disguise the high grade security locks on many of them. One stack of dark green containers were imprinted with the letters IRF – Indian Republic Forces – the ground combat arm of one of Earth's four great powers. Nearby, a large black container was embossed with the words Nanjing Industries, the People's Federation of Asia's largest armaments manufacturer. Alongside it were containers marked with Naskhi calligraphy, the Second Caliphate's cursive script, which my threading told me translated to 'seeker grenade launcher'.

Four cargobots emerged from the central hold carrying a white domed structure the size of a small house, which my threading profile matched as a Union manufactured mark forty one cruiser turret. The bots carefully placed the big naval gun on the ground and returned to the *Merak Star* for another load. It was an impressive collection of weapons drawn from all four of Earth's collective governments, but while gun running was banned, it hardly rated an aleph-null classification. The EIS left such cases to UniPol as there were usually no Access Treaty implications.

I was beginning to wonder if Tiago Sorvino had overstated the importance of his find when a distant rumble rolled down out of the sky, growing rapidly in volume, then a charcoal black ship passed overhead. It was a squat cylinder with three large maneuvering engines mounted amidships, external to her hull and equally spaced as if at the points of a triangle. I recognized the hull geometry immediately, having ridden in her like years before. She'd once been a navy assault carrier, a heavily armored transport designed to land ground forces under fire. Her navy livery was gone, replaced by blast scars and a ring of point defense polarity guns above her maneuvering engines. As she came down, a single massive turret atop her blunt bow came into view, dwarfing the cruiser weapon the cargobots had unloaded and leaving me in no doubt, whatever she'd once been, she was now a brawler with a punch no navy frigate could match. My threading had no record of such a ship operating in this part of Mapped Space, perhaps because anyone unlucky enough to cross her path had not lived to tell the tale.

When her thrusters fell silent, the black assault carrier stood like a dark fortress, looming above the fourteen thousand tonne *Merak Star*, and no doubt drawing a few apprehensive looks from the smugglers in the Rashidun Souk. Before the dust had settled, an armored door lowered to form a ramp wide enough for the heaviest combat vehicles and revealing the thickness of her armored hull. With all that mass, she'd fly like a pig, but she'd be the devil in a fight.

A woman in tight fitting, bright red body armor appeared wearing a gun slung low to her thigh. She wore a slender commband which wrapped across the right side of her forehead and vanished beneath her auburn hair. Two well armed men in bulky, mismatched battle armor followed her across to the stacked containers. A moment later, Domar Trask, Julkka Olen and Stina Kron emerged from the *Merak Star*. They were followed by an unarmed spacer who looked like he'd rather be anywhere else than there. I cranked up my bionetic listener to maximum gain as Trask and the red suited woman met.

"You were supposed to have finished unloading before we landed," the woman snapped. "You know

Rix hates being on the ground longer than necessary."

"What Rix wants isn't my concern," Trask replied coldly.

"If we're caught down here, you'll be the first to die. I promise you."

"Spare me your threats, Anya," Trask said, genuinely unconcerned. "Every ship here is slower than the Cyclops. You'll have plenty of time to run if there's a raid."

That must have been why they picked the Souk, to use the other ships as interference while they got away.

"Rix wants a report on the security breach," Anya said.

"We took care of it," Trask snapped. "That's all he needs to know."

"Our agent said a crewman hacked the Merak Star's nav log. That puts us at risk!"

"If your man had waited at Nisport, instead of running as soon as your ship picked him up, he'd know we eliminated Sorvino and recovered the data taps."

"He didn't run. We only made this rendezvous because he left when he did," she said coldly. "Did this Sorvino communicate with anyone?"

"Only his maker!" Julkka Olen said with a cruel grin.

"There was a trader in the street," Kron reminded him.

"Yeah, but I cracked his head like an egg," Olen boasted. "He's as dead as Sorvino."

Good thing Julkka Olen was not well acquainted with Nisk medical technology.

"Who was he working for?" Anya demanded.

"His snooper-tech was mil-spec," Kron replied. "Too fancy for UniPol. Could have been naval intelligence."

Anya's eyes flared with anger. "Rix will have your head if you lead Earth Navy to us!"

"You Drakes worry too much," Trask said dismissively.

Drakes? They were the Pirate Brotherhood faction operating in Outer Draco. Anya and her two gun humpers looked the part, but I'd never heard of Drakes cooperating with mercs before.

"So you killed the spy before you interrogated him?" Anya persisted.

"He wouldn't have talked," Trask said. "His kind never do."

"Rix won't be happy."

"Rix is never happy," Trask growled indifferently. "Comes from sneaking around out here all his life, running from every fight."

She bristled. "I wouldn't say that to him if I were you!"

"You're not me."

I tried DNA-locking Anya but she was just out of range.

"How long will it take to load the Cyclops?" Trask demanded, glancing at the black Drake ship as four cargobots emerged carrying a polished white hemisphere almost as large as the cruiser turret. The bots moved slowly, either in fragile transport mode or because the machine was unusually heavy.

"If the Merak Star's bots help, two hours," Anya said.

I focused the monoscope on the white hemisphere. It was encircled by a translucent ring and had a flat base with a conical protrusion at its center. My threading couldn't profile match it and the monoscope couldn't even get a basic spectral read on its composition. With a sinking feeling, I realized it was alien-tech, and by the size of it, no mere trinket. *Aleph-null!*

Trask glanced past the four cargobots edging down the ramp into the *Cyclops's* cavernous vehicle deck. "Where's the other one?"

Anya shook her head. "They didn't have it. They said it'll be ready next time."

"It better be," Trask said irritably. "We're running out of time." He nodded for his two merc companions to follow, then started across to the *Cyclops*.

Anya glanced at her two guards, nodding toward Trask. Without a word, they followed the three Orie mercs past the alien-tech hemisphere into the *Cyclops*. Clearly Anya didn't like Trask prowling around her ship unescorted. When Trask had disappeared from sight, she turned to the swarthy spacer who'd stood quietly by during the exchange. "Is the stasis cradle ready, Nazari?"

"Yes Miss Anya, exactly as Captain Rix specified." From his accent and bearing, he was obviously a Cali trader. Perhaps he was how the Drakes had gotten landing rights at the Souk. Considering their mutual distrust, a lot of credits must have changed hands to stop the Rashidun and the Brotherhood from blasting each other on sight.

Anya looked bemused. "Rix didn't specify anything. He knows as much about this stuff as I do!"

Nazari looked puzzled. "The instructions were very precise. If they did not come from you, then who?"

"Trask's technical advisor. I've never met him, no one has, except Rix. Trask's got ten men guarding him night and day."

"What does Rix say about him?"

She laughed. "Not a thing. I've never seen him so

secretive."

"Do you wish to inspect the installation?"

"No point. I can fly the Cyclops through a pin hole blind folded, but this stuff is beyond me."

Nazari looked puzzled. "I don't know why I couldn't use pressure restraints."

"Me neither," she said as they started toward the *Merak Star*. "So, how'd you like being cooped up with Trask for five weeks?"

"Mr. Trask is a bully, but he is not the one who scares me. It's that other one, the one they have watching me. He is a killer."

Nazari gave her a frightened look, then they passed inside the *Merak Star* and out of range of my listener. I waited, but they didn't reappear. Instead, the Drake cargobots loaded more alien-tech aboard the *Merak Star*, then began moving the weapon containers onto the *Cyclops*.

According to my threading, the standard navy complement for the Drake assault carrier would have been two hundred and eighty, plus bots and a combat team of a thousand grunts. Fitted for raiding, she'd carry at least four hundred with plenty of room for captured cargo. It was too many for me to risk going after Trask, but the alien-tech was on the freighter and her crew would be minimal. That's what Sorvino had sacrificed his life for, not a bunch of Earth weapons that could be bought in any one of a hundred arms bazaars across Mapped Space.

Pocketing the monoscope, I crept back into the boggy forest and moved through the proto-trees until the *Merak Star* stood between me and the *Cyclops*. Based on what Anya had said, the Drake ship would be scanning space, more worried about being caught on the surface by Earth Navy than being spied upon from the ground. The smuggler ship would be doing the same, only with less sophisticated sensors and with most of her crew catching up on bunk time. Neither would be expecting trouble to come sneaking out the Permian swamp.

Using the freighter for cover I darted from the forest, under the *Merak Star's* engines to the nearest landing strut, then crept beneath her hull toward the aft most cargo door. The cruiser turret and the stack of weapon containers obscured the door-ramp from the *Cyclops* while my bionetic listener confirmed no human sounds were coming from inside the freighter's cargo hold. Satisfied I was alone, I pulled myself up onto the ramp and slipped inside.

The cargo hold filled the body of the *Merak Star*, with large rectangular space doors on either side and connecting pressure hatches in the forward and aft bulkheads. This one hold alone could have stowed a ship the size of the *Silver Lining*, although the Drake assault carrier, with its immense vehicle and hangar decks, had a greater carrying capacity overall. The aft side of the hold was stacked with VRS containers while a square metal frame reaching from the deck to the ceiling dominated the center. The alien-tech hemisphere floated in the center of the frame within a glowing stasis field. Alongside it, magnetic deck clamps secured four small cube-shaped containers and one long rectangular chamber with a transparent upper surface, all loaded from the *Cyclops*.

I approached the stasis cradle looking for a control console to sabotage, but it must have been operated from the bridge because there was nothing evident. I drew my P-50 and fired twice at the hemisphere, aiming high, but the stasis field absorbed the slug's kinetic energy, suspending them both a few meters from the white metal machine.

"Worth a try," I muttered to myself, holstering my gun and turning to the nearest cube container.

It had a simple control panel of recessed surfaces which I tapped experimentally until the top of the cube hinged up to the vertical, revealing four metal circles lying flush with the top of an inner panel. When I pressed lightly on one of the circles, it rose up revealing a twenty centimeter long cylinder with metallic end plates and a transparent body. A blue substance glowed within, held in place by an invisible field preventing it from touching the sides. I lifted the cylinder out of its storage space, finding it surprisingly light and cold to the touch, and held it up for the bionetic receptors in my eyes to optically scan. After a few seconds, my threading projected its nonsensical conclusion into my mind.

BALL LIGHTNING.

Deciding to keep it for later analysis, I slid the cylinder into a pocket inside my jacket and resealed the cube, hiding my thievery. Finally, I turned to the three meter long rectangular chamber. Its curved, transparent upper surface was frosted with ice crystals and a faint hum issued from its base. I wiped frosting from the transparent surface revealing a frozen alien lying within. Unable to tell if he was alive or dead, I released the transparent coffin-like lid which lifted up with a hiss of misty air. A frosted life signs display above his head indicated he was barely alive, sustained in hypothermic suspension by the cryochamber.

The frozen alien was from a race I'd never seen, a species my threading could find no optical match for. He had a squarish head covered with taut, light brown skin, with large round eyes deeply inset below a protruding brow. Below his eyes was a flat nose with a single horizontal nostril and an almost human-like mouth, although his ears were little more than vertical slits in his bony cranium.

Over his body, he wore a dark flexible body suit with matching boots and a belt that had been stripped of attachments. Several thin rectangular plates lay beside him, having fallen from his suit, although there was no clue as to their purpose. I retrieved one of the plates and wiped it clean of frost, revealing a column of finely engraved symbols that my threading couldn't identify. Whatever the language, it wasn't from a species the EIS had ever encountered. The symbols appeared to be control points, but when I touched them, there was no response, indicating whatever the device it was, it was as lifeless as its owner.

At a guess, his brain to body mass was close to man's, so if he was ahead of us on the evolutionary ladder, it wasn't by much. I considered trying to revive him, but the metallic click of the pressure door unlocking sounded behind me. I quickly pocketed the rectangular plate, closed the cryochamber and took cover among the VRS containers at the back of the hold. A moment later, Anya and Captain Nazari stepped through the aft pressure door and started across the cargo deck toward the open door.

"I won't use marked navpoints," Nazari said in his slurring Cali accent. "It will allow me to avoid Earth Navy inspections. I just hope your Drake friends know enough to leave me alone."

"I wouldn't count on it," Anya replied as they approached the stasis cradle. "Rix is a secretive bastard. He hardly tells me anything and I've been with him five years."

"If I'm attacked, I'll tell them I work for the great Captain Rix."

"They wouldn't believe you. And even if they did, they'd kill you just to stop you telling Rix what happened." She gave him a meaningful look. "He's not the forgiving type."

"So, I'm on my own," Nazari concluded nervously.

"You've got fast bubble. You'll be OK."

They stopped close to the white hemisphere to study it a moment. The two slugs I'd fired were on the opposite side, out of sight, and were slowly being expelled by the stasis field.

"You don't know what it does?" Nazari asked without noticing where I'd wiped frost from the cryochamber's transparent surface a few meters away.

She shook her head. "Only Trask and his technical advisor know, and they won't even tell Rix."

They continued on toward the open cargo door. Nazari produced a small red stimhaler, pressed the spout to one nostril and breathed deeply, then exhaled a crimson vapor.

Anya stepped away with a scowl on her face. "Be careful with that stuff, you've got a ship to fly."

"It calms my nerves. You saw how the skinny one looks at me? Like he is waiting to slit my throat! On my own ship!"

"Do you have a gun?"

"I have three," Nazari said, "but I am no fighter."

"You won't be if you fry your brains with that stuff," she said, nodding toward his stimhaler.

He sniffed, wiped his eyes, then grinned mischievously. "You want a try? First one free!"

Anya scowled. "No thanks, I like to keep a clear head."

"I'll be glad when this is over and I'm back running contraband through Ursa."

"Over?" Anya gave him a surprised look. "This is just the beginning."

Nazari looked miserable. "See? They tell me nothing. I am less than dirt to them."

One of my slugs finally reached the edge of the stasis field surrounding the alien-tech machine and fell to the deck, landing with a reverberating clang.

Anya spun around, drawing her gun. "What was that?"

Nazari turned more slowly due to his tranquilized reflexes and waved dismissively. "Ah! This old ship is always creaking!"

Anya studied the cargo hold, missing the remaining slug floating high in the stasis field. She holstered her gun and turned back to him. "I'll see you at Loport in four weeks. Don't be late." She studied his bloodshot eyes, adding, "And lay off the stims. They'll kill you!"

The *Merak Star's* captain nodded weakly. "Maybe, when they let me go back to Ursa."

Anya strode down the door-ramp, then Nazari ambled back across the cargo hold and passed through the forward pressure door. When the hold was deserted again, I crept from my hiding place to the cargo door. Anya was walking up the vehicle ramp into the black hulled *Cyclops* behind a laden cargobot. When she was out of sight, I jumped down to the ground and hurried back under the *Merak Star*, then slipped back through the Permian proto-forest to the tent market.

Once back on dry land, I headed for the *Silver Lining* through narrow tent alleys, past endless black market stalls, careful to keep the bottle of ball lightning well hidden inside my jacket.

* * * *

Once aboard the *Silver Lining*, I went straight to engineering and handed the alien-tech cylinder to Izin for analysis. He turned it over curiously, then placed it in his particle analyzer.

"Do you have any idea what it's used for, Captain?" he asked, watching the output screen.

"That's what I want you to tell me."

After the analyzer had completed several passes, he said, "There's a containment field surrounding the material. Whatever it is, our analyzer can't penetrate it."

"Can we open it?"

"I wouldn't recommend it. If the substance is highly reactive, there may be an energy release of unknown proportions. If you must open it, Captain, I would do so in a remote location, such as the other side of this planet."

While I was still deciding what to do, an alarm sounded.

Izin turned to his console, searching for the cause. "It's the Rashidun," he said. "They've declared a general evacuation. The Souk is over."

"Stow that thing in our smuggler compartment!" I said, pointing at the cylinder of ball lightning as I ran out.

By the time I reached the flight deck, sixteen ships had already launched and were climbing into the sky, brilliant points of light on divergent trajectories. Among them was the *Cyclops*, which had abandoned whatever of its cargo remained unloaded. The energy levels of the remaining ships were all spiking as they powered up to lift off.

"Jase," I said over the communicator. "Get up here, we're leaving."

The belly sensor had him in its sights. He was

engaged in animated discussion with two Republic dealers. In one gesture, he terminated the negotiation, scooped the niskgel containers from the table and charged up the ramp. Before he got to the top, I ordered it to lift and seal.

By the time Jase got to the flight deck, I'd finished a rushed preflight. More than fifty ships had now launched. Most were activating their maneuvering engines as soon as they left the ground with no regard for the down blasts that were tearing the flimsy tent city apart.

Jase slid onto his acceleration couch holding a sculpted bust of a demonic creature. He placed it at the top of his console. When he saw the direction of my gaze, he said, "That's Kogol, Lord of the Syrman Underworld. It's a rare art treasure."

"What did it cost?"

"Eighty grams. The republic dealer told me it's worth half a million credits to an Earth museum. All we have to do is get it back to Earth!"

I didn't have the heart to tell him he'd been conned, but I shouldn't have been surprised. His cabin was already overflowing with rare 'treasures' that were just waiting to make him rich.

"There's only one ship outside the gravity well," Jase said, quickly checking his sensors. "It's a merc escort broadcasting the alert."

"That's a picket ship."

It was right where I expected it to be. It had been stationed in the outer system, then had bubbled in to the planet to sound the warning when unwelcome company had arrived. It could be hours before the newcomer's signatures reached Novo Pantanal if they kept their distance, or they could be here any minute if they jumped in after the picket.

Jase saw that preflight was complete, but we hadn't started powering up. "What are we waiting for?"

"The Merak Star." If they were recording profiles and we launched, they'd know from our Society registered energy signature we were here. I had to wait until she was gone so we could slip away unnoticed. High above us, the *Cyclops* cleared orbit and began racing toward minimum safe distance.

"There she goes!" Jase said at last, as the *Merak Star* lumbered into the air. At fifty meters, her big engines came to life, pushing her into a powerful vertical climb. "The Rashidun escort just bubbled out."

True to their word, they'd given us one warning, then saved themselves – contract fulfilled.

We watched on the big screen as the remaining ships launched, completing the destruction of the tent city and leaving the *Silver Lining* alone on the ground. When the raging wind storm finally ended, collapsed tents and tables littered the ground, strewn with valuables abandoned in the rush to evacuate, while high above, several hundred brilliant white stars filled the sky, scattering in all directions.

"Who do you think it is?" Jase asked, wondering what had triggered the end of the Souk.

"Navy or UniPol." We still weren't showing any ships in orbit, indicating whoever they were, they were cautious. If they were still out near the edge of the system, they'd have no idea the Rashidun Souk had been abandoned. Only when they jumped in close and started picking up all the energy signatures would they know what had happened.

One by one, the brilliant points of light winked out, then when the *Merak Star* finally vanished, I turned to the intercom.

"Izin, light her up, we're going!"

"Right away, Captain."

Once we had enough power for thrusters, we started climbing. Below us, the Rashidun trading post looked like a tiny village surrounded by a patchwork quilt. Incredibly, for all its notoriety, the floating black market had come to a successful conclusion with no arrests made.

"So, no payback?" Jase asked.

"Not yet, but I haven't given up."

He nodded approvingly. "I wouldn't want to be them."

"They were Ories," I said. "O-Force turned merc."

Jase looked impressed. "Wow, you're lucky to be alive!"

"Domar Trask is their leader. Ever heard of him?"

"No, I never had much to do with O-Force. Saw them exercise a few times. Crazy bastards," he said with a touch of admiration. "Maybe you should let this one go."

"Good advice. If I was smarter, I'd take it."

"I always wondered how I'd go against those O-Force types," Jase said thoughtfully. "Guess I'm going to find out."

"Captain," Izin's voice sounded over the intercom, "are you tracking any other ships close by?"

Jase checked his sensors and shook his head. "We're all alone."

"I'm detecting a powerful magnetic field a thousand meters to starboard," Izin said, "and a friction avoidance shockwave from the same area."

Izin routinely monitored ambient influences we didn't, especially anything that could interfere with energy and propulsion systems. If he was picking up a pressure wave, something had to be generating it, something our navigational sensors couldn't see.

Jase double checked his command console while I angled our optics to starboard, filling our screen with nothing but clear blue sky.

"Zero neutrino emissions," Jase said, confirming if there was a ship out there, it wasn't running on reactive energy. That meant they'd progressed beyond nuclear physics as a power source, putting them way up there with the Tau Cetins!

"It began following us as soon as we launched," Izin said.

"Maybe they're just curious," Jase suggested, knowing advanced civilizations sometimes buzzed human ships without contacting them just to have a look at tech they'd abandoned long ago, but those were always chance encounters at deep space nav points. This was different. We were inside a planetary atmosphere far from any choke point. Whoever they were, they'd come looking for us.

"Izin, give me a marker," I said.

A contact icon appeared on the flight deck's wraparound screen, indicating the anomaly's position as we continued to climb.

"Time to say hello," I said, deciding to let them know we weren't as blind as they thought. I rolled the *Lining* sharply, threw hard g's at our internal acceleration field as I opened up the engines and headed straight for the invisible contact.

Jase braced, startled. "Skipper!"

The contact marker flashed off to the side of the screen with a burst of super acceleration, easily avoiding us. "That's what I was afraid of."

"What?"

"They're too fast to ram."

Jase looked at me like I'd lost my mind. "I'm glad of that!"

"Izin, are they still matching us?"

"Yes, Captain, same distance, same aspect as before."

I nosed the *Lining* up, putting her back on course for our bubble out point. "Enough games." Whoever they were, we couldn't catch them or stop them following us. I figured they'd let us know what they wanted when they were ready to talk.

We continued climbing out of the atmosphere, pursued by our invisible shadow, then three new contacts appeared beyond minimum safe distance.

"There they are!" Jase said as their signatures appeared on screen. "No transponders!"

They couldn't be Earth Navy or UniPol, both of whom broadcast who they were to ensure law abiding ships heaved to when ordered to do so.

"Let's see them," I said, angling our trajectory away from the new contacts.

Jase refocused our optics, putting the three incoming ships on screen. They were chevron shaped vessels, painted in elaborate red and orange livery, each individually larger than the Rashidun escorts.

"Shivas?" Jase said surprised.

They were the Rashidun's main rivals, a Republic syndicate who objected to the success of the floating black market. They would have seen us the moment we saw them, but they made no move toward us. Instead, the three Shiva gunships headed for geostationary orbit above the trading post. As the distance between us widened, I relaxed, certain they were going to let us escape unmolested.

"So now what?" Jase asked.

"We find out what's in the bottle." He'd caught a glimpse of it when I'd returned, as mystified by it as I was.

"How are we going do that?"

"Ask the alien-tech experts?" I said, entering our destination into the autonav.

When Jase saw where we were headed, he gave me an incredulous look. "They'll never let us in!"

I grinned knowingly. If a lowly human trader had been doing the asking, he'd have been right, but an Earth Ambassador was a different matter.

Just before we bubbled, the three Shiva raiders began bombarding the surface from orbit. Jasim Hajjar and his people would already be safely in their shelter, riding out each earthquake sized blast far below the surface. When they emerged in a few weeks, they'd find all that remained of Kedira Town would be a field of steaming craters. In six months, another Kedira would exist close to the remains of the first, ready for the next Souk.

It was the Rashidun way.

Chapter Three : Ansara

Restricted System – Non-Communication Class
Pelani System, Outer Ursa Minor
0.89 Earth Normal Gravity
904 light years from Sol
Tau Cetins

The *Silver Lining* exited superluminal flight at the edge of the Pelani System's heliopause, the outer edge of the system's physical and legal boundaries. Our sensors extended into space as bubble heat rapidly bled from the hull, then Pelani's tiny yellow orb appeared in the center of the flight deck's wraparound screen. A single circular marker indicated the location of the only planet in the system, while concentric rings of indicators identified the locations of thousands of artificial objects orbiting the star. It was a view few human eyes had ever seen, because only our diplomatic ships ever approached restricted systems. Like most Forum members in contact with mankind, the Tau Cetins refused to allow us open access to their inhabited worlds while our probationary status remained.

"There's only one terrestrial planet orbiting a hundred and forty million clicks out," Jase said as he studied the sensor data. "No moons, no asteroids, no gas giants, but lots of optical contacts, none of them natural. And the only neutrinos are from the star."

No surprises there. The TCs had moved beyond reactive energy sources long before *Homo sapiens'* distant ancestors had begun roaming the plains of Africa.

"Just your run of the mill Tau Cetin system," I assured him, knowing from my diplomatic training that all TC systems we'd visited looked like this.

The Pelani System was no mere colony. It had been transformed long ago into a fully developed home for the Tau Cetin Civilization, following a pattern they'd developed over millions of years. The TCs didn't terraform single planets, they reengineered entire systems to support their way of life. In a real sense, they had home systems rather than home worlds.

The solitary planet was called Ansara, a blue-green orb devoid of natural satellites with an engineered biosphere ideal for avian life. Once, other planets and moons had orbited Pelani, along with billions of pieces of rock and ice circling far out into the frigid depths of interstellar space, but no more. Now nothing larger than a grain of sand remained within a light year of Ansara's yellow sun. In their place, precisely positioned in concentric orbital rings beyond the planet were thousands of silver hexagonal prisms: two equal flat sides connected by six square surfaces. Each prism was hundreds of kilometers across with a circular hole at its center for ship docking. They'd been constructed from Pelani's now vanished planets and moons and from material drawn from nearby star systems. Some orbitals floated alone, others were mated side to side forming massive honeycombs in space or were joined end to end creating long multi-segmented super prisms. It was a simple, infinitely expandable design that had served the Tau Cetins for eons.

The silver prisms were the productive base of the Tau Cetin Civilization in this part of the galaxy, synthesizing everything they required with automated efficiency. A handful of human ambassadors had toured similar creations in the Tau Ceti system itself, the epitome of the model followed by the Pelani System, only on a vastly larger scale.

"Three thousand, four hundred and sixty one orbitals," Jase said impressed, "and over eighty seven thousand high velocity visual contacts."

"That we can see," I added, certain their system defenses were invisible to our sensors.

A powerful signal suddenly blanketed the *Silver Lining's* comm system. There was no image, just a terse audio message that blared from the speakers.

"Access Treaty provisions governing probationary species prohibit entry to inhabited systems class two and above. As no exemption has been provided, you are required to withdraw immediately. Failure to do so will result in relocation of your ship to the nearest human system and a formal protest being lodged with your government."

"Not very friendly, are they?" Jase said.

"They're not friends or enemies. They're Observers."

Observers were the arbiters of interstellar law, the supreme representatives of the Galactic Forum and the greatest technological and military powers in the Galaxy. They were meant to be impartial in all matters, although sometimes I wondered if the Tau Cetins didn't bend the rules just a little when it suited their interests. And with Earth only twelve light years from Tau Ceti itself, the TCs had more of an interest in us than if we'd been at the other end of the Orion Arm and we had no option other than to seek good relations with them. Proximity to such a powerful civilization made some nervous, but there were undeniable advantages in progressing from the stone age to the stars under the watchful, generally benevolent gaze of a galactic superpower.

"They're half a click above us," Jase said, orienting our optics toward them.

A sleek, silver dart appeared floating in perfect synchronization over the *Silver Lining*. It was small by their standards, hull polished to a mirror sheen with no visible sign of weapons or shields, but that meant nothing. Whatever armament it carried would be formidable, making this a very short conversation if I couldn't convince them to change their minds.

I switched off the ship's intercom. It was normally open so Izin knew what was happening on the flight deck, but any electrical signal would be easily read by the Tau Cetins. "Go tell Izin to stay in his stateroom. He's not to use the intercom or anything electromagnetic."

"Right!" Jase said, sliding off his acceleration couch.

Izin's ancestors had attacked the Tau Ceti System over two thousand years ago. If there was one species the TCs had cause to dislike, it was the aggressive and ultra-advanced Intruders – although that wasn't why I was ordering Jase off the bridge. Trying to hide Izin's presence from the Tau Cetins was pointless, as they would already know everything about us. What I wanted was to talk to them in private.

When Jase was gone, I transmitted a tight signal at the patrol ship. "I request diplomatic entry to Ansara. My recognition code is as follows..." I said, then recited an ambassadorial code from the vast array of security clearances stored within my bionetic memory.

The perimeter guard's response was immediate. "Ansara does not accept interspecies envoys. Diplomatic contacts can only be made through the Tau Ceti System."

"I understand, but this is an emergency. If I have to go to Tau Ceti, it'll take eight months to get there in this ship. I need help now. Today. It's an Access Treaty matter."

"What is your emergency?"

At least he was prepared to talk, which meant he could grant exceptions.

"I'm investigating a possible Treaty violation for Earth Council. I request Tau Cetin technical assistance to help me assess the scope of the potential breach."

"Access Treaty matters are the responsibility of the Observer Executive in the Tau Ceti System."

"In that case, I request a full exemption for any Treaty violations that occur in relation to this matter while I spend the next eight months going to Tau Ceti."

I threw that last bit in to tweak his beak, knowing the Tau Cetins would never provide mankind with a get out of jail free card – I wasn't even sure they could do such a thing – but they also couldn't ignore that I was trying to meet our obligations within the limits of human technological capabilities. It was a sneaky way of roping them in and they'd know it, but they'd have to swallow it because Observers never ducked their responsibilities.

The perimeter guard fell silent, presumably

communicating with his masters on Ansara even though the planet was many light hours away. After several minutes, he said, "Temporary diplomatic entry is granted pending assessment of your request."

I breathed a sigh of relief. "Thank you. What flight path should I follow to Ansara?"

"None. Your ship's spacetime distortion drive will not function inside the Pelani System."

No bubble? "Why not?"

"Ansara is protected by a system wide suppression field. We will move your ship to the planet, Ambassador. Standby."

Confirmation that the TCs had a means of collapsing spacetime bubbles on a system wide basis was a tantalizing piece of intel, even if it would be a very long time before we could replicate such technology. That wouldn't stop the EIS assembling a team to try to figure out how they did it.

The flight deck's wraparound screen distorted to white noise momentarily, then a garden world appeared below us. It looked the way Earth must have tens of thousands of years ago, before mankind had begun transforming its surface. Ansara's four continents were covered in temperate and tropical forests, vast islands of green surrounded by pristine blue oceans. White capped mountain ranges dissected two of the land masses, although there was a peculiar absence of barren regions. More strangely, there were no cities, no farmlands, no pollution, none of the indicators of civilization.

From high orbit, Ansara appeared to be a perfectly preserved natural environment – the opposite of what might be expected from the beating heart of an interstellar superpower. If I hadn't known better I'd have been surprised, but I'd read enough diplomatic reports describing their ancient origin world in the Tau Ceti system to know this was a close copy. To the Tau Cetins, planets were places where they lived according to their avian tastes, not places to spoil with cities and pollution.

The flight deck speakers sounded with the same synthesized voice that had greeted us at the Pelani heliopause. "Do not engage your reaction engines. Another ship is coming to transport you to the surface."

I swiveled the optics looking for the patrol ship, but it had already vanished. Instead, streaks of light flashed across the screen as TC craft went about their business, travelling at incredible velocities so close to a planetary mass. With their vehicles too fast to study, I focused on Ansara where millions of tiny, equally spaced gray dots were suspended above the endless expanses of green. Before I could investigate further, the screen filled with white noise again.

The *Silver Lining's* landing struts extended without me touching the controls, then the screen came back to life. We now sat on a circular gray platform high above a mist shrouded forest. It was one of the tiny gray dots I'd glimpsed from orbit, identical to thousands of others stretching as far as the eye could see. The platforms stood on thin, pole-like towers that rose through the trees to exactly the same height.

"Skipper," Jase said over the intercom, "the energy plant just shut down. One moment it was fine, next it was stone cold dead, like it had the life sucked right out of it."

No power, but the lights were still on? According to my console, life support, sensors and a thousand and one invisible machines that kept the ship going were all still functioning normally. Only weapons, propulsion and the E-plant were down. Somehow, they were feeding us juice even though there were no umbilicals attached.

I couldn't blame them for taking precautions. Human religious fanatics had detonated their ship's energy plant on the Mataron homeworld in 3154, triggering a thousand year suspension of mankind's interstellar access rights and turning the Matarons into our enemies – a big mistake considering the snakehead's xenophobic culture flourished when they had someone to hate. The Embargo had caused some human colonies to collapse, others to regress and had fractured Human Civilization for a millennium.

"They're just playing it safe," I said, slipping off my acceleration couch. "Stand watch up here while I go talk to our avian friends."

"On my way."

I headed for the hidden smuggler compartment amidships, passing Jase in the main corridor.

"How'd you talk them into letting us land?" he asked.

"They couldn't resist my charm and good looks."

"Now I know you're lying," Jase said, continuing on to the flight deck.

After retrieving the alien-tech canister, I headed down to the cargo hold's belly door. Once outside the ship, I found the landing platform was shielded from high altitude winds by invisible pressure fields. Just as I began wondering how I was supposed to get down, a synthesized voice sounded from the center of the platform.

"Remain where you are. A liaison is being synthesized."

Unsure how long I had to wait, I paced the platform, peering over the edge. A thick forest canopy obscured the ground below, while a tremendous variety of birds soared above the trees. If not for the landing platforms visible in all directions, Ansara would have appeared to be uninhabited.

A slender, highly reflective craft soon flashed down out of the sky, seemingly coming to an instantaneous stop as it landed. There was no sign of thrusters or exterior sensors or even an airlock, but moments after it touched down, an oval opening dilated in the hull and a beautiful, human female emerged. She had blue eyes, dark hair and perfect features, definitely not what I was expecting. I glanced back at the *Lining*, knowing Jase was cursing that he was stuck up on the flight deck instead of down here with me.

She approached me and smiled. "Ambassador Kade, I am your liaison while you are on Ansara," she said, offering her hand.

"I wasn't aware there were human diplomats on Ansara," I said, finding her touch warm and soft.

"There aren't," she replied in a cultured Unionspeak accent.

Her demeanor was professional and feminine, yet in spite of her beauty, I felt no rapport with her. That fundamental connection eliciting everything from love to loathing which all humans felt toward each other was missing, then I realized they'd meant exactly what they'd said: *synthesized.*

"You're an android?"

"I am. As you know, Tau Cetins are incapable of producing human vocal sounds. I will act as translator during your stay. If this form is unsuitable, we can synthesize another."

"No, you're fine," I said, adding, "they really made you since we arrived?"

She nodded. "Ansara has no facilities for dealing with human diplomats, so I was created for that

75

purpose. I have a full understanding of human customs, culture and languages for your convenience."

I whistled softly, not because she – it – was a flawless piece of engineering, but because they'd produced her in one of their prism orbitals in a matter of minutes. "Fast work. Do you take requests?"

"Galactic Forum protocols prohibit transfers of advanced technology to less developed species, Ambassador, with some exceptions of course. Unfortunately, your civilization does not qualify for any exceptions at this time."

"What do we have to do to qualify?" I'd thought galactic law prohibited advanced civilizations from accelerating primitive societies, but I shouldn't have been surprised there were exceptions. In a rules based pan-galactic civilization that had evolved over millions of years, there seemed to be a law and an exception for everything.

"A compendium of technology transfer protocols endorsed by the Forum could be sent to your ship if you like."

"Is it a quick read?"

"With addendums, annotations and case histories, it would translate to forty three million words."

"Tempting, but no thanks. I won't be here that long."

"As you wish."

"Do you have a name?"

"My design designation is 'Artificial meta-human species liaison'."

"Hmm … it's a bit dull, no offense."

"I understand. Human emotionalism has a need to anthropomorphize inanimate objects. I could adopt a simpler name if that would make you more comfortable."

"What's a meta-human?"

"A human-like abstraction that is beyond human."

"Beyond?"

"Millions of years beyond," she said simply, "from an engineering perspective."

It was typically Tau Cetin. "OK, how about I call you Meta for short? That satisfies my human emotional need to anthropomorphize you."

"As you wish, Ambassador. I will respond to Meta." She motioned for me to follow her. "This way."

She led me to the center of the platform, then there was a momentary blur of gray metal around us as we were transported down through the tower to the ground. I found myself facing a large round room with lounge chairs laid out in quarter circles at the center. Floor to ceiling windows surrounded the room revealing a dark, misty forest beyond.

Meta led me through a rounded doorway to a tiled patio where a solitary Tau Cetin sat by a small table. He looked like every other member of his species I'd seen: almond green eyes, pale dappled skin, a wide face with a small mouth, pointed chin and a tiny ridge-like nose. He rose to greet me, speaking in short sharp clicks that rattled off his tongue with machine-like speed.

"This is Jesorl," Meta said. "He will advise you."

"Thanks for agreeing to see me."

Meta didn't translate what I said, only Jesorl's clicking response to me. "What is it you require, Ambassador?" she asked on his behalf.

"I'd like to talk to an Observer named Siyarn."

Meta again translated for Jesorl, confirming this was how we were going to communicate. "Observer Siyarn is unavailable."

"When will he be available?" I'd counted on

contacting the one Tau Cetin I knew. Last time we met, he'd left me with the impression that he was favorably disposed toward mankind.

"There is no possibility of contacting Observer Siyarn at this time," Meta replied. "Intermediary Jesorl has been assigned to advise you. Please state what you require of us."

Taking that as final, I removed the alien-tech container from my jacket pocket. "I want you tell me what this is."

"Why?"

"Because it relates to an impending Access Treaty violation. If you can help me understand what it is, I hope to prevent it occurring." Technically, stealing alien-tech and kidnapping its owners was already an infringement, but the Tau Cetins didn't need to know that – not yet anyway.

Jesorl took the container and turned it over slowly before replying. "We will do as you request. Do you wish to return to your ship while we conduct our analysis?"

"No, I'll wait. I know you guys work fast."

* * * *

Meta showed me around Jesorl's estate while the Tau Cetins figured out what was in the cylinder. The house comprised a circular hub containing family living areas and three spokes for sleeping quarters and work spaces. It felt like a secluded country lodge hidden deep in a tranquil, mist shrouded forest. Similar houses were visible in the distance, each with their own landing tower and manicured paths, although none had gardens. Tau Cetins may have loved trees, but clearly had no particular affection for flowers.

"Does Jesorl live alone?" I asked, as we strolled along a path leading away from the house.

"There are seven inhabitants, including the Intermediary," Meta replied. "Two are away with the Ansara Squadron. One is quite old."

After Jesorl's white walled house faded into the mist, a small round vehicle barely wide enough for one passenger raced silently through the trees, reminding me Ansara's nature reserve appearance was a carefully crafted illusion.

"Why no cities?"

"They are not to our liking."

"But you had them once?"

"A long time ago," she conceded. "Ansara's population density is low by Earth standards, but its inhabitants are more closely connected on a planetary scale than on any human world."

"How many live here?"

"Eight hundred million."

"That's more than I expected."

"Eliminating agriculture and industry from the surface creates a great deal more room for habitation, and of course, agricultural and industrial production is more efficient in controlled, microgravity environments."

"When did you make the switch, from cities I mean?"

"We have lived this way for millions of years, Ambassador."

When I'd first received my EIS briefings on the Tau Cetins, it had seemed strange that such an advanced society had evolved beyond urbanization, had abandoned cities to return to a simpler way of living. Now that I was seeing it for myself, I understood why. They'd overcome every challenge the universe had thrown at them only to adopt a lifestyle paralleling their distant evolutionary origins, when their ancestors had roamed vast forests in small groups foraging for food. It was their natural state, now invisibly integrated with an all pervasive technology that served their every whim. What at first seemed strangely regressive was in fact a triumph of their genius and individuality. Technology no longer dictated how they lived, but served the ideal of who and what they were. It was a lesson humanity had yet to learn.

We walked on in silence, between trees that rose high above a sea of ferns carpeting the forest floor. In the canopy above, winged creatures flew among the branches, rustling leaves from sudden movements and occasionally screeching at each other, breaking the tranquility of the vast Ansaran wilderness.

"Earth used to have forests like this," I said thoughtfully.

"I know," Meta said. "Many trees on this world are from Earth."

"You have Earth trees here?" I asked surprised.

"Of course. Earth was one of the galaxy's richest biospheres before the human initiated mass extinction. Many civilizations took life forms from your homeworld for use in their own planetary engineering activities, or simply to feed their people."

"I never knew that."

"Earth flora and fauna are scattered across the galaxy. It is a mark of how rare your homeworld was, even on a galactic scale." She pointed to a stand of massively tall trees to our left. "Those trees over there are from Earth. You call them Sequoiadendron chaneyi. They are related to your present day sequoia."

"Related? Did you genetically reengineer them?"

The great trees looked similar to the few surviving sequoias I'd seen preserved on Earth.

"They are from your Miocene epoch, five to twenty three million years ago. They are extinct on Earth now. Perhaps I should have said your sequoia are descended from them."

"You brought them back to life?"

"No. Many civilizations study and catalogue the life forms of other worlds. The richer the world, the greater the interest. When we were engineering Ansara's ecosystem, we selected species suited to this world which we also found to be aesthetically pleasing."

Suddenly it hit me. The TCs had terraformed Ansara during Earth's Miocene era, when a now extinct species of sequoia had been alive on Earth. They hadn't revived it, they'd transplanted it!

"Over there," she continued, "that smaller tree with the radiating leaves is a species you call Annularia. It is from your Carboniferous period, three hundred million years ago."

"Hey! Even I know the Tau Cetins aren't that old."

"It was a gift from another species, one that had utilized it on their worlds."

Aliens taking plant samples from Earth a third of a billion years ago was almost impossible to conceive. "Anyone we know?"

"It was a Precursor Civilization, one that arose long before the Tau Cetins."

"I'll take that as a no."

"Such civilizations no longer involve themselves in the Galactic Forum. Their responsibility in that regard has passed to us and others like us." She stopped walking, distracted for a moment, then added, "I can say no more."

"Is someone listening?"

"All knowledge is shared freely on Ansara. It is an aspect of our interconnectedness."

"Is that why you don't translate what I say to Jesorl, only what he says?"

"He hears through my ears in his language."

"And you're only allowed to translate, not tell me about Precursors."

"I exceeded the parameters of allowed discourse with your species."

"You made a mistake? I kind of like that you're not perfect. It's something we have in common."

"My awareness is still integrating."

"With what?"

"My outer interacting awareness is simulated human, my inner consciousness is imprinted Tau Cetin. They are quite different. Getting them to work together takes time."

"Sounds schizophrenic."

"My human awareness was eager to share with you."

"So, you're still learning to channel your inner Tau Cetin." I was tempted to suggest she was an android with a multiple species disorder, but restrained myself.

We reached a fork in the way. Meta chose the path taking us in a circle around Jesorl's house.

"What happens to you when I leave?" I asked.

"My resource elements will be resynthesized."

"They'll scrap you?"

"Unless they decide it would be more efficient to retain me for future interactions with humans."

"How do you feel about them ending your existence?"

"I'm not opposed to it. I have no inner drive to exist beyond my created purpose."

"So no will to survive? Nothing?" I asked, strangely revolted at the prospect of Meta being recycled.

"A survival instinct is a necessary requirement for evolution, Ambassador, however, I'm not alive."

"You think, you reason, you make mistakes, why shouldn't you survive?"

"Do you feel the same way about your ship's processing core?" She smiled, adding, "Maybe you would, if it looked human."

"Right, I'm anthropomorphizing you again. Force of habit."

"And thinking is not the key to life, Ambassador, having a soul is."

I stopped, stunned. "Are you telling me Tau Cetins have souls?"

"Every species has a center from which they determine right from wrong. Such fundamental concepts are essential prerequisites for a rules based universe built upon responsibility and ethical principles acceptable to all sentient life. If there were no common agreement on ethics, there could be no galactic civilization. Without each life form having such a center, the universe would be chaotic. The strong would crush the weak. No species could coexist with any other. Not every species responds equally to the ethical impulse, but the vast majority do."

"It'd be a dog eat dog universe all right, not a place I'd want to live in." Not when mankind was the weakest dog in town.

"It would be a universe you would be *unable* to live in. Your planet would have been conquered long before your species had ever come into existence."

It was an astonishing thought. Not having been crushed before *Homo sapiens* had even evolved meant we'd been living in a rules based universe all along. It was a universe governed by an ancient galactic civilization created by species so old we'd never met them and probably never would. If it had been the other alternative, our distant ancestors would have been hunted down and killed before they'd ever climbed out of the trees. Sometimes, it paid to be lucky.

Jase's voice sounded urgently in my earpiece. "Skipper, can you hear me?"

I activated my communicator. "Loud and clear."

"The TCs have taken Izin! I tried stopping them, but my weapons wouldn't work."

I turned to Meta. "What's going on?"

Her face went blank for a moment as she tapped into Ansara's global network. "Izin Nilva Kren has been arrested."

"What for?"

"An Intruder Force has attacked the Forum Fleet blockading the Minacious Cluster. Izin Nilva Kren is therefore a member of an aggressor species at war with the galaxy."

* * * *

"He's a citizen of the Democratic Union of Earth!" I shouted undiplomatically at the silently impassive Jesorl at the entrance to his house. "I'm an Earth Ambassador and Izin is part of my diplomatic staff! You can't touch him!"

Jesorl clicked his reply for Meta to translate, "Considering the danger posed by his species, Izin Nilva Kren has been detained as a spy."

"He's not a spy! He's an engineer."

"Izin Nilva Kren is a member of the most dangerous species in this galaxy," Meta said on

Jesorl's behalf, "a species that has already invaded the galaxy once before and has attacked the Alliance Fleet several times since. That makes him a threat."

We knew the Intruders had invaded the galaxy during Earth's twenty first century – unbeknown to mankind at the time – but the tight lipped TCs had omitted to mention any other attacks. "So this is not the first time they've tried to break out?"

"They have made two other attempts in the last two thousand five hundred years," Meta replied. "Both were defeated."

"And you'll defeat them again, right? So why lock up Izin?"

"The Forum's blockade fleet has been forced to withdraw from the Minacious Cluster with heavy casualties."

"You lost?" I asked, stunned.

"We suffered a setback."

"But you're technologically superior to them!"

Meta gave Jesorl a human look seeking permission to speak, then he emitted a single click, assenting to her request.

"Our general levels of development are not equal," she said, "however, the Intruder Civilization focuses upon developing military technology in a way no other species does, not even the Matarons. For all our achievements, we are essentially a peaceful society. The Intruders are not. For thousands of years, they have been trying to surpass the leading Forum Powers in military technology, through research and espionage. Knowing this, we have followed their advances closely, retaining a marginal lead in military technology, however, they are extremely resourceful and our lead is not decisive."

"They caught you, didn't they?"

"They have achieved approximate parity, however, it wasn't technology that gave them the decisive advantage."

"I don't understand."

"The Alliance Fleet was betrayed. The locations of our early warning systems, our spacetime suppression fields and our fleet dispositions were all known to the Intruders prior to the battle. This allowed them to sabotage our detection measures and launch a surprise attack. Someone had to give them that information. It's the only possible explanation."

"How does anyone surprise ships like yours?" I asked incredulously.

"Surprise is measured in billionths of a second," Meta explained. "The Intruder forces knew precisely where our ships were. They appeared alongside them and fired blind. They could only have done that if they'd been provided with precise targeting information before they arrived."

"There's no way Izin could have anything to do with that!"

"Izin Nilva Kren is the only member of the Intruder species currently on any Tau Cetin world. The timing is highly suspicious."

"That's crazy. We don't even have the technology to find out what you're having for lunch, let alone where your fleet is! And even if we knew, we couldn't tell anyone. Do you know how long it would take us to get a message to the Intruder Fleet – wherever it is?"

"It would take your ship forty eight years to reach the Minacious Cluster, if you had the astrographics data required to navigate such a voyage."

"Which we don't, because you haven't given it to us!"

With the galaxy full of undetectable gravitational

hazards able to collapse superluminal bubbles with catastrophic consequences, our ships were restricted to the limits of the astrographic charts provided by the Tau Cetins. Those charts gave mankind access to a sphere of colonization and expansion that stretched approximately twelve hundred light years from Sol. It was why Mapped Space wasn't simply a collection of star charts, but the physical extent of Human Interstellar Civilization.

"You may lack the technology to communicate with the Minacious Cluster, but the Intruders do not. If Izin Nilva Kren is working for them, he has access to their technology."

"But he's not! And he doesn't!"

"If he were, Ambassador, you would never know."

I knew because I trusted him, but if I said that, they'd consider me a naive fool.

"We've never had contact with an Intruder ship – ever! I don't even know what they look like. As for this Minacious Cluster, I'd never heard of it before today and have no idea where it is."

"The Minacious Cluster orbits high above the galactic disk, approximately sixty five thousand light years from Earth."

"Sixty five thousand light years!"

"It may seem a great distance to you, but Intruder spies have penetrated this far into the galaxy before."

"So they regularly beat your blockade?"

"We contain their battle fleet. We cannot stop every ship from escaping, particularly small craft they have designed to evade detection. Some slip through. Most are caught and destroyed."

"But not all!" I said, beginning to realize the Tau Cetins weren't as infallible as they wanted us to believe.

Meta nodded. "Their spies are particularly interested in the Tau Ceti system. With Earth only eleven point nine light years away and home to an indigenous Intruder population, it is an ideal location from which to spy on us. Contact could have been established with Izin Nilva Kren, before he left Earth, by an Intruder spy hiding there. As a member of your crew, he has a freedom of movement no Intruder has, making him an ideal choice."

"Only in your paranoid imaginations!"

Jesorl emitted a short rapid fire burst of clicks which Meta translated, "The container you brought us suggests otherwise."

I hesitated, sensing from Meta's simulated humanity that I was missing something important. "What do you mean?"

"It contains a material beyond anything your civilization can currently synthesize, a material which relates to technologies able to undermine our security."

Her words were like a kick in the guts. I'd given the Tau Cetins the smoking gun that made Izin look like an Intruder spy! It was my fault he was under arrest. "It's mine, not his. He has nothing to do with it."

"The presence of such a substance in human hands is a concern to us, Ambassador, because you have no use for it. Intruder spies on the other hand do."

I was beating my head against a Tau Cetin brick wall. "So what now?"

"The Alliance Fleet is regrouping at the edge of the galaxy, awaiting reinforcements. That is why Observer Siyarn is unavailable. He has taken command of the Tau Cetin Fleet."

Siyarn commanded one the most powerful warships in this part of the galaxy, so it made sense he would lead their fleet. "And the Ansara Squadron you mentioned before, what's that?"

"It is this system's contribution."

Suddenly I knew why Jesorl was so intractable. Meta had said two of his family members were away with the Ansara Squadron, but I hadn't realized at the time what that meant. "And Jesorl has family members heading into the fight?"

"Yes Ambassador, one of his sons and his only daughter."

With Jesorl's own family at risk, my hopes of freeing Izin sank. "What are you going to do to Izin?"

"He will be interrogated. The results will determine his fate."

The way she said it gave me a feeling he was not being subjected to mere questioning. Whatever it was, Izin would hate it. "I want to see him – now!"

* * * *

When Jase saw the Tau Cetin android and I arrive on the landing platform above Jesorl's house, he hurried down from the *Silver Lining*.

"They had him before I even knew they were aboard," Jase said, giving Meta less attention than he normally would have paid a beautiful woman.

"It's not your fault," I said, it was mine. "This is Meta. She's an android, talks like a human, but is really a Tau Cetin at heart."

"Technically, I'm an artificial Tau Cetin consciousness within a simulated human self aware shell sustained by a synthetic human female bioform."

"And I thought human women were complicated!" Jase said, looking her up and down uncertainly before turning back to me. "They wouldn't tell me where they were taking him."

"We're going to see him now." A TC craft streaked down from on high and landed opposite the *Silver Lining*. "That must be our ride."

"I'm coming," Jase declared.

"Someone's got to stay with the ship," I said.

"What for? She can't fly and they can do anything they want to her."

He was right, the *Silver Lining* was completely helpless. "OK."

We followed Meta to the spindle-like craft. It was typically Tau Cetin, all polished reflective metal with no sign of a propulsion system. As we approached, an oval shaped opening dilated in its hull, then once aboard, the walls became transparent giving us unobstructed views outside the craft. Only the floor and the two rows of seats running lengthwise through the craft were visible.

"Wall screens?" I asked as the hatch irised shut.

"No," Meta replied. "Quantum refraction. The hull is designed not to impede visible light passing through it."

"Wouldn't that make the ship vulnerable to radiation?"

"Why would it?"

Having no idea what quantum refraction was, I let it go. Outside, Ansara fell away in the blink of an eye. Within moments, the planet shrank to a tiny dot as the craft hurtled toward the outer system, past massive hexagonal prism orbitals organized into a vast array of modular configurations, no two the same.

"Where's the prison?" I asked

"We have no prisons. Izin Nilva Kren is in a medical facility in the ninety eighth stratum."

"So what do you do with the hard cases?" Jase

asked. "The Saturday night stimheads?"

She gave him a quizzical look. "So it's true? Humans periodically inject toxic chemicals into their systems for recreational purposes?"

"Inject, snort, sniff and swallow," Jase said elaborately. "What do Tau Cetin androids do for laughs?"

"Study humans," she said deadpan.

"Ouch." Jase gave me a pained look. "There really is a Tau Cetin under that face, isn't there?"

I nodded. "And millions listening in."

"Not that many," Meta said. "They don't find primate behavior that interesting." She looked us both over curiously. "Which of you is the more prototypically human?"

"He is," I replied.

Jase inhaled impressively, "I'm a prime example of Oresund manhood, a lover and a fighter!"

"Really?" she said, silently dropping us a few more rungs on the evolutionary ladder.

An immense, flat sided hexagon loomed out of the darkness ahead. Several other prism orbitals drifted in the distance while the star Pelani had shrunk to a tiny glowing orb and Ansara was no longer visible. Our small craft entered the circular tunnel at the center of the prism, then passed through a huge space door into an enormous cylindrical chamber that could have docked dozens of ships. We glided to a stop close to the curved wall as a narrow bridge extended toward us forming a sealed walkway between our craft and the orbital.

"Is this entire station a hospital?" I asked as Meta led us across the walkway.

"It is more a laboratory than what you would think of as a hospital. It is equipped to remedy any Tau Cetin physical condition, conduct biological research and synthesize replacement components as required."

"Like cloning body parts?" Jase asked.

"No," she replied as we entered a long, softly lit corridor. "Cloning copies the patient's own genetic material. We construct new components from elementary biomatter and program the genetic coding directly. It is a process that eliminates replicative failure."

"Is that how they made you?" I asked.

"I am biomechanical. My outer dermal layer is human-like, but more durable and long lasting than your skin. My interior structure is flexion-carbon."

"Flexion-carbon?"

"It's a material we use extensively, extremely light and many times stronger than your polysteel. It is the strongest artificial substance in the universe. This orbital is constructed of it, as are our ships."

"Any chance of getting a sample?" I asked.

She smiled, amused at the prospect, then led us through a sliding door into a darkened room where Izin floated naked, bathed in soft beams of light. Three curved metal strips forming segments of a circle slowly orbited his head emitting thin beams of yellow light that swept up and down rhythmically over his long cranium. I started toward him, plowed straight into a pressure field and was pushed back with a gentle, unyielding force.

"What are you doing to him?" I demanded.

"Copying the electrochemical structure of his brain," she replied. "I assure you, he feels nothing."

"This is how you question a suspect?"

"The method is flawless. Once we have copied his memory and mental processes, we will disable any deception or resistance inherent in the original, creating a compliant duplicate which will answer every question with absolute honesty. If Izin Nilva Kren is a spy, the duplicate will confess."

"Does he get to testify in his own defense?"

"That is neither necessary nor desirable."

"So his life depends on what the copy says?"

"Yes. Such confessions have far greater weight under our law than his own testimony because there is no possibility of deception."

"What about his right not to incriminate himself?"

"We recognize no such right. That concept is nothing more than a piece of legal trickery used by primitive societies to allow criminals to avoid responsibility for their actions. Advanced societies are built upon a fundamental concept, that justice avoided is injustice. That applies as much to an individual as to an entire civilization. We seek truth. Once we know it, we act upon it."

"You have no secrets," I said, realizing in their society, no one could ever lie and get away with it. If they did that to me, my copy would reveal everything I knew, my threading, my work for the EIS, every dirty trick and double cross I'd ever pulled.

"Secrecy stands in the way of justice," she said simply. "In this case, it threatens the safety of the Tau Cetin people and of the galaxy itself."

"Is he asleep?" Jase asked, peering through the darkness toward Izin.

"He's conscious, but disconnected from all sensory inputs. A certain degree of cognition is required for the process."

"What does he think is happening?" I asked.

"He knows he's being interrogated, but is unaware of the method being used."

"Can he see me?" Jase waved a hand

experimentally, then yelled, "Izin!"

"He cannot hear or see you," she said.

"Free him now!" I demanded.

"Not until the copying process is complete."

"You have no right!"

"We have every right. The interrogation of Izin Nilva Kren is being conducted according to galactic law and with the full authority of the Forum. We must determine if the terrestrial amphibians of Earth are in contact with the Minacious Cluster."

"That's crazy," Jase said. "The tamphs couldn't keep something like that a secret from us!"

"We disagree," Meta said calmly.

"Is that why you've been following us?" I asked. It was a theory I'd been considering since Izin's arrest.

She gave me a puzzled look. "Why do you think we are following you?"

"There was a ship tracking us on Novo Pantanal. It wasn't emitting neutrinos. The only ships we know that can do that are yours."

Meta fell silent, listening to a conversation among those who were eavesdropping on us. Finally she said, "No Tau Cetin ships are following you."

"You expect me to believe that?"

"What you believe is of no concern to us, but it is the truth."

As an android, she could have lied through her teeth without any of the human signs of deceit, yet I believed her. The Tau Cetins played their games, but they'd never directly lied to us. "Who else has ships like yours?"

"No one in the Orion Arm. There are others elsewhere in the galaxy with similar capabilities, but why would they be interested in you?"

"What about the Intruders?" Jase asked.

"They have recently acquired a theoretical understanding of aspects of our technology, but they are still some way from being able to practically deploy it."

Damn! "They're catching you aren't they? And not just in weapons!"

"They have a remarkably single minded focus, at least for what they want. In any event, you would find their existing ships difficult to detect."

If it was an Intruder ship, why would it be following us? Were they trying to contact Izin? He'd been the one who'd detected them, proof he wasn't working for them, but other tamphs might be – especially the females. It made frighteningly good sense for the Intruders to use the tamphs of Earth to spy on our closest neighbor, who also happened to be their greatest enemy.

"Suppose there are Intruder spies among the tamphs. What then?"

"Skipper!" Jase exclaimed. "What are you saying?"

"Izin isn't a spy," I said, "but he's only one tamph in ten million."

"If the terrestrial amphibian population of Earth are cooperating with the Intruders, then they are implicated in the attack on the Alliance Fleet, in which case the tamph population will be returned to the Minacious Cluster."

"But Earth is their home!" Jase snapped.

"The Minacious Cluster is their home," Meta corrected. "Their presence on Earth is an accident of history, our mistake for not detecting them at the time."

"How can you return them?" I asked. "You've lost control of their home cluster."

"They'll be placed in suspension until the present

hostilities have ceased." She motioned to Izin, indicating he was in the state she was referring to. "An orbital is being prepared as we speak."

"You'd turn them all into sleeping zombies?" I asked.

"They will not be harmed, but if they pose a danger to us, they will be returned to where they belong."

"Does Earth Council have any say in this?"

"They'll be advised of the sentence, but will not be allowed to interfere in its execution."

"We'll protest to the Forum!"

"You are not yet members. Even if you were, you would find such a decision is in their interest as much as ours."

Suddenly, it hit me. They were looking for an excuse because the tamph presence so close to Tau Ceti made our mighty avian neighbors nervous. It was an abject lesson in how powerless we were when their interests and ours conflicted. All it would take was one tamph traitor and Izin would be condemned to their collective fate whether he was a spy or not.

It wasn't justice, it was a great power flexing its muscle.

* * * *

After watching Izin float helplessly for almost an hour, Meta said, "Jesorl wishes to speak with you."

"Has he made a decision about Izin?" I asked.

"No, he wishes to discuss the substance you brought to Ansara."

In my fury over Izin's arrest, I'd almost forgotten my reason for being there. "Does he know what it is?"

"I only know to take you back."

96

"I'm staying here, Skipper," Jase said, "until they let him go."

I glanced at Meta. "Any objections?"

"It is permitted. We will provide sustenance and accommodation while our investigation proceeds."

I left Jase there and followed Meta back to the boarding bridge. Floating above our spindle shaped transport was a large Tau Cetin ship. She was a sleek metallic dart hundreds of meters in length. Her normally mirror-like hull was pockmarked with circular black scars and her sharp bow had been completely blown off. Amidships, two ragged holes exposed melted interior decks. The only other TC warship I'd seen had been Observer Siyarn's Arbiter a year ago. It had left me with an impression of immense military power while this smaller version warned there were limits to Tau Cetin power.

"She looks pretty beat up," I said, stopping to watch as the stricken ship glided toward several docking bridges extending to meet her.

"She was lucky to survive," Meta conceded. "Many weaker allied ships did not." Once docked, lines of small silver capsules began streaming across to the prism orbital's open doors. "Those survival modules contain our wounded."

No wonder the TCs were mad. I hoped for the sake of all tamphs on Earth that they weren't on the wrong side of this fight. I hid my concern as I followed Meta into our transport, not taking my eyes off the damaged warship until we shot away from the prism orbital toward Ansara.

"That didn't look like you have much of a lead on the Intruders," I said.

"Once all laws of the physical universe are fully understood, technological advancement plateaus," she explained. "The differences between mature civilizations narrow even when they are of greatly different ages."

"That's why you're paranoid about being spied on, isn't it? They're closing the gap."

"They have always been a threat, now more than ever."

"But if the Tau Cetins are on the plateau, you must be closing in on the Precursors?"

"Progress exists on the plateau, but it is slow. Nevertheless, ten million years of gradual advance is an insurmountable lead."

"Does anyone ever pass someone ahead of them?"

"Only when civilizations stagnate or collapse. Generally, everyone advances together, at their own pace, only slowing as they near the plateau."

So, no matter how hard we tried, our place in the universe had been determined by a clock we didn't control and could never adjust. My mind turned back to the battered TC warship. "Did your allies survive?"

"Only the Yhinsar and the Ovani escaped."

"I haven't heard of them."

"They are Observers," she said as we plunged into Ansara's atmosphere. "The Yhinsar are from the Cygnus Arm. They fought with us against the Intruder Fleet two and half thousand years ago when it transited your Solar System."

"And the Ovani?"

"Their homeworld is very far. I don't know if they've ever visited Earth."

"So if only three of you survived ..."

She nodded. "Hundreds of ships belonging to minor powers were destroyed, including more than forty ships from the Orion Arm."

"Anyone we know?"

"The Syrmans, Minkarans, Matarons, Carolians and Gienans all lost ships."

"The Matarons were there?" I asked incredulously. I'd assumed the idea of cooperating with anyone would have repulsed them.

"Since the Vintari Incident you were involved in last year, they've been actively seeking to improve relations with us and the Forum Membership."

"Doesn't that strike you as strange? I mean, the Matarons hate you. Why would they suddenly want to help you?"

"We have embarrassed them on numerous occasions. After Vintari, they sought to improve relations with us. It is normal behavior for a weaker power to seek good relations with a stronger neighbor. Such a decision is rational and inevitable, even for inherently aggressive, fearful societies like the Matarons."

The snakeheads might just be sneaky enough to cozy up to the Tau Cetins, hoping one day to catch humanity out. I didn't like it, but Meta seemed unconcerned by their change of heart.

"How many ships did they lose?"

"Five. Mataron ships are as inferior to Intruder vessels as they are to ours. They could have escaped, but chose to stay and fight. A commendable, if rash choice. You see, even the most xenophobic species can learn in time to become valuable galactic citizens."

Once the transport settled on the landing platform above Jesorl's house, we took the elevator down to the surface. Jesorl was waiting for us on one of the curved lounges in the center of the main room. He began clicking in his native avian language before I'd even taken the seat opposite him.

"He wishes to know how you obtained the

cylinder?" Meta translated.

"I removed it from a human ship on a planet we call Novo Pantanal."

Jesorl twittered again in bird-speak, then Meta said, "And how did this human ship obtain the material?"

"I don't know, yet." If Siyarn had been there, I might have mentioned the frozen alien and the strange tech the *Merak Star* was smuggling, but with Jesorl threatening to turn every tamph on Earth into mindless zombies, I wasn't in a trusting mood. "I was suspicious. I couldn't identify it so I came here, because I thought we were on the same side of the galactic fence."

"Galactic fence?" Meta asked.

"Figure of speech. I don't suppose there's any chance of contacting Siyarn?"

"We have already communicated with Observer Siyarn."

"He's back?"

"No. He is with our fleet assembling along the Halo Threshold." The galactic halo was a long way away. For us to send a message even one light year required a courier ship, which took time. When she saw the puzzled look on my face, she added, "Our communications do not operate under the same limitations yours do."

Or course they don't. "What did he say?"

"He said we can trust you."

If my android liaison could read human expressions, she would have seen relief wash over my face. "What did I tell you!"

"But," Meta added slowly, "he could not vouch for Izin Nilva Kren."

"OK. You trust me, I trust Izin. Now tell me

what's in the cylinder?"

Jesorl clicked once, giving Meta permission.

"It is a form of matter, with negative inertial mass and negative energy density."

She might be translating for Jesorl, but if she was going to talk like that, I'd need Izin to translate for me. "That means absolutely nothing to me."

"It reacts oppositely to normal matter."

"So it's antimatter?"

"No. Antimatter has positive energy and mass, like normal matter. This material has negative energy and mass. Matter with a like electric charge repels. This material attracts. Your scientists call it exotic matter."

"Is it dangerous?"

"No. If released from containment, particularly in a planetary environment, it would instantly dissipate. Unlike normal matter, exotic matter is repelled by gravity. Its reaction to an applied force is opposite to what you would expect. Some prestellar civilizations believe they need it for superluminal flight, but lose interest once they learn to amplify the Casimir Effect, as mankind did."

The smuggler Nazari had been trading it for weapons. I wondered if it was a like for like trade? "You said it's not dangerous, so you're sure there's no possibility of a negative energy bomb?"

"We are certain."

"OK," I said with some relief, "so what's it good for?"

"Opposing positive energy."

"Give me an example."

"Stellar core engineering, wormhole stabilization, several quantum mechanical field solutions and certain forms of stellar communications."

Considering mankind didn't use this exotic stuff

and couldn't do any of the things she'd mentioned, I was left with a sinking feeling. "What's the communications range?"

"Transgalactic," she said slowly, exactly what a spy needed to spill the beans on Tau Cetin activities to a bunch of malevolent Intruders plotting their destruction in the Minacious Cluster.

"Humans don't have that kind of technology," I said, "so if someone on Earth wanted to call long distance, they'd need help doing it."

"They would," she agreed.

Was that what the alien-tech hemisphere on the *Merak Star* was for? "What would a transgalactic communicator look like?"

Meta and Jesorl fell silent while another discussion excluding me took place. "Any size," she said at last, "any shape, depending on the degree of miniaturization."

It was the proverbial how long was a piece of cosmic string. "Who knows how to make all this stuff?"

"Many mid level civilizations have the capability."

"How many?"

"Thousands."

"That narrows it down," I said bitterly, well aware that the Drakes could be dealing with any of them, swapping alien-tech contraband for Nazari's weapons.

"The energy requirements for exotic matter based technologies are very high," she added, "considerably above your current generating capabilities."

Sorvino's aleph-null warning was now ringing loudly in my ears. The Tau Cetins had suspected Izin of espionage, because he was descended from Intruders, but they'd missed the most obvious answer. The spies might not be tamphs at all, but humans!

102

There were plenty of scum sucking lowlifes rotten enough to be working with the Brotherhood and their alien-tech suppliers, people who'd sell out all of Human Civilization for a mountain of credits no matter what the consequences.

Whoever they were, I had to find them fast before this whole dirty business blew up in mankind's face.

* * * *

Jesorl left Meta and I alone for several hours. She wouldn't comment on how Izin's interrogation was proceeding, leaving me to pace anxiously while she kept me company in silence. When night fell, the forest became immersed in a misty darkness broken only by the distant lights of neighboring estates. Occasionally, other members of the household appeared, glanced at me curiously, then withdrew when our eyes met. Eventually, Jesorl returned late in Ansara's thirty hour day, greeting me with a short burst of avian chatter.

"Intermediary Jesorl says Izin Nilva Kren's questioning is complete," Meta announced.

My heart pounded in my chest. "And?"

"He has not been in contact with the Intruder Civilization."

I knew he was innocent, but I breathed a visible sigh of relief anyway. "So he's free to go?"

"He is being returned to your ship as we speak."

"What about the exotic matter container?"

"We have decided to keep it."

"That wasn't part of the deal."

"There was no deal, Ambassador."

"But it's mine."

"Technically you stole it, negating any lawful ownership right, whereas we have the authority to

103

retain it for further analysis and as evidence in any future Forum Inquiry." She hesitated, perhaps asking permission to speak further. "There is another reason why this material should remain with us."

"I'm listening."

"Whoever produced it would be able to detect it aboard your ship. That could pose a danger to you."

I hadn't thought of that. The last thing I needed was a glowing sign over my head warning some teched up alien spy I was onto them. "Consider it a loan, but I may want it back some day."

"We make no promises," she replied. "We are however prepared to transport you and your ship to Earth should you wish to make an immediate report to your Earth Council."

"No thanks." Whatever was going on, the answer lay out here a thousand light years from Earth. Anya and Nazari had mentioned meeting at a place called Loport. The only Loport I knew of was far enough off the space lanes that it made an ideal spot for shady deals beyond the reach of Earth's long arm.

"If you intend to continue your investigations in this region," she said, reading my expression with unnerving precision, "Intermediary Jesorl requests you provide him with a report when you have finished."

"Sure thing," I said, deciding it was better to work with the Tau Cetins than trying to freeze them out, although they'd only get a cut down version of what I sent Lena Voss. "Tell him Earth will deal harshly with anyone working against our mutual interests."

Jesorl considered my assurance before answering. "You are entitled to resolve matters relating to tamphs or humans internally, Ambassador. However, the extent to which other species are adversely affected by members of Human Civilization will determine the scale of our intervention."

It was an ominous warning and there'd be no getting around it. If there were traitors in our midst, if humans or tamphs had betrayed the Tau Cetins, it would go very badly for us. "I understand."

"Any action you take on behalf of your government to mitigate the situation will, of course, be given due consideration by the Forum."

It wasn't much, but it was a ray of hope. I considered telling Jesorl any humans or tamphs involved in betraying the Alliance Fleet were dead men walking, but I figured he'd interpret that as my primitive need for revenge, so I tried to sound ambassadorial instead. "I can assure you, Earth will meet all its Treaty obligations in full."

"If that is true, then we are indeed on the same side of the galactic fence," Meta said.

Now that I was leaving, I realized she was only minutes away from being reprocessed. It seemed a harsh end to such a short existence. "I hope you'll still be around if I ever get back this way."

"Anthropomorphizing me again, Ambassador?" She smiled with simulated human amusement.

"Call me a sentimental primate."

"Intermediary Jesorl has decided that considering how rapidly your species is expanding, he will need a permanent liaison for future human contact."

"Glad to hear it," I said, genuinely relieved. "I guess that means you owe your continued existence to humans."

"Goodbye, Ambassador," she said with no sign of appreciation.

I took the elevator up to the landing platform. A small TC transport was parked on one side, the twin of the craft that had carried us out to the medical station.

Jase and Izin had already exited and were about to board the *Silver Lining*.

"Izin!" I said. "Good to see you in one piece!"

"Thank you, Captain," he replied, "but the Tau Cetins did not dismember me."

"They might as well have!" Jase snapped, "Keeping you hanging up there like a lab rat!"

Izin glanced at Jase. "It was not an experience I care to repeat, but thank you for being there."

"Hey, we're shipmates!"

Izin considered Jase's reply, as if seeing him in a new light. "Indeed we are."

Whether Jase knew it or not, Izin had his back from now on in a way he never had before, the same way he had mine – the way I had both of theirs.

"What did it feel like?" I asked.

"I was a bystander, aware but powerless, reminded of every memory I ever had … It was a remarkably irritating experience."

"Well, let's get out of here before they change their minds," I said as we headed up into the ship.

When Jase and I reached the flight deck, a synthesized TC voice sounded from the intercom. "Prepare for relocation to interstellar space." The belly door sealed shut without any action from us, then the wraparound screen filled with white noise.

"This is one place I'm in no hurry to come back to," Jase said as we took our positions on the acceleration couches, waiting to get back control of the ship.

"It's a beautiful planet."

"If you like trees," he said sourly. "The best thing down there was the android."

"They're keeping her intact."

Jase gave me an intrigued look. "Hmm … I

wonder how good a simulation she is?"

"I'm sure she's perfect in every way."

He looked thoughtful. "I guess I could do worse."

The screen flickered to life revealing we were back where we started and the TC tow ship was already gone.

"Not ones for chit chat, are they?" Jase said.

"They chatter a lot, just not with us."

"So did you get what we came for?"

"More than I wanted," I replied grimly, entering our destination into the autonav.

"Captain," Izin's voice sounded from the intercom, "I'm detecting the same magnetic anomaly we saw on Novo Pantanal."

I glanced at Jase. "Anything?"

He checked the sensors and shook his head. "There's nothing out there."

"It's approaching the port airlock, Captain," Izin said. "They mean to board us!"

Would an Intruder ship risk revealing itself so close to Ansara? I guessed it depended on how badly they wanted us. I considered hailing the Tau Cetins for help, but if they had no ship nearby, it would be hours before our signal reached the nearest prism orbital. And if Intruder spy ships were as sneaky as Jesorl had implied, the TC system defenses might not even see it once it locked onto us.

"Pull sensors!" I ordered, pushing the maneuvering engines to their maximum inertially shielded acceleration. Thirty-five g's was nothing for a ship with TC level tech, but we only needed a few seconds to button up. I rolled the *Lining* hard away to starboard, hoping our engine blast caught the prowler by surprise.

"Go!" Jase said the moment our delicate sensors

were safely stowed.

I released the autonav, praying we weren't about to get a nasty surprise. A moment later, the bubble formed and the screen filled with telemetry confirming we were superluminal.

"How's it tracking us?" Jase asked.

No signal could penetrate a bubble's quantum distortions. That's why we always flew blind when we were superluminal. As far as I knew, no one – not even the TCs – had a way around it. It made tracking another ship through interstellar space a physical impossibility, yet somehow, Izin's magnetic anomaly had followed us from Novo Pantanal.

"Izin," I said over the intercom, "check every system diagnostic we have from Novo Pantanal to now."

"What am I looking for, Captain?"

"That bastard's tracking us. I want to know how. You've got ten days before our next stop." I exchanged wary looks with Jase. "If I'm right, they'll be there waiting for us."

Chapter Four : Hardfall

Union Mandated Colony
Lornat System, Outer Draco
1.43 Earth Normal Gravity
939 light years from Sol
58,000 humans

Moments after we unbubbled half a million clicks out from Hardfall, eight long range surface batteries began tracking us. The speed with which they had us target locked and the size of the energy spikes emanating from the planet warned that we weren't facing a bunch of half trained farm boys. It wasn't the reception I was expecting from a tiny colony on a dying world.

"No one here but us," Jase reported after a quick review of the sensors.

"Izin, are you picking up that magnetic anomaly?"

"Not yet, Captain," Izin replied from engineering. After a week and a half reviewing every system log in the ship, he'd found no clue as to how we were being tracked.

"Give them the transponder," I said, eager to land before we had company.

If the grunts on the ground didn't like the look of us, we'd never know it. Any flash from the surface batteries would reach us the same moment the blast did, giving us no time to run. Being only eight light years from the Acheron Abyss dark nebula, a known Drake hot spot, I couldn't blame them if they were a bit twitchy. Hardfall was a Union colony so they rated some protection, but the firepower aimed at us looked more like it belonged guarding a military base than a bunch of dirt-loving freeholders.

A cluster of threat indicators appeared on screen over the southern hemisphere, marking the space gun's location on the planet's only substantial land mass, a super continent known locally as Prairieland. It stretched from the southern pole to the northern tropics, occupying a third of Hardfall's surface area, with the remainder taken up by receding oceans and isolated island chains. Large river valleys snaked from towering mountains in the east, across vast plains to the desolate west coast, although only the great rivers of the south still held water. Their northern cousins were now dry and barren scars across a once fertile land.

The decline was due to Hardfall's dying star which grew imperceptibly in luminosity each century, slowly transforming the planet into a hot, dry wasteland. It was why Hardfall's previous inhabitants had abandoned the planet long before humans had arrived. Now only the crumbling ruins of a great megacity sprawling unbroken along Prairieland's vast northern coast remained as a monument to their faded glory. The equatorial city had flourished when the tropics had been dominated by lush rainforests and monsoonal rains, neither of which had been seen on Hardfall for thousands of years. In their place, baking desert had consumed the northern lands, turning to arid plains at the mid latitudes and rolling grasslands in the far south.

After Hardfall's original rulers had departed, the planet's predatory wildlife reclaimed what was left in a desperate fight for survival that triggered one last evolutionary gasp of adaptation. As the northern grasslands dwindled and competition increased, the hunters grew in ferocity and size while the hunted became tough, armored creatures ready to trample any attacker. Land that had once been frozen tundra became the last grasslands Hardfall would ever know, drawing the dwindling herds of bone-plated herbivores south, followed by the fiercest predators that had ever walked the planet's surface.

It was then that humans arrived.

They found the predatory wildlife so aggressive that they were forced to live in fortified communities atop defensible plateaus, veritable island fortresses amid an ocean of hostile land. While their weaponry could defeat any single animal, they couldn't defeat them all, especially not at night. Every attempt to set up farms on the banks of the surviving southern rivers had ended in disaster.

More pervasive than the dangers of the lowlands was the high gravity. The colonists had endured broken bones and fatal falls for three generations before the Union had provided genetic enhancements that turned the colonists into a stocky, thick boned offshoot of mankind. It was partly the gravity that gave Hardfall its name and partly a salute to the first colony ship, the *Dahlia*, which had landed hard and never flew again.

Hardfall was one of the few defended locations close to the Acheron, inhabited by people adapted to their environment, yet with no chance of surviving their dying star. It was the lot of mankind – latecomers to the galaxy – to pick up what no-one else wanted and make something of it. Watching the brown-blue planet floating on the screen, I felt a twinge of regret that it wasn't a few billion years younger, but then it wouldn't have been abandoned and we wouldn't have a colony there now if it were.

"Silver Lining," a woman's voice sounded from the flight deck communicator, "proceed to Hiport. Our guide beam is enabled. Do not vary your flight path or activate your weapons. Shields are permitted for atmospheric insertion. Be advised you are entering Union controlled space and will be fired upon if you deviate from these instructions. Acknowledge."

My listener told me her accent was East Euro descended, not a native of Earth or Hardfall, but from Ardenus, a large Core System world a hundred and forty two light years from Earth. Ardenus had been colonized by the Democratic Union centuries before the Embargo and had resumed a loose affiliation with the Union after contact had been restored a thousand years later. Both Earth Navy and the Union Regular Army recruited from there, but as neither stationed unmodified humans on high gravity worlds, her presence here was somewhat surprising.

"I don't suppose she'll let us land at Loport?" Jase asked.

"She wants us under those big guns in case we're not who we say we are."

Four of the colony's surface batteries had direct line of sight to the Hiport Landing Zone, while Loport had only one battery and it covered the approaches, not the landing field itself.

"Hardfall control, acknowledged," I replied, then

followed the guide beam down.

The approach path kept us squarely in the firing envelopes of all eight batteries, making sure we did exactly as we were told. A thousand clicks out, we began passing over outlying plateaus that had been leveled and sealed off from the plains by the colony's engineers. They were all covered in rows of tightly packed green houses, providing the colony with its only source of agricultural produce. Homesteader families operated them, guarded by sheer cliffs and linked to the main settlement by air. Some had armored ground vehicles strong enough to withstand attacks from the larger predators, but the distances were great and vehicle hoists were expensive.

After dropping through a cloudless blue sky, Hardfall Colony came into view. It comprised one large mountaintop city known as Citadel, a smaller flattened plateau called Hadley's Retreat and two landing grounds perched atop leveled ridges, Hiport, which was almost as high as Citadel, and Loport, which rose barely above the plains. They were joined by heavy cables supporting capsule-shaped transport pods that shuttled passengers and cargo between them, safely out of reach of the dangers below.

Since the colonists arrival over a hundred and sixty years ago, every natural path to the mesa tops had been destroyed, ensuring the only way up was by air, internal elevator or aboard one of the massive vehicle cranes that reached out over the cliffs. The cranes had been brought in by the Union in an effort to make access to the plains easier, but old habits die hard. Most colonists still preferred flying to riding, even though their multi-wheeled vehicles were armored and mounted automatic weapons.

Citadel was perched on a flattened mountain top

surrounded by sheer cliffs. We passed to the north of it, riding our thrusters down to Hiport, tracked all the way by dome-shaped turrets that looked like they'd still be firing long after the city had been reduced to a molten slag heap.

"No wonder the Drakes steer clear of this place," Jase said, suitably impressed.

"They look new." Considering Hardfall exported nothing of value and had gravity high enough to discourage migration, someone must have had good political connections to convince the Union to invest so heavily in the colony's defense.

"What's that on the ground?" Jase asked, motioning toward a large rectangular cage between Hadley's and Citadel. Inside the cage was a four legged creature the size of a small elephant. It was covered in shingle-like bone plates, had a massive angular head and a thick stump where its horn had been sawn off.

"They call them tankosaurs."

"I can see why."

"It's a harmless herbivore," I said, "unless you make it mad."

"What happens if you make it mad?"

"It'll disembowel you with its horn and trample your body into mush."

"Why's it in the cage?"

I hadn't been to Hardfall in years, but seeing the tankosaur staked out like that told me when it came to this, little had changed.

"It's a bait trap."

Jase gave me a curious look. "That thing's bait? For what?"

"Dinner. There's no farming on the plains but there's plenty of meat, if you can kill it before it kills you. There are gun platforms set into the cliffs to shoot whatever takes the bait. It's good training for the local militia and it helps feed the colony."

Dark blood stains surrounded the bait trap from decades of slaughter while a well worn track led back to the foot of the cliffs. Above the track was a giant crane, used to lower the armored recovery vehicles to the plain and hoist the catch up to the city.

We flew over the bait trap, then began our descent onto Hiport's flattened crest. The summit was long and narrow, only wide enough for ships to berth side by side. A group of small aircraft were parked near the spaceport building at the southern end, close to a cable car station linking Hiport and Citadel. A small orbital transport and an old intersystem ferry, both overdue for the scrap heap, were parked north of the aircraft. When the guide beam finally dropped and the spaceport's crude docking system took over, we were ordered to land north of the old ferry, then the Approach Controller's voice gave us the obligatory warnings.

"Hardfall is a Union Mandated Colony subject to all Earth Council directives. As such, Access Treaty violations are punishable by death. Should you choose to go onto the flatlands, the colonial government accepts no responsibility for your safety and will not mount rescue missions. Freelance hunters will assist you for a price, providing you pay in advance using a valid Earth Bank vault key. Be advised, conventional side arms with less than Union Regular Army level seven armor piercing projectiles are ineffective against some indigenous species. The people of Hardfall welcome you to the colony and hope you enjoy your stay."

URA level seven? My P-50, even with hardtips, was only L5.

"Friendly bunch," Jase said. "I don't suppose

there's much night life here?"

"If there is, I'm sure you'll find it. Just remember, if you fall down drunk, the gravity's going to hurt." His initial eagerness wavered, then I added. "Finish the shutdown and you'll see what I mean."

When he killed the ship's inertial field, we sank into our acceleration couches. "Ooh, that is kind of heavy," he said lifting his arms, testing the planet's pull.

Humans normally didn't settle worlds with gravity more than ten percent above Earth normal. Hardfall was an exception, but only because the first colonists didn't have the option of moving on.

"Plus forty three percent," I said. "Not enough to put you in g-braces, just in hospital if you stub your toe. And remember, the women are genetically engineered."

"So they're what? ... Stronger than me?" A curious look crossed his face as he wondered what it might be like to be dominated by a Hardfall woman.

"Increased bone density, muscle mass, enlarged heart, improved lung efficiency and reduced body height," I said.

"Oh, so it's a planet of dwarves? Izin will fit right in!"

Izin's synthesized voice immediately sounded from the intercom. "I'll have you know, I'm considered tall for my kind."

I leaned towards the intercom. "How are you finding the gravity?"

"Mildly unpleasant, Captain."

"Better get used to it, there are no powered walkways here," I said, easing myself onto the deck and testing my weight. Ultra-reflexed or not, I'd have to be careful in Hardfall's gravity. "And cover up, I don't want you spooking the locals."

"Considering the creatures humans hunt on this planet," Izin said, "they're unlikely to be frightened by my appearance."

"I don't know," I said, feigning uncertainty, "tamphs are a lot scarier than fleshrippers."

"I find that comment strangely gratifying."

Jase gave me a wary look. "Fleshrippers?"

"Piranha with legs," I said with a grin, then went to prepare to reconnoiter Loport.

Now that we were here, I was wracked with doubt. Had I guessed wrong? Was there another Loport? Last time I'd been here, Hardfall had been a toothless backwater. Now it was a fortress with fangs. So how did a gun runner and a Drake raider expect to land under the noses of Hardfall's space guns without getting blown to bits?

Why would they even try?

* * * *

The Skylink terminal at the southern tip of Hiport plateau was a simple white building beneath a massive cable support tower. We bought three tickets from an automated vendor, walked up a metal ramp and caught the next southbound capsule to Citadel. It was an eight kilometer journey along a gently sagging polysteel cable through still air to the colony's only city. Far below, armored herbivores appearing no larger than black dots grazed dry grassland in scattered groups.

"I wouldn't want to be in one of these things if it fell," Jase observed, leaning against the window, looking down.

"I'd rather we not discuss that possibility," Izin said, sitting as far from the windows as he could. He wore a one piece coverall over his pressure suit with his helmet set to opaque to hide his amphibian features. The locals would know he was an alien off a ship, but not what kind of nonhuman, reducing the risk of some trigger happy redneck shooting him simply because he was a tamph.

Jase took on a mischievous look, remembering Izin's aversion to heights. "If we fell, how many seconds would it take before we hit the ground? Ten or eleven?"

"Less," Izin said, "considering the higher gravity. Perhaps you should try jumping to put it to the test."

Jase and I exchanged amused looks, leaving Izin to suffer in silence.

When we approached Citadel's rust colored cliffs, I directed Jase's attention to a gun platform jutting from the rock face close to the ground. It was manned by a group of uniformed troopers. One sat behind a short barreled field gun mounted on a metal column while the others scanned the plains with biscopes looking for targets. A narrow ladder led down from the gun platform to a ten wheeled, armored recovery vehicle waiting to tow their kill to the nearest vehicle hoist. A track led out from the cliffs to a bait trap containing a tankosaur calf. The creature had a nasty wound in its side, inflicted by the hunters so the smell of blood would attract their prey.

Jase studied the surrounding dry plains and shook his head. "No meat for dinner tonight," he said, unable to spot any approaching predators.

"They're out there," I said, "you just can't see them."

"In that case," Jase said lightly, "I'm glad I'm up here."

As we neared the cliffs, the gunner started firing,

sending tracer screaming out into the plain. While Jase tried to discover what the hunters were shooting at, my attention was drawn to two of the dome-shaped surface batteries covering Hiport. They were perched on the cliff tops five clicks apart, scanning the sky now that the *Silver Lining* had been assessed as no threat. They were heavies, designed to kill large targets at suborbital ranges and beyond, but would struggle against fast moving targets at close range. It was a strange choice for a colony so close to the Acheron where Drakes often used small, fast raiders rather than frigate sized warships.

A couple of Union Regular Army troopers were visible guarding the nearest battery. They were tall lean types, definitely not Hardfallers. Considering the gravity, I'd expected the URA to have trained local militiamen to man the guns, not station offworlders here. Maybe the colonists would rather farm and hunt than subject themselves to military discipline? It wouldn't have been the first time freewheeling frontier types had eschewed military service.

We passed over a low wall encircling the city and came to a halt inside Citadel North station. Passengers and cargobots exchanged places for three minutes before the transparent doors sealed and we were moving again, this time over crowded, narrow streets wedged between neatly ordered buildings, some ten stories high. Above the frenetic streets, flat topped roofs joined by a network of foot bridges were filled with gardens and entertainment areas, serving as refuges for the local residents from the press of the city.

Stocky colonists and small solar powered vehicles filled the streets, although curiously for a frontier world, no one wore weapons. It was a custom they'd developed celebrating the safety of their high mountain fastness. The fact that Jase and I wore our guns openly was not lost on the other passengers, who gave us suspicious looks but otherwise ignored us.

We stopped once more, this time at the station on the south side of the city, before gliding out over the cliffs for the long ride down to Hadley's Retreat. Far to the south, beyond a few grazing tankosaurs, a six wheeled armored beetle raced across open ground, kicking up a dust trail that hung in the air long after the vehicle had disappeared into the distance. Eventually, the low island of Hadley's Retreat took shape as the cable car carried us in a long sweeping arc over the plains. It was a slender mesa with a bulge in the middle filled with sun bleached, one story stone buildings and a thinning tail pointing south toward an even smaller and lower mesa in the distance.

The Skylink ended in a terminal building at the northern end of Hadley's. From there, a dirt road led south through the town to Loport Link, the colony's second suspension system joining the smaller inhabited plateau with the backup landing ground further south. Unlike Citadel, which loomed in the distance like an urban giant against a cloudless sky, Hadley's dusty little town was dissected by broad avenues and open plazas, had no street vendors, few vehicles and scarce signs of life.

As we marched south, I realized the gun emplacements perched above Citadel's southern cliffs commanded Hadley's Retreat, but none of the smaller town's weapons had line of sight back to the city. It was as if whoever had sited the colony's defensive firepower had intended for the micro-city to dominate the rest of the colony unopposed.

"What's up?" Jase asked, wondering what I was

staring at.

"It's probably nothing."

The few inhabitants of Hadley's Retreat we saw viewed us with even more suspicion than those on Citadel. Their eyes followed our every step, then as we approached, they retreated, closing doors and shutters as we passed. Only once we'd moved on, did they reappear behind us, whispering and staring.

"I feel like every shadow's watching us," Jase said as we entered Hadley's central bulge.

"I know what you mean," I said.

"At least they're not armed."

"They're all armed," Izin corrected, "and there are snipers in the windows."

"You can see them?" I asked, noticing that some shutters were open but the interiors were impenetrably dark.

"Yes, Captain. Their weapons are primitive, but heavy caliber. Starting a fight here would be inadvisable."

The town's main square was paved in stone with a stand of small Earth trees providing shade at its center. Several children playing among well tended flower gardens were ushered out of sight by their mother as my DNA sniffer warned we were being followed. He was easy to spot, a stocky colonist with a weather beaten hat, leathery skin and an ugly black metal articulated claw for a left arm. His prosthetic must have been a local device, but from the ease with which he rubbed the back of his neck with it, its neural interface was as efficient as any Earth-made attachment.

Jase followed my gaze. "What's Clawhand up to?"

"He's their leader," I said.

"How can you tell?" Jase asked.

"The others watch him, waiting for a signal," Izin

said, having seen the same signs I had.

Clawhand leaned against a wall, waiting for our next move. I considered approaching him, but decided that might trigger a response I wasn't ready to deal with, so we continued on, never passing out of the gaze of our one armed shadow.

At the southern tip of the mesa, the paved avenue ran out along a tongue of land flanked by stone walls and sheer cliffs to a decrepit cable station. A pair of cables ran off toward a rocky promontory called Lone Peak where a support tower took their weight before they passed out of sight for the second leg down to Loport.

I produced my monoscope and zoomed in on Loport mesa, visible beyond Lone Peak. The summit was barely twenty meters above the plains, low enough for predators to have been a constant threat before engineers had sealed it off. There were no ships on the landing field, only two URA uniformed guards patrolling the cliff tops, too tall and slim to be genetically modified Fallers.

"What are all those bones, Captain?" Izin asked, pointing toward a large expanse of bleached white skeletons in the distance.

I lowered my scope, glancing in the direction he'd indicated. "That's the Boneyard." I pointed to a dull gray shape lying in the baking sun toward the south eastern horizon. "And that's the wreck of the Dahlia, the first colony ship. The landing broke her back, cracked her hull wide open."

Jase borrowed my monoscope for a better look, whistling slowly as he studied the hundred and sixty three year old wreck. Beside him, Izin polarized part of his helmet to give his naturally telescoping eyes a better look.

"They fought their way here," Izin said, correctly interpreting what the animal bones meant.

"That's right," I replied slowly. "When she came down, she attracted a lot of attention. The colonists didn't realize what they'd walked into until the fleshrippers were inside the hull. By then it was too late. They fought for three days before abandoning ship. Some women and children got here in ground vehicles, most came on foot. By the time they started across, the smell of death had attracted every meat eater for a hundred clicks."

"Nowhere else to go, I guess," Jase said, studying the horizon, realizing Hadley's was the nearest elevated land to the wreck.

"A third didn't make it, but that was just the beginning. Their supplies and equipment were on the ship and the plains were crawling with death, all kinds of creatures fighting over human and animal corpses alike. They nearly starved."

"They were lucky," Jase said, handing back my monoscope.

"They were stupid," I said. "If they'd surveyed the planet properly from orbit, they could have landed up here, or on Citadel, and lost no-one."

"A costly mistake," Izin observed.

"Ready for another ride?" I asked, starting toward Loport Link station.

When we reached the entrance, four URA uniformed guards appeared carrying heavy assault weapons. None were Fallers.

"The Link is closed for maintenance," a guard with sergeant's stripes and an Ardenan accent snapped.

I looked past our welcoming committee to the small control room and the spherical gondolas crawling along the parallel cables. There were no mechanics in sight, no sign of any breakdown.

"For how long?" I asked.

"Five days."

The obvious lie immediately irritated Jase. "Since when does maintenance require an armed guard?"

"Since we said it did," the sergeant replied with an arrogance that Jase instantly took as a challenge.

I placed a restraining hand on his arm. Starting a fight without knowing who we were up against wasn't what I was here for. "We'll come back in five days," I said, nodding for Jase and Izin to follow me.

Once we were out of earshot, Izin said, "We can return after sunset. They'll be no challenge at night."

"They're no challenge now!" Jase snapped. "Did you see the look on that grunt's face?"

"Did you see the weapons they were carrying?" I asked.

"Yes, Captain," Izin replied, "Vel penetrators."

"That's Indo gear," Jase said, puzzled.

"Republic standard issue," I agreed. Named after a Hindu war god's spear, Vels were high end infantry assault weapons. They were just the kind of thing the *Merak Star* was feeding the Drakes on Novo Pantanal, but not a weapon the Union Regular Army used.

"So those troops are …?" Jase asked uncertainly.

"Imposters."

Hardfall might have a Union mandate, but it was at the ass-end of nowhere. It would be years before anyone on Earth had any idea the colony was under criminal control and it would take at least another year before anything could be done about it. No wonder the local colonists viewed outsiders with suspicion!

"Captain," Izin said, motioning subtly toward the southern sky. His remarkable eyes had been the first to see it, a long silver gray slab dropping from orbit on a

124

power glide toward Loport. "It's the Merak Star."

I watched through my monoscope as the freighter came down, braking all the way. When she was over the tiny spaceport, she flared on thrusters, then settled onto the shaved rock landing ground. No hatches opened, no one went to meet her and the two guards continued pacing the perimeter as if she was a common sight.

"What now?" Jase asked.

"You two get back to the ship," I said. "Calculate the firing envelopes of those big guns in case we have to bust out of here. I'm going to check who's got landing rights on Hardfall."

We headed back to the Skylink terminal, watched every step of the way by Clawhand. When we boarded the transport capsule back to Citadel, he took a seat at the opposite end, making no secret of his interest. All through the long climb back, I felt his eyes on me as I wondered if we were about to be arrested. When the gondola stopped at Citadel South, I waited until the doors were about to close, then jumped out. Clawhand hurried after me, but the doors slid shut in front of him, trapping him inside. He gave me an irritated look, then produced a communicator and spoke rapidly into it as the gondola carried him away from the station.

While Jase and Izin continued on toward the ship I hurried down into Citadel's narrow, crowded streets. My threading's map of the city was almost a decade out of date due to infrequent Earth Navy surveys, but the Society's offices hadn't moved in half a century. They were located in a relatively modern looking five story building with the usual security precautions that required me to surrender my gun at the door.

The Exchange was small, just four terminals on the ground floor offering Society underwritten contracts, mostly off world fetch and deliver type deals, but as this was high threat space close to the Acheron, the completion bonuses were sky high. Most were sponsored by the Union colonial administration, although a few were put up by local farmer co-ops desperate for spare parts. Some were many months old, indicating few traders visited the planet, which in itself helped drive up prices. Hardfall might have been the place to come for fast money, but only for those few willing to run the Drake gauntlet.

A quick search of actives found no inbound or outbound consignments for the *Merak Star*. It had been a long shot, hoping Nazari had picked up side contracts revealing where he'd come from or where he was headed. Whoever he was working for, they were paying him well enough to prevent him from moonlighting. As far as the Society was concerned, the *Merak Star* wasn't even in Outer Draconis. She was supposed to be doing monotony runs in Ursa Major for colonial governments and blue chips. According to the Society – who auto-tracked ship transponders – the only trade ship in port or even to have landed in over seven months was the *Silver Lining*. The only way Nazari could have got down without the Society knowing was if the *Merak Star* had her transponder off, something genuine URA surface batteries would never have allowed. If they hadn't blasted the *Merak Star* out of the sky for hiding her identity, there was a good chance they'd turn the same blind eye toward the *Cyclops* when she got here.

My last task was to check the threat advisories, looking for specifics on the *Cyclops*. There was no ship known by that name, but there was a phantom who matched her description, who was blamed for every ship that inexplicably vanished near the Acheron. She was only known of at all because a handful of modern freighters with fast bubble had escaped before she'd got within weapons range. Nothing was known of her captain, only a dozen guesses as to his name, none of which were Rix. Whoever he was, he liked his privacy, not easy to keep in his line of work, but at least that explained why my threading had no matches on him or his ship.

With more questions than answers, I retrieved my gun and stepped out onto the street. My DNA sniffer had barely begun area-scanning when four men converged on me at once. Two grabbed my arms while the others pressed guns into my ribs from both sides, giving me no chance.

"Give us an excuse, spacer," one of the men said with a distinctly Ardenan accent as he pulled my P-50 from its holster. He was dressed in Faller street clothes, but his height and build showed no sign of genetic adaptation to the local gravity.

They pulled my hands behind my back and snapped restraints on my wrists as a small solar powered three wheeler pulled up in front of us. Its rear cargo door popped up, then they threw me inside, slamming the door shut behind me. In complete darkness, I felt the vehicle pull away from the curb and begin swerving through Citadel's narrow streets, certain I'd made a good first impression on someone.

* * * *

They hung me by my wrists from force clamps inside a shadowy cold storage room, surrounded by enormous carcasses rendered microbe free by irradiation. To avoid freezing to death, I performed leg lifts and had my threading trigger muscle tremors, but it was a losing battle. By early evening, my shoulders were straining under the heavy gravity and a layer of frost had formed across my face as cold clawed my body. I'd started thinking it was only a matter of time before I'd be as frozen as the carcasses around me when the cold room's metal door swung open.

A small machine with four articulated legs riding on ball rollers stepped over the door seal and trundled in. It was followed by a tall, slender man and one of the thugs who'd bundled me into the three wheeler outside the Society's office. As they crossed the room, the rollerbot was careful to remain close to the tall man at all times. It wasn't until it stopped below my dangling feet, immediately reducing the strain on my shoulders, that I realized why. It was equipped with a personal acceleration field, reducing ambient gravity to something fractionally less than Earth Normal. Such devices were extravagances on any world and certainly unexpected on a place as remote as Hardfall. Whoever my visitor was, he had no intention of going native anytime soon, of enduring years of discomfort to build muscle and bone density the old fashioned way.

My guest studied me with a curiosity colder than the freezing air while I stared blankly at the floor, feigning hypothermia.

"This is Sirius Kade?" My visitor asked.

"Yeah Gov'nor, that's him."

Governor? Union mandated colonies usually elected one of their own to run things, but their accents told me they were both from Ardenus. Offworld appointees were only sent to restore worlds riven by corruption and incompetence, but I doubted that was the case here. My DNA sniffer tried pattern matching them, but couldn't identify the Governor. His muscle man was Stas Riscani, a URA deserter facing five years in the stockade once the Union army got their hands on him.

"What do we know about him?" the Governor asked.

"He's a local trader. Second generation. Seems genuine."

"He wouldn't be watching Loport or running searches on the Merak Star and the Cyclops if he were genuine!" the Governor declared irritably.

The Society were obsessively secretive about their member's activities. The only way he could have known what searches I'd run was if he had the Exchange bugged, which was a flat out breach of the Union Colonial Charter – something no genuine Union administrator would ever break.

The fake Governor stepped toward me causing the little rollerbot to readjust its position. "Why are you here, Kade?"

I maintained my frozen stare on the floor, hoping he'd believe I was close to an icy death.

"You left him in here too long!" the Governor snapped.

"He's not dead," Riscani said, stepping forward and shaking me by the knee. "Hey! Kade! Wake up!"

"What do you know about the Merak Star and the Cyclops?" the Governor demanded.

When I didn't answer, Riscani produced a short rod shaped stun-jabber and shoved it into my side. For a moment, my body tensed from the charge, then I relaxed.

"My name is Rykard Metzler. I'm the Governor of this colony. The only way you're getting out of here is by answering my questions. Now tell me, who are you working for?"

"Nazari," I wheezed.

"You work for Captain Nazari?" Metzler asked surprised.

"He owes … me money."

"How did you find him?"

"His … stim … dealer."

Anger swept over Metzler's face. "I knew we couldn't trust that Cali stimhead! We should have used our own people! What do you know about the Cyclops?"

"Nazari … making deliveries … Don't want … trouble … just money."

"He don't know nothing," Riscani said dismissively.

"Maybe …" Metzler said warily, unconvinced by my act.

"Want me to shove him in the food processor?"

"No, the Society knows he's here. We don't want them asking questions. Not now, not this close."

"So he's bait then?"

"Yeah. Where are the other two?"

"Back at their ship. My people are watching them."

"Grab them when they come out looking for him," Metzler said. "And have the garrison target their vessel in case they try to run."

"We could use their ship, Gov'nor," Riscani suggested.

"Hmm … OK, capture it intact. I'll tell the Society it was impounded for charging weapons in a no fire zone. Prepare fake sensor logs in case they want proof."

"We'll need a crew."

"Some of the those Drake scum might want a pardon. If not, I'll send for a crew from Hades City."

Riscani nodded. "When do you want us to dump

Kade?"

"Tonight," Metzler said, stepping back, drawing the little rollerbot after him. "He won't be the first offworlder to underestimate the danger of the flatlands."

* * * *

Sometime after midnight, Stas Riscani and his three musclemen snapped restraints on my wrists and ankles and carried me up to the rooftop where they loaded me into an aging cargo lifter. It had two vectoring thrusters mounted high above the fuselage, a small one seat cockpit up front and a tiny swivel mounted tail thruster for maneuvering. Both side doors had been removed, making it windy and noisy in flight, and the cargo deck stank of manure and was stained with blood, nonhuman blood according to my threading.

We flew briefly above Citadel's rooftops, then once clear of the cliffs, power glided toward the southern plains. Soon we were skimming low rolling grasslands, then just as the colony's lights receded to the horizon, the lifter slowed, coming to a hover above an abandoned bait trap. Its massive door hung by a twisted hinge, while inside the rusting square cage were the bleached bones of a long dead tankosaur. It was a first generation trap, abandoned because it lacked the required strength and was too far from Citadel to tow the catch back safely.

Riscani pulled my P-50 from his pocket and fired repeatedly through an open side door. "Some folks beg for one round, so they don't have to live through it," he yelled over the roar of the thrusters, glancing at me quizzically. When I said nothing, Riscani shrugged, "Suit yourself, Kade." He fired several more shots then tossed the gun out, watching it clatter through the bait trap's metal bars to the artificially smooth rock floor below.

One of the guards moved to the rear of the fuselage where he pulled back a tarpaulin covering an old quad-bike. He activated its four ground effectors, floated it forward to an open door then shut it back down. Another of the guards switched power packs, then tried starting the quad-bike himself. This time it whirred weakly, unable to lift itself off the deck. The pilot, who'd been watching over his shoulder, dropped the cargo lifter close to the ground, then the two guards pushed the quad-bike over the edge and watched it crash onto the rock flats below.

"You hired it this afternoon," Riscani explained, producing my vault key. "Paid for it with this." He slid the key into my pocket, shaking his head with mock sadness. "When will you spacers learn? This ain't no place for joy riding!" He laughed, then motioned for the others to drag me to the edge.

With my face hanging over the side, Riscani unlocked my restraints while I lay as limp and helpless as when they'd first removed me from the cool room.

"You could try hiking back to Citadel," he said. "You might even make it, if you're lucky."

One of his companions laughed. "There ain't no one that lucky, Stas."

Riscani stepped back with the restraints to let his companions throw me out onto the ground. As their weight shifted, I twisted suddenly, spearing my knuckles into the throat of the guard to my left. He fell back choking, then before the others knew what was happening, I whipped my arm back, crashing my elbow into the forehead of the guard to my right. He reeled away, stunned, blood welling from the split skin above his eyes.

The third guard launched himself at me, but I rolled onto my back and caught him with my heel and hands and catapulted him over my head through the side door. The guard caught the landing skid as he fell and swung beneath the cargo lifter as I jumped to my feet only to find myself staring into the business end of a short barreled shellgun. It fired armor piercing, exploding shells ideal for taking down the heaviest beasts on Hardfall and making a mess of any human.

"You don't fight like no spacer," Riscani said, glancing at his companions. One was turning blue from lack of air, another lay unconscious with blood smearing his face while the third desperately clawed his way back up into the lifter. "Maybe the Gov'nor's right, you're not what you appear to be."

"I just don't like walking," I said taking a step toward him.

Riscani raised his gun to eye height in an unmistakable warning. "The Gov'nor wants it to look like an accident, but I'll finish you here Kade, right now, and dump your body down south where it'll never get found. Makes no difference to me. You get eaten all the same."

"What's Hardfall to a bunch of Ardenans?"

He gave me a sour look. "Nothing! I hate this stinking place, but it pays better than the army."

"When Earth Navy finds out what's going on here, they'll burn you to the ground."

"We're ready for them," he said with surprising confidence.

"Don't bet on it."

"There ain't a navy ship within five hundred light years could stand up against our defenses."

It was more than an idle boast. The colony's eight

armored turrets could be hiding enough firepower to knock out a frigate before it ever got within range, but why would anyone want to fortify an isolated outpost like Hardfall? Its proximity to the Acheron made it attractive to smugglers and Drakes, but no one else.

Riscani nodded toward the open door. "Jump!"

I glanced down at the ground, hesitating.

"Or I'll blast you out the door," Riscani added malevolently. "Your choice!"

I moved to the edge, stepped down onto the skid and dropped lightly to the ground.

Riscani looked out across the plains, searching for movement. "They can smell you already, Kade," he yelled from the open door as the lifter climbed away. "You don't have long!" He grinned as the aircraft turned away toward Citadel's distant lights.

I clambered over the fallen door into the giant cage, recovered my P-50 and checked the ammo counter. It was empty. I holstered my gun, becoming aware of how eerily quiet and empty the flatlands were at night. A soft light came from the stars above, partly obscured by the impenetrably black depths of the Acheron Abyss, while far to the north, Citadel floated like a glowing island above the dark plains. A point of light close to Citadel marked Hiport's location, although Hadley's Retreat and Loport were both hidden from sight, too low and far away to be seen. I could have hiked back to the city in a day, but Riscani was right, trying to get there on foot would be suicide. My best chance was to stay with the cage and hope Jase and Izin found me in the morning.

I cranked my listener to high gain and my infrared optics to maximum as a distant howl came rolling in across the plain. Sometime later, I spotted a thermal ghost slinking through long grass, working its way toward me.

I soon discovered it wasn't alone.

* * * *

Prowling apparitions crept toward the ruined bait trap while I searched desperately for a weapon. In spite of having been abandoned for more than a century, the cage was still strong enough to provide protection on three sides forcing any attacker to come in over the broken door. Some cage bars were rusting, others were bent from having been charged by creatures larger than a tankosaur, while several bars in the wrecked door rattled loosely but wouldn't twist free.

Frustrated, I retreated to the enormous skeleton in the middle of the cage. Its ribs were thicker than my chest and twice my height, jutting from a spine composed of immense anvil-like bones. They were too heavy for me to lift in Hardfall's oppressive gravity, but eventually I found a small joint-bone that had the makings of an adequate hammer. I lugged it to the broken cage door watched by a lone sawtooth perched on its haunches off to the right and a pair of four legged nightstalkers creeping through the long grass further out. Most dangerous of all, a few knee-high infrared blurs hopped in the distance with growing agitation. Most of the fleshripper pack were sleeping, but my alien scent was drifting their way, rousing them from their slumber.

The hulking sawtooth gave off a lazy howl as it sniffed the air, forcing me to act. I drove my bone hammer into the ruined cage door, shattering the night with a thunderous crack that startled the skittish nightstalkers. They scampered off into the darkness while the big shouldered sawtooth just sat watching me through the grass.

I lifted the hammer again, smashing the twisted bars until one broke free. It clattered onto the rock floor noisily, then several blows later, a second bar came loose. I dropped the hammer and carried my makeshift spears back into the cage. They were heavy polysteel tubes with blunt ends incapable of piercing tough hide, but were as long as medieval pikes, giving me reach.

I took cover behind the tankosaur skeleton, hoping I could hide there until help came, but the sawtooth stood on his muscled forearms and started toward me. The infrared orbs of its eyes glowed brightly above a blockish snout sniffing uncertainly as it savored my scent. Even though we were in sight of the colony, it had little knowledge of humans. Colonists either kept well clear of the plain's predators or dispatched them with armor piercing slugs, giving Hardfall's monsters no chance to learn to fear men.

After resting one of my metal bars against the tankosaur's skeleton, I held the other ready as the sawtooth approached. It paused at the edge of the grass, studying the artificially smooth rock base and the unfamiliar cage. The creature seemed strangely misshapen with large powerful shoulders, muscular forelegs and short rear legs for balance. Its head was square with broad jaws lined with thick, yellow teeth. It wasn't armored like a tankosaur, but its hide was tough and its teeth could tear bone plate from flesh with a flick of its head.

Sniffing tentatively, it started forward again, shifting its angular head slowly from side to side as it neared the cage, never taking its recessed eyes off me. It hesitated at the fallen door, confused by its strangeness and by my alien scent, but like every predator roaming Hardfall's dry plains, it was racked by a hunger that overcame any fear. It pawed the trap door warily, causing it to clatter noisily against the rock, then bent its forelegs and leapt over the door, landing fully inside the cage.

Now its demeanor changed, from prowler to killer.

The sawtooth's head dropped slightly as its eyes bored into me, its lips curling back to reveal serrated teeth in a snarl dripping with saliva. When it saw I wasn't easily flushed from my hiding place, it moved forward growling constantly, never letting me out of its sight. When only the tankosaur skeleton separated us, the creature opened its wide mouth and gave out a ferocious roar, then seemed puzzled that I refused to run.

Realizing it would have to drive me out, it started around the skeleton. Thick muscles rippled under a dark brown hide pulled taut against bone from days without food. As the big meat eater skirted the tankosaur's rounded skull, I moved back, trying to keep the skeleton between us. Suddenly it leapt forward sweeping a massive forearm at me, but I rolled away with ultra-reflexed speed, coming to my feet and slamming my clumsy weapon onto the point of its black snout.

The sawtooth roared angrily, shaking its head in surprise as I darted away. Seeing me run, it immediately charged, leaping with both forelegs outstretched, but I dodged sideways around the skeleton. When it landed, it slid across the smooth rock floor into the cage wall causing the entire structure to vibrate from the impact.

"You like to chase, don't you," I said to myself, realizing it had evolved to bring down fleeing prey. It expected me to run, because that's what herbivores did out on the flatlands. As soon as I ran, its instinct was to charge after me, but it couldn't keep its footing on the laser smooth rock floor.

The sawtooth scrambled to its feet, then we circled the skeleton again in a deadly stalking game. After one full circuit, I broke into a sprint, testing my theory. The sawtooth instantly charged around the end of the skeleton, losing its footing and sliding on its side across the slick rock floor. Before it righted itself, I rushed forward and hurled my bar like a spear, striking the beast's sloping forehead with a thud that filled it with fury.

It got to its feet, exploding with rage as I ran back to the rib cage, triggering the sawtooth's pursuit instinct again. Its large feet scrambled on the smooth rock as it rushed to chase me down. A threading indicator flashed into my mind, warning it was almost on top of me, then I dove between the tankosaur's ribs, landing on the segmented anvil spine. I rolled and dived again, leaping through the other side of the rib cage and scooping up my second iron bar.

The sawtooth charged blindly after me, hurling its massive shoulders against the giant bones, shattering them on impact. Its chest bounced off the anvil-jointed spine, then its head speared between the far side ribs, coming to rest with its shoulders wedged against the tankosaur rib cage. Its head and shoulders were pinned by its own weight and its small rear legs were left sprawled across the backbone, flailing helplessly in the air.

Seeing my chance, I charged, holding the metal bar above my shoulders with both hands, then drove the blunt end like a lance into the creature's eye. It roared in anger, twisting its torso, trying to break free, but for all its immense physical strength, it couldn't move backwards. On Hardfall's endless plains, it had evolved incredible power going forward, but no ability to step back.

There wasn't room for it to move its forearms, only to push its enormous shoulders against the bone edifice trapping it. Knowing I didn't have long before the tankosaur skeleton collapsed, I drove the metal bar deeper into the sawtooth's eye socket, trying to puncture its brain, but the metal bar struck bone and would go no further. I released the bar, now firmly wedged in its skull, and stepped back as the creature whipped its head from side to side, causing the metal pole to carve wild arcs through the air.

When the sawtooth lifted its head, raising the bar vertically, I leapt forward, catching it and vaulting my weight toward the tankosaur skeleton. As I passed over the sawtooth's head, I jerked the bar forward, hearing a loud crack as the creature's neck snapped, then its head rolled sideways limply, forcing me to jump clear.

Before I was even on my feet, my DNA sniffer was flashing another warning, of multiple contacts approaching from the west. Fast, hopping contacts! Dozens of them! The roars of the sawtooth and my scent had attracted them and now the prospect of food was sending them crazy. Knowing I couldn't stay inside the bait trap, I ran to the entrance as a swarm of infra red wisps appeared out of the darkness, bouncing toward me through long grass on short, powerful hind legs. My listener amplified the patter of little feet and a chorus of barking growls as the plains piranha closed in.

With nowhere to run, the only direction was up. I clambered from the fallen gate to the top of the cage, then turned and kicked furiously at the trap door's rusted hinge, trying to knock the gate down. Suddenly, fleshrippers surged out of the long grass in a wave of growling, bouncing death. They swarmed over the flat rock toward the bait trap, then as the first one reached the fallen gate, the rusted hinge snapped. The ripper leapt off the gate toward me, slashing at my leg with blade-like claws extending from its small forearms. I pulled back as it carved the air and wrapped one deadly paw over the edge of the cage, then tried to scramble up, but I smashed the heel of my boot into its little round face, sending it flying.

The fleshripper pack swept into the bait trap toward the dead sawtooth, yelping with glee to have found one of their most dangerous enemies dead before them. They swarmed over its carcass, tearing its thick hide open with their claws and gorging themselves on its still warm meat. The big animal's blood spread across the bait trap floor as more of the ravenous little creatures swarmed into the cage, eager to join the feeding frenzy. The sawtooth's carcass disappeared beneath a mass of squawking, slashing fleshrippers, then once the food was gone, their attention turned to me.

Dozens of blood crazed little carnivores squealed furiously as they tried to find a way to reach me, clawing the bars, hopping onto the tankosaur skeleton and leaping hopelessly up at me. Perched on top of the cage, I was trapped, but just out of their reach. Even if my P-50 had been fully loaded, I could never have killed them all. There were too many and they were too aggressive. Watching those ravenous, little fleshrippers staring up at me, it was abundantly clear why every attempt the colonists had made to move down from their high fortresses had failed.

It was the uncompromising brutality of life on Hardfall's dying plains.

* * * *

Several hours after the fleshrippers had swarmed the bait trap, a dozen of them still prowled the rock floor below, staring up at me in frustration. The rest had drifted away into the grass, some to sleep after gorging themselves, others to wander restlessly nearby waiting for their next victim.

Far off in the distance, the lights of a speeding ground vehicle pierced the darkness of the plain as it raced south. For a long time, it seemed unaware of my presence, then it slowly turned toward the bait trap, following an old dirt road linking the trap to the colony.

When it was still some way out, my infrared optics picked up another heat source approaching from the opposite direction. As it drew near, I realized it was larger than a fleshripper, smaller than a sawtooth, heading toward me at a leisurely pace. There was no stalking, none of the initial caution shown by the sawtooth or the frenzied charge of the rippers. Soon the ghostly apparition took on the form of a man, walking alone across the plain, seemingly unaware of the danger.

When he was several hundred meters out, he stopped to study me and my little friends below. I tried DNA-locking him, but got nothing. I considered shouting a warning, but feared that would rouse the rippers sleeping in the grass between us. I tried waving him back, but he ignored my efforts, renewing his approach. Soon he was close enough for my threading to read his body temperature – a few degrees above the human norm.

On the rock flats outside the bait trap, a fleshripper got wind of his scent and hopped uncertainly into the long grass, toward him. Its red blur moved leisurely at first, then it emitted an excited barking sound, rousing the others. Suddenly the long grass was alive with movement as rippers surged toward him. The creatures below immediately lost interest in me and raced after the pack, fearful of missing their share of the prey.

The humanoid stopped as he became aware of the wave of death rolling toward him, then calmly reached over his shoulder and retrieved a two-handed weapon. When the rippers were almost upon him he fired a steady energy blast, sweeping left to right and back again, creating a cone-shaped inferno that incinerated all before him. High pitched squeals of shock and agony filled the air as the ripper pack died while the alien continued to unleash controlled destruction upon them. The glow of the flames revealed his dark helmet and body armor, identical to what the large humanoid who'd pursued me on Krailo-Nis had worn.

Suddenly I realized neither the Tau Cetins nor the Intruders were following us. It was him! He'd tracked me from the streets of Nisport to the plains of Hardfall, making me – not Izin – the target!

More infrared fleshripper ghosts converged on his position from the right. For a moment, I thought he'd hadn't seen them, then as they were almost on top of him, he leapt away. Ionized light glowed from the base of his boots as he power jumped through the air, drawing them after him. When he landed, he waited for the second wave to swarm after him, then he fired again, calmly annihilating his attackers. When the only thing left alive out there was him, he locked his weapon on his back and power jumped over the spreading grass fire toward the bait trap.

Wheels skidded on smooth rock behind me, then the metallic click of a hatch opening sounded. I turned to see a six wheeled, all-terrain vehicle with four powerful floodlights mounted on top parked alongside the bait trap. It was painted in savannah camouflage, shielded by rectangular plate armor that gave it a faceted look and crowned by a round roof turret mounting an impressive seventy five millimeter autocannon. Painted across the side of the hull were images of plains animals and in red letters the words 'Prairie Runner'. Above the middle pair of wheels, a hatch lifted up vertically, gull wing style, pushed up by a black prosthetic claw.

The same weather beaten face that had followed me across Hadley's Retreat looked up from the ATV's hatch. "Kade," Clawhand yelled, "Down here." He was holding a triple barreled scatter gun in his real hand, but it wasn't aimed at me. It was pointed low, ready to blast the first ripper that showed its beady little face.

I hesitated, glancing back at the approaching alien now walking toward me, certain this was one fight I wasn't going to win, then slid down the side of the bait trap to the ground. The humanoid power jumped to the top of the cage, landing with a heavy metallic thud as I dived head first into the open hatch past Clawhand, who pulled the armored door down behind me.

Inside, the Prairie Runner was all raw metal, roll bars, gun racks and ammo lockers. A pair of padded bench seats ran down the middle, back to back. I landed on the metal floor as an attractive young blonde in her early twenties turned from the steering position up front and flashed me a broad smile.

"Hey mister! Glad you're still alive."

"So am I," I said uncertainly, climbing onto the bench seat.

"Last fella we tried rescuing," she added, "was dead by the time we got here!"

"That's Emma," Clawhand said. "My daughter. Ain't she pretty?" He nodded to her. "Let's go honey!"

Emma turned and pushed the twin throttles halfway up. The armored all terrain vehicle lurched forward with a roar, skidding on the smooth rock as its tail spun out, crashing into the bait trap, then it straightened as glowing boots appeared out of the sky ahead of us.

"What the hell …?" Emma said confused as the alien landed in front of us.

"Go!" I yelled.

Emma glanced at her father uncertainly. "He's not one of ours."

"Do as the man says, honey."

She slammed the throttles to full, driving the ATV straight into the large humanoid, bouncing him off the sloped frontal armor and hurling him into the air. The Prairie Runner bounced off the rock flats into the grass and picked up speed. Through the slit rear window, I saw him float to the ground on his glowing boots, apparently unharmed.

Clawhand followed my gaze to the alien who stood watching us race away. "Friend of yours?"

"I very much doubt it," I said, wondering if the ATV's armor could survive a blast from the alien's energy weapon. I waited, but he didn't fire. Either he judged the ATV too tough a target or he wanted me alive.

When the dust obscured the alien from sight, Clawhand turned to me with an appraising look. "Let me get this straight. You been here less than a day and already Metzler and his bully boys want you dead and you got some big-ass alien after you as well. Son, you got a talent for making enemies."

I smiled. "It's a gift."

"If you're looking for trouble, you've come to the right place."

"How'd you know I was here?"

"After you jumped off the Link, one of my boys saw them grab you off the street. When they flew you south, we knew they were dropping you at this old trap."

"Good guess."

"No guess. You're not the first man they dumped out here. Won't be the last."

"Why are you risking making an enemy of the Governor by helping me?"

"I'm already his enemy and if that lying, murdering dog wants you dead, I want you alive."

"Why?"

"Because I want him off my planet – or dead," he looked thoughtful. "Preferably dead."

Emma turned back and grinned. "Metzler feels the same way about Daddy."

"He wants me in that bait trap," Clawhand said, "but I'd rip open his guts and tear out his spine if he tried." He flexed his metallically brutal prosthetic meaningfully.

"What'd you do?"

"It's not what I did, it's who I am." When the blank look on my face told him I had no idea who he was, he added. "I used to be the Governor. The name's Quentin Tobias Hadley, direct descendant of old A.M. himself!"

* * * *

We drove through the Boneyard south east of Hadley's Retreat as the sky began to lighten, past bleached skeletons, wrecked vehicles and triangular obelisks

145

engraved with lettering I couldn't read. Each time we passed one of the memorials, Emma dimmed the ATV's lights in respect.

"They got the names of everyone who didn't make it," Hadley said when he saw me trying to read the inscription on one of the stone monuments. "The locations mark where they were taken. Most of the bodies were never recovered."

Once we left the bones behind, we drove north along the eastern side of Hadley's Retreat as Hardfall's sun began to peak above the horizon. There were glimpses of buildings perched atop the cliffs and of a few people out walking before breakfast, safely out of reach of the dangers prowling the flatlands.

Soon, two cylindrical turrets standing like sentinels in front of the cliffs came into view. They were armed with long barreled autocannons placed to cover each other and destroy any creature pursuing an incoming vehicle. Emma turned the ATV onto a well worn track between the two guns and headed for a large rectangular door set into the cliffs. It lifted up as we approached, revealing a long cavern filled with many vehicles. They ranged from fast two seaters to crane equipped tow trucks all the way up to massive ten wheeled transports. All were armored, most had portable weapon mounts and a few – like Hadley's ATV – were fitted with turreted cannons.

The cavern had once been a natural feature, but the colonists had smoothed and expanded it, drilling a vertical elevator shaft down from the top of the mesa. The armored door closed behind us as soon as we were inside, showing that even with two robot guns guarding the entrance, Hardfall's colonists took no chances. Emma parked the Prairie Runner in a large space close to the cavern door, then we took the elevator up to the mesa top.

Hadley's house was the largest on the plateau. It had been built more than a century ago, with a stately grandeur befitting the colony's founder and a view over the eastern cliffs toward the wreck of the *Dahlia*. A rocky promontory, which doubled as a memorial lookout, hid the house from the surface battery a few clicks south. When we arrived, Emma went to fix breakfast while Hadley directed me to a chair in front of open concertina doors and offered me a cigar from an ornate box.

"Hardfall's own," he said proudly.

When I declined, he lit one up and settled into a nearby chair. He was a typical Faller, almost a head shorter than me with hard muscle and thick bones engineered for the planet's uncomfortable gravity. His face was tanned, framed by white hair and apart from his robotic arm, he appeared to be in excellent health.

He pulled on his cigar, then exhaled blue smoke slowly. "We don't get many traders here, Kade."

"I'm not surprised. The Acheron's a little close for comfort."

"It is and yet, here you are … and with Metzler in a God awful hurry to see you dead. I'm wondering why?"

I wasn't sure I could trust Hadley and I certainly wasn't about to share classified information with him, but he had rescued me from the bait trap and the alien and that counted for something.

"Maybe I ask too many questions."

"You seemed real interested in Loport and you got here right when that smuggler ship landed. I'm guessing that's no coincidence."

"You know the Merak Star?"

"I've seen her before." Hadley fixed a penetrating

gaze upon me, deciding how useful I might be. Eventually, he said, "Most of the time Loport's used by hydro farmers. They land their hilljumpers down there to avoid Hiport's fees. Then every few months, Metzler shuts it down. Sends in his private army. Won't let anyone near it, not ever the croppers. That's when we know we're getting visitors."

"Like now," I said thoughtfully.

"Uh huh." Hadley tapped ash from his cigar. "I figured it was only a matter of time before someone like you showed up."

"Like me?" I said, feigning innocence.

"Someone with an unhealthy curiosity in Metzler's side business," he said, giving me a quizzical look.

I could have spun him a song and dance cover story he wouldn't have believed, but I wanted his trust and his help. "He's got my interest," I conceded, telling Hadley nothing about myself and leaving him in no doubt I was not what I appeared. A flicker of hope flashed across his face, then I asked, "How'd Metzler get control of the colony?"

"He was appointed by the Union's Colonial Administration."

"He could be an imposter."

"I saw the commission myself. It was genuine."

"His soldiers aren't," I said. "None of them are URA."

"Hmph! Figures," Hadley said grimly. "What are you planning to do about it?"

"Make him regret not killing me when he had the chance."

A crooked grin slowly appeared on Hadley's face. "How can I help?"

"Tell me what you know."

He took a moment to gather his thoughts, then

said, "Three or four times a year, that old freighter sets down at Loport. Always meets a dark, cylindrical ship. Nasty looking brute, bristling with guns – exactly the kind of thing those surface batteries are supposed to destroy."

"The Cyclops. I've seen her."

"Sometimes the Merak Star is by herself, sometimes she comes with other ships. Big haulers. All new, all exactly the same."

"Armed?"

He shook his head. "No weapons that I could see, but I'm no expert."

"Unarmed ships don't enter high threat space," I said doubtfully.

"These do. You want to see?"

"You have holos?"

"This isn't Hades City!" he said indignantly. "Two-dee only." He touched a control sensor beside his chair, bringing a wall screen to life above the mantelpiece. "I told you I've been waiting for someone to show up. Took these just in case. Got a whole lot more if you're interested."

An image of a vessel painted in Pan Core Shipping livery appeared. Pan Core was one of the giants of interstellar transport with links to the Consortium, the largest white collar criminal organization in Mapped Space. The ship looked like she was straight out of the builder's yard, spotlessly clean with a flawless paint job and lacking any kind of defense, even shield emitters. No one in their right mind would send such a valuable prize in this close to the Acheron unless they knew they had nothing to fear from the Drakes.

The ship reminded me of a Saracen class freighter, only longer and thicker in places where she'd undergone structural reinforcement – a strange modification for a noncombat ship. She had the same four cargo doors each side, although her four maneuvering engines arranged in a diamond formation were twice the size of those on a standard Saracen. The bigger engines would have made her tactically faster and more maneuverable at the cost of reduced cargo capacity and higher mass.

"When they land," Hadley continued, "the crew goes aboard the Merak Star while a new crew transfer over from the dark ship."

If the *Merak Star* was Consortium owned, then they weren't just selling weapons to the Drakes, they were building ships for them as well. It was a marked change for the Brotherhood, who used ships captured in deep space or rescued from the scrap yard. They didn't place orders, or they never used to.

"I want copies," I said.

"I was hoping you'd say that. I've been trying to get these pictures out for two years, but Metzler's got offworld comms sewn up so tight, we can't even send a weather report without his say so."

"You must get traders in here."

"Some, but they're either gone in a day or end up the same place you did."

"I see," I said, wondering how many Metzler had killed to keep his operation a secret.

"This was a good place, once. Never had a need for an offworld governor, not since old A.M. died, and he was one of us."

"A.M.? That's the second time you've mentioned him."

Hadley looked surprised as he realized I'd never heard of his distinguished ancestor. "Andrew Mordechai Hadley, founder of Hardfall Colony! If not for him getting everyone out of the Dahlia when he did, they'd all of died right then and there. I won't say this is our family's colony, but no one has a bigger stake in it than we do."

"And being A.M.'s descendant, you have the respect of the colonists, which is why Metzler wants you in jail."

"It's why he wants me dead! Only he can't kill me outright or he'd have half the colony up in arms. Yes sir! Metzler's got to find a way to get rid of me nice and legal like. Considering my wife is the daughter of Hardfall's Chief Justice," Hadley smiled, "that isn't going to be easy."

After a few hours with Quentin Tobias Hadley, I knew he was neither a crook or a traitor, giving the Union no reason to replace him. That made Metzler's appointment a fix. Whatever was going on, the Drakes wanted the colony nearest the Acheron under their thumb, although pulling strings on Earth wasn't a game the Brotherhood played. They'd leave that to the Consortium, who had the wealth and the contacts to subvert entire planets. Considering hardly anyone on Earth had even heard of Hardfall, bribing colonial officials to get Metzler appointed would have been child's play.

"Is there a way I can get a message to my ship?" I asked.

"Not by communicator. Metzler has everything tapped. One of my boys could take a message over for you."

"Metzler's men are watching my ship."

Hadley smiled. "That won't be a problem."

* * * *

While we waited for his men to return from the *Silver Lining*, Hadley and his daughter showed me their home movies of hunting trips and expeditions through the crumbling remains of a lost alien civilization.

"It was a resources colony," Hadley explained. "After the northern plains turned arid and the planet was mined out, they had no reason to stay. Even so, it took them a long time to abandon the planet."

"It's hard to imagine anyone farming with the kind of animals that live here," I said, recalling my experience of the previous night.

"They almost exterminated the planet's wildlife," Emma said, "except for small breeding populations they kept alive in nature reserves. They got away with it because there were no proto-intelligent species on the planet."

"Hardfall's officially classified as a dead end world," Hadley added.

The appearance of intelligent life was random and didn't occur on every habitable planet, but where it did, it was protected by galactic law.

"The Tau Cetins called them the Birali," Emma said, "but that's all they'll tell us."

Maybe they'd been one of Meta's Precursor Civilizations. It was hard to know with the Tau Cetins drip feeding us information based on rules they wouldn't explain.

Hadley used his prosthetic arm to activate the next recording. When he noticed my gaze, he flexed his black claw arm demonstratively. "Lost it to a sawtooth more than ten years ago. Gun jammed. Lucky it didn't cut me in half." He pointed to the dark brown head of a square jawed beast mounted in pride of place on a wall of hunting trophies. "Good thing for me it took time swallowing my arm. I cleared the breach one handed while it had me pinned!"

"Why don't you get a full cosmetic job?" I asked.

"Then who'd know I'd looked death in the face and survived?" He grinned mischievously. "People respect that kind of thing around here. I'm Hardfall, pure and simple."

"'We fall hard but always get up,'" Emma said, quoting a local saying. "Just ask them, they'll tell you!" She glanced at her father's prosthetic, shaking her head. "Sometimes I think he fed his arm to that sawtooth on purpose, just so he could wear that hideous thing to show how tough he is."

Hadley grinned. "Old A.M. lost a leg. He hobbled around on a metal stump for years before the colony got a new one sent out from Earth. It's a family tradition."

"Not a tradition I'll be following!" Emma declared, every bit as tough as him, but without the bravado.

Hadley grinned and leaned towards me. "She says that, but she saved me that day. Tied off my arm and kept me alive until the evac arrived. Old Doc Tanner couldn't have done better himself, and she was only a kid at the time."

She avoided his eyes, almost embarrassed by his praise.

"So you live under a burning sun on a dying planet," I said, "mined out by aliens, swarming with creatures that'll eat you on sight, with gravity too heavy for most humans and nothing but planetary extinction to look forward to?"

Hadley chuckled. "That about sums it up."

"Ever thought of moving?"

"This old rock's seen better days, no doubt, but it's

home and it'll be here long after we've turned to dust,"
he said philosophically, then started the next recording.

* * * *

Hadley's men returned late in the afternoon with Jase
and Izin, having smuggled them in Hiport's vehicle
crane down to the Prairie Runner for the cross country
drive back to Hadley's Retreat.

"How'd you get past Metzler's men?" I asked
when we met in the trophy room.

"Izin took care of it," Jase said absently, passing
me the fresh ammo I'd requested as his eyes wandered
over Hadley's collection of snarling animal heads.
"Are they real?"

"Oh yeah," I replied. "The big one in the middle
bit Mr. Hadley's arm clean off."

Hadley held up his prosthetic arm proudly.
"Swallowed it whole. Didn't even thank me."

Izin removed his pressure suit helmet, revealing
his streamlined features and the vocalizer over his
mouth, much to Hadley's surprise. "The arrival of Mr.
Hadley's men provided a useful distraction, Captain."

"Are Metzler's men dead?" I asked.

"Merely unconscious," Izin replied.

"And locked in a VRS container at the spaceport,"
Jase added.

"The auto timer should release them before they
suffocate," Izin said, "unless my air consumption
calculations were incorrect."

I glanced at Hadley. "We'll give you the container
number. You can let them out in a day or two."

"If I remember," Hadley said indifferently.

Emma entered with two of Hadley's men. Jase
locked eyes on her immediately, flashing her a smile as

154

she approached.

"And I thought they called this place Hardfall because of the gravity, not the girls!" He took a step toward her. "Jase Logan," he said, taking her hand. "Starship pilot, soldier of fortune, lover extraordinaire of beautiful women."

She smiled, flattered by the attention. "Emma," she said, introducing herself.

"Pleased to meet you ... Emma." Jase glanced at me. "No wonder you stayed out all night, Skipper!"

"Emma's Mr. Hadley's *daughter*," I said with a warning look.

"And I'm a very protective father," Hadley added, snapping his prosthetic claws meaningfully.

"I'm still very pleased to meet you, Miss Hadley," Jase said with an admiring look.

"Been in space a long time?" she asked, intrigued by his attention.

"You have no idea." He sighed, reluctantly releasing her hand.

She turned to her father. "They just changed the guards down at Loport Station. Next change won't be until morning."

"We're going somewhere?" Jase asked, clearly preferring to stay and try his luck with Miss Hadley.

"We're paying the Merak Star an unexpected visit." I turned to Hadley. "Have you got somewhere to put the station guards?"

"We'll lock them in the vehicle park storeroom. No one goes down there but our people."

"Good," I said, sliding a gelslug mag into my gun. "They won't be alone."

* * * *

Four guards wearing URA uniforms lounged inside the Loport cable station paying scant attention to the street outside. Hadley and his people stayed hidden to avoid future reprisals while we made our way along the cliff wall out of sight of the entrance.

"Are you sure about this, Izin?" I asked. "They might shoot you on sight."

"Ardenans are unused to tamphs," Izin replied. "They won't shoot if I'm unarmed."

When we reached the terminal, he handed me his shredder pistol, removed his helmet revealing his face, then stepped into the station's entrance.

"I still think we should have tossed one of your fancy stun grenades in there," Jase whispered.

I'd suggested it, but Izin had argued one grenade wouldn't take them all out, giving the survivor a chance to summon more guards than we could handle.

When Izin had their attention, he walked unhurriedly into the station while Jase and I waited outside, guns drawn.

"Hey, isn't that one of them fish men from Earth?" one guard asked in surprise as Izin approached.

Another laughed. "It don't look so tough!"

"Hold it right there, fish head," one of the guards said, casually aiming his weapon at Izin.

"I seem to be lost," Izin said, continuing past the guards to where the cables ran out toward Loport, drawing them after him.

"I told you to stop!" the leader yelled.

Izin turned to face them, "I'm looking for the ocean."

One of the guards laughed. "It wants to go swimming!"

"That's five thousand kilometers from here!"

Ocean was Izin's signal. We stepped into the

entry, Jase with a fragger in each hand, but under strict instructions not to shoot unless I missed. Fraggers were rapid fire gunfighter weapons designed for killing only. They couldn't take the nonlethal gelslugs my P-50 was loaded with. The low kinetic energy round popped an elastic polymer moments after leaving the barrel, turning it into a short range haymaker ideal for taking down targets you didn't want to splatter across the room.

Holding my P-50 two handed, I put gelslugs into the heads of two guards before they knew what was happening. The third guard dodged sideways, avoiding my shot and bringing his penetrator around to fire. He got it halfway up before Izin darted forward, snatched the weapon from his hand and kicked out his legs. A moment after he hit the floor, Izin slammed the weapon's stock into the guard's head putting him to sleep. I switched to the fourth guard who was running for the comm panel. I aimed low, put one into his back knocking him down followed by a second into his head ensuring he didn't get up. All four would wake up in Hadley's storeroom with concussion, but they'd still be breathing. Good for them, good for me, as I had no desire to leave a trail of corpses behind. I was here for information, not a bloodbath.

I motioned at the entrance, then a solar powered delivery van emerged from a side street and drove up to the terminal. When it stopped, Hadley and his people climbed out. They loaded the guards and their weapons into the vehicle, then drove off leaving Hadley and Emma behind.

"Give us time to get down there and take the ship," I said to Hadley.

"We'll head out past the Dahlia tonight, swing around and come up from the south. We'll be there in the Runner about two in the morning."

If everything went according to plan, we'd control the *Merak Star* by then, but they weren't the only eyes down on the low mesa. "What about Loport Battery's sensors?"

"We'll stay beyond the horizon as we circle out, then come up in the mesa's blind spot. They won't even know we're there. We just got to be gone by dawn so Citadel don't see us, otherwise they're likely to open up on us with their big guns."

"I understand."

A spherical cable car was gliding up from the south. It was half the size of the Skylink gondolas with only a single door each side and transparent walls. While it offered no cover, it would be dark when we got to Loport. With *Merak Star's* bridge crew relying on Metzler's men to keep the landing ground secure, I hoped they wouldn't be paying too much attention to the gondolas.

Izin moved up to the boarding platform while Jase struck up a last minute conversation with Emma Hadley. From the look she gave him, his charms weren't lost on her.

"Jase, we're going," I said, heading toward the platform as the cable car slid to a stop and its automatic door opened.

Jase talked fast and she smiled, touching his arm lightly, then he raced up to the platform, jumping aboard just before the door closed.

"I thought we were going without you," I said as the gondola glided out over the low cliffs for the long ride south.

"Hey Skipper, you know I never miss a party!" He said, looking back toward Emma Hadley standing hands on hips watching us go.

"You know she's genetically engineered?" I said. "Tougher, stronger and probably smarter than you."

"Yeah," he agreed philosophically, "but at least she's human. The last female you introduced me to was an alien robot!"

* * * *

The cable support tower on Lone Peak, between Hadley's Retreat and Loport mesa, was equipped with a small maintenance platform and a narrow ladder down to the ground. During the long climb toward the tower, Loport was increasingly obscured by the pillar of rock, only coming into view once we rose above the summit. The *Merak Star* was now clearly visible, perched on top of the low mesa with hatches sealed. The only signs of life were the two man foot patrol pacing the cliff tops and the rotating dome of the surface battery standing alone on the low plateau's eastern promontory.

"We'll lure the guards into the cable station," I said as our gondola approached the maintenance platform, "then take the Merak Star after dark."

"Is attacking a ship on the ground considered piracy?" Jase wondered.

"Depends if we keep it."

"Technically, Captain," Izin said, "attacking a noncombatant ship, whether on the ground or in space, is a crime punishable by death."

"Then we better not get caught," I said as the cable car reached the maintenance platform and came to an unexpected halt. A moment later, a small metallic disk crashed through the window and shot into the center of the gondola. The device hovered at eye height, blasting a piercing, rapidly increasing tone at us, then it emitted a brilliant white flash.

I didn't remember hitting the gondola floor, but when I came to, my bionic clock told me I'd been out for only seconds. While the stun itself had been short lived, the after effect lingered. A persistent white fog pervaded by a monotonous tone filled my mind. I wanted to open my eyes, but couldn't remember how. I'd been stunned before, but never like this, never so completely isolated from my body. I gave up trying to see and forced my scrambled thoughts to form a single word.

Analysis.

After what seemed an unusually long delay, my threading responded as best it could:

NEUROLOGICAL AREA EFFECT WEAPON, TYPE UNKNOWN.

My biological senses were out, giving my threading nothing to amplify. No hearing, no sight, no touch. All my addled mind could do was fall back on its training, requesting a mode switch.

Bionetic receptors to direct input.

My listener wasn't as effective without my body's auditory inputs, but it was all I had. I now heard the click of metal on metal through the monotonous tone, the sound of heavy boots approaching across the cable car's metal deck. My threading automatically analyzed the sound and fed its conclusion into my mind.

KRAILO-NIS HUMANOID CONTACT, 74% PROBABILITY.

It was the alien who'd tracked me from the Nisk colony to the bait trap! He must have seen me board the Loport cable car and set an ambush at the Lone Peak tower.

PHYSICAL MOVEMENT DETECTED.

I still felt nothing, but my bionic receptors were

sensing my body being dragged off the cable car.

Restore physical, disable safeties.

It was going to hurt – it might not even work – but if I stayed like this, I was sure to wake up with no options, if I woke up at all.

40% FUNCTIONING POSSIBLE.

That was low. Against Earth-tech nerve pulses with revival safeties off, my threading could get me much more, but the alien had hit me with something that had really scrambled my senses.

Suppress twitch response. Activate restore.

My threading tried kick starting my body while preventing involuntary muscle movements that would warn the alien I was coming out of it. The ringing grew louder as bionetic controllers released a massive blast of adrenalin, spiking my metabolic rate and blood glucose levels. Neurotransmitters flooded through my body while bioelectrical impulses shocked unresponsive muscles to life. To my captor, I appeared as lifeless as ever, while inside, partial feeling returned.

My head exploded with pain, wiping away the white fog as I felt myself being dragged face down from the cable car. Realizing he couldn't see my face, I pushed my eyes half open, trying to focus. Blurry metal boots passed in and out of view as he pulled me across the maintenance platform. When we reached the edge, he released me and touched his wrist, then a narrow metal walkway extended to the maintenance platform from an oval shaped airlock suspended in empty blue sky a few meters away.

I tensed feeble muscles, then spun on my hip and clumsily kicked out at his legs. It was a weak blow, but it caught him by surprise, knocking him forward off the platform. With lightning fast reflexes, his hand snapped out and caught the stealth ship's walkway. He swung like a pendulum as his helmeted head turned to me, then I slammed the back of my boot onto his gloved fingertips. The alien lost his grip, reached for the walkway with his other hand, but missed and fell. Halfway to the ground, his boots glowed in the fading light, slowing his fall, letting him land unharmed – not the result I'd hoped for. He immediately launched himself in a tech-assisted jump onto the tower and began scrambling up the narrow ladder back to the maintenance platform.

"Tough bastard," I slurred, starting to drag myself back toward the cable car. He'd manipulated the controls, forcing it to stop, but a bar light over the door was filling, counting down the seconds until it continued on its way.

"Clear doors," a synthesized female voice ordered, "the car is leaving the platform."

I forced rubbery arms and legs to push myself across the platform. As I neared the gondola, the door slid shut and it glided away, carrying Jase and Izin – both still unconscious – with it. I crawled to the edge of the platform and looked down. The humanoid was already more than halfway up the tower. I drew my P-50 with semi-paralyzed fingers and fired several poorly aimed shots. The first few gelslugs went wide, another bounced off the tower near his shoulder, then by luck alone one glanced harmlessly off his helmet. He immediately swung around the tower and continued climbing using its metal framework for cover. He was climbing so fast, he'd reach the platform long before the next cable car arrived. I rolled onto my back, then with fumbling fingers ejected the gelslug magazine from my gun and replaced it with armor piercing hardtips. When I finally got the lethal ammo loaded and rolled back to the edge, the tower below was deserted. I turned and aimed at end of the platform, waiting for him to show himself, then large metal boots crashed down either side of me. Before I could lift my gun, he snatched it out of my hand.

"Enough!" he said in a deep voice.

I rolled over and kicked my leg up, driving the toe of my boot into his back and catching his ankle as he stumbled forward, but he tucked and rolled gracefully over me, coming easily to his feet.

"You recover fast for a human," he said in stilted Unionspeak.

"What do you want?"

"Information."

"What kind of information."

"Not from you human, for you."

He was trading me for information? "You're a bounty hunter?"

He grunted in disgust. "I'm a tracer."

I sat up slowly, feeling the numbness beginning to fade. "What's that?"

"I find what others cannot."

"Do you have a name?"

"I am Gern Vrate."

"Never heard of you."

"I am Kesarn."

"From the Orion Arm?" I asked, forcing myself to stand on wobbly legs.

"No." He ran a disdainful eye over my P-50 before tossing it onto the platform behind him. "I am from what you call the Perseus Arm."

That was over five thousand light years away, far beyond the edge of Mapped Space. I'd certainly never been there and was unlikely to ever reach it. "You've come a long way just to kidnap me."

"I'm not here for you," he said motioning me

toward the walkway.

I ignored his order, gauging the distance to the next cable car now climbing to the platform. "How'd you track me?" I asked, stalling for time.

"I scanned your navigation system. Easy to do if I can get close enough." He reached over his shoulder, retrieved the bulky weapon he'd used near the bait trap and aimed it at me one-handed. "Don't make me use this."

"You won't shoot. You want to trade me."

"You only need to be alive, not whole."

A persuasive argument if ever I'd heard one. I started hobbling toward the walkway, accentuating my unsteadiness, watching the cable car approaching behind him. I figured he'd made the last car stop at the tower, but the next one showed no sign of slowing.

At the edge of the platform, I feigned a stumble and dropped to one knee. "I'll fall."

Vrate aimed at my legs. "Crawl."

"I can't," I said as the cable car reached the platform.

Gern Vrate stepped forward, reaching for my jacket collar. I caught his wrist, dragging him forward and tripping him with my outstretched leg. He fell onto his face, then I threw myself at my gun, scooped it off the deck and leapt into the air at the cable car as a blast from Vrate's weapon flashed behind me. The gondola's door was shut, but the landing skids underneath should have been an easy ultra-reflexed jump, only I was still battling the after effects of being stunned. My hand narrowly missed the skid, then I was falling, sailing beyond Lone Peak's ragged cliffs toward the plain far below. A wall of weathered rock flashed past, then a powerful hand caught my gun belt. I twisted, trying to shoot Vrate over my shoulder, but he struck my hand with the butt of his gun, sending my P-50 spinning away into the air beside us, then the base of his boots glowed brightly, slowing us both.

"You don't give up easy, do you?" I said.

"Kesarn never give up."

Vrate planted his two big boots wide apart as we landed, absorbing the shock with his powerful legs, then he dropped me on the ground and kicked me in the stomach, sending me flying.

I landed on my back, gasping for air. "What was that for?"

"You are beginning to irritate me."

Vrate strode toward me, then wrapped a thin metallic strip around my wrists. I felt cold metal form a tight bracelet, then my arms went numb. Before I knew it, he slapped another strip around my ankles, paralyzing my legs.

"I don't suppose we can make a deal?" I asked as he stepped back.

Vrate ignored me as he walked a short distance out from the cliff, then touched a dark control surface on his forearm.

"Are you carrying me back? It's a long climb, even for you."

Night was descending, rapidly reducing visibility. My sniffer could already reach out further than I could see. It began warning of a contact at the edge of its range, approaching from the south west, something it hadn't scanned before. Whatever it was, it had spotted us from a long way off and was coming in fast. My gun wasn't far away, but it would do me no good while I was wrapped in Kesarn restraints. Vrate had secured his weapon in his back harness while his attention was fixed upon the sky, following something I couldn't see.

"Bringing your ship down?"

Vrate kept his fingers touching his arm control. I couldn't tell if he was piloting the ship remotely or merely feeding it instructions, but it kept him busy as the large creature, still no more than a shadow, appeared in the distance.

"Having an invisible ship must make the kidnapping business very profitable," I said.

"It's for infiltration," he said absently, "not that we do that anymore."

Infiltration of what? "Maybe if you told me what you were looking for–?"

"I've found what I'm looking for!" Vrate snapped as he watched his invisible ship glide toward the ground.

When it landed, he hoisted me over his shoulder and started out onto the plain. In the distance, the lights of Hadley's Retreat were just coming on, and further away and much higher, Citadel's lights were also visible.

"We going far?" I asked as my listener picked up a distant pounding on the ground and the contact marker floating in my mind's eye turned from orange to red. Whatever had us in its sights, my bionetics had decided it was time to get out of the way.

"Further than you've ever been," he said.

"I've travelled a lot."

"That's what you think."

"Considering you're from Perseus, a place no human has ever been, you know my language well." His command of Unionspeak was impressive, considering it was a physical impossibility for some of our Orion Arm neighbors.

"We know many languages."

"Met many humans?"

Vrate grunted. "You're the first."

166

"How am I doing so far? Making a good first impression?"

"No."

My infrared optics illuminated a dark red blur of daunting size heading straight for us.

"And here I thought we were getting along so well."

Vrate's helmeted head turned toward me, puzzled why I would think such a thing. "The Kesarn do not like idle chatter."

"That's a pity, because I have one more question?"

Vrate grunted irritably. "What?"

"How's your hearing?"

"Why?"

The dark mass was now as big as a house and charging at us like a Rigosian swamp bull protecting its young. "Well if your hearing was as good as mine," it was almost on top of us, "you'd know to … look left."

Vrate glanced to the left as the bonecrusher surged out of the darkness. He threw me to the side, freeing his hands so he could reach over his shoulder for his gun, but the massive creature scooped him up in its jaws before he got to it. The huge six legged beast lifted him off the ground, trying to crush him as it slowed. It tossed its head back and forth, shaking him like a rag doll. For a moment, I thought he was already dead, then I saw he had an arm free and was reaching for his gun as his legs kicked vainly against the beast's enormous jaw.

"Vrate!" I yelled, unable to move my legs or arms. "Free me!"

"No," he wheezed, giving up on his gun and clawing with his free hand at the bonecrusher's eyes.

"We'll both die!"

"No!" he declared obstinately.

The bonecrusher lifted its head high, then threw Vrate's body down hard. For a moment, he lay motionless then he reached up for the gun strapped to his back. He got it free just as the bonecrusher scooped him up, sending his gun spinning off into the darkness. It lifted its head high as it tried snapping him in two.

"I can save you!"

The metal bands binding my wrists and ankles dropped away, instantly restoring feeling to my arms and legs. I pushed myself to my feet and stumbled to where my P-50 lay. Its armor piercing hardtips wouldn't be enough to kill the huge creature pounding Gern Vrate to death, but they might tickle it enough to let him go. I glanced at the cliff face, knowing if I started climbing now, I'd be out of reach by the time the bonecrusher finished with him and came looking for me. Leaving him was the smart thing to do, but I saw the giant creature hurl him onto the ground again, then incredibly he stirred, broken but still alive.

"Damn it," I said, then ran toward the bonecrusher as it scooped Vrate's shattered body up to finish him off.

Twenty meters from the creature, I fired high, aiming above its deeply recessed eyes, fearful of hitting Vrate if I went too low. The armor piercing slug ricocheted off its immense skull, but had so little effect the bonecrusher hardly reacted. I fired twice more as I ran to them, hitting its bone-plate covered chest and its knee, but it simply ignored me. When I was almost alongside, Vrate lay pinned in its jaws, now completely helpless.

"Stupid human!" he wheezed. "You made it angry!"

I fired at the creature's eye, but its head was moving so fast, all I managed to do was chip a piece of bone off its skull.

"Lower," Vrate ordered.

It took me a moment to realize what he meant. He could see my weapon wasn't powerful enough to kill the bonecrusher, only him. "No!"

"Don't miss!"

Vrate's armor covered head turned to me, waiting for the kill shot, then the bonecrusher reared up and threw him down onto the ground with tremendous force, trying to break every bone in his body. I darted forward, switching to full auto as I reached Vrate's body. The creature roared above its shattered prey, then I emptied my P-50 into the roof of its open mouth. The hardtips cut up through soft flesh, shattering its tiny brain, then the bonecrusher froze in confusion, staring blankly ahead before collapsing to the ground.

Gern Vrate lay breathing shallowly at my feet. Dark blood stained his body armor, but miraculously, he was still alive. He turned toward the creature, surprised it was dead, as green phosphorescence oozed from his suit and spread along every tear, into every open wound, wrapping him in glowing green threads.

"I guess it takes a lot to kill a Kesarn," I said, surveying his wounds.

"More than a human."

I had to admire that, he was almost dead and still throwing insults. "Don't thank me for saving your life."

He sat up coughing as fluorescence ran up his neck, defying gravity and entering bloody fractures in his helmet, then incredibly, he got to his feet.

"How come you're not dead?" I asked.

"The suit."

"It's not very good armor! You're a mess!"

"Not armor. Kesarn healsuit," he staggered a short

distance, barely able to walk, then reached down and picked up his gun. Weakly, he turned and aimed it at me.

"Are you out of your freaking Kesarn mind?" I yelled. "I just saved your worthless life!"

"Your fault ... you jumped."

I raised my gun, aimed at his chest and fired, but my gun clicked empty. I'd drained the magazine when I'd fired into the bonecrusher's mouth!

"My ship ... that way," he said, nodding out toward the plain.

"No."

"Yes." He aimed at my right leg and touched his gun's firing surface. Sparks exploded from the weapon's side where the bonecrusher had damaged it.

I quickly reached into my pocket, pulled out another mag and reloaded. "Now, do you want to tell me why you're tracking me?" I said, raising my gun, finding I was suddenly alone.

I turned, searching for any sign of him, scarcely able to believe he could even walk, let alone run. Even my bionetic sensors, boosted to their limits, could find only a few drops of alien blood leading out into the plain, showing the way he'd gone. I DNA-locked the sample, gaining mankind's first ever genetic code from the Perseus Arm, but decided not to risk following the trail and getting too close to his ship's weapons.

Suspecting I hadn't seen the last of the big Kesarn, I retreated toward Lone Peak. There above a solitary flashing light high up on the summit marking the way up. When I reached the cliffs below the safety beacon, I found an old metal ladder bolted to the rock face. It had originally been built to provide a safe haven for anyone stranded in the open on the way to Loport, before the cable car system had been constructed.

There were many such safe havens dotted across the plains, because only humans – and one crippled Kesarn – could climb ladders on Hardfall.

I holstered my P-50 and started up the rickety ladder, hoping Gern Vrate's recovery would be a long one. Whatever his motives, I had no desire to find out why I was wanted in the Perseus Arm!

* * * *

Loport cable station's lights were out when I stepped off the gondola several hours after sunset. The dark silhouette of the *Merak Star* could be seen by starlight a few hundred meters away. For a moment, I heard nothing but the creaking of suspension cables and the hum of the gondola as it moved away, then a voice sounded from the darkness.

"What happened to you, Skipper?" Jase asked, holstering his twin fraggers as he emerged from the darkness wearing a URA jacket and carrying a Vel penetrator slung over his shoulder. "Something hit us, then we woke up and you were gone."

"It seems I'm wanted in the Perseus Arm."

"Edge of the galaxy Perseus Arm?"

"Yeah, that one," I said as Izin appeared at the top of the ramp.

"Perhaps we should discuss your galactic infamy another time, Captain," he said, carrying another URA jacket and a Vel.

"We cut the power and took care of the guards when we got here," Jase added, glancing at the sergeant's stripes on his jacket. "It seems I outrank you."

"Just don't expect me to salute you," I said switching back to gelslugs, then I pulled on the army jacket and shouldered the assault gun as we hurried down the ramp. Two guards lay unconscious and bound in the shadows, waiting for Hadley.

"The Merak Star's buttoned up, Skipper," Jase said. "There's no easy way in."

"Let's hope their bridge crew didn't take a close look at those guards," I said, then Jase and I followed the guards' patrol route across the landing apron, strolling at a leisurely pace while Izin slipped away into the darkness to sneak along the cliff tops. By the time we neared the freighter, he was waiting for us behind the landing strut nearest the bow airlock.

I activated the airlock intercom, with Jase in view behind me, "Hey, open up. I have to use your communicator."

"You know I can't do that," a young crewman answered.

"The power's out at the cable station. I've got to get a repair crew down here before the Cyclops lands."

"No one's allowed on board."

"No one but us," I said sharply.

"Use the cable car."

"I can't abandon my post. Look, all I want to do is send a message. We'll be on board for two minutes."

"I have my orders."

"And I have mine!" I said feigning irritation. "I want to speak to Captain Nazari!"

"He's ... unavailable."

"Let me make this real simple. The Governor will have Nazari throw you in the brig when he finds out you delayed the transfer. It's all on your head!"

The junior officer hesitated. "We don't need power from the cable station to do the transfer."

"Rix has a meeting with the Governor. Do you expect him to bumble around in the dark?"

"I don't know about any meeting."

"You're wasting my time!" I snapped. "Get someone up there who knows what's going on, right now!"

There was a long pause this time, then the young officer relented. "Leave your gun outside."

I tossed my Vel to Jase in clear view of the comm panel and held up my empty hands. "Satisfied?"

The outer hatch unlocked with a click, then I placed my hand over the thumbnail sized optical sensor and nodded to Jase. He stepped forward and shot the airlock's interior sensor with his Vel before entering, then Izin darted up into the airlock after him.

"What happened to the 'lock sensor?" the watch officer asked as I stepped into the airlock.

"How should I know, it's your ship," I said as Izin hurried to the hatch control panel.

Jase handed my Vel back to me as the outer hatch closed.

"I can't see you," the officer said with growing anxiety.

"Where's the sensor?"

"Above you."

"Oh yeah, the round thing," I said peering up at the shattered device, sparking with electricity. "It looks OK from this side."

When the inner hatch opened, Izin darted through with his long barreled shredder in hand to secure the companionway. Fortunately for the crew, it was empty. The kid on the bridge hadn't had the sense to send anyone down to check us as we boarded.

"Izin, take engineering. Jase, get the bridge. I'll clear crew quarters."

I figured most of the crew would either be catching up on sack time or relaxing in the mess. In a guarded port with hatches sealed, not expecting boarders, they'd be unarmed. That only left the young watch officer on the bridge for Jase and hopefully no one in engineering for Izin, who was quietly reloading his shredder with highly lethal shattershot.

"We agreed to take them alive," I said.

"–if possible," Jase added.

"If I'm going to commit an act of piracy, Captain, I intend to be the last tamph standing."

"Hmm." I couldn't blame him for being cautious. "OK, but no kill shots."

"If you insist, Captain," Izin said.

It wasn't much of a concession. Shattershot would take a man's leg off and with Hadley unable to take Izin's victims to hospital until we were gone, there was a good chance they'd bleed to death.

"Remember, they're just spacers," I said, suspecting the crew were merely hired hands with no idea what they were really involved in.

With muted agreement, Jase took the elevator up to the bridge, Izin headed aft toward the energy plant and I moved into crew country. After passing through two pressure doors, I heard the pounding beat and wailing sopranos of Indosync blasting down the companionway. What passed for music on the *Merak Star* was popular in the Republic, but it was an earsplitting assault on the senses to Union ears. It came blaring from an open hatch that led into the ship's exercise room. Two heavily muscled pan-Afros and a lean Indo-Asian were sweating hard, pumping pressure field resistors as I stepped through the hatch. They looked up surprised as I bounced gelslugs off their heads, then used the Vel to blast their sound system. With peace and quiet restored to the *Merak Star*, I continued on through the galley to the ship's sleeping quarters.

Izin's voice sounded in my earpiece, "Engineering is secure, Captain."

"Keep it locked down," I said, then pushed open the hatch to the last sleeping compartment.

Inside was a large lounge and office in one. Knowing only the Captain would rate such luxury, I crept toward an open inner door, hearing snoring coming from within. It was Nazari, lying flat on his back on a double bunk, feet still on the floor, a stimhaler in one hand and an empty glass in the other. I slapped his face, but he was so stimmed out, he continued snoring oblivious to my presence.

"Bridge is clear, Skipper," Jase said, "but the navlog's encrypted."

It's what we'd come for. I wanted to know who and where the *Merak Star* was delivering its alien-tech cargo to. "Did you get the watch officer?"

"Yeah, he's alive. He nearly died of fright when I stuck this Vel in his face."

"Ask him who can access the log?"

After a moment, Jase replied, "He says only the captain knows the combination."

Nazari lay with his mouth open snoring like a man who could sleep through an Indosync beat fest. If I couldn't revive him before the *Cyclops* arrived, capturing the *Merak Star* would have been for nothing.

* * * *

While Izin arranged for cargobots to carry the three stunned crewman and Nazari down to the cargo hold, I went up to the bridge. It was a large triangular compartment with the officer's acceleration couches and command consoles facing the base of the triangle

175

where four screens were mounted two by two. Jase had one of his fraggers leveled at a swarthy Cali watch officer with a wiry physique and shifty eyes.

"What access do we have?"

"Everything except the log and weapons," Jase replied.

I turned to the young officer. "Did Nazari have the log access key memorized or written down?"

He gave me a sullen look. "Uncle Naz keeps his secrets up here," he said, tapping his temple.

"You're Nazari's nephew?"

He nodded slowly. "I am Mouad."

I activated my communicator. "Izin."

"Yes, Captain?"

"Nazari has the log key memorized. Revive him. I'll be down soon."

I'd been careful to avoid racking up a body count of flunkies and hired muscle, but I needed access to the *Merak Star's* log fast and if Nazari was anything other than agreeable, I'd let Izin loose on him.

I turned back to Mouad. "Where'd you go after Novo Pantanal?"

He shrugged. "I don't know. Uncle Naz tells me nothing."

"What about the screens?" I asked, pointing at the quad display. "You must have seen something up there?"

Mouad shrugged. "We meet ships in space."

"Drake ships?"

"All kinds," he said evasively.

"Where are the Drake's getting the alien-tech from?"

"What alien-tech?" Mouad asked innocently.

"The stuff you got on Novo Pantanal. Where'd it come from?"

He shrugged. "A box is a box. It's all the same to me."

"He's lying," Jase said, aiming at the young officer's head. "Want me to take off his ear?" He was bluffing, but Mouad didn't know that.

"My uncle tells me nothing!" Mouad said, raising his hands. "He makes me sit here while he sleeps!" He pointed to the sensor console. "If that light flashes, I call him. That's it!" His voice was filled with fear, his body cringed, yet his eyes were more calculating than afraid.

"Captain," Izin's voice crackled in my ear, slightly distorted by the ship's decks separating us. "I've given Nazari an analeptic booster from sickbay. He's regaining consciousness."

"I'll be right down."

Jase motioned with his fragger for Mouad to move, then we went down to the cargo deck where a groggy Nazari was sitting up. Izin had bound and blindfolded the other three crewmen who now lay unconscious alongside a stack of munitions containers. On the far side of the hold, the cargo door had been opened to the ground, waiting for Hadley's ATV.

Jase whistled as he ran his eye over the vast array of weapons stowed in the hold. "They're giving all this to the Drakes?"

"There's more in the other holds," Izin said. "Naval guns, shields, combat vehicles."

"The Drakes will outgun the navy at this rate," I said, kneeling beside the *Merak Star's* captain. "Nazari, can you hear me?"

His half opened eyes looked as if he was surfacing from a deep, stim-induced dream, then as he realized where he was, surprise spread across his face. "How'd ... I get ... here?"

"I control your ship," I said. "If you want to get out of here alive, tell me the log access code."

"Log?" He looked at me with genuine confusion. "Don't ... understand."

"Your ship's log is encrypted. What is the key?"

"Don't know."

His brain was obviously so stim-soaked, he couldn't think straight. "Nazari, how do you access your ship's log?"

He smiled sourly. "Not me ... Con ... sort'm ..."

"You work for the Consortium, but the log is your responsibility."

"I haven't ... been Captain ... since ... they took over."

"If you're not in charge, who is?"

His head turned slowly, looking around. When his eyes settled on his nephew, he nodded weakly. "Him."

I glanced at Mouad, confused. "Your nephew's in charge?"

"Ne-phew?" Nazari's face twisted in revulsion. "He's not ... my–"

A silver shard flashed past my shoulder, slicing through Nazari's throat. Blood spurted from the wound as I instinctively rolled sideways and another metal shard cut the air where I'd been only a moment before. I came up on one knee, P-50 drawn, as Jase went down from an elbow to the head and his fragger went skidding across the deck. Mouad – or whoever he was – dived after it, scooped it up and fired at Izin, but the little tamph was too fast. He darted sideways in a blur of speed, then brought his shredder up with an instinctive intention to eliminate Mouad as a threat.

"Don't kill him, Izin!" I yelled desperately. "I need him alive!"

Izin shifted his aim, sparing Mouad's life, then

fired. The shattershot broke into a torrent of tiny, rapidly spinning slivers the moment they left the barrel, severing Mouad's arm between wrist and elbow. His severed hand still holding Jase's gun fell onto the deck, then Mouad clamped his good hand over the bleeding stump to stop the flow and ran for the open cargo door.

"My shot!" I declared, knowing if Izin fired again, Mouad would bleed out before I could question him.

Izin kept the fleeing watch officer in his sights, but didn't fire, while I put two gelslugs into Mouad's spine. He fell forward under the twin hammer blows, rolling down the ramp as Izin and I ran after him. When we reached the open cargo hatch, Mouad was lying on his back at the foot of the ramp, wheezing from the air knocked out of his lungs. Sweat was beading heavily on his face and the whites of his eyes were turning a sickly yellow. I aimed my P-50 at him as my threading interpreted the signs and flashed an alert into my mind.

WARNING : KANOZON-7 METABOLIC ACCELERATOR DETECTED!

K-7 was a banned drug, giving a tremendous burst to physical strength and endurance while suppressing all moral constraints. The PFA military had invented it, but abandoned it when they discovered it turned disciplined troops into paranoid psychopaths. High on K-7, he was likely to kick me so hard he'd break both our legs without blinking.

"Who are you?" I demanded

"Mouad," he said, giggling in a crazy breathless way.

"Why is the Consortium shipping guns to the Brotherhood?"

"You're about to find out!" he said, jabbing his blood soaked thumb into his jaw.

I grabbed Izin with my free hand, lifting him off the deck, and dived sideways behind the ship's bulkhead as Mouad's body exploded. Shrapnel, bloodied flesh and bone fragments showered the cargo hold as we landed together.

After a moment, Izin glanced at my arm pinning his chest to the deck. "Thank you, Captain. You can release me now."

I rolled off him, then stepped back to the open cargo door. The explosion had torn Mouad's body apart, but barely dented the heavy cargo door.

"How did you know?" Izin asked.

"His eyes. He was juiced on K-7. That stuff will make anyone crazy – crazy enough to trigger a detonator implanted in their jaw. "

"It would appear the Consortium like their hitmen to be young and psychopathic," Izin said. "A formidable combination."

Jase sat up slowly, blinking, holding the side of his head. "Whew! Never saw that coming."

Izin and I returned to where Nazari lay dead in a pool of his own blood.

"You are fortunate he wanted Nazari dead more than you, Captain" Izin observed.

He was right. If Mouad had gone for me first, I'd be dead on the floor instead of the Cali smuggler. The metallic blade intended for me had struck the bulkhead behind Nazari's corpse and fallen to the deck. It was three centimeters long, razor sharp with a flared tail that expanded after firing, giving stability through the air and extra cutting power. There'd been one hidden beneath the skin of each of Mouad's forearms.

I retrieved the blade from the bulkhead, turning it over in my fingers.

"What is it?" Jase asked.

"A subcutaneous flechette." An assassin's weapon. It was lightly smeared with Mouad's own blood as it had cut its way out of his arm.

Jase winced. "What kind of sick freak uses a weapon like that?"

Izin peered at it curiously. "Ingenious."

"So Nazari wasn't the boss? Beady eyes was!" Jase said, picking his shredder up by the barrel and shaking Mouad's severed hand from it.

"Nazari flew the ship," I said, "Mouad gave the orders."

"I guess that's it then," Jase said. "No Mouad, no log."

"We still have the navlog – and we have Izin!" I said glancing at the little tamph. "You'll have to break the encryption before the Cyclops gets here."

"It's unlikely I can do that in the time available, Captain," Izin said warily.

"Then you better get started. We'll clean up the mess down here."

"We will?" Jase asked, glancing at the blood splattered cargo deck with revulsion.

"You know I like a taut ship," I said, enjoying the worried look on his face, then added, "Those bots must have a scrubber function."

Relief washed over his face. "Yeah, scrubber bots! That'll work!"

For an Orie trained gunslinger, he was surprisingly squeamish at the sight of the splattered remains of a psychopathic Consortium hitman.

* * * *

Hadley arrived in his ATV as the cargobots finished cleaning the last of Mouad's remains from the deck and the ground outside surrounding the cargo ramp. The Prairie Runner had come across from the vehicle hoist with its lights off so spotters on Citadel didn't see it. When Hadley strode up the ramp with two of his men, he couldn't help but be impressed with the quantity of armaments stowed in the *Merak Star's* cargo hold.

"So this is where the Drakes get their weapons from," he said, recalling the sporadic raids the colony had endured before the first URA batteries had been set up.

"Not for much longer," I promised.

He looked pleased, then motioned for his men to load Nazari's body, cocooned in cargo wrap, and the other prisoners into the Prairie Runner. "Considering what they've been doing," he said bitterly, "I'm inclined to dump them on the flatlands."

"Then you'd be no better than Metzler."

"Now why'd you have to go spoil my fun!" Hadley replied as Izin entered the cargo hold and hurried to us.

"I need the Silver Lining's processing core to access the Merak Star's navlog, Captain. I've made a copy," he said, holding up a data chip.

"How long?"

"A few days, maybe a week."

"All we need is the last drop off location." I was certain the alien-tech delivery point was the key to whatever the Drakes and the Consortium were up to.

"The log is protected by a multiplex-encryptor," Izin said. "It's broken into randomized, individually coded blocks. I have to break each block separately until I find the one we're looking for."

It wasn't military grade encryption, but it was more sophisticated than any mere smuggler needed.

Izin turned to Hadley. "I need to get back to the

Silver Lining as soon as possible."

Hadley nodded. "I'll drop you at the Hiport hoist before dawn."

"We'll meet you at the Retreat in the morning," I said to Hadley.

"You're not coming with us?" he asked.

"We have one more to job do here, then we'll catch the Link back."

"What job, Captain?" Izin asked.

"Put the Consortium out of the arms business, at least for a while."

"How are you going to do that?" Hadley asked.

"I'm going to blow up the Merak Star," I said simply. It would take the Consortium at least a year to get a replacement ship sent out from Core System space. That would give Lena Voss and Earth Navy time to figure out how to put a permanent end to the Consortium's gun running racket. It was the best disruption I could manage at short notice.

"This is a big ship," Hadley said. "How are you going to destroy it?"

"An energy core collapse ought to do it."

Hadley's eyes widened. "How big an explosion will that cause?"

"Izin?" I said.

He thought for a moment. "Based on the size of the energy plant, a collapse would generate a two kilometer hypocenter surrounded by a ten to twelve kilometer blast wave."

"That puts Hadley's Retreat outside the danger zone," I assured him.

Hadley look shocked. "But you'll destroy the cable station and the spaceport!"

"Loport mesa itself will cease to exist," Izin said.

"More than that," I declared. "If we time it right, we'll vaporize the Cyclops as well!"

* * * *

The *Merak Star* was equipped with safeguards designed to protect densely populated Core System worlds from the kind of attack human religious fanatics had launched against the Matarons fifteen hundred years ago. Disabling them proved to be a slow process, made more difficult by Izin's absence. We were far from finished when the ship's sensors detected a large contact plunging through the atmosphere toward us. Soon thermal and optical images of the *Cyclops's* dark cylindrical mass filled the bridge's four screens, while heat blooms on her bow and amidships revealed she was coming down weapons hot. With her transponder off, the colony's surface batteries should have been hammering away at her, but they simply watched and did nothing.

"She's got targeting beams on us and all eight gun emplacements," Jase said.

"Not exactly trusting are they," I replied.

The *Cyclops* set down close to the *Merak Star* leaving her weapons charged and her maneuvering engines on standby in case she needed to jump back to space at short notice.

"Now what?" Jase asked.

"We bluff," I said, loading detonators into my gun. If it came to a fight with the Drakes, area effect exploding ammo would even the odds.

We hurried down to number one hold and waited above the door-ramp as the ground cooled beneath the *Cyclops*.

"Give them a good look," I said, certain they had

us on screen and were wondering where Nazari was.

"You think they can see my knees shaking?" Jase asked lightly.

"Act like an Orie merc. Make them believe you belong."

Jase assumed a swaggering bearing, leaned against the bulkhead and crossed his arms. "I belong everywhere!"

A mechanical whir sounded from the *Cyclops* as its massive armored door lowered to the ground, then Anya appeared, followed by Domar Trask and his two O-Force bookends. They eyed us suspiciously as they approached, stopping at the foot of the cargo ramp. I opened my mouth, about to introduce myself, when Jase cut me off.

"JAG-40s?" He said contemptuously, nodding at the weapons the three Orie mercs carried. He straightened, placing his hands on his hips. "I guess kissing Drake butt don't pay well."

Trask's eyes narrowed while his two cannon humpers bristled. I realized Jase had initiated some kind of Oresund ego-flexing ritual designed to determine who was the alpha of alphas. Either he'd get us killed or earn us some grudging respect.

"I'd take one of these over those popguns you're wearing," Trask growled, taking the bait.

Quick as a flash, Jase had both fraggers out and aimed at Trask's head. "Are you sure about that now, squaddie?"

Trask blinked, surprised at Jase's speed and ready aggression. "I'm ready to put it to the test right now, if you are." As he spoke, Julkka Olen and Stina Kron moved out to the flanks, placing distance between themselves and turning their guns on us.

Jase gave him a cocky grin. "Anywhere, anytime,

grandpa."

"Before you boys start blasting each other," Anya said, "do you want to tell me where Captain Nazari is?"

"He's dead," I said. "Binge snorted four stimhalers in one night. Never came out of it."

Anya's eyes arched, but she didn't look surprised. "I warned him about that stuff."

"A lot of people did," I said.

"What about Mouad?" Trask demanded.

"He's dead too," Jase said with cold menace. "I retired him for letting Nazari die."

Understanding appeared on Trask's face as he guessed Jase was the new Consortium hitman, sent to replace his failed predecessor, then he turned to me, "And you are?"

"Sirius Kade, Nazari's replacement. The Consortium gave me the job because I don't use 'halers and they don't want any more mistakes."

"I've never heard of you," Trask said bluntly.

"That's because I'm discreet."

Anya gave Trask a slight nod of approval, then the three Orie renegades lowered their guns. Jase made a show of twirling his fraggers and sliding them back into their holsters.

"She just saved your life," Jase said.

Trask scowled. "There's three of us and only one of you."

"Yeah, but I have two guns, which means I'd have shot you twice before they got me once." He grinned, making a show of enjoying himself. He was so overbearingly confident, even I was almost convinced he lacked any fear. Not for the first time, I wondered how Oresund had developed such a strangely militaristic culture. Clearly, any sign of weakness was punished, while a reckless disregard for death earned respect.

"So do you want the cargo?" I asked. "Or are we going to stand here all day arguing about who has the biggest pistol?"

"We want it," Anya said, "but there's been a change of plan."

"What change?"

"You're coming with us to pick up the return shipment," Trask said.

"Why didn't you bring it with you?"

"It was too large for the Cyclops," Anya said.

"I don't have orders to go anywhere with you," I replied, taking a risk that no such order had been issued to Nazari.

"You do now," Trask snapped.

"Go where?" Jase demanded, asserting his authority as the Consortium representative.

"That's not your concern," Trask replied.

"I'll be programming your autonav," Anya said. "You'll never see the coordinates."

"You expect me to let a bunch of Drakes take control of a Consortium ship?" I asked.

"The Consortium and the Brotherhood are both being well paid to follow orders," Trask said. "If you have a problem with that, we'll terminate your involvement now and take the ship."

His tone was a thinly veiled threat to terminate more than my contract, but it was his other words that shocked me. Neither the Consortium or the Brotherhood were calling the shots! They were both working for an unknown third party, someone with the resources to recruit both the largest organized crime syndicate in Mapped Space and the notoriously treacherous pirate collective.

"I'm just doing what I'm paid to do," I said,

"looking after the Consortium's interests."

"And I'm looking after the Brotherhood's interests," Anya said, "which is why we'll be loading a bomb aboard your ship. It will detonate if you try to access the autonav or look at your destination's coordinates."

I'd wanted to destroy the *Merak Star*, but not with us aboard!

"How am I supposed to fly the ship?"

"You'll have thrusters and maneuvering engines," she said, "but no control over your bubble. It will activate automatically once you reach the jump off point."

Jase and I exchanged wary looks. We were about to become prisoners aboard a Drake controlled flying bomb, heading to coordinates unknown, to collect a cargo whose purpose remained a mystery while masquerading as Consortium agents.

At least we'd be rid of Hardfall's onerous gravity.

* * * *

"Two people aren't enough to operate this ship," Anya said suspiciously as her engineer knelt at the back of the bridge's central console. He slid a spherical device inscribed with Chinese hanzi graphemes into the console and attached it to the *Merak Star's* autonav. My threading had identified it as an orbital diver warhead, a weapon designed to destroy ground targets from space and more than capable of vaporizing the *Merak Star*.

"There wasn't time to recruit a full crew after Nazari's death," I replied.

"What was wrong with the old crew?"

"They wouldn't serve on the same ship as him," I

nodded toward Jase who was watching the engineer, hoping to find a way to undo his work. "We've got enough maintenance bots to keep her going until I sign more crew."

The engineer looked up at Anya. "Ready."

She approached one of the control consoles, then motioned Jase and I to the far side of the bridge. Once we moved to where we couldn't see the console's interface, she entered our destination's coordinates into the autonav.

"Are you ready to launch?" she asked.

"Why?"

"I'm activating the autonav timer. When it runs out you bubble, ready or not."

If the ship's superluminal bubble tried to form while we were still in space steeply curved by the planet's gravity, it would be a very short trip. "I was planning to strip the port engine –"

"There's no time for that," she said. "How long do you need to clear the planet's gravity well?"

"Two hours," I said playing for time.

"You've got thirty minutes."

"Nazari was a stimhead, not a maintenance engineer! That's why we've only got one good engine. With the load we're carrying, even if we burn thrusters all the way, we won't make it. Either give us more time or detonate your bomb right now!"

She gave me a long, dubious look, then relented. "You have one hour." She entered commands into the console then closed the interface. "Don't be late."

The Drake engineer leaned in to the open console, made a final connection, then replaced the rear panel. "It's armed," he said as he stood, turning to me. "If you touch the autonav or try to disconnect the bomb," he smirked, "– boom!"

"What happens at the other end?" I asked.

"We'll be waiting for you," Anya said. "If you don't show up, we'll assume you did something stupid." She followed her engineer to the bridge's pressure door. "In case you're thinking of jumping ship, the Cyclops will stay grounded until you launch. We've also disabled your lifeboat."

"You've thought of everything."

"You better get started," she said, then headed for the corridor outside.

When they'd taken the elevator down to the cargo deck, Jase removed the panel concealing the bomb. "There must be a way to disarm this thing."

"If there is, we don't have the time or the skills to do it." Even if we did, I wanted to see where we were going and what cargo Trask had waiting for us. "Start preflight," I said as Anya and her engineer appeared on one of our bridge screens hurrying back to the *Cyclops*.

"We're going?" Jase asked surprised.

"You heard the lady, we've got one hour," I said, sliding onto the pilot's acceleration couch and ordering the cargo door sealed. "Struts-up in two minutes."

"What about Izin?"

"That depends on him."

Jase slid into the copilot's station and began checking systems while I familiarized myself with the *Merak Star's* flight controls. She was four times the mass of the *Silver Lining* with much greater internal volume, and by the look of her propulsion systems, she was underpowered. Flying on one engine would be tricky, but I had to make the Drakes believe I'd been telling the truth.

"Ready," Jase announced at last.

We launched with the port engine feathering at twenty percent, climbing into the sky like a feeble elephant. Once we cleared the landing ground, the *Cyclops* blasted off. The old assault carrier was big and heavy, but she went barreling past us like we were standing still, eager to escape the vulnerabilities of being planet bound. She quickly reduced in size to a point of brilliant white light, shooting out of the upper atmosphere before we'd even cleared the stratosphere. While we limped skywards, feigning engine trouble, the *Cyclops* hurtled toward flat space, showing no interest in nursemaiding us away from Hardfall.

"We can land after they bubble," Jase said, "jump a cable car and let her blow."

"No we can't." When Jase gave me a puzzled look, I explained. "They waited for us to launch. Now that we're committed, they're leaving us behind because they know we can't go back. The bomb must be rigged to explode if we land."

"Why didn't Anya warn us?"

"Because she's testing us. If we go back now, we fail and the Consortium will be looking for a new ship."

Realization spread across his face. "What a bitch!"

"Let's see what's happening below?"

Jase oriented the sensors toward Hardfall Colony. All eight surface batteries were tracking us, but none made any attempt to stop us, or even offer a parting hail. Over at Hiport, the *Silver Lining* sat on the ground showing no sign of life.

"Switch on the transponder," I said.

Jase looked puzzled. "Those grunts know who we are. They're not going to fire."

"It's not them I'm signaling."

Jase started broadcasting our identity while I kept our climb rate to a steady crawl, hoping the *Cyclops* wouldn't get suspicious and Izin was paying attention.

The *Silver Lining* remained asleep at Hiport while, to my relief, all eight surface batteries continued to track us. Better they were locked onto us than the *Lining*.

"That stupid tamph's got his head stuck in the processing core again!" Jase said.

"He's waiting." Far out beyond the edge of Hardfall's gravity well, the *Cyclops* vanished from our screens as it bubbled away. "For that."

The *Silver Lining's* maneuvering engines immediately glowed to life. She lifted off, but instead of climbing, she power dived over the cliff toward the ground, leveling off at the last moment and heading north west, away from the colony. Her engines went to full power, sending her streaking fast and low over the plains. She was halfway to the horizon before Hardfall's surface batteries began target locking her. The north side domes rotated slowly, bringing their guns to bear, but they were anti-orbital weapons not designed to track fast, ground skimming targets at close range. Agonizing seconds passed before the Hiport battery fired, sending a blast of energy flashing above the *Silver Lining*. Citadel's northern batteries followed suit seconds later, but it was all too slow, too late. The *Lining* followed the planet's curvature, putting ground between her and the big guns. When she was safely beyond the horizon, she stayed low for another five hundred clicks then began climbing, never letting Hardfall's batteries see her.

"Not bad flying for a tamph," Jase admitted grudgingly.

"I'll tell him you said that."

"If you do, I'll mutiny!"

While we lumbered away, the *Silver Lining* cleared Hardfall's atmosphere above the planet's north pole and headed for deep space, keeping the planet's bulk between her and the colony's heavy weapons. Only once she was outside their effective range, did she begin a long curving trajectory toward us.

Jase nodded to himself. "That's why you were playing for time! So Izin could catch us outside Hardfall's range."

"I couldn't leave my favorite tamph behind!"

"So we're transferring over?" he said relieved.

"Nope."

We were halfway to the bubble point when the *Silver Lining* became visible to Hardfall's space guns again, already further from the planet than we were. The surface batteries began firing as soon as they saw her, but their blasts dissipated with distance, flashing harmlessly against her battle shield. Soon the *Silver Lining* rolled bow over stern and began decelerating toward a point ahead of the *Merak Star*.

We weren't yet out of range of Hardfall's guns and I didn't want to make Izin's job harder by taking evasive action, so I began transmitting on all channels. "Mayday, mayday, this is the Merak Star. We are being pursued by a hostile ship. Request assistance."

Jase gave me an incredulous look. "Skipper, what are you doing?"

"Confusing the grunts. In their eyes, we're the good guys. I don't want them shooting at us." We only needed to keep them scratching their heads for a few minutes, then we too would be out of their reach.

Izin was listening and knew immediately what I was doing. His synthesized voice come back on all channels. "Heave too Merak Star and prepare to be boarded. We will open fire if you do not obey."

Jase shook his head slowly. "A pirate tamph! Now I've seen it all!"

I smiled. "He does seem to be enjoying this."

"Merak Star, you are moving out of our firing envelope," the same female controller who'd given us instructions on our arrival said. "Reverse course immediately. Enter orbit above Hardfall Colony's meridian."

"Say again Hardfall! They're jamming our communications," I yelled, then switched off the communicator.

I cut our engines, giving Izin an easy matching maneuver as we drifted out of range of Hardfall's heavies. Izin immediately fine tuned his course, coming alongside a few minutes later. Hardfall stopped firing at the *Lining* for fear of hitting us, then I pumped the pressure in the stern cargo hold to ten atmospheres, released the magnetic deck locks holding the cargo in place then opened the hull doors on both sides. The hold explosively decompressed, hurling hundreds of containers full of Drake munitions into space.

"Park her in hold four," I said on a tight beam to Izin once the containers had floated clear of the *Merak Star*.

He didn't acknowledge my instruction, but came in above us, then glided down to the open cargo hold. The *Silver Lining* was crescent shaped, with a large maneuvering engine at each 'wingtip', giving her a beam four times her bow to stern length. When her starboard engine was alongside, she thrusted gently sideways into the aft hold. Once inside, Izin killed her lateral drift and nudged her down onto the deck where magnetic locks caught her landing struts. When she was secure, I sealed the cargo doors and repressurized the hold.

"Welcome aboard, Silver Lining," I said over ship-to-ship. "Shut her down cold, Izin. We don't want the Drakes knowing you're there."

"Right away, Captain."

I started up the *Merak Star's* engines again, this time at full power, and headed for Anya's bubble point, rolling and decelerating only at the last possible moment. We came to a dead stop with barely a minute to spare.

"We could use the Silver Lining to abandon ship," Jase suggested as we waited for the autonav to take over.

"We could," I agreed, "but I still have a score to settle," and an aleph-null code to unravel!

Jase nodded understandingly. "Now that I've met them, I don't like the look of them either. They give all Ories a bad name."

The first indication of the autonav taking over was when our sensors suddenly retracted and the spacetime distorters began charging.

"Here we go!" Jase said.

I relaxed, hands behind my head. "Time to see what the Drakes are hiding."

"Captain," Izin's synthetic voice sounded from the intercom.

"Yes Izin, what is it?"

"I'm detecting that electromagnetic anomaly again. It's very close."

I smiled, this time knowing what it meant. Gern Vrate was alive! "Don't worry about it, Izin. It's just a nosy neighbor from the Perseus Arm."

Before he could question me further, the *Merak Star's* bubble formed, sending us hurtling at a thousand times the speed of light toward Anya's secret destination.

Chapter Five : Acheron Station

Drift Station
Acheron Abyss Dark Nebula
Non-System Space, Outer Draco
945 light years from Sol
Population Unknown

The *Merak Star* was bubbled up for three days, and thanks to Anya, the autonav refused to share its real time coordinate simulation with us. I was used to flying blind – there was no way to avoid it, no signal of any kind could penetrate a superluminal bubble – but not seeing the autonav plotting our progress against the infallible Tau Cetin charts was strangely unnerving.

Jase and I took turns standing watch while Izin locked himself in the *Silver Lining* trying to crack the Consortium's navlog encryption. In my spare time, I studied the armaments the *Merak Star* was still carrying for the Drakes in three of its four cargo holds. At first glance, they appeared to be everything the

Brotherhood could want, except they were all hard hitting military grade weapons designed for war fighting, and that was the problem. The Brotherhood wanted loot, not glory. The only booty they'd get with these weapons would be corpses and radioactive wrecks. There was no profit in that.

"Skipper," Jase's voice sounded over the intercom in hold two. "We've arrived."

"On my way," I said, pushing off in zero gravity toward the forward hatch. Like many large ships, the *Merak Star* was rigged for artificial gravity only in crew areas in order to lower build costs and reduce energy consumption.

Izin met me halfway to the bridge elevator, as eager to see where Anya was taking us as I was.

"Any progress on the log?" I asked.

"I've decrypted a fifth of the entries, but have found nothing useful. Nazari was even more ineffective at keeping records than you, Captain."

I was sloppy on purpose, because I didn't like anyone knowing my business, especially my EIS business. Nazari on the other hand was a stimhead who'd have lost his license the moment he set foot in Core System space.

"You've been reading my log?" I said, feigning indignation.

"I assure you, Captain, deciphering your cryptic annotations is more difficult than decrypting the Merak Star's log, and far less stimulating."

When we reached the bridge, Jase was scanning nearby space. All four screens displayed a thin black mist devoid of stars with only a single point of light in the distance, blurred by the gas and dust between us.

"Where are we?" I asked, climbing onto my

acceleration couch.

"The autonav isn't talking," Jase replied, "but from the looks of it, I'd say we're inside the Acheron Abyss."

The dark mass of the *Cyclops* floated in the mist several clicks to port. Being significantly faster than the *Merak Star* at both super- and subluminal velocities, she must have been waiting there for almost a day.

"Incoming signal," Jase announced.

"Izin, they don't know you're here" I said. "Let's keep it that way."

Izin hurried into the corridor, then Jase put Anya on screen.

"Follow us in," she said without preamble. "Don't try to access your autonav or you know what'll happen, and whatever you do, don't activate shields or weapons. If you do, we won't be able to protect you."

The screen went blank, then the old assault carrier's three maneuvering engines glowed to life as she started toward the distant light.

"If they can't protect us," Jase said, "what are we doing here?"

"They want us looking like a prize, not a threat," I said, laying in a course behind the *Cyclops*.

Jase parked his annoyance, turning his attention to the sensors. "There's over a hundred ships out there, all sizes, all types, all Drake!"

It explained Anya's insistence on secrecy. She was a Brotherhood navigator, a member of an elite group who knew the coordinates of every pirate base in Mapped Space, places so secret that such knowledge was a death sentence to all but the anointed. Bases like Acheron Station were the beating heart of the

Brotherhood, where booty, hostages and ships were bought and sold and the long arm of Earth Law was entirely unknown. If Earth Navy ever discovered this location, they'd send in a fleet and blast it out of existence. It was why no Brotherhood navigator had ever been taken alive – or ever would be.

"Welcome to pirate central," I said, wondering if I'd made a terrible mistake coming here.

* * * *

Ten thousand clicks out we passed through a field of gravity mines forming a spherical shell around our destination. The curved space the mines generated was strong enough to collapse any bubble passing through it, providing an impenetrable barrier to superluminal flight. In the event of an Earth Navy attack, the barrier gave the Drakes a chance to escape while the navy wallowed through curved space trying to reach them.

"Fancy stuff for a bunch of raiders," Jase said.

"It's old technology," Izin said, back on the bridge now that our commlink to the *Cyclops* was closed. "Only new knowledge is difficult to acquire. It's why there were no pirates during the early centuries of human interstellar travel. Back then, Earth's collective governments had a monopoly on superluminal technology. Now interstellar flight is commonplace and pirates are everywhere Earth Navy is not."

"Greed always finds a way," I said.

After more than two thousand years of interstellar travel, any thug could buy or steal a ship, equip it with weapons and menace the space lanes – at least the human lanes. Initially the pirates had fought each other for the spoils, then the Brotherhood had been formed, turning raiding into an organized, highly profitable business. The captains pooled their resources, built support bases in locations shrouded in secrecy where Earth Navy couldn't find them.

The navigators who knew where those bases were hidden received the largest share of the booty, even more than the captain, because they bore the greatest risk, being the first to die if Earth Navy boarded their ships. The commband Anya wore on her forehead was more than just a communications device, it was her death sentence if she or her ship were ever captured. All navigators had them surgically attached, knowing they would wear them for the remainder of their lives. The commbands carried within them the coordinates of every Brotherhood base and allowed the navigator to communicate directly with Brotherhood ships, negating the need to enter coordinates into pirate autonavs that might be seen by bridge crews.

The rewards in terms of wealth and power for bearing such risks were great, and should they pay the ultimate price, the Brotherhood ensured all they were owed went to their chosen beneficiaries. It was a harsh but effective system, one neither Earth Navy or the EIS could penetrate, and in spite of the risks, the rewards ensured there was no shortage of volunteers.

Inside the sphere of gravity mines was a layer of long range sensors monitoring the approaches to the minefield. There were no gun platforms, no robot sentries to engage an attacking fleet because the Brotherhood knew if Earth Navy came, it would be in overwhelming strength. The defenses were designed to warn and delay only, not for a stand up fight the Drakes could not hope to win.

Once inside the early warning system, the *Cyclops* performed a half-roll and began decelerating. We followed suit, mimicking the Drake ship's every move.

Soon the station came into view. It was a long, linear structure with cruciform arms branching out from the central spine every fifteen hundred meters. Attached to the arms was a haphazard mix of VRS containers, ship hulls, habitats, storage tanks, agridomes, hangars and shipyards. The derelict ship hulls had long ago been stripped for parts and were now no more than pressurized structures organically integrated into the station's cross-arms. Small craft and maintenance bots orbited the station like insects around a rotting corpse while scaffold-like docking gantries containing flimsy pressure tubes extended from the station's arms to battle worn combat vessels of every type. Floating near the station were other Drake ships, maneuvering to dock or preparing to set off to plunder the shipping lanes grazing the edge of the Acheron.

"Sure is a lot of them," Jase said warily.

"Too many," I said, surprised at how well organized they were.

In spite of their numbers, the odds were with the traders. Space was vast and a smart captain could avoid the choke points favored by the Brotherhood if he didn't mind spending a little longer underway. Even so, ships were lost, prizes taken and the Brotherhood flourished on the promise of instant riches.

"Lots of space docks," Jase observed, noting how many ships were laid up, surrounded by cranes and thrusterbots.

"Maintenance docks," Izin corrected. "They have repair facilities only, no construction."

There were many docks of different sizes, but they all held completed ships. There were no partially constructed super structures, no massive hull blocks being aligned, just darkly scarred ships that should have been scrapped years ago.

"He's right," I said, "the Brotherhood are scavengers, not builders."

"Then what's that doing here?" Jase demanded, pointing to a distant dock. He zoomed our optics, revealing a pristine ship surrounded by cranes and gantries. Her hull was as spotless as if she'd just been launched and her four large engines in diamond formation showed no sign of wear. She had a squat bridge amidships, a rounded bow and four cargo doors each side.

"It's not a new build," Izin said, "it's an upgrade."

Closer inspection revealed large thrusterbots were fitting slab armor, big naval turrets, small point defense weapons and shield emitters to the hull. She was unmistakably a structurally reinforced Saracen, the same class Hadley had imaged landing at Loport, now being transformed by the Drakes into the equivalent of a purpose built, cruiser sized warship. It didn't take long to discover other maintenance docks performing similar transformations on seven more Saracens.

"That's quite an upgrade," I said uneasily.

"Cyclops hailing," Jase warned.

Izin hurried from the bridge, then Jase opened a channel.

"Follow us around," Anya ordered, on screen for only a moment.

"Yes, ma'am," Jase said to a blank screen as the *Cyclops* pitched slowly and thrusted along one of the station's massive cross-arms.

"Her captain's watching her," I said, sensing her tension.

Jase gave me a puzzled look. "I thought she was the captain."

"She's the navigator. Rix is the captain. We haven't seen him yet."

202

I copied the *Cyclops's* maneuver, then as we drifted up past the cross-arm, nine more Super Saracens came into view parked off the far side of the station. They stood with their upgrades complete in block line abreast formation – three rows of three stacked together. Compared to the chaotic structure of the station, the precision of their formation displayed an order and discipline unlike anything the Drakes had ever shown.

"The Brotherhood appear to have learnt station keeping discipline from Earth Navy," Izin observed from the hatchway.

Brotherhood ships were adept at working in teams, but they never flew tight formations. They kept their distance from each other, always ready to run, every man for himself in the face of Earth Navy. Formation flying was the navy's specialty, designed to bring all weapons to bear upon a single target. Even standing to, these Super Saracens looked ready to fight in the same way, indicating they were fitted with Earth Navy level combat systems that would enable the ships to fight as a single unit.

"Maybe the Drakes are recruiting Earth Navy tactical officers," Jase suggested.

The more I watched the Drake fleet, the more apprehensive I became. Several Super Saracens fighting the way the Drakes normally did, sharing sensor data and targeting at will, would challenge the solitary Earth Navy frigates that patrolled Mapped Space's outer regions. A fleet of them, fighting as a compact, integrated force could strike any target outside Core System space with impunity.

"She's back," Jase said, eyes on the comm system.

"Ride the docking beam into theta one niner," Anya said.

Jase did a quick check of our incoming signals and nodded. "I see it."

"Lock up to the station, and open your outer doors. Cargobots are waiting to unload you."

"We've got cargo in holds one to three," I said. "Four is empty."

She looked puzzled. "We were expecting a full load."

"The manifest says we're full, but that's not what we're carrying." I shrugged. "Nazari sold the rest for stims."

She gave me a disgusted look, but swallowed the story. "Once you're empty, we'll begin preparing you to receive your outbound load. Until then, you're free to access the station, but I wouldn't recommend it."

"Why not?"

She gave me a scornful look. "It's full of Drakes, all drunk and looking for fights. You should stay there ... where it's safe." She cut the signal.

Jase exhaled slowly. "I'm not one to pass up shore leave, Skipper, but in this case ..."

"I agree. You stay here." Knowing Jase's quick temper, he was likely to get into a fight the first time a drunken Drake breathed on him. "I'll check it out."

Jase gave me a surprised look. "If you're going, I'm going."

"No, you and Izin make sure their bots don't find the Silver Lining," I said, calculating how far it was to the nearest Super Saracen. "The kind of sightseeing I have in mind is better off done alone."

* * * *

I cycled through the airlock with a stun grenade in one pocket and a combination scanner in the other. The grenade was in case Anya's horde of drunken Drakes took a dislike to me and the c-scanner was so I could stick my nose where it didn't belong.

A flimsy pressure tube, twisting through vacuum from the station's outer hull, had been attached to the ship by thrusterbots with barely a safety check. It was old and patched and there was a disturbing hiss of escaping air warning of an unseen pinhole leak, but the pressure seemed stable so I quickly pulled myself along the guide cable to the station's outer door. Once through to hard deck and gravity, I headed toward the station's backbone, the massive shaft holding the cross-arms in place. The air was musty and laden with a foul mix of human and chemical smells, but tolerably breathable. Somewhat reassuringly, grimy maintenance bots crawled over the bulkheads checking for leaks indicating there was some semblance of pressure discipline.

The corridor led past dozens of docking ports to a crowded plaza lined with bars, brothels and merchants. It rang with raucous laughter, music and loud voices and smelled of stale drink, sweat and roasting meats. Unlike most human ports, there was not a single nonhuman among them, testament to the fact the Brotherhood shared no secrets with aliens. One look told me I was underdressed in my brown flight jacket, dark pants and magnetic boots – workmanlike clothes but dull compared to what the Drakes wore.

The men dressed in mismatched body armor sprayed in bright colors, the bolder the better. The Drakes were scroungers, grabbing any piece of personal protection they could find and customizing it according to their gaudy tastes. Punctuating their garish body armor were gold rings: on their fingers; in their ears, and every possible piercing. Beneath the armor, they wore white or gray shirts and loose black pants. Few wore space boots. Most preferred armored combat boots painted with various decorations suggesting they were sufficiently adept in zero-g that they didn't need magnetic anchoring. It was a competition of sorts, between alpha males jostling for dominance, all armed to the teeth and ready to shed blood at any perceived slight.

By contrast, the women came in two varieties: those who inhabited the station and those who did not. The enterprising ladies who lived aboard and maintained a revolving door of clients wore clothes as bright as the men, although more skin was displayed than concealed. Bulges in the wrong places hinted at weapons secreted about their bodies and the freedom with which they moved from one group to another showed they did as much of the choosing as the men. Some were young and beautiful, most were not, but all had eyes alert to the next opportunity.

The second type of woman showed little flesh, choosing instead to clad herself in body armor painted in matching colors. They were the spacers like Anya, visibly armed and as lethal any man, with a strength that ensured liberties were offered, not taken.

Many pairs of suspicious eyes followed me as I slipped through the rowdy throng. My sniffer area-scanned them all, comparing their signatures to my bionetic memory's most wanted list, finding many hits. Several times I sidestepped drunken men beating each other's brains out. Bare knuckles, elbows and knees flew but no matter how much blood splattered the decks, no weapons were drawn. These were 'friendly' fights, cheered on by laughing onlookers who drank, snorted, sniffed and wagered as the men – and sometimes the women – pounded each other to pieces.

A few times, derisory voices yelled at me, but I ignored them, slipping away through the crowd before an insult could develop into something more threatening, hoping they were too drunk to follow.

Where the open plaza met the station's spine, a raised platform displayed a line of male and female captives, most dressed similarly to me, facing a large audience. One Drake stood on the podium shouting over the jeers and laughter of the crowd as other buccaneers pushed one of the captives forward. He was in his forties, face bruised with his hands tied behind his back.

"Here's a likely fellow!" the auctioneer on the podium yelled, glancing down at the data screen in his hand. "Skilled in vacuum welding, structural assembly and corrosive decontamination!" The auctioneer nodded approvingly as he turned toward the man. "What experience you got?"

When the prisoner didn't reply, one of the guards open handed his ear. "Answer the man, scum!"

The prisoner winced, then said, "Nine years. I was a construction worker on Onyx Four, in the Kazaris Belt."

The auctioneer turned to the audience, impressed. "You hear that boys? A construction worker from the Kazaris Belt! He's trained. Send him out to fix your hulls when you don't want to risk a crew brother or a hullbot. Do I hear a thousand credits?"

"How much for the girl?" someone shouted from the crowd.

"More than you can afford, Gadnar Pit! Now get back down to old Lulu on K deck where you belong! Thirty seconds with her is all you need!" the auctioneer declared, followed by jeering laughter from the crowd. "Brothers! How much for this highly trained Kazaris 'roid hugger?"

"Five hundred," a man declared in a vaguely familiar, Afro-east accent. He was a tall, dark skinned cutthroat with braided hair and a face half melted from plasma burns. In spite of his gruesome scars, I recognized him instantly. It was Gwandoya, a regional leader of the Brotherhood I'd had a run in with a year ago. I'd left his ship a fiery wreck, which almost certainly made me responsible for his face. A single lifeboat had launched, which I now knew had carried him to safety as he abandoned his crew to their fate.

Knowing I'd be a dead man if Gwandoya saw me, I hurried away from the auction, regretting again my spacer clothes. After slipping through a large corridor equipped with an auto-sealing safety door, I entered the station's spine, listening for any sign I'd been spotted. Here the riotous sounds of the plaza faded into the muted thrumming of machinery essential to the drift station's life. While the cross-arms had grown organically from derelict ships and salvaged parts, the spine had been carefully engineered to sustain a complex and ever changing artificial habitat deep within the Acheron's freezing darkness.

Satisfied I wasn't being followed, I caught the transit tube running through the station's spine to the next cross-arm, then headed out toward the maintenance dock where a Super Saracen was being transformed. The only people on this level were dock workers, and pairs of Orie mercs dressed in light and dark gray fatigues manning access checkpoints. The guard's quiet discipline was a stark contrast to the chaotic Drakes and the thoroughness of their identity checks told me they wouldn't let me anywhere near the Super Saracen.

Before I attracted attention, I headed back to the

spine, then walked up a series of broken conveyor ramps to the level above. It was poorly lit, used by cargobots carrying sealed containers to and from the storage facilities located there. I immediately fell in beside a fully laden cargobot as if I was supervising its delivery. When I was back out to where the Super Saracen was docked, I pressed my combination scanner against a sealed pressure door and hoped Drake security locks weren't deviously encrypted. It took only seconds for the hatch to unlock, revealing a dark compartment full of storage shelves stacked with equipment. I slipped inside, pocketing the c-scanner and easing the hatch shut behind me.

"State your part number!" a mechanical voice snapped from the darkness.

I spun around, hand going to my gun as a conical spotlight blinked on and swiveled toward me. Out of the darkness, a metallic column twice my height glided to me on a circular base. Below the spotlight were two thin, telescoping arms that independently slid up and down its sides as if on rails.

"What?" I asked uncertainly.

It came to a stop in front of me, aiming its light down into my eyes. "I require a UniLog Catalogue Number to access your required part." The spotlight narrowed from a cone to a tight beam. "You do know your part number, don't you!"

"No," I said slowly, "can't you tell me?"

"I am a Universal Logistics Support System able to catalogue, store and access over ten billion components manufactured by more than two million industrial facilities on fifty one human worlds. I am not a mind reader!"

Either a bored station tech had been tinkering with the Drake logistics system's interactives or this warehouse bot was about to short circuit. I decided to play along. "I'm looking for a Superdyne Vectorex thruster assembly."

The tight beam flashed back to a cone. "We do not carry that component!"

"Yes you do! A shipment came in last week, to this location. I ordered it especially."

"Impossible! No such delivery was received."

"You lost it? A UniLog SS lost my component?"

"No components have ever been lost, except for when humans failed to transmit the correct dataset – which was not my fault!"

"Maybe you were affected by the power failure?"

"What power failure?" the machine asked indignantly.

"The one that caused you to lose my thruster assembly."

"I have no record of any power failure!"

"Well my thruster assembly's here. You better find it or you can catalogue yourself as a spare part for your replacement!"

The columns' arms slid up and down its sides alarmed. "I will conduct an immediate stocktake of all components."

"How long will that take?"

"Twenty six hours, thirty one minutes."

"I'll wait."

The erratic warehouse bot turned sharply and glided off through the darkness to the far end of the compartment, giving my eyes a chance to adjust. While it busily counted nuts and bolts, I hurried down an aisle between crowded shelves to an industrial sized airlock flanked by a row of thrusterbots. Beside the airlock was a grimy viewport overlooking the Super Saracen.

The ship was bathed in beams of light and

anchored to the maintenance dock by gantries extending from the station. Thrusterbots floated around her, guiding heavy naval turrets into indentations in the cargo doors precisely engineered to match the weapon mounts. Other thrusterbots attached armor and installed ship defenses, all supervised by human engineers in thruster suits. It was an efficient, automated process my threaded optics recorded for later analysis, although it didn't take a naval architect to realize the Super Saracen and its various armaments had been manufactured separately, perhaps in locations hundreds of light years apart, then brought here for assembly far from Earth Navy's prying eyes.

A thrusterbot lifted off its cradle behind me and glided toward the airlock door, rotating and twisting its two articulated arms as part of its carefully choreographed preflight readiness check. Emblazoned on its side were the words: *SHINAGAWA STATION, UNIT 5076*, although I doubted the machine had ever seen service at the giant Japanese shipbuilding orbital in Core System space. More likely, someone was using Shinagawa as a cover for building thrusterbots prior to shipping them to Acheron Station.

An operation on this scale required coordination and access to construction facilities across Mapped Space, all under the noses of Earth Navy, UniPol and the EIS. It was something that could only have been done by the Consortium and might have gone unnoticed if not for one dead EIS agent who was never far from my thoughts.

After imaging every part of the Super Saracen for Lena and her EIS analysts, I slipped quietly back into the corridor, unnoticed by the eccentric UniLog warehouse bot, and headed for the *Merak Star*. I gave the prisoner auction – and Gwandoya – a wide berth, then when I was halfway across the plaza, a bearded Drake with thick, tattooed arms and wearing a dark purple chest plate stepped in front of me.

"What have we got here?" he slurred drunkenly, grabbing my arm as he looked me up and down. The bearded bully carried a metal jug sloshing with ale that splashed over the sides as he turned to his crew mates sitting around a table. "Looks like he should be on sale!" The other Drakes and their female companions laughed, smelling blood, then he turned back to me. "You wouldn't be escaping now, would you?"

"I'm off the Cyclops," I said, trying to wrench my arm free of his vice-like grip without overly provoking him.

"The Cyclops! You?" He belly laughed. "What's it like taking orders from that tight assed bitch?"

"I take orders from Rix," I said, shifting my position.

"Rix?" the Drake declared in surprise. "Does he even exist? I've never seen him." He turned to his crew mates. "Any of you ever seen Rix?"

They shook their heads, impatient for blood. One of the women yelled, "Anya made him up so she could be captain!"

The big brute in front of me took a swig from his jug, then turned toward the auctioneer and yelled, "Hey Skunkweed, I got one of your boys here trying to run!"

A hundred heads turned toward us, leaving me no quiet way out. I stepped back dragging the Drake's arm after me, caught his wrist and twisted, locking his elbow then drove my palm into it. There was an audible crack as the joint snapped, then rage exploded across his face.

"I was just being friendly!" He declared angrily, throwing his mug onto the deck and reaching into his trouser pocket with his good arm. Instead of a gun, his clenched fist emerged holding a knuckle stunner. The curved metal knuckle shield glowed to life, warning one punch would land with ten times its normal force. In the hands of a drunken mountain like him, one blow would be fatal – if he could land it. His eyes narrowed menacingly. "Now I'm going to be *un*friendly!"

With one arm limp by his side, he threw a surprisingly well aimed punch. I dodged with ultra-reflexed speed, more worried about the growing number of eyes on us than my opponent's teched-up fist. Before he realized it, I was beside him, kicking out his knee and breaking his jaw with an elbow that sent him flying into the table where his shipmates sat. All around him, angry Drakes jumped to their feet, hurling women off their laps and scattering their drinks, murderously intent on settling the score.

"Get him!" one of the Drakes growled through gritted teeth as I pulled the stun grenade from my pocket.

"Not today," I said, rolling one of Armin's Armaments finest toys their way.

The gang peered through intoxicated eyes at the silver metal sphere skating across the deck toward them, at first confused then with growing alarm. I turned and ran, barging between two inebriated Drakes who moved to block my escape, then pressed my hands to my ears and squeezed my eyes shut as the G-Max Sensory Assault Grenade detonated. I saw the flash through closed eyes, heard shocked screams through shielded ears, while the two brutes who'd tried to stop me took the worst of it. Even though I'd reached the edge of the effect zone, my ears still rang and spots danced before my eyes. I managed to keep my feet and stumble away from the plaza, now full of cursing, angry Drakes with vengeance on their minds.

Everyone near the G-Max was down, while anyone standing on the far side of the plaza was looking my way, including a tall, dark skinned man with an ugly plasma scar. For a moment, our eyes met and recognition flashed in Gwandoya's eyes, then I turned and ran as every Drake standing came charging after me.

I knocked people aside, dodged through empty spaces and evaded drunken attempts to block my escape while heavy footsteps and belligerent voices sounded behind me. As I neared the end of the plaza, I darted into a crowded bar, then slipped quietly out a side entrance and hid in a narrow service passageway behind a stinking garbage processor. Moments later, a herd of Drakes stampeded past, demanding to know where I'd gone. I waited out of sight for a long time, letting the chase peter out, occasionally stealing glimpses of my pursuers as they filtered back in ones and twos. When it was all over, I moved calmly through bars and brothels and back passageways, staying out of sight until I reached the main corridor leading back to the *Merak Star's* berth. After ensuring no one was still searching for me, I hurried to the airlock and pulled myself through the leaky pressure tube to the freighter.

Izin was waiting for me when I cycled back in. "They're demolishing the bulkheads between the cargo holds," he said.

"Who are?"

"Drake thrusterbots. They've already removed the plating between holds one and two. Now they're breaking into hold three."

"Why?"

"To make room for the cargo," Izin replied.

"They're bringing it over now."

"What is it?"

"Nothing I've ever seen before."

"Can you get to the Lining without them seeing you?"

"I can use the maintenance crawlway below the cargo deck. "

"Get ready to power up, but only if they start cutting into hold four. As soon as you go hot, the Drakes will detect you."

"Captain, there are over a hundred neutrino emitting energy cores within twenty clicks of the ship. The Drakes are unlikely to notice one more this close to the station."

I hadn't thought of that. With the Drake fleet right on top of us, the *Silver Lining* could hide in plain sight. "You're right, but keep her idling until you need to power up."

While Izin made his way back to the *Silver Lining*, I went up to the bridge. Jase was watching thrusterbots on three screens demolish the *Merak Star's* interior with laser torches, while an aging ore transporter standing off our spaceward side filled the fourth screen. She was equipped with a single cargo door that ran almost her full length and opened toward us as a dozen thrusterbots glided into her long dark hold. The light from their thrusters showed hints of a streamlined structure inside, then they towed a long gray shape out of the ship's hold. It was vaguely tower-like with a round base, a long inward sloping body and eight curved arms at the top shaped like the folded petals of a flower bud. Each arm ended in a blackened point, while a short silver needle extended from the apex of the body, pointing toward the heart of the bud. Stains from long exposure to cosmic radiation covered every part of its skin, suggesting great age.

"Ever seen anything like that before?" Jase asked as thrusterbots eased the alien-tech tower toward us.

I was slow in answering, waiting for my threading to complete a pattern match. Eventually, OBJECT UNKNOWN flashed into my mind.

"Nope," I replied at last.

A small, blunt nosed drop ship emerged from the transport's cargo hold and followed the tower at a distance. Once the alien-tech structure and the drop ship were clear, thrusterbots converged on the old ore carrier and began towing her away, not trusting such a decrepit vessel to maneuver under her own power so close to the station.

"Get me Anya," I said, climbing onto the command couch.

When her face appeared on screen, I said, "What are you doing to my ship?"

"Making room for your cargo."

"What is my cargo?"

She stiffened, suppressing irritation. "That's not your concern."

"I disagree, considering you're wrecking my ship to make room for it!"

"No critical systems will be affected."

"Then what? You leave me with a ship in pieces? How am I supposed to explain that?"

"After this delivery, the Merak Star will no longer be required. Now stay off this channel until further orders," she snapped, cutting the signal.

Jase scowled. "Not very helpful, is she?"

"She doesn't know what it is." That was what really annoyed her. Anya was a Drake navigator, used to knowing things even her captain didn't, yet this time she was as much in the dark as we were. "Triangulate how long that thing is. We need to warn Izin if they're going to cut into hold four."

Jase routed the optical feed into the processing core and got an immediate answer. "They can squeeze it diagonally into three holds."

The thrusterbots halted the alien-tech structure close to the ship, waiting for the demolition of the interior bulkheads to be completed. Once the forward three cargo holds were joined, they threaded the tower in through hold one while the drop ship came in via cargo door three. When they'd both settled on the deck, I locked them down with deck clamps, then Anya's face appeared on screen.

"Seal and pressurize your cargo deck," she said, then vanished.

Jase carried out her instructions, then a dozen men in armored fighting suits exited the drop ship. Using a combination of impressive zero-g acrobatics and suit thrusters, they approached and destroyed every optical sensor in the forward three holds with their armored fists rather than risk puncturing the hull with their high powered suppressors.

"Too late," Jase said. "We've already seen their toy."

"Unless that's not all there is to see."

An Orie accented voice sounded in the bridge without any visual feed. "Transfer magclamp control to deck panels."

Jase gave me a quizzical look.

"Do it."

With a shrug, he gave our guests local control of the deck locking system, then I secure linked to Izin in the *Silver Lining*. "Izin, there's a bunch of guys in fighting suits in the cargo holds forward of you. You're about to have company."

"I'll be ready, Captain." Izin didn't need to elaborate. The first Orie merc to set foot in the aft cargo hold wouldn't live long enough to warn the others, even if he was wearing an armored fighting suit.

"If they find the Lining," I said to Jase, "get back there fast and get out with Izin."

"Where are you going?"

"To find out why they blinded us."

"I'm not leaving without you, Skipper."

"You may have no choice," I said, then went down to the cargo deck and zero-g.

When the elevator door slid open, I heard the hollow click of armored magboots echoing through the passages, signaling at least one guard was patrolling in a fighting suit. There was no sign of him, so I floated silently along the corridor, past the cargo hold's main pressure door to a small emergency access hatch on the starboard side. The safety lock indicated the cargo deck was now fully pressurized, so I eased the half height hatch open a little. The lights were dimmed and the base of the alien-tech tower partly obscured the hatchway from the rest of the deck. Way over in hold three, Orie mercs wearing gray and black shadow fatigues had climbed out of their fighting suits and were maglocking them to the deck in front of the drop ship. The suit's clamshell torsos were cracked open down the side as they stood with parade ground precision in a straight line. As each fighting suit was locked down, its operator floated into the drop ship, returning moments later wearing a JAG-40 and a utility belt. Once armed, they returned to their fighting suits and began field stripping and cleaning them.

I was about to move in for a closer look at the tower when Domar Trask emerged from the drop ship with Stina Kron and Julkka Olen, all wearing shadow fatigues. They kicked off from the drop ship and glided in a line through the three cargo holds to the forward bulkhead's pressure door. Before they got too close, I pulled my hatch back, leaving only a crack to watch them through. Trask rolled expertly, landing his boots on the bulkhead, then pulled the hatch open for Kron and Olen to glide through without stopping. Once they were clear, he somersaulted boots first after them, pulling the door closed behind him, as comfortable in microgravity as any man I'd seen.

Once Trask and his two lieutenants were gone, I slipped into the cargo hold and floated through the shadows to the tower's circular base. It was flat except for a small lip around the outer edge and three squat cylindrical silver legs evenly spaced halfway in. A narrow shaft at the center ran up through the middle of the tower, quickly disappearing into darkness. I touched the silver legs curiously, finding them extremely cold. The threaded contact sensors in my fingertips measured the heat drain and flashed an immediate warning.

HYPERCONDUCTIVE METAL, TYPE UNKNOWN.

Whatever it was, it shed heat faster than any known substance while the material surrounding the legs was comfortably warm, giving my contact sensors another mystery to solve with equally disappointing results.

SUPERINSULATIVE MATERIAL, TYPE UNKNOWN.

Whatever the tower's purpose, it was built to handle high energy with great efficiency.

Soft footfalls sounded close, so quiet I hadn't noticed them approach. Whoever he was, the tower had hidden him from my sniffer. The footsteps weren't the metal click of magboots, but the soft scraping of civilian gripshoes. When he was close, a panel door unlocked in the tower's side followed by the muffled clatter of precision instruments. I guessed he was an engineer or a scientist, not a grunt, making him an easy target for abduction and questioning. And with the Orie mercs way over on the far side of hold three, I could take him down without being seen.

Using the superconductive legs as anchors, I pulled myself to the edge of the tower's base and listened to the scientist working nearby, oblivious of my presence. I stole a glance around the edge, finding an open gray maintenance door obstructed my view of him. Only the edge of his back was visible, clothed in a dark green coverall.

Beyond the access panel, the trunk of the tower hid us from the Ories. With growing confidence, I eased myself forward, preparing to swing around the panel door, disable him with a paralyzing blow and drag him to the galley storeroom for a private conversation.

The scientist finished his task, straightening as he prepared to close the maintenance panel. I tensed, about to launch myself at him when I realized something was wrong. There was a fluidity in his back as he straightened that didn't seem right. There were too many joints and it curved in an unnatural way. The hairs on the back of my neck stood on end as an unusually thin – *inhuman* – hand wrapped long, skinny fingers around the door's edge. I pushed myself back as the alien hand closed the panel door, revealing dark penetrating eyes and a long triangular reptilian head.

A Mataron head!

I dragged myself back toward the center of the tower – heart pounding! – listening for any sign he'd seen me. Tools clicked as he carefully returned them to his kit, oblivious to my presence, then his gripshoes scuffed the deck as thin reptilian fingers wrapped around the side of the tower. He was headed my way!

Pushing down on one of the superconductors, I launched myself away from the deck as the Mataron ambled around the base of the tower. Just as his fingers dropped, I caught the protruding lip of the tower base and cart wheeled over, gripping hard to slow myself, knowing contact between my boots and the tower would ring like a clash of cymbals. My thighs absorbed the impact silently, then my hands fought white knuckled to prevent my body rebounding away from the tower.

Even in the shadows, the Orie mercs would have seen me if they'd looked my way, but they were focused on servicing their fighting suits. Below me, the soft scraping of the Mataron's gripshoes marked his progress past the tower base to the other side. Any thought of taking him prisoner was gone. Fighting any Mataron hand to hand was a bad idea, even a scientist unfamiliar with microgravity. Whoever he was, he moved like a common planet hugger, but that meant nothing. Not every member of the Mataron Guard, or even the Black Sauria, were zero-g trained. Our reptilian nemesis might have been seven hundred thousand years ahead of us technologically, but they needed microgravity training every bit as much as we did – something this ambling snakehead clearly lacked.

The scientist opened an access panel on the other side of the tower and began working again, my signal to slip back over the edge and wait. My mind raced as I floated high above the deck, trying to understand why a snakehead and a bunch of human mercs were working together. No, not working together. The Ories weren't helping the Mataron, they were *guarding* him! He was

Trask's technical expert, the one Anya had mentioned on Novo Pantanal, the one she'd never been allowed to meet.

He was why they'd killed the cargo hold's sensors, so we wouldn't know a snakehead was aboard. Did that make this tower Mataron-tech? If so, it was unlike anything I'd seen them produce and I'd seen as much snakehead gear as anyone alive. Even more strange was the idea that a Mataron would cooperate with humans. They were xenophobes who instinctively despised anyone not of their race – particularly humans. They were members of the Forum out of necessity, because they feared the consequences of not joining, not from any desire to partner with other species. The Tau Cetins had said the Matarons had been cozying up to them. Now I wondered if that had been a ruse to lull the TCs while the snakeheads plotted a punitive strike against us?

When the reptilian scientist closed the second panel and padded off alongside the tower, I pushed down toward the hyperconductors, then glided silently back to the emergency access hatch. Once in the corridor, I resealed the hatch and headed back up to the bridge. To my surprise Jase was gone. All four screens were hissing static and Domar Trask and his two blonde bookends were studying the flight consoles with puzzled looks.

When Trask saw me, he aimed his JAG-40 my way. "One of my men is missing. You wouldn't know anything about that, would you?"

"No," I said, but Izin might. "What was he doing?"

"Routine ship search." Trask nodded to the static filled view screens. "Why are they down?"

Jase must have sabotaged them when he saw Trask coming. "They were working when I left. What did you

222

touch?"

My listener detected footsteps approaching in the corridor outside, but with no line of sight, my sniffer couldn't identify who it was.

Trask gave me a suspicious look. "Why'd you go into Acheron Station?"

"I've never been to a Drake base before," I said as a man stepped into the hatchway behind me letting my sniffer get its first look and begin pattern matching.

"Curious enough to carry stun grenades," Trask said suspiciously.

"Would you rather I gunned down a bunch of drunks with bad fashion sense?"

"You attract a lot of attention for a smuggler." He glanced at the screens thoughtfully. "If that's all you are."

My sniffer got a match and flashed a warning, but it was already too late. I'd made a fatal error coming back to the bridge. I'd only done it because I thought Jase was waiting for me and I couldn't leave without him. My mistake for being soft.

"You done wit' him?" a basso voice demanded behind me.

Trask considered his options and nodded. "Yeah, done."

From the bridge hatchway, Gwandoya let me have it with a brain scrambler on full power. I never saw his face, his stun gun or even the deck as it raced to meet my face.

* * * *

The scrambler's effect lifted slowly as heavy footsteps, slamming hatches and tortured screams haunted me like a nightmare. When I opened my eyes, I discovered

I lay in a dark cell illuminated by a grimy slit window set high in an ovoid hatch. Occasionally shadows obscured the window as guards and their prisoners passed outside while the screams continued unabated. As my eyes focused, I realized the filthy cell lacked furniture or water and had only a small drainage hole in one corner decorated with feces.

The stark metallic clunk of a locking bolt sliding back rang through the cell, then the door swung in on rusty hinges and two men entered. The shorter one wore a gun holstered at his hip, carried a pain baton in one hand and a slender no-doze stimrod in the other. He jabbed me in the shoulder with the rod, ignoring the fact I was already conscious, forcing me fully awake.

The taller one leaned forward, studying me with hate filled eyes. "Sirius Kade! I been waiting for you!" Gwandoya declared in his distinctive Afro-east accent. He rubbed the melted flesh on the side of his face. "You did this to me. You cost me my ship. Now Gwandoya take payment in full."

I pushed myself into a sitting position, back against the cold metal wall. "I'll give you ten credits for the ship, but the face was an improvement."

"Silence slave!" the gravel voiced jailer shouted, jabbing me with the pain baton, forcing my body to convulse uncontrollably. When he pulled the baton back, he asked, "Do you want him matched or unmatched?"

"Unmatched," Gwandoya said. "Fight him every day, but he no die. Not yet."

"I won't be able to stop them killing him, not if they're fighting for their freedom. Once he's down, they'll finish him."

"If he die, they die."

"He'll need patch ups. That'll cost money."

"Do what you have to. Gwandoya leave Acheron in ten days. I kill him then."

"Ten days in the pit?" the jailer said doubtfully. "There won't be much left of him."

"There better be," Gwandoya said menacingly, "or you will take his place."

The jailer grunted uncomfortably, then threw a metal anklet at my feet. "Put that on, slave."

There was a tiny flashing green light on one side and a miniature power pack on the other. It was a tracking device with a stunner that would paralyze me if I tried to escape the Drake dungeon. I left it where it was.

"He doesn't know where he is," the jailer said. "Thinks he still has a life. We'll break him of that."

"No. Let him resist," Gwandoya said. "It will make his time in the arena more entertaining."

The jailer shrugged indifferently. "I've seen his kind before. They never last."

"Feed him well. Give him strength to resist."

"Do you want anything special in the arena?"

"Corrosives."

"If they throw acid in his eyes," the jailer said apprehensively, "he won't be able to keep fighting."

"If they blind him, take out their eyes. Burn him, burn his skin, but not his eyes!" Gwandoya said, rubbing his hideous plasma burn absently.

"I'll warn them," the jailer said uncertainly.

"Have they found his crew?"

"Not yet."

"They die in front of him." Gwandoya studied me, savoring what was to come. "You will beg for death before Gwandoya is done with you, Kade."

"Don't count on it," I said. If they let me keep my strength and it was anything like a fair fight, he'd be the one doing the begging.

Gwandoya grunted. "Who will he fight first?"

"The big Tanosian's ready. I had him slated to kill three spacers we couldn't ransom, or there's Girok."

"The Tanosian will do."

"He's good with an acid whip."

Gwandoya tried smiling, but his melted face made it look like a grimace. "You were a fool for coming here, Kade," he said, then walked out with the jailer close behind.

The metal hatch slammed shut, plunging the cell into near darkness again. My eyes settled on the slave anklet's feeble green indicator light blinking monotonously beside me as the no-doze coursing through my body revived me, negating any need for bionetic tricks to recover my strength. After several hours, the locking bolt slid back and the cell door creaked open.

I expected the jailer, come to throw me into the arena for my first beating, but instead a dark silhouette stepped into the cell. He had an athletic physique, wore light weight black body armor and had a pistol holstered at his right hip. In his left hand was a straight bladed charge knife dripping with blood and still sparking with tiny electrical flashes. He flicked blood from the knife, switched the weapon off with his thumb, then slid it into a scabbard at his left hip.

Leaving the cell door ajar, my visitor advanced a few paces, studying me in silence. There was something strangely familiar about him, his movements, his bearing, but my sniffer couldn't find a match and it was too dark to see his face.

"Quite a mess you've got yourself in, little brother."

His hushed words came like a thunderclap from

the darkness. It was a voice I hadn't heard in more than twenty years, a voice I never thought I'd hear again. For a moment, I was too shocked to speak.

"Don't tell me they've cut your tongue out already!" he said.

"Canopus?" I wheezed, surprised at the hoarseness of my own voice.

"I haven't used that name in a long time," he said slowly. "I hear you still call yourself Sirius, but then you always were his favorite."

It had been our father's idea. He'd called me Sirius, my brother Canopus, after the two brightest stars in Earth's sky. How else would a navigator, who'd crossed every light year of Mapped Space, name his sons? Only later, when my brother and father began to fight, did the fact Canopus was the second brightest star begin to anger my brother. He came to believe in our father's eyes, it meant he was second best.

"Canopus is brighter," I said. "Its true brightness is hidden by distance."

"Hmph! A navigator's explanation," he said bitterly, "but then you always were the better pilot."

"You won the fights."

"I was two years older and I cheated."

He'd always used his size against me and fought dirty, although this was the first time he'd ever admitted it. "What are you doing here?"

"I was about to ask you the same thing."

"I brought a ship in here—"

"No!" he snapped. "I know all about the Merak Star! What I don't understand is what you're doing *here*!"

He knew? How could he know?

For a moment I considered telling him the truth, that I was an EIS deep cover agent and there was a

Mataron scientist aboard the *Merak Star*, then I caught myself. If he already knew everything, then maybe he knew about the snakehead, which made him the enemy. I remembered how hard he could be, how calculating, certain if he were the enemy, he was far more dangerous than Gwandoya or Trask. We might have grown up together on the old *Freya*, plodding from one dead-end outpost to another, both suffering under the harsh discipline of a father who cared more about his ship than his sons, but that had been a lifetime ago. He might have been my brother back then, but now we were strangers.

"I didn't plan on coming here," I said. "A Drake navigator, a woman, she forced me–"

"Yes, Anya Krol," he said, cutting me off. "I know how you got here." He took a few more steps into the prison cell. "What really happened to Nazari?"

"He fried his brain with stims."

"What type of stims?"

It had been a long time since I'd read between the lines with my brother. He wasn't asking for information – he already knew the answer. He wanted confirmation I was telling the truth. I tried to remember what kind of stimhaler Nazari had been using. All I could recall was that it had been dark red in color. That narrowed it down to three choices.

"Crimson Sky," I guessed, suspecting Nazari's tastes leaned more toward psychedelic dream states than sensory or sexual enhancement. "I had to clean up the mess."

My brother showed no sign as to whether I'd guessed right. We'd had our disagreements, but I'd rarely lied to him. Deception was a skill I learned much later. "So you're working for the Consortium now?"

"Not if I can help it. I've had some bad luck. I

needed money. This job came up, so I took it. They said nothing about going into the Acheron."

"And Gwandoya?"

"He jumped me a year ago," I replied. "We were competitors. It didn't end well for him."

"So, you gave him that face."

"You know Gwandoya?"

"We sit at the same table. He thinks that makes us equals. He's mistaken."

His tone told me there would be a reckoning between them one day, no doubt when Gwandoya least expected it. I relaxed a little. If I crossed my brother, that was one thing, but I knew he wouldn't let Gwandoya murder me. That was personal.

"He doesn't know we're brothers?" I asked.

"He'd have tried to kill me by now if he did, as revenge against you."

"How'd you know I was here?"

"I saw you," he said simply.

"On the station?"

"Before that."

Before Acheron Station? I searched my memory, wondering where he could have seen me. "I don't understand."

"When you were on Hardfall."

"You were on Hardfall?" Was he working with Governor Metzler?

"At Loport," he added.

There was only one way he could have seen me there. "You were on the Cyclops!"

"I knew it was you as soon as you set foot on the Merak Star's cargo ramp, when you met Anya and Trask."

"What were you doing on the Cyclops?"

There was a clatter of metal on metal as my P-50

skated across deck plates to my feet. "You'll need this."

I retrieved my gun, holstering it as I climbed unsteadily to my feet. "Canopus, what were you doing on the Cyclops?"

"You always were slow, little brother. Still are, even after all these years."

I realized there was only one way he could know about the *Merak Star*, the alien-tech smuggling, the gun running and about my meeting with Anya and Trask on Hardfall.

"You're Rix!"

"You don't think those dimwitted Drakes could have put this together, do you?"

He stepped closer, letting the feeble light from the entrance catch his face, revealing a curved black metal skull plate that enclosed the top of his head and wrapped down over where his eyes should have been to his nose. Instead of human eyes, a large optronic sensor was mounted in the center of his metal enclosed forehead. Other sensor nodes were evident around the skull plate, although their purpose was disguised.

When he saw the shocked look on my face, he said, "Like you, Sirius, I have enemies. They left me for dead, eyes burned out, crippled. Their mistake was not killing me when they had the chance."

"I'm sorry."

"Don't be. Cybernetics suit me." He smiled grimly. "I spent four years hunting them down. Killed them all. Took their ship, their crew, everything they had."

"And the name?"

"Regoran for vengeance," he said simply. "It describes my present, with no link to my past."

Regor II was over three hundred light years from

Earth, inhabited by a minor humanoid civilization in diplomatic contact with Earth, but not a species I'd ever dealt with. "I didn't know you spoke Regoran."

"I know enough not to insult them. They take '*rhiix*' very seriously," he said, pronouncing Rix as they would, "as do I." He motioned to his optronic sensor. "And I named the ship after this."

"Cyclops!" I whispered. I'd thought the ship had been named for the massive single weapon on its bow, but now I realized it was a sign of my brother's dark humor and his defiance at the horror that had been inflicted upon him.

Disfigured, lost among the Brotherhood with an alien name, it was little wonder there'd been no trace of him for twenty years. A lot could happen in that time, perhaps enough to make him an enemy of the entire human race.

"There's a Mataron on the Merak Star," I said.

"Yes, an arrogant bastard named Inok a'Rtor." The Mataron's name rolled off his tongue with a familiarity that told me he was no stranger to their language. It was almost enough to convince me he was a traitor willingly collaborating with the enemy.

"How'd you get involved with the Matarons?" As soon as I said it, I knew it sounded more like an interrogation than simple curiosity.

"You ask a lot of questions for a freighter captain down on his luck, Sirius," he said suspiciously.

"I want to know what kind of mess the Consortium's got me into."

"The kind that pays well."

"Not well enough to be executed."

"Then don't get caught," he said coldly. "The Mataron's a technical advisor, a renegade. Trask told me he's wanted by his own people. I don't know where

Trask found him. Don't care."

"So it's Mataron equipment?"

"No," he said with certainty.

"You know what'll happen if you're caught stealing alien-tech?"

"We pulled the tower off an abandoned station. It hadn't been used in thousands of years. It was more like salvage than theft, and no one saw us."

An Observer ship could have been watching and he'd never know, yet the Tau Cetins hadn't questioned me about it, so maybe he'd gotten away with it.

"What about the other alien-tech, the stuff before Hardfall?"

My brother stiffened. "How do you know about that if you only replaced Nazari for the Hardfall transfer?"

"The Consortium told me there'd been other alien-tech shipments. Obviously, that hadn't required tearing the insides out of the Merak Star."

He nodded slowly, trying to decide if he could trust me. "I don't know where they get it from."

"The Matarons? They're your supplier?'

He nodded. "We've done a few pick-ups from them, all arranged by Inok a'Rtor."

A cold chill ran down my spine. Stealing alien technology would drag humanity into an Access Treaty violation and whatever the Mataron involvement was, they'd make sure we were left holding the bag when the Forum powers came calling.

"If the Matarons are helping you, they're playing you."

"Not me. Trask. He's the customer. I'm just the middle man."

Suddenly, it made sense. The snakeheads were using the Brotherhood to secretly deliver stolen alien-tech to the Consortium, ensuring there was no way to tie them into the deal.

"What's Trask up to?"

He smiled evasively. "He's making the Brotherhood very wealthy. And the richer we get, the more powerful I become." He leaned forward, studying my face with his bulging robotic eye. "I thought you'd look older."

I would have, if not for the EIS genetic engineering which had dramatically slowed my aging rate. The optronic sensor wired to his brain would have told him I looked barely thirty, even though my chronological age was forty eight.

Sidestepping explaining my appearance, I said, "With what you know, Earth Navy would offer you a deal. You could start again."

"As what? Captain of a space barge living on scraps!" he snapped scornfully. "My ambitions reach far higher than that, little brother." There was a dark finality to his words, then he seemed to brighten for a moment. "I could use a mediocre pilot, one that would have to learn to stop asking so many questions."

It was more than an offer. It was a promise to eliminate my troubles with Gwandoya and elevate me into the higher ranks of the Brotherhood. If that was the cost of reconciling with my brother, it was too high a price. He saw from the look on my face it was an offer I couldn't accept.

"Guess not," he said, genuinely disappointed. "The Cyclops is docked at Delta Zero Nine. Stay out of the transit tubes. Use the backbone crawlway. My crew's expecting you. I'll drop you in the Duranis System in a few weeks. You can catch a ride out from there."

"Duranis?" It wasn't anywhere I'd been before.

"I'm headed that way. There's not much there. It's

kind of a temporary transit hub."

"I'll pass."

"You can't get out on the Merak Star, not now," he warned. "The Brotherhood are crewing it for Trask."

"I've got more than a hundred ships to choose from," I said with a grin. "I'll be fine." Either I was getting out on the *Silver Lining* or I wasn't getting out at all, but he didn't need to know that.

He gave me curious look, wondering how I was going to escape Acheron Station. "Suit yourself, little brother." He stepped forward and hugged me once, then released me. "Canopus *is* brighter than Sirius, once you leave Earth."

"Not from here it isn't."

"Maybe when this is over, I'll move to Outer Carina," he said with a crooked grin, knowing it was where his namesake was brightest. "I don't know ... Canopus Rix? ... Has a ring to it, don't you think?"

"You'll be the terror of the space lanes," I said, knowing we were almost certainly enemies and one day, one of us may be forced to kill the other.

"I already am," he replied with a hint of the same bravado he'd shown after beating me zero-g racing through *Freya's* cavernous holds. "Don't come back, Sirius, this is no place for you." There was a menace in his tone that revealed he also suspected we were enemies.

"I couldn't find my way back, even if I wanted to." If I knew how to get back to Acheron Station, I'd return with an Earth Navy fleet and obliterate it.

He walked to the cell door and turned to me one last time. "Give me two minutes," he said, then vanished into the corridor outside.

Rapid footsteps echoed away from my cell as my brother disappeared into the station's maze of passageways, then I crept out into a dimly lit corridor lined with identical cell doors. Halfway along the corridor, I found the jailer lying in a pool of his own blood with his throat cut. He undoubtedly deserved it, but it reminded me again of what my brother was capable of. He'd always been good with a gun, but the knife was something new, a skill he'd acquired after we lost contact.

I stepped over the jailer's corpse and hurried along the corridor to the station's spine where a transit tube access point and a maintenance crawlway hatch were located. I realized I didn't know which way to go, up or down? Suddenly, the hiss of microthrusters signaled the arrival of a high speed transit capsule, then the tube's airtight doors slid open revealing two armored fighting suits standing inside, identical to those worn by Trask's men.

Backing away, I drew my P-50, knowing I had little chance against two armored battle units. They marched robotically out of the transit capsule in perfect synchronization, a head taller than me and several tons heavier. My bionic memory identified them as OA-5's, obsolete Union Regular Army orbital assault suits. They mounted a weapon on each arm, were covered in ablative flak armor and according to the rotating schematic projected into my mind, had a tiny weak spot at the back, above the thruster pack. Considering I was already in their sights, I had no chance of flanking them for a shot.

"Don't move," the lead fighting suit ordered in a strangely synthesized voice, "Captain."

Captain?

Both suits cracked open along the clamshell seams running down the side of their torsos, then a tamph head leaned out of the first suit.

"Izin!" I said surprised.

"The second suit is for you, Captain. It's slaved to this unit. I'll release it to you, once you're inside."

"How'd you find me?"

"Gwandoya's been boasting on the station-net for several hours about how he's going to have you repeatedly beaten in the slave arena before burning you alive. Once we knew you were marked for the arena it was a simple matter to locate the prison. I'm surprised you managed to escape, Captain."

"I had incentive," I said, climbing into the second fighting suit. "Where'd you get these things?"

"Trask's men were over confident," he said before sliding back into his suit and sealing up.

Once inside, I took a moment to familiarize myself with the controls. I'd done three days of suit orientation with the URA years ago, then hadn't touched one since. The main lesson the instructor had stressed was to let the suit do the work. Most of the controls were at my fingertips, inside the hand spaces, while the large spherical head space was all screen, except for the padding behind my head. The curved display in front of my face was splattered with blood and a flashing indicator warned of a microleak behind my neck, exactly where the heat exchanger regulating suit temperature was located. Somehow, Izin had found and exploited the suit's only weakness and clearly, the OA-5's auto-patcher hadn't been able to fully seal the hole made by his weapon.

Izin's synthesized voice sounded inside the suit's head space. "Releasing control to you, Captain."

I remembered the instructor's words: 'thumb-lock to seal', but couldn't remember which of the five thumb points did the job. I tapped one experimentally, heard the suit's thruster begin to power-up, then fearing

I was about to be launched into the ceiling, tapped it again to shut it down.

"Perhaps I should initiate suit command functions," Izin suggested. "Sealing you now."

My fighting suit slowly clamshelled shut around me, then pressure field sensors activated, allowing the suit to read my every movement, turning it from a rigid sarcophagus into responsive armored skin.

"Aren't you a little short to be operating one of these things?"

"I can reach the controls. The pressure fields do the rest," he said as his suit came to life.

"Can anyone hear us talking?"

"No, Captain," he replied as his armored robot turned to face me. "These suits have secure tactical communications."

"Have they found the Lining?"

"Not yet, but with two of Trask's men missing, we had to move her out of the Merak Star."

"Did they see you?"

"I don't believe so. They still haven't got the internal sensors working and I fuse-locked access to hold four. They were cutting through when we left. I expect they were surprised to discover the hold was depressurized."

A nasty surprise, no doubt. "So how do we get out of here?"

"We take the transit tube six kilometers then walk."

My brother had said to stay out of the tube, but he wasn't to know I'd be riding it in an armored fighting suit, so I followed Izin into the capsule without protest. It accelerated briefly, then braked to let three drunken Drakes and a station engineer squeeze aboard. We rode together as one of the drunks leaned against my suit for support, causing his face to loom large on my headscreen.

He belched, then rapped on my suit's head armor. "Hey! What's it like in there? Can you see me?"

I ignored him, then the capsule stopped, letting the drunks stumble off in search of more ways to blow the last of their stolen credits while the technician studied Izin's suit.

"They're OA-5 mark twos aren't they?" he asked.

"I don't know," Izin replied, trying to terminate the conversation.

"That's what they are all right. The thruster controls have a habit of freezing at high altitude."

"I'll remember that, next time I jump from orbit," Izin said.

The engineer ran a professional eye over the bulky thruster pack, craning his neck to get a better look. "If you bring them down to maintenance, I can insulate the controllers for you. It'll take about an hour. Should raise your drop ceiling to–" He stopped mid sentence, standing on his toes to study the rear of the suit above the thruster pack. "Hey, there's a tiny hole back here. The auto-seals on these old models always were a bit iffy." He reached up and touched the microleak, then studied his fingertips, finding them smeared red. "Is that blood?"

Izin's arm snapped up, slamming the fighting suit's elbow into the engineer's face, sending him flying into the elevator wall. The tech's limp body crumpled like a rag doll to the floor as Izin resumed waiting for us to reach our destination.

"That's one way to end a boring conversation," I said to myself.

When the elevator door opened, the people waiting to enter peered curiously in at the unconscious engineer. Making no effort to explain, Izin marched out through the crowd as if he owned the place, forcing everyone in his path to scatter.

Following close behind, I said, "I don't recognize this level."

"The cross-arm the Merak Star is docked at is now heavily guarded," Izin said. "They're searching for Jase and me. In any event, the Silver Lining is not docked at an airlock."

"How are we getting aboard?"

"We're going to jump."

"Izin, this thing isn't airtight!"

"Neither suit is. Unfortunately, shooting through the heat sink was the only way to penetrate their armor."

"How'd you find the weak spot?"

"Superior amphibian eyesight."

Crippling a combat suit in a darkened cargo hold without the benefit of my bionetic encyclopedia to draw on was impressive, but leaping a pair of leaky suits through hard vacuum was nuts.

"Do we have enough atmo for the jump?"

"I do," he replied. "You may have to hold your breath."

It was tamph humor as he knew as well as me that holding my breath was useless when cells started popping.

"That's your plan?"

"Air supply is not the problem, Captain. Power is. These suits are not designed for autonomous space flight and their power cells are already somewhat depleted."

"How far are we jumping?"

"Fifteen hundred meters, the distance between cross-arms."

Izin stopped at a large security door, lowered his right arm and blasted the lock with his rapid fire suppressor, then kicked the door in. A cool white mist billowed out as several nearby station hands looked at us in surprise.

Izin turned and aimed his suppressor at them. "Run!"

Their eyes widened, then they raced back to the station's spine to raise the alarm while Izin led the way into the refrigeration compartment.

"How do we set the suit's nav targeting to get us there?" I asked.

"If we allow the suit to plot the course, Captain, it will select the most energy efficient course. That would be a slow transit, giving station security time to locate us."

"We can't doing this manually."

"Not you, Captain. I will fly both suits at maximum acceleration."

He'd have to crunch two sets of numbers simultaneously in his head, something I needed an autonav to do. "Are you sure about this, Izin?"

"You could try flying your own suit, Captain, but I wouldn't recommend it."

No tamph humor this time. Long distance space jumps weren't seat of your pants flying, they were complex mathematic problems with no room for error. "OK, let's get this over with."

"Assuming control now."

My suit ceased moving with me. It now mimicked Izin's every action, forcing me to move with it.

When he approached the bulkhead closest to the station's hull, he said, "Remember, Captain, any unnecessary movement inside your suit will have an inertial effect I will have to compensate for."

"Suppose I have to scratch?"

"Fidgeting will require offsetting thrust which will consume power, reducing your chances of survival."

"OK, no scratching," I said, suddenly itchy all over.

Our right arms came up together, firing their suppressors as one, blasting a hole through the double lined hull. A torrent of escaping air erupted around us, sweeping us off the deck and hurling us out into space. Inside the station, alarms sounded and emergency pressure doors slammed shut, sealing off the decompressing section from the rest of the habitat.

We tumbled away from the massive station cross-arm, out of the local acceleration field into zero gravity, then Izin fired the thrusters bringing us around to face the *Merak Star* docked one and a half clicks away. The sound of thrusters filled my suit's headspace – there was no helmet – as Izin wasted no time going straight to full power. Acheron Station had few genuine viewports, but it was well lit to give nearby ships good visibility. Those same floodlights now lit us up, although from a distance we'd be indistinguishable from thrusterbots.

I forced myself to relax, to make Izin's job as easy as possible. There was a constant hiss of escaping air behind my neck now that we were in vacuum, while in front of my eyes, a flashing indicator warned life support was eating through my air supply as it fought to prevent the suit's atmosphere from thinning. In the distance, our destination cross-arm appeared like a band of light against the nebula's impenetrable blackness.

When we were halfway there, Izin rolled the two OA suits head over heels in perfect unison and began decelerating, bringing the cross-arm we'd left behind into view. Spider-like hull crawlers were already working to patch the rupture, which station engineers would have discovered by now had not been caused by a mechanical failure.

"How long, Izin?"

"Three minutes, twenty seconds."

"They know we blew a hole in their space station."

"Captain, it would be better if you refrained from speaking while I'm performing simultaneous sets of complex delta-vee calculations."

I shut up, letting him do his thing while I watched for company. Soon I noticed a pair of bright lights moving toward us, growing rapidly in size. It didn't take long to realize they were thrusterbots on an intercept course. Knowing Izin's calculations were about to get a whole lot more complicated, I retrieved my suit's suppressor specifications from bionetic memory.

"Izin, the muzzle velocity of my suppressor is twelve thousand, one hundred and forty meters per second per forty six gram projectile."

"If I wasn't so busy calculating ways to save your life, Captain, I'd wonder why you've memorized such an obscure number."

"Yeah, well we've got company and I'm about to start shooting." I dialed up the suppressor's fire controller and set the rate. "Twenty rounds per second, three second bursts. Got that?"

"The recoil will be severe, Captain. I will lose control of your suit."

"That's why I gave you the number, because they're not coming out here to give us a wash and a wax."

When the two thrusterbots were only a few seconds out, they focused their floodlights on us, ensuring anyone watching saw exactly what we were.

"I need my suit back," I said. "Now!"

The Shinagawa thrusterbots yawed as they slid in behind us on a collision course. They were unarmed, but they didn't need weapons. With industrial strength arms able to move starship hull segments, they could rip our arms off like butterfly wings.

"Releasing control," Izin said.

My suit came to life around me as a proximity alert began flashing. I rotated a quarter turn, bringing my suppressor to bear on the machine headed for me, but held fire, knowing I had one chance before the recoil would send me spinning away uncontrollably. When the giant bot was almost on top of me, it reached out with both its massive arms, its finger-like manipulators snapping open ready to crush me. I thrusted up, dodging the arms, then fired at its body. A muted burping sound filled the suit, spewing neutronium tipped rounds into the thrusterbot as the suppressor's kick sent me tumbling backwards.

My suit rang like a bell as one of the thrusterbot's massive arms struck me side on, sending me flailing away even faster, then there was a flash as it exploded behind me. Spinning fast, close to blacking out from the g-forces, the blur of the station's lights raced across my screen, over and over again against the nebula's blackness, then my suit's stabilizers fired automatically, slowly killing my spin. When I saw the thrusterbot again, it was adrift, wracked by secondary explosions flashing within.

Off to my left, Izin was being pursued by the second Shinagawa machine. He was firing a constant stream of suppressor rounds into its hull while he manually fired his stabilizers to soak up the recoil. The thrusterbot froze as Izin circled it, continuing to fire until it exploded, hurling a giant arm at him. He narrowly dodged a collision, then glided quickly to me, assuming control of my suit and turning us both toward the *Merak Star* without a word. I knew he was moving fast because of the energy we'd burned through, so I kept quiet as we started decelerating again. To my surprise, we didn't fly side by side as before. Instead, Izin flew up to me and planted his boots on my shoulders, pinning them to my suit's head bulge.

"What are you doing?" I asked at last.

"Neither suit has sufficient power to complete the jump," he said without any attempt to sugarcoat the bad news.

Below my boots, the station's cross-arm was racing up at us, too fast and too close now for us to stop in time.

"I suppose crashing into the station is out of the question?" I suggested.

"The suits would survive the impact, but our bodies would not."

Once again a helpless passenger, I watched Izin aim for a point astern of the *Merak Star*, intending to graze the cross-arm rather than crash into it. Another alert began flashing on my headscreen, warning my suit's power supply was dangerously low. Soon, the *Silver Lining's* crescent shaped hull came into view, hiding between the *Merak Star's* stern and the station's hull.

When we were close to the freighter, Izin's thruster died, shut down by his suit to preserve energy for life support. His power cell's early depletion was the price of his fancy flying against the thrusterbot. With only my thruster slowing us now, Izin climbed down until we were chest to chest, locking arms as we swept past the *Merak Star's* huge engine exhausts. For a moment, we were almost close enough to touch the *Silver Lining* sheltering behind the freighter's stern, then we skimmed the station's hull on an oblique trajectory. A few seconds later, we cleared the cross-arm, then my suit shut down the thruster, saving enough juice to keep life support going until my air ran out.

Arm in arm, we drifted toward the Acheron's inky blackness.

"Nice try, Izin. We almost made it," I lamented as he locked our legs together. If it hadn't been for the thrusterbots, he'd have got us to the ship, but even his mighty tamph brain couldn't calculate every possibility. "I wonder if Jase knows where we are?" One of my metal coffin's arms wrapped itself around Izin's shoulders as his arms embraced my torso. "I hadn't expected to die cuddling a tamph, but I guess there are worse ways to go. You could be a snakehead, or Jase's mother."

"We are where we need to be, Captain. And so there is no misunderstanding, I'm not cuddling you, I'm anchoring you. Standby."

"For what?"

My suit's free arm extended straight out from my chest, past Izin's head, then my suppressor fired a six second burst into space. The heavy recoil stopped our forward motion and sent us drifting slowly back to the station, rotating slightly. He'd angled my arm to minimize spin, but the angle had been off a little. When I was facing the *Merak Star*, Izin fired a single shot behind me, offsetting our rotation and slightly increasing our drift toward the station.

"You planned to use the suppressors all along!" I said incredulously. He'd got his calculations right after all!

"It was your idea, Captain. Each suit has ten thousand rounds. That's a lot of kinetic energy."

"When exactly did you work this out?"

"As soon as you told me the muzzle velocity."

No wonder he'd flown like a fighter pilot against the thrusterbot! He knew he had energy to spare!

"You could have told me."

"I assumed you knew."

"Is this going to be a hard landing?"

"I'll try not to break you, Captain."

Now that I knew I wasn't going to die in the Acheron Abyss cuddling a tamph in a tin box, I began scanning apprehensively for more thrusterbots. This close to the station with our thrusters cold, we'd be hard to detect, but if they'd plotted our trajectory correctly, they'd know where we were. Fortunately, nothing approached us as we drifted back past the station, heading for the *Merak Star*.

Izin shifted his arm slowly away to the right, turning us to the left, then my suppressor fired once, nudging us toward the *Silver Lining*. There was very little space between her hull and the freighter on one side and Acheron Station on the other.

"It took some sweet flying to get her in there," I said appreciatively.

"That's what Jase said – repeatedly – when he did it."

"In that case, I'll bawl him out for scratching the paint work."

"I don't believe he did any damage to the ship's outer coating, Captain."

"We'll scratch it on the way in," I said mischievously. "Just a little scratch, enough to dock him a day's pay!"

Izin fired a shot from his arm cannon and another

from mine, pushing us toward the *Silver Lining's* starboard airlock. A short distance away, the flimsy pressure tube snaked its way between the *Merak Star* and Acheron Station.

"I'm tempted to put a burst into that tube," I said, "just for laughs."

"That would be inadvisable, Captain. The reaction force would push us away from the ship and alert the station to our position."

"Yeah," I said disappointed as we reached the airlock, "and we still have to get out of here."

With over a hundred Drake ships docked within weapon's range, that would be no easy task.

* * * *

We parked the fighting suits in the corridor outside the airlock, then Izin went to engineering to power up the ship while I went to the bridge.

"The station's broadcasting an escaped prisoner alert," Jase said as I hurried to my acceleration couch. "Killing the jailer has got them real mad."

"It wasn't me," I said, switching my display to sensors and searching for Acheron Station's energy plant. One look told me the station's neutrino emissions were indistinguishable from all the Drake ships alongside, forcing me to shelve any thought of putting an anti-ship drone where it would do the most good. "We'll blink to the gravity mines and run through before they can catch us." Izin already had us half way to full power, making the *Silver Lining* visible to any Drake ship bothering to look. "I assume you can get us out of here?"

Jase grinned. "Getting out will be easier than getting in."

He took the helm, tickled the thrusters and sent us drifting out of our cramped hiding place. The big screen wrapping around our control positions all the way to the aft bulkhead showed how close Acheron Station and the freighter were as we slid into view of a Drake raider berthed astern of the *Merak Star*. Her hull was blackened and scarred, and she could have crippled us with a single shot, but we turned across her bow without a response.

By the time we were clear, I had the autonav ready for a sub-light hop out to the minefield, having overridden its protest at being unable to find any stellar reference points. For a machine designed to fly blind across Mapped Space, it had a peculiar dislike of not knowing where it was.

"There are four ships maneuvering off the station and one powering up to undock," Jase said as he returned helm control to me. "None heading our way."

Five ships that could give chase at short notice was bad luck for us. I'd hoped the Drakes would all be docked and manned by skeleton crews when we ran.

"What about the Super Saracens?"

"The fleet's gone. Only the refits are left."

A gruff voice sounded from the flight deck's comm system. "Ship in zone theta, identify yourself."

I nodded for Jase to open a channel. "This is the Cormorant. What do you want?" I barked aggressively, bringing our maneuvering engines to life to put distance between us and the station.

"Who's your Captain?"

"Gwandoya," I replied. "Big guy, melted face, bad teeth. You've heard of him."

"Shut down your engines!"

"I don't take orders from you," I snapped, buying time.

"I'm the station master! No one undocks unless I say so!"

"Screw you! I have permission!"

"And I have six pulse cannons targeting you. Last chance, tough guy!"

We had good inertia now, enough to carry us into clear space. "OK, OK, shutting down."

For several valuable seconds, we drifted away from the station, then the station master's voice sounded again. "What are you doing? Get back to the station!"

"You told me to shut down my engines!" I said. "Now you want them back on?"

"Use thrusters, you idiot!" the station master ordered with rising anger.

I nodded for Jase to pull sensors as I starting charging our spacetime distorters.

"Hey!" the station master yelled as he detected the energy build up around the *Lining's* hull. "Where do you think you're going?"

We blinked to the inner edge of the gravity minefield. Before our sensors had even deployed, I kicked the maneuvering engines to thirty-five g's and began accelerating blind toward the mines. Soon we were slip sliding through heavily curved spacetime, slewing into one artificial gravity well after another.

We soon picked up the station master broadcasting on every channel. "All ships! An unknown vessel is heading for the minefield! Zero six five by one eight nine. Intercept and destroy!" The urgency in his voice was laced with fear that we were spies about to escape with Acheron Station's most closely guarded secret, its location. Once Earth Navy knew how to find their base, the Drakes would have to abandon it, leaving them crippled for years until a replacement could be built.

"Here they come!" Jase warned as three of the ships maneuvering for berths suddenly went to full power.

"They won't risk the minefield," I said, glancing at the screen now filling with rotating ovoids. Each gravity mine was equipped with a pair of acceleration fields that created an hourglass depression in spacetime strong enough to collapse any bubble with devastating consequences.

"We've got company," Jase said, orienting the port side of the screen toward a stretched disk-shaped passenger ferry with maneuvering engines above and below the hull. Two short range energy weapons on her bow glowed hot as they charged to fire. Moments later, a space tug unbubbled several clicks to starboard. She was little more than a huge circular engine behind a tiny trapezoid hull armed with a belly mounted turret. Its massive engine went to full power, sending it speeding into the minefield after us.

"The big ferry's about to fire!" Jase warned, raising our battle shield.

"It's the other one I'm worried about," I said, concerned its belly turret showed no thermal build up.

The flash of an explosion flared ten clicks away as a third Drake ship overshot, jumping into the minefield where its fragile bubble collapsed, tearing its hull apart and detonating its energy core. A brilliant white blast sphere inflated rapidly, vaporizing every gravity mine in its path and washing over the *Silver Lining*'s shield. Our view screen dimmed, automatically saving us from flash blindness as the blast momentarily hid us from the two surviving Drake ships.

"Those crazy bastards!" Jase exclaimed.

Once the blast wave had passed, the *Silver Lining* stopped floundering in curved space, now free of the gravity mines destroyed in the explosion.

"Have we got flat space ahead?" I asked, charging our distorters, waiting for the white noise to clear.

"I can't tell," Jase said, staring helplessly at his overloaded sensors.

I ordered the autonav to plot a tenth of a light year bubble thirty degrees to starboard, hoping that would throw off the Drakes and carry us clear of the Acheron without crossing any natural gravity hazards. By the time the screen cleared, the space tug had moved well ahead of the ferry. Her belly turret was still ominously cold, and now a dark square of an open hatch had appeared, marking it as a launcher, not a gun.

"This is going to hurt," I said softly, surprised to find any Drake ship armed with anti-ship drones. Brotherhood ships preferred crippling weapons, so they could capture and loot their victims, but ASDs were dedicated ship killers, most designed to target a ship's energy core.

"Must be a station defense ship," Jase said.

The tug's ASD flashed into space on a brilliant blue-white tail, heading straight for us. There was no way we could outrun it without going superluminal, and if it was anything like our drones, its electromagnetically charged penetrator would easily punch through our shield. A moment later, the ferry opened fire with its two beam weapons at extreme range, barely tickling our shield, but that was all they needed to do. Those beams prevented us dropping the shield to bubble, holding us for the anti-ship drone.

I woke up our drones hidden in the *Silver Lining's* bow and ordered them to compute parabolic firing solutions against the two Drake ships. We had one on the launcher and three in the loader, and thanks to Lena Voss, the EIS had upgraded our old black market weapons to Earth Navy Vulcans.

"Are we fighting or running?" Jase asked when he saw our ASDs come to life.

"Both." With a hundred Drake ships preparing to come after us, the last thing I wanted was to stick around, but we weren't going anywhere with those beams on us.

Our first two anti-ship drones plotted best guess solutions, then launched in quick succession, planning to figure out the rest in-flight. They swung around behind the *Silver Lining* on high-g trajectories, one heading for the ferry, the other for the tug. I set three and four to defend rather than attack, then let them loose too. For the first few seconds, they followed the same path as our first two Vulcans, but rather than go after the ships, they angled away, going head-to-head with the Drake ASD running us down.

Jase looked surprised as he realized what three and four were targeting. "I didn't know they could do that!"

Black market drones couldn't, but expensive navy drones were multi-mission. He'd seen the new birds when they'd been loaded, but thanks to the EIS scrubbing them clean of any navy identifiers, didn't realize what they were.

When the space tug saw it had one of our drones bearing down on it, it fired a second ASD then quickly turned and ran, showing no sign of preparing to bubble as the crew bet their lives on their big engine. It was a bad choice. The Vulcan had long legs and would run them down long before it ran out of power.

While Vulcan three continued to go after the first Drake ASD, number four switched targets, locking onto the tug's second drone. Our two defenders started moving apart, each now locked in single combat with a rapidly accelerating robot opponent.

The Drake ferry suddenly decided it was time to save itself, veering away before it had even shut down its energy weapons, sweeping space with parallel beams. Seconds later, its twin beams winked out, its shield dropped and it streaked back toward Acheron Station. Our Vulcan immediately switched targets, joining the hunt for the tug.

The two Drake drones heading after us now tried to avoid our Vulcans. The first narrowly dodged an impact, but our drone detonated close for a proximity kill, catching its target in the blast, triggering a double flash as both weapons vaporized. The second Drake weapon pitched sharply one way then another, forcing the heavier Vulcan to slew off course as it tried to shut down its target's escape vectors. Under high acceleration, two brilliant points of lights raced toward each other, then at the last moment, the Drake drone nosed up sharply. Vulcan four detonated, swallowing its target in a brilliant ball of light, then the Drake ASD burst out of the blast sphere and swung toward us.

"That's not good!" Jase said anxiously.

"Are we clear ahead?" I asked as our distorters charged to full. If there was just one gravity mine ahead, bubbling would be suicide.

Jase focused on his console, searching for any holes in space blocking our course. "Sensors are still foggy," he said uncertainly as the collision alert sounded, warning the Drake ASD was about to hit us. "Just a few more seconds."

"Too late!" I declared. "Sensors in!"

Almost a hundred clicks away, Vulcan two fired its penetrator into the tug's shield. The armored warhead punched through the Drake ship's hull into the energy plant and detonated. An intense flash forced our screen to dim, then a brilliant white blast sphere bloomed where the tug had been, swelling rapidly. Suddenly, our screen went blank as our sensors locked inside our hull, safe from our bubble's searing heat. I cut shield and maneuvering engines, then let the autonav take over. For a moment, we drifted naked through space, then a muted thud rang hollowly through the ship, followed immediately by telemetry filling our screen, telling us we were superluminal.

"We made it!" Jase said relieved.

"Something hit us," I said warily. "How close was their drone?"

"Right on top of us," Jase said, "but it must have missed. We're still alive!"

I knew the Drake ASD had struck the hull, and it couldn't have been a dud. Thousands of years of development had engineered misfires out of existence. Suddenly, the telemetry on screen disappeared, replaced by a flashing warning:

Bubble collapse in 30 ... 29 ... 28 ... 27 ...

Jase stared at the screen, confused. "What the hell is that?"

The message wasn't coming from any of the *Silver Lining's* systems and no signal of any kind could pass through the bubble.

"Izin, what's our hull integrity?" I demanded, suspecting the truth.

24 ... 23 ... 22 ... 21 ...

"Within safe limits, Captain," he replied.

"No! Exactly! What is it?"

17 ... 16 ... 15 ... 14 ...

"Ninety nine point seven percent, Captain," Izin replied, still unaware of the danger.

"That signal's coming from outside the ship, but inside our bubble!" Jase declared confused.

8 ... 7 ... 6 ... 5 ...

254

"Emergency stop!" I yelled, ordering the autonav to dump the bubble. There was no slowing down, no decrease in intensity. The bubble just vanished, subjecting the *Lining* to a sudden spring back of spacetime. Internal inertial fields absorbed the effect, but when the sensors locked in place, we discovered the ship was rolling and spinning out of control. The thrusters quickly stabilized the ship while the timer was frozen on screen with two seconds to spare, then a new message appeared:

Disable your weapons and shields and prepare to be boarded.

It was a message from a dead ship and a dead crew.

Jase scanned nearby space. "There's nothing out there, Skipper."

"It's not out there, it's on the hull!"

Lucky for us Drakes wanted cargoes and credits, not worthless radioactive wrecks. Not so lucky was the fact that the Drake fleet had seen the space tug's drone hit us just before we bubbled. They knew we were either dead or trapped. We'd flown for only twenty eight seconds, but it would take ten and half hours for our energy plant's neutrino emissions to get back to Acheron Station. They'd be there now, listening and waiting. When they picked up our emissions, all they'd have to do was jump out and grab us. There was no point having our E-plant go dark, it was already too late for that.

"Captain," Izin's voice sounded from the intercom, "I've sent a crawler out to investigate a hull breach ten meters forward of our port engine."

"Check for an acceleration field. It would have started when the timer finished, so we can't bubble without blowing ourselves up."

"Did we ram a gravity mine?" Jase asked as Izin's eight legged robotic spider scurried across the hull, sending us its optical feed.

"Not a mine," I said, eyes glued to the screen as the round bulge of our port engine appeared above the gentle curve of the *Silver Lining's* hull. The crawler ambled forward, revealing the glowing exhaust of a hypervelocity engine, then the cylindrical body of a drone embedded at an angle into our hull. Five harpoon like clamps had shot out from the drone's body, anchoring it to the ship.

"That's no ASD!" Jase exclaimed, surprised. "It's got claws!"

My bionic memory identified it as a Caliphate device, used by their security forces to prevent suspect ships from escaping patrol vessels, the ideal weapon for raiding Rashidun Souks. Considering the connections the Drakes had, it was no surprise they had access to weapons ideal for capturing freighters with their cargos intact.

"It's a shackle drone," I said, "and we're not going anywhere while it's out there!"

* * * *

"Any progress on the drone?" I asked as I entered engineering.

Izin sat in the middle of his six screen setup viewing separate feeds from the hull crawlers he'd sent out to study the shackle drone. Without taking his eyes off the screens, he pulled on his vocalizer to reply. "Only the outer hull was penetrated. The inner pressure hull remains intact."

"Lucky for us." No explosive decompression.

"It did what it was designed to do, keep us alive so

we could shut down the ship, then generate a directional acceleration field that intersects our bubble seventy meters from the hull. It's also equipped with a homing beacon that began transmitting as soon as we unbubbled."

"As good as a gun to our head. Cut it loose. We'll patch the hull later."

"I can't. It's equipped with a self destruct device that will detonate if I remove its arms or body panels. The explosion would not destroy the ship, but it would wreck the port engine and prevent superluminal travel. To disarm the detonator, I have to cut in through the drone's engine exhaust."

"How long?"

"It could be done safely in two days."

"You've got ten hours."

"Ten hours, thirteen minutes," Izin corrected, well aware how long it would take the drone's locator signal and our energy plant's neutrino emissions to reach Acheron Station and for them to jump out to collect us. "While you're waiting, Captain, you may wish to check your reader. I've completed decrypting the Merak Star's log."

"Anything interesting?"

"They used seven rendezvous locations, never the same place twice in a row. After meeting the Cyclops, the Merak Star always returned to the same system to unload and pick up another cargo."

"What system?"

"The Duranis System."

It was the same place my brother had offered to take me to! He'd called it a transport hub, although I'd never heard of it and I'd visited almost every human port within a thousand light years. "What's there?"

"Nothing, according to the navy's astrographics

catalogue. No colonies, no stations, only a Forum safety advisory."

"Good work," I said, then headed to my stateroom, eager to trace the *Merak Star's* movements for myself.

My cabin's light came on automatically as I entered, illuminating a thin metallic sliver floating above my bunk. It's movement caught my eye as it shot toward me, forcing me to duck instinctively and dart away as it turned and came after me again. It was as long as my little finger, with no markings revealing what it was or where it came from.

Wary of firing my P-50 inside the ship, I grabbed a datapad off my desk and swatted at the sliver, but the slender device easily avoided my attacks. As it circled around, I tried striking it twice more, then it flashed toward me. I leapt sideways, but it was too fast. Cold metal latched onto my neck, instantly paralyzing me. I crumpled, dropping the datapad, then it caught me before I hit the deck, isolating me from the ship's internal acceleration field. A moment later, I was floating face down above the deck, completely helpless.

My listener flashed a proximity warning into my mind's eye as a large, dark form stepped into my stateroom's doorway. I couldn't turn my head to see who it was, but my listener pattern matched the heavy footsteps immediately.

WARNING! ALIEN CONTACT! IDENTIFIED AS GERN VRATE.

"The chase is over, human," he said in a low voice, removing my gun from its holster and dropping it on the deck.

He touched a control surface on his forearm, then I floated face down into the corridor and along the passage toward the airlock. I tried to yell, but the paralysis prevented me speaking. Izin's security systems should have been flashing alerts to the bridge and engineering, but Vrate's lack of urgency told me he'd disabled them all.

We cycled through the *Lining's* airlock into a narrow, cylindrical chamber. The Kesarn ship had attached itself to the port airlock without Jase receiving any warning on the bridge, and Izin was so absorbed in disarming the shackle drone, he hadn't noticed the magnetic anomaly signaling its approach.

After passing through a high arch-shaped inner door, Vrate floated me along a short oval passage, past several sealed compartments, to a spherical chamber. Its walls were non-reflective black which instantly became transparent the moment we entered. Only the dark metal floor, the frame of the passageway and the rounded shoulders of his ship behind us diminished an otherwise uninterrupted view of space. The *Silver Lining* was just visible astern, mated to Vrate's aft facing airlock, while ahead lay the blanketing darkness of the Acheron void. The spherical chamber extended from the short body of his ship like a fishbowl. In the center of the chamber was a circular platform rising a meter above the deck. On it were two hip high, silver metal poles, each crowned by a polished silver sphere.

Vrate rotated my body to the vertical, then a pressure field pushed me securely against the bulkhead beside the entry. The metal sliver then detached itself from my neck, immersing me in the ship's gravity, and floated into Vrate's hand. He slid it into a thin belt compartment, then strode up the short ramp to the circular platform.

With his back to me, he stood between the two metal poles and placed his hands on the spheres. The moment he established contact with the ship, thin glowing lines marked with unfamiliar characters appeared across the fishbowl walls surrounding him. Silently, we slid away from the *Silver Lining* into the Acheron darkness. As the ship's orientation changed, the lines glided across the transparent surface, suggesting they were a form of navigational aid.

I craned my neck to see the *Silver Lining* fall away behind us. The shackle drone was just visible forward of the port engine, surrounded by Izin's hull crawlers, one of which was using a laser cutter to slice through the drone's engine. Once we had moved away from the *Lining*, the Kesarn ship bubbled. To my surprise, the gray blur of the bubble was visible, indicating Vrate's sensors could withstand the exterior heat. Vertical navigational lines surrounding the piloting platform slid aft across the fishbowl's inner walls with increasing velocity. Most surprising of all was the geometry of the bubble. Unlike our spheroidal bubble, the shape surrounding Vrate's ship was biconal, reaching forward to a distant point and even further behind to a trailing point.

A point!

It was as if we were inside a long narrow spear, racing through spacetime in a way I'd never dreamt possible. I tried to speak, but found my voice hadn't yet recovered from Vrate's paralyzer.

His helmeted head turned to watch me. "You should be proud, human. You're about to be the first member of your species ever to leave this galaxy."

Chapter Six : Solitaire

TransGalRef: 89X4-03g5-8fH3-Ui30
Red Dwarf Star, Extra-spiral Zone 0714
Galactic Halo
22,462 light years from Sol
Uninhabited

The Kesarn ship was smaller than the *Silver Lining*, with a narrow body designed to fit inside its biconal bubble. Throughout the flight, Vrate paid me no attention, standing like a statue with his hands on the silver spheres at his hips as the navigational lines and their symbols slid smoothly across the spherical shell surrounding us. Incredibly, he showed no sign of the injuries he'd received on Hardfall, demonstrating a miraculous healing ability.

"How come you're not dead?" I asked when my power of speech returned.

"The healsuit regenerates me," he said without turning.

He'd certainly suffered broken bones and massive internal injuries, yet he moved as if the bonecrusher had never attacked him. "That's some suit."

"Self reliance is the key to survival, when one travels alone."

He'd been standing on the circular platform for hours, manually piloting the ship even though he could no more see through his biconal bubble than we could see through our spherical equivalent. I assumed the strange bubble geometry was an ominous sign of how fast we were travelling. It was certainly at a velocity only an artificial intelligence could control, so why hadn't he handed flight control to the ship? On the *Silver Lining*, once we were underway, the autonav did all the work, turning Jase and I into passengers who did little more than watch the course simulator calculate our progress.

"I don't suppose we can discuss this?" I asked.

"If you keep talking, human, the neural blocker goes back on."

I fell silent, knowing if he paralyzed me again I was finished. For several minutes, I watched the circles on the inside of the fishbowl slide toward me, noticing there was one thicker circle inside the sphere that was parallel to the rear bulkhead. As it crawled slowly aft, it reminded me of a horizon line, representing a reference plane of some sort. He'd said we were leaving the galaxy, which made me suspect the horizon line was the galactic ecliptic, marking our progress out of the Milky Way's great spiral.

After a few minutes, I tried again. "Your bubble shape should be impossible."

"Why?"

"Propulsion geodesics are fragile. That bubble should collapse."

"Hmph. You've been out here over two thousand years, and you've learnt nothing!"

"I wouldn't say … nothing."

"You continue to place limits on the unknown, unknown to you."

Is that what I was doing? I thought I was trying to build rapport so I could talk my way out of this mess. I gave him some more silence, then asked, "How long have you been out here?"

"Two hundred and eighty thousand giran."

"Giran?"

He grunted. "Three hundred and … forty six thousand Earth years."

The answer surprised me, being much less than I'd expected. It was obvious from his ship that the Kesarn were far ahead of Human Civilization, yet extragalactic travel was normally accessible only to much older species. In cosmic terms, the Kesarn and humanity were almost peers on the lower rungs of the galactic ladder.

"Cross-species kidnapping is prohibited by the Access Treaty," I said.

"I'm not subject to your Access Treaty."

My Access Treaty? Every species in the Milky Way was subject to the Treaty. None were excluded, no matter how young or old, not even primitive civilizations who knew nothing of its existence. Observer civilizations had ensured for eons there were no exceptions, certainly not a species whose existence was measured in mere hundreds of thousands of years. Even the Matarons, who were twice as old as the Kesarn, couldn't opt out. Only the Intruders, who had evolved far beyond the galactic disk, had evaded its reach – ultimately to their detriment – but Gern Vrate was from the Perseus Arm. Galactic law applied to him as much as it did to me.

"Where are we going?" I asked.

"Nowhere you've ever heard of."

"Try me."

"No more talk, human," he said sharply.

I wanted to press him further, but couldn't risk being silenced again by his neural-blocker, not if I hoped to escape. On the fishbowl wall, the horizon line of the galactic ecliptic had fallen behind where Vrate stood, indicating we'd left the disk behind.

I wondered, even if I could escape, where would I go?

* * * *

The spear-shaped gray blur surrounding Vrate's ship vanished, revealing a great black void, broken only by isolated misty pearls of light. It took me a moment to realize they were globular clusters, orbiting high above the galaxy in halo space, while dimmer points of light marked distant galaxies. Behind us lay the Milky Way with its distinctive glowing bar at the center of a vast whirlpool of light isolated amid an infinite night. At that distance and perspective, I couldn't tell where human space was located, so tiny was it against the vastness of the galaxy.

Gern Vrate lifted his hands off the two control spheres, paying no attention to the spectacular panorama behind us. He massaged his palms without turning, visibly relaxing.

"Why are we stopping?" I asked.

"I need to rest." He stretched his thick neck, showing signs of fatigue.

"No autonav, huh?"

"The ship can fly only when I'm part of it," he said

simply.

"Suppose you have to sleep?"

"I stop."

"That's not too smart."

"As if you would know."

"Hey, even human ships fly themselves!"

"It's the price we pay."

"The price for what?"

"For what we are." He pointed to a feeble, red point of light directly ahead. "That is our destination."

Without instruments, I had no way of knowing how far it was. "Looks close."

"Ten light giran."

At that distance, it could only be a solitary star thrown from the galaxy by a cosmic quirk of fate. Considering how far we'd come in such a short time, we could have covered the remaining distance in a matter of seconds. So why rest now?

"Are you just leaving me here?"

"Yes," he said, marching down the ramp from his piloting platform.

"You could at least put me in a cabin where I could get some sleep."

"There's only one sleep pod on this ship."

"Suppose you have company?"

He stopped in front of me. "I travel alone."

I nodded, feigning sympathy. "No friends, huh?"

"I am Kesarn."

"I take it you're the aloof loners of the galaxy?"

Vrate studied me like I was a bug. "You humans have no concept of individualism. Compared to us, you are a docile herd species."

"I've been called a lot of things, but that's the first time I've ever been compared to a cow!" The Tau Cetins were herbivorous avians who considered humans to be an aggressive hunter-predator species. I guess it depended on your perspective. "So, do you want to tell this docile herd creature what's waiting up ahead?"

"You ask a lot of questions for a condemned prisoner," he said, then strode out into the corridor.

His footsteps receded as I fixed my eyes on the solitary star ahead, wondering what interest I could possibly hold for its inhabitants.

* * * *

When Vrate returned, he offered me a fist sized cube with a thin tube extending from the top.

"This will sustain you," he said as the pressure field released my arms, letting me reach for it.

I took a sip, gagged on the bitter liquid and spat it out, spraying his boots. "I thought you had to deliver me alive, not poison me!"

"One container will keep you alive for a week," he said glancing disdainfully at the spittle on his boots.

"Do I have a week?"

"That is not my concern."

He touched his helmet at ear height, causing his dark visor split into two horizontal slices that slid apart revealing his face for the first time. He had light brown skin, large round eyes beneath a prominent brow and a flat nose with a single nostril. He was the same species as the frozen alien I'd seen on the *Merak Star*!

"You're Kesarn?" I asked surprised, wondering how any Drake could ever have captured one of his race.

"Drink!" he ordered, then strode up the short ramp to the circular platform.

I glanced down at the alien food substitute

uncertainly. It tasted like acid, but I needed my strength, so I took a breath and gulped it down, then tossed the cube away in disgust when I'd finished. "Argh!"

When I looked up, Vrate was studying me from the piloting platform. "Your survival instinct is strong, human. Many species would not have drunk."

"You actually like that stuff?"

"It tastes like doongpa!"

"It sure does!" I agreed. Whatever doongpa was, I now considered it to be the vilest tasting substance in the galaxy.

Vrate turned and placed his hands on the control spheres at his hips. Almost immediately, the stretched biconal bubble appeared around us, sending us hurtling toward the solitary halo star.

"I've seen your kind before," I said.

"That, I doubt! We are rarely seen and never by the likes of you."

"No, really. I'd recognize your ugly face anywhere." I hoped an insult might draw him out, but he simply ignored me. "They must be paying you well, to go to all this trouble."

"You would think that."

"You don't like us much, do you?"

"You are what you are."

"A docile herd creature?"

"Talkative."

The bubble vanished, revealing a small red orb a quarter the size of Earth's sun. Whatever gravitational cataclysm had ejected the red dwarf star from the galaxy had also stripped it of planets, hurling it toward the emptiness of intergalactic space. Whoever Gern Vrate was delivering me to, they couldn't be inhabitants of this system. The solitary star was nothing more than a rendezvous point far enough outside the Milky Way that it was beyond the gaze of those who enforced galactic law.

Vrate waited while his ship searched nearby space, then when three markers appeared on the fishbowl wall to starboard, he nosed his ship toward them. Considering the speed the Kesarn ship was capable of, it took a surprisingly long time for the contacts to resolve into dark hulled ships. Indistinguishable at first, they slowly grew in size as we crept up on them, taking on a flattened teardrop shape marked by ridges running bow to stern. I knew at a glance what they were – snakehead armored cruisers, Ortarn class.

"You're selling me to the Matarons?" I asked incredulously. "I thought you weren't a bounty hunter."

"I'm not," he replied, his eyes fixed on the three ships floating in line ahead formation still some distance away.

We slid in astern of them with a caution that showed Vrate didn't trust the Matarons any more than I did. He matched their velocity while keeping his distance, then Kesarn script began appearing below each ship, identifying them in ever more detail.

"You're scanning them?"

Vrate acknowledged my question with a distracted grunt.

"They can't see us, can they?" I asked, knowing Mataron cruisers wouldn't just sit there and let themselves be scanned, unless they knew nothing about it.

"Not yet."

The Matarons might have been militaristic xenophobes, but they were also hundreds of thousands of years ahead of the Kesarn. There was no way Vrate should have been able to sneak up and scan them without being detected. "I know humans are slow learners and all, but how can you hide from them?"

"Easily."

"You obviously don't trust them, so why are you doing their dirty work for them?"

"I don't trust anyone." He lifted his hands off the two control spheres. The Mataron ships immediately broke formation, circled toward us at high speed and took up firing positions forty five degrees apart. "Now they see us."

A holographic image of a triangular reptilian face appeared directly ahead of Vrate. I normally couldn't tell one snakehead from another, but this one wore a thin black circlet around the top of his head and an ornate black uniform with a chest scabbard holding a ritual blade. I'd only ever seen one other Mataron dressed like that. He'd been a high ranking commander of the shadowy Black Sauria organization, but surely this couldn't be him. Not out here.

"Identify yourself, Kesarn!" the Mataron Commander snapped, angry that Vrate had gotten so close without being detected.

"Gern Vrate. You are Hazrik a'Gitor?"

"I am."

It wasn't the first time I'd been wrong, but it might be the last. Hazrik was the same Mataron who'd sworn a year ago to have my head. Thanks to Vrate, he was about to get his wish.

"I have the prisoner," Vrate announced.

The Mataron's anger began to abate. "We nearly destroyed you!"

"If you had, you would not get the human."

"Do not be so careless approaching Mataron warships in future."

"I am never careless and it was not my defenses

that were penetrated."

The Mataron emitted a low sound, a sign of anger, confirming Vrate had a genius for irritating everyone he came in contact with, even the snakehead he worked for.

"Reveal yourself next time, or you will not be so lucky."

"There'll be no next time. Do you have the information?"

"Yes."

"Transmit it now."

"Not until Sirius Kade is in my possession."

"He is here," Vrate said, motioning toward me.

My image must have become visible to Hazrik, because he leaned forward studying me closely. "I told you we would meet again."

"And here I thought all snakeheads were liars," I replied lightly.

"My daughter waits for you on Kif-atah. You murdered her husband, now you will die by her hand, my gift to her."

"That'll give me plenty of time to kill you and escape," I said, relieved to discover I wasn't going to die today.

"You will be on the Mataron homeworld in three weeks," Hazrik said, "and you will not escape."

Knowing roughly how fast Mataron ships were, three weeks to Kif-atah put us approximately twenty two thousand light years from Mapped Space. It was a long way for the Black Sauria commander to come just to capture me, and he'd brought three top of the line cruisers with him as escorts. I knew he wanted me dead, but that seemed like overkill, even for a vengeful snakehead.

"Transmit the data," Vrate said.

"I will send a transport to collect Kade. When he is aboard, you will have your payment."

Vrate hesitated, but realized he had no choice. "Agreed."

Hazrik's triangular face vanished, then I said, "You can't trust him."

"But I can trust you?"

"I saved your life on Hardfall."

"You almost got me killed trying to escape," he said as a small transport emerged from Hazrik's cruiser and glided toward us.

"As soon as you hand me over, he'll cheat you."

"Betray the Kesarn once, never deal with us again. He knows that."

While the Mataron transport maneuvered to dock, Vrate reached over his shoulder for his gun and leveled it at me. The pressure field pinning me to the bulkhead dropped, then he motioned me to the passageway.

"I will shoot if you try anything."

"And risk disappointing Hazrik's daughter?" I said, stepping through the doorway.

"Her feelings are not my concern."

"I don't suppose we can make a deal?" I said, starting along the short corridor leading to the airlock.

"No."

"What's this information Hazrik has? Maybe, I could help you?"

"You can't even help yourself," he said, irritated by my stalling tactics.

"I can put you in touch with people who could help you, like the Tau Cetins."

"I trust them even less than I trust you or the Matarons!"

I took several more steps, then turned to face him. "How about..."

271

I swept my hand with ultra-reflexed speed at his gun, caught the thick barrel and pushed it wide as he fired. Before he could wrestle the gun free, I kicked him in the abdomen, but his healsuit absorbed the blow, then Vrate threw a jab at my head with his free hand. I ducked, trying to twist the weapon out of his hand as he grunted in pain, but not from anything I'd done. Realizing his wounds from Hardfall hadn't fully healed, I threw myself at him, slamming my elbow into his chest, aiming for where the bonecrusher had held him in its jaws.

The healsuit was tough, but it wasn't armor. The breastplate flexed under the impact, causing Vrate to stagger back holding his chest with his free hand, never letting go of his gun with the other. Before he could recover, I kicked him again, aiming for his thigh where the bonecrusher had bitten down on his legs. Vrate stumbled back, wrenching the gun barrel out of my hand as he dropped to his knees in pain, proving no matter how good his healsuit was, bone needed time to knit, even Kesarn bone.

I dived sideways as he fired from his knees, sending a white blast flashing past me. He followed me with his gun, forcing me to dive through an open hatchway onto a small landing as he fired again. I bounced off the far bulkhead and fell down steep, narrow metal grill stairs to the deck below where I lay momentarily stunned as Vrate staggered onto the landing above. He aimed down at me as I scrambled away behind storage containers, then his heavy boots sounded on the stairs as he came after me.

From the far side of the compartment, a static electric hiss filled the air, throwing flickering yellow light and sharp shadows toward me. I couldn't see the source as I crawled between containers, looking for a way out.

"There's nowhere to run, human," Vrate declared as he landed on the deck. He fired once, shattering a container's contents behind me, then made a short tech-assisted jump over the containers, landing in front of me and aiming his bulky weapon at my head. "It didn't have to be this way," he said as the yellow flickering light played over his healsuit.

I glanced toward the light source, a white metal hemisphere floating in the center of the chamber – the twin of the alien-tech device I'd seen loaded aboard the *Merak Star* on Novo Pantanal. A brilliant yellow beam emanated from the flat cylinder protruding from its base and poured into a dish shaped receptor in the deck.

"Wait!" I yelled.

He adjusted a control on his weapon. "It's set to stun. You will not see me again."

"What is that?"

"No more talk!" Vrate said, extending his arm to fire.

Suddenly I knew why he'd brought me out here, far beyond the gaze of any Observer civilization, and it wasn't for the reason he thought!

"It's not me they're after! It's you!"

He hesitated. "What are you talking about?"

"I told you, I've seen your kind before!" I pointed to the hemisphere floating at the heart of Vrate's ship. "And that thing! Whatever it is!"

"Impossible."

"I can prove it!"

"How?"

"In my pocket!" I said reaching toward a sealed section inside my flight jacket.

"No tricks," he said, ready to fire, but letting me

proceed.

I retrieved the rectangular plate I'd taken from the frozen Kesarn on the *Merak Star* and tossed it to Vrate, who caught it one handed. "I took that off one of your people. He was in cryostasis alongside one of those things," I said, nodding toward the hemisphere.

He turned it over suspiciously, studying it. "He was alive?"

"Frozen. His life signs were low, but he was definitely alive."

"This could be a fake, a copy," Vrate said, lifting the control plate, comparing it to an identical device on his wrist, the same device he'd used to remotely pilot his ship.

"That's your language! Humans don't know your language!"

Vrate glanced at the control plate once more, then slid it into his pocket. "Do you know *why* he was alive?"

It was a trick question, but I had no idea what the trick was. "No. For questioning maybe?"

He stared at me, deep in thought, then slowly lowered his weapon. "I believe you."

"You do?" I asked surprised.

"He was alive because the siphon cannot exist without him," Vrate said, his mood changed. "You could not know that."

"You're right! I didn't! And I still don't know what you're talking about!"

He motioned toward the hemisphere. "That is a dark energy siphon, my ship's power source."

"Dark energy?" I turned to the Kesarn machine with renewed interest. "Really?"

"It taps into the force driving the accelerating expansion of the universe."

"I've heard of it." Dark energy made up seventy percent of the total mass-energy content of the universe. "I just never knew it could be harnessed."

"It is the ultimate energy source in the universe, infinite and free."

"That's why we can't detect your ship's emissions."

"Yes. There are none."

"But we can detect Mataron ships," I said, struggling to understand how the Kesarn, who should have been far behind the Matarons, were so far ahead of them.

"Their ships are reactively powered, although not in the same way yours are."

If Hazrik was involved, then the Black Sauria had orchestrated everything. That meant the snakehead technician on the *Merak Star* was no renegade. He was Hazrik's agent! The Black Sauria would kill any Mataron who dared help humans, unless he was following their orders. Being the only link to the Matarons, Inok a'Rtor would disappear at the first sign of trouble, leaving us holding a dark energy siphon in one hand and a frozen Kesarn in the other.

Considering what I'd seen of Gern Vrate, no human – not the Brotherhood, not the Consortium, not even my brother – could steal his technology without help. Snakehead help! If the Consortium genuinely believed Inok a'Rtor was a renegade scientist, they wouldn't know who their alien-tech supplier really was.

That left only my brother, who was in this up to his cybernetic skull cap! He was the one dealing directly with the Matarons, the only member of the *Cyclops's* crew who really knew what was going on, and that made him the biggest traitor of all. But he was human, and anything he did was – under galactic law – mankind's responsibility. No excuses. It was a harsh law, but it was our job to police ourselves because when it came to interspecies relations, no buck passing was tolerated.

But there was more here than simple cross-species piracy. The Matarons were taking a huge risk attacking the Kesarn, who were clearly more advanced. And why were the snakeheads simply handing such advanced tech to humans, rather than keeping it for themselves?

Certain Vrate wasn't going to shoot me, I climbed to me feet and asked the one question I had no answer for. "How'd you get so far ahead of the Matarons?"

Vrate lifted his gun over his shoulder and locked it to his back. "It's not our technology. It's Tau Cetin."

"You stole tech from the TCs?" I asked, genuinely impressed.

"No one steals from the Tau Cetins!"

It took me a moment to understand. "They gave it to you?"

The Tau Cetins were millions of years ahead of the Kesarn, the Matarons and us, and one thing they weren't was generous with their secrets. For them to simply gift technology to a vastly inferior civilization went against everything I knew about them, about how the galaxy itself worked!

"Everything to do with the Tau Cetins comes at a price," he said bitterly. "Remember that."

A dull clang rang through the ship as the Mataron transport docked with it, then Vrate's eyes lifted toward the airlock above, deciding what to do next.

"Sounds like there's a bunch of armed snakeheads about to kick in your airlock and kill us both."

"They will kill you. Me, they need alive."

"Alive or dead, it's a bad deal for both of us, so

let's get out of here."

"It's too late," he said. "They've locked onto my ship."

"It's a Tau Cetin ship! Let's kick their scaly asses from here to the other side of galaxy!"

"This is a Kesarn ship equipped with Tau Cetin technology. There's a difference."

"But you've got TC weapons, right? So let's fry these snakeheads!"

"If I had Tau Cetin weapons, the Matarons would already be dead for what they've done. All I have is the siphon, the star drive, sensors and masking technology. I'm no match for them in a fight."

"Then hide!"

"I can't, not while they're clamped onto my hull. Come," he said, then limped back up the metal stairs.

I followed him up to the airlock and said, "They'll be wearing skin shields."

"This weapon is ineffective against their micro-contour shielding," Vrate said, tapping his wrist panel. A circular hologram appeared in front of the airlock, revealing its interior. Four snakeheads were squeezed inside, all dressed in Black Sauria body armor. They were so tall, they were hunched over with their shoulders pushed against the ceiling.

"A quantum blade would do it," I said.

"Do you have such a weapon?"

"Yeah, a real fancy one – back on my ship."

"Very helpful," Vrate said, then strode off down the passageway to the flight deck. I hurried after him, then watched as he stepped up onto the piloting platform.

"This is Gern Vrate. Your ship is disrupting my airlock system. I cannot release the inner seal."

Hazrik a'Gitor appeared before him. "We are

showing no disruption to your ship."

"My systems do not recognize the outer seal is closed. You will have to undock your vessel."

"Correct your malfunction and open your airlock immediately."

"I will try again," Vrate replied, closing the commlink.

"You can't let them inside," I said.

"Obviously not," he replied tersely, studying the locations of the three Mataron ships, calculating his chances of escape. Once sufficient time for a systems check had elapsed, he reestablished communications. "I cannot solve the problem. I am a tracer, not a technician. If you want this prisoner, undock your ship!"

Hazrik hesitated, but his desire to enter Vrate's ship got the better of his innate suspicion. "Very well."

The Mataron Commander's image vanished, then the snakehead transport released the Kesarn ship and moved away from the airlock. Vrate placed his hands on the spheres at his sides, then the biconal superluminal bubble appeared, accompanied by a bright flash as the transport's bow was sliced off by the bubble's extreme quantum forces, fortunately missing its energy core. The transport's sharp nose remained trapped inside the bubble while the rest was left behind, adrift in space. Almost immediately, the three Mataron cruisers fired together, but the Kesarn ship was much too fast for them. We were a quarter of a light year away before the blast of their weapons reached the point in space we'd occupied an instant before.

Inside the bubble, the transport's bow section drifted against Vrate's hull aft of the fishbowl flight deck, sending a tremendous shudder through the ship, then it tumbled slowly away. For a few seconds, it hung in space over our heads, then it slid into the bubble and vanished in a brilliant flash.

"Ouch!" I said. "Never seen that before!" It occurred to me a bubble was fragile in highly curved space, but could be a deadly weapon in flat space.

"No damage," he said without any data displays appearing.

"The four snakeheads in the airlock will wonder why they've lost contact with their ship."

Vrate didn't answer.

"We could take them prisoner and hand them over to the Tau Cetins," I suggested, thinking it wouldn't take the TCs long to probe their minds.

"Why would I do that?"

"Oh, I don't know, because you're a good galactic citizen and you want to make the Tau Cetins mad at the Matarons." That was certainly my motivation.

"I am not a good galactic citizen," he said ominously.

The bubble dropped, revealing empty halo space around us. The distant red point marking Solitaire's position was now dozens of light years away. The visual feed from the airlock appeared in front of Vrate showing the two closest snakeheads firing at the inner door.

"How long before they blast their way in?" I asked.

"Long enough," he said, then the airlock's outer door snapped open, hurling all four Matarons into space.

"Blowing their scaly asses out the airlock wasn't exactly what I had in mind," I said, disappointed I'd lost the chance of handing the reptilians over to the Tau Cetins for questioning.

Vrate turned the bow of his ship toward the four Black Sauria operatives drifting helplessly in space. They were still alive, protected by their suits, although they wouldn't survive long stranded in halo space. One by one, they began firing at us in a futile act of snakehead defiance. From the bow of the ship, four rapid energy blasts flashed out, shattering the Matarons into a million pieces.

"Neither was vaporizing them with your cannon!" I muttered, realizing he hadn't simply killed them, he'd summarily executed them for their crimes. I could hardly blame him for that.

In silence, we watched a cloud of Mataron droplets drift away into the transgalactic void, then Gern Vrate turned and fixed a cold stare upon me. "Now ... tell me what you know of Kesarn in cryostasis?"

* * * *

"Three Kesarn disappeared in your part of the galaxy," Vrate explained after I finished recounting my experiences on the *Merak Star*. "I was sent to find them."

The tiny red solitaire glowed in the distance, our nearest companion in the halo void. Even if the Matarons had extrapolated our course and were searching for us, Vrate assured me they couldn't penetrate the Tau Cetin masking technology now hiding his ship.

"What led you to me?" I asked.

"The Matarons discovered I was asking questions. Hazrik a'Gitor offered me information in exchange for a condemned human who'd killed a member of his family. You."

"It was self defense."

"What humans and Matarons do to each other is of no interest to me."

"OK," I said slowly. "Obviously, the Matarons took your people. You could lodge a protest with the Forum."

"The Kesarn are not members, haven't been for a long time."

For two millennia we'd been told the only way to be granted interstellar access rights was to join the galactic political system and commit ourselves to the principles that had governed interstellar relations for eons. Refusal would force the Tau Cetins to take back their astrographics data and neutralize the precious novarium we needed to power our ships, trapping us in our scattered systems. Yet somehow, the Kesarn had found a loophole, been allowed to follow a different path.

"How can you not be members?"

"We were once, for hundreds of thousands of giran, until the Intruder War."

The war had been fought centuries before mankind had developed interstellar travel, lain waste to many worlds beyond the Orion Arm and made Izin's people the pariahs of the galaxy.

"What happened?"

"They invaded our homeworld in the Perseus Arm, fortified themselves behind massive shields we couldn't penetrate, then swarmed our planet with robotic armies and millions of their kind. We couldn't match their technology and even if we hurt them, it made no difference. They breed so fast, casualties mean nothing to them."

"But they do to you."

"We are individualists," Vrate said. "Our numbers are small."

"The Forum couldn't help?"

"They were driven from the Perseus Arm, leaving us to fight alone. Vastly outnumbered, we could not win."

"Why'd you stay?"

"It is our way," he said, as if that explained it all. "We raided and spied upon the Intruders, but always, they found us. The Tau Cetins changed that. They gave us what we needed to evade Intruder sensors, to become the eyes of the Alliance in enemy controlled space. With Tau Cetin technology, our ships reached the Intruder home cluster, established contact with conquered races, scanned Intruder ships and brought information back to the Alliance. We even warned the Tau Cetins when their homeworld was about to be attacked."

"So why don't the Matarons keep your TC-tech for themselves?"

"Because they can't use it. No one can, but us."

"I don't understand."

"Nothing is ever simple where the Tau Cetins are concerned. They are peaceful and old and deceptively cunning. They gave us their technology to use, not to understand. They were desperate for information we could provide, but not so desperate as to advance our civilization millions of years even when theirs faced destruction."

"That was thousands of years ago. Your ship looks new."

"It is. The Tau Cetins gave us machines to produce the equipment we needed to spy for them, but there were conditions."

"There's always a catch," I said.

"We provide the raw materials the Tau Cetin fabricators need ... including ourselves."

"Yourselves?"

"We are a solitary species. We travel alone, we mate infrequently, have few children, just enough to survive. The Tau Cetins knew this. Everything the fabricators produce is linked to one of us – only one. It is the price we pay. I was present when my ship was formed. When I die, so does my ship. I can never be further than a light second from the siphon or it will destroy itself. The same is true for every Tau Cetin component aboard. If the siphons are separated from their Kesarn imprint, or if any attempt is made to disassemble them, there will be a very contained, very Tau Cetin annihilation."

"That's why you have to touch the control spheres."

"I must be one with the ship. No other can fly it, not even another Kesarn."

"And you're still using the same construction machines – fabricators – the TCs gave you during the Intruder War?"

"The Tau Cetins build to last and we have taken great care to preserve them, much better care than the they expected."

"I'm surprised they let you keep them."

Vrate was slow to answer. "They owe us."

"Because you helped save their homeworld?"

"Because they didn't save ours. The Intruders destroyed my homeworld when they discovered we were spying for the Tau Cetins. They couldn't subdue us, so they exterminated us. It is a debt the Tau Cetins can never repay."

"I'm sorry."

"It was the price of our freedom. Now we go where we please, we answer to no one, although continue to respect the law."

"So they don't sanction you, and the Tau Cetins turn a blind eye because they feel guilty." They might be the shrewdest super-intelligent birds in the galaxy, but I found it reassuring that they were capable of remorse.

"They are patient. They hope we will rejoin one day."

"Will you?"

"No. The Tau Cetins continue to inform us of galactic affairs, but we keep our distance. They are how I knew of the tension between humans and Matarons. Hazrik a'Gitor's claim that he was settling a blood feud with a human seemed plausible, and as Matarons cannot use our Tau Cetin technology, there was no reason to suspect I was his target."

It was a double win for Hazrik, capturing the Tau Cetin technology and taking his revenge on me in one operation, although I was simply icing on his snakehead cake.

"So why are the Matarons giving your energy siphons to us humans?"

"I don't know. Humans lack the technology to utilize limitless energy. Even we Kesarn would have no need of the siphons if not for Tau Cetin star drives."

"And it all works, providing you're alive," I said thoughtfully. "Cryostasis is not dead."

"We have never put it to the test, but ... I believe you are correct."

"The siphons must be needed to power some other alien-tech in human hands. It has to be the tower they loaded aboard the Merak Star, and Hazrik's snakehead scientist is there to show them how to plug it all together."

"The Matarons could tell your people any lie about that technology and they'd never know."

Considering the scum of humanity's propensity for self interest, they'd believe anything they assumed was to their advantage. They might well have no idea what that tower's real purpose was!

"Your missing people will be where that tower is. If you take me back to my ship, I'll lead you to it." Izin had already told me where the tower was headed, but I didn't trust Vrate enough to tell him, not while I was still his prisoner.

"The Kesarn and their technology are to be returned to me. The humans are your problem."

"And the Matarons?"

"Them, we will share," he said menacingly.

"Deal," I said, offering my hand. Vrate glanced at my hand curiously, making no move to shake, then I withdrew it awkwardly remembering shaking hands was an ancient Earth custom from the era of sword fighting – a meaningless gesture to the Kesarn.

"We have an agreement, Sirius Kade, but that does not make us allies."

He stepped onto the piloting platform, placed his hands on the control spheres and turned his ship toward the Milky Way's great spiral disk. A moment later, the biconal bubble formed around the Kesarn ship, sending us hurtling back down into the galaxy.

Gern Vrate might not be my ally, but he'd referred to me by name for the first time, signaling he was no longer my enemy.

* * * *

We docked with the *Silver Lining* without Izin or Jase becoming aware of our presence. Izin's hull crawlers had removed the shackle drone's thruster assembly and a crawler now clung precariously to the drone's tail, reaching into its interior.

"There are no other human ships nearby," Vrate informed me as he removed his hands from the control spheres and escorted me to the airlock.

"Will you deliver a message for me?" I asked as I stepped into the airlock, past black scars burnt into the bulkhead by Mataron weapons fire.

"I'm not a courier."

"It's to your advantage as much as mine."

"What message?"

"There's an Earth Navy ship waiting in the Paraxos System. The message is for Lena Voss. Tell her to come to the Duranis System with everything she has."

"Paraxos … Duranis … these are human names. They mean nothing to me."

"I'll enter the Tau Cetin coordinates of Paraxos into my autonav, then delete it, then enter Duranis. You can read them both before we bubble."

Vrate gave me a noncommittal look as the inner door sealed shut between us, then I cycled through into the *Silver Lining* and hurried to the flight deck.

"Skipper!" Jase exclaimed with an astonished look as I appeared in the open hatchway. "Where have you been?"

"To halo and back," I said with a wry grin.

He gave me a puzzled look. "Where?"

"Later," I said, shrugging off his question. "How long until Izin disarms the shackle drone?"

"Soon. A crawler's working on the self-destruct now and two more are standing by with a skin-patch as soon as we push it off."

"No sign of the Drakes?"

"Not yet." He nodded to a timer counting down on the screen. We still had an hour and forty three minutes left. "That's assuming they're waiting at Acheron Station. If the Drakes jumped out to listen, they could be here anytime."

They didn't know which way we'd gone, so they'd have to disperse a lot of ships to find us early. More likely they'd wait for our signature to reach them, then come out with overwhelming force. "We're getting underway as soon as Izin gives us clearance."

I left Jase watching the sensors and hurried to my stateroom to skim the *Merak Star's* log. She'd rendezvoused with the *Cyclops* and other Brotherhood ships every six to eight weeks for several years, delivering munitions and often receiving nothing in return. Only three times had she picked up return cargo, including the transfer on Novo Pantanal. Nazari had simply logged it as 'sealed containers', his cryptic way of describing kidnapped Kesarn and their stolen tech. The common denominator was every voyage started and finished in the Duranis System.

When I finished reviewing the *Merak Star's* log, I returned to the flight deck where the timer was down to twenty minutes. The shackle drone was drifting away from the ship and Izin's hull crawlers were patching the hole in our hull.

"Izin is almost done," Jase said.

"Just in time," I said, activating my console's nav-mode and selecting the Paraxos System from our TC astrographics database, unnoticed by Jase who was watching for Drake ships. After a minute, I reset the autonav for Duranis-A, just as Izin arrived on the flight deck and climbed onto the third couch behind the two piloting positions.

"If a Drake ship appears, Captain," he said, "you can engage the superluminal drive. We'll lose the hull crawlers, but the ship is safe to fly."

"The crawlers have time," I said, more concerned that Gern Vrate got a good read of our destination than I was for a couple of replaceable hullbots.

Izin glanced at the destination visible on the autonav display in front of me. "There's no Society Exchange in the Duranis System, Captain, only the Merak Star's customers."

"That's right."

"Are we continuing a vendetta we cannot hope to resolve?" he asked. "Perhaps we should drop it now and wait for a better opportunity to deal with Domar Trask."

Jase gave me a furtive look, clearly having been thinking the same thing. If I was just settling a personal score, they'd be right.

"If you're looking for a paying job, the Orie mercs all have prices on their heads." It wasn't true, but Lena would ante up to preserve my cover, making it true. The Society ran a bounty board for Earth Navy and for private security contractors, some of which were EIS kill missions in disguise. I steered clear of them all, even the EIS hits, because I was deep cover, not assassination. That didn't mean I couldn't pretend to be dishing out vigilante justice, if it convinced them to go along with it.

"Are we bounty hunters now?" Izin asked. "Or is this a Captain Ahab obsession?"

And Trask was my Moby Dick? Izin must be thinking I'd lost my mind taking such risks simply for revenge.

Jase brightened, declaring with bravado, "I always thought I'd make a good bounty hunter!"

"It's neither," I said, deciding to give them part of the truth. "It's my brother."

"Your brother? I thought he was dead."

288

"He's Rix, Captain of the Cyclops." And a Mataron collaborator!

"He's a Drake!" Jase exclaimed incredulously.

"Not just any Drake. He's a leader, maybe *the* leader of the Drakes."

"Damn!"

"There's more," I said. "The Mataron, Hazrik a'Gitor – you remember him? He's behind this. It's why Gern Vrate was after me, to hand me over to the Matarons, except I made a deal with Vrate. He doesn't give me to the snakeheads and I track down the three Kesarn he's looking for. The only way to do that is to find my brother and he's on his way to Duranis right now." I turned to Izin. "It's beyond revenge, beyond obsession, it's family."

Izin's bulging eyes blinked horizontally, a long slow sweep he only did when his prodigious intellect was overloaded with indecision. "A spawn matter is a heavy burden, Captain."

"Especially when you only have one brother, not twenty thousand," I added meaningfully.

Izin pondered the differences between our two species, then said, "I understand."

I gave Jase a quizzical look.

He grinned. "I was charging weapons as soon as you said there was a price on their heads!"

I made a mental note not to have Lena pay too many credits for the Orie mercs. I didn't want Jase getting a taste for bounty hunting.

Chapter Seven : Duranis-A

Type 1A Supernova Progenitor Companion
Red Giant Star, Duranis Binary
Evacuation Zone, Outer Draco
802 light years from Sol
Transient population

Duranis-A was a red giant, a doomed star slowly expanding as it consumed the last of its fuel. It had already swallowed three terrestrial planets and was threatening to do the same to the inner most gas giant, but time was against it. Duranis-B, its tiny white dwarf companion, was now pulling vast quantities of super heated gas from the red giant's surface, creating a glowing river of light arcing through the blackness of space between the two stars. The red-orange gas spiraled down into a radiant disk surrounding the white dwarf before falling onto the tiny white star's surface, dramatically increasing its mass and core temperature.

It made little Duranis-B a cosmic time bomb.

The white dwarf had entered the supernova convection phase three centuries ago, which in cosmic terms placed it a mere heartbeat from catastrophe. In human terms, Duranis-B would not explode for another seven hundred years, but when it blew, its few weeks of glory would produce more energy than the entire Milky Way galaxy would in a year.

Five thousand years ago, the Forum had ordered every inhabited world within thirty light years to begin evacuating, within eighty if they were aligned with the white dwarf's axis. It was a ban on settlement Earth Council had endorsed, which was why there were no human settlements within forty light years and why I'd never been near the Duranis Systems.

"No ships close," Jase reported.

"The Cyclops is out there somewhere," I warned, raising our battle shield.

Jase studied the transponder signals, then shook his head doubtfully. "I don't think so, Skipper."

Dozens of contact markers began appearing on screen, none of which were combat vessels. They were all civilian ships parked halfway across the system above a yellow-brown gas giant orbiting Duranis-A twenty five degrees from the river of gas dissecting the heavens. Far from immediate danger, the gas giant provided an ideal vantage point for one of the most spectacular panoramas in Mapped Space.

"No shields up, no weapons charging on any ships," Jase confirmed with growing confusion.

"They're all lit up like they don't care who sees them," I said, surprised.

"Wait a minute!" Jase said as he oriented our optics toward the civilian flotilla. "I've got four hot spots, big ones, no transponders. There! At the edges!"

Four dark, prolate ellipsoids turned slowly on their

axes, silently guarding the flotilla. They were Nortin Armory's defense platforms, the kind used for the planetary defense of Core System worlds. Bristling with heavy weapons and loaded with shields and armor, they were reason enough for the civilian flotilla to have no safety concerns.

At the flotilla's center was an enormous starliner with two rows of small ships docked along each side and dozens more in synchronized orbits nearby. The small ships were mostly luxury yachts, executive transports and commercial vessels while the whale in their midst was the super starliner *Aphrodite*, an eight hundred thousand tonne palace that had no place being outside Core System space. She was lit by thousands of lights and by her neutrino signature which dwarfed the energy emissions of all the other ships combined. If she was a secret raider base, she was a very conspicuous one.

"Open a channel," I said.

"Which one?" Jase asked perplexed as his eyes scanned all the designated commlinks. "They're all in use." He patched them into the flight deck's sound system, surfing through one channel after another.

"I want to confirm dinner reservations for a party of ten at Pharaoh's ..."

"... promised me an exclusive interview!"

"What do you mean KXN have the ball room?"

"... OK, ten thousand credits, but I have to be near Vice-Chancellor Liang."

"... our Denedus hub has twelve distribution ships on standby, but it'll take five months to get the datacast back there from here!"

Jase silenced the chatter. "They're all like that."

"I guess we should crash the party," I said. "Switch on the transponder."

"If the Drakes are out there–"

"They know enough not to tangle with those Nortin platforms, and I don't want them blasting us when we jump in."

Confident we weren't going to put Nortin Armory's fabled auto targeting systems to the test, we performed a sub-second superluminal leap across the Duranis-A system to join the insects swarming around the majestic *Aphrodite*. No one even noticed our arrival. We tried contacting the starliner and were politely transferred from one department to another until we were finally put in contact with a tired young woman in a smart blue hotel uniform.

"I'm sorry, sir, but all permanent ship berths are taken and I have a waiting list," she said in a courteous, mildly bored tone. "Your chauffeur can drop you at a boarding station if you wish to use the ship's facilities, but docking is limited to fifteen minutes per twelve hour rotation. One thousand credits per docking cycle."

Jase gave me an incredulous look, silently mouthing the word 'chauffeur'?

"What if I book a cabin?"

"Paying guests are permitted one free docking per twenty four hours, sir. Starburst Cabins start at ten thousand credits per twenty four hours, ranging up to one million credits per day for our Grand Galaxy Suites. This includes full access to all facilities and complimentary drinks in any of our casinos."

Jase eyes widened at the exorbitant prices. "We're in the wrong business!"

"I'll take the cheapest cabin," I said.

"Unfortunately sir, the Starburst Cabins are fully booked. The first vacancy is in four days."

"Are you always this full?"

"Not usually. It's because we're hosting the Core

Systems Trade and Development Congress. If you wish to purchase Congress admission, we have individual, corporate and sponsor level packages, however, the Opening Night Gala Dinner is sold out."

"Isn't Duranis kind of remote for something like that?"

"They wanted somewhere with a spectacular view, sir, for the networks."

"What networks?"

"There are thirty four data streamers and over a hundred sim-casters here, sir, including the six all-band majors from Earth. Not all are hotel guests, of course. If you'd like the full list, I could connect you with traffic control. This is reservations."

"No thanks. Just give me one of your fifteen minute, thousand credit docking slots so my chauffeur can drop me off." I gave Jase a wink.

He scowled, unimpressed at his ignominious demotion from starship pilot to chauffeur.

* * * *

The *Silver Lining* docked at an airlock adjoining one of *Aphrodite's* many hangar decks. The hangar was crammed full of small craft: ferries, sub-light transports, pleasure yachts and a row of the liner's own white hulled, gold trimmed launches. A huge space door dominated the hull-side bulkhead while the aft facing wall opened into a sophisticated engineering workshop filled with white clad engineers and state of the art repair bots.

As soon as I set foot inside the hangar, a ship security officer in a dark uniform pointed me to a vending panel on the inboard bulkhead, located beside a transparent pressure door. Beyond the door was a carpeted corridor lavishly decorated with holosculptures and lightboards advertising the *Aphrodite's* many diversions.

"Purchase your all-day Pleasure Pass here, sir," the vending panel announced as I approached. A glowing red arrow pointed to an Earth Bank reader which scanned my vault key and quickly relieved me of a thousand credits for docking the *Silver Lining* and another two thousand for unlimited access to the ship's amenities. In return, I received a digitized rectangular tag that opened public doors and allowed the ship to track my movements.

"Please familiarize yourself with the immersion code before entering. The Aphrodite's captain and crew thank you for your purchase and hope you enjoy your stay."

The transparent door slid open as a lightboard illuminated, explaining what the immersion code was. In terse language it advised me that no stims, pressure suits, predatory creatures, toxic organisms or weapons of any kind were permitted beyond that point, and that scanners throughout the ship ensured the code was obeyed at all times. While it didn't say what the penalty for breaching the code was, I was glad I'd followed the pre-docking advisory and left my gun on the ship.

I started down the corridor, holding a small communicator to my lips, "Jase, can you hear me?"

"Loud and clear, Skipper."

The signal was encrypted, nothing fancy, just enough to give me a few hours of anonymity.

"I'm in. Stay close in case I have to get out fast."

The corridor opened into a small area bordered by an arc of translucent infopanes, beyond which was a huge tropical pool and garden area hundreds of meters across.

"Trade congress," I said to one of the rectangular infopanes.

A ship's schematic appeared showing my present location relative to a ten thousand seat theater called Constellation Hall, the center piece of the congress. It was flanked by smaller auditoriums and a media center that coordinated coverage of the proceedings.

"What's happening at Constellation Hall?"

"The Plenary Session is in progress, sir. Official delegates only," it replied, obviously aware the pass I carried didn't give me access. "If you would like to purchase a Congress Package, I am authorized to–"

"No thanks." Buying a package would let the *Aphrodite* know where I was headed. I was already acutely aware my all-day Pleasure Pass would tell the Nortin Armory's robot guns outside which ship to shoot at if I got into trouble, which was why I needed to get my hands on a replacement.

I stepped between the infopanes and headed toward a towering fountain spraying water over white nymph statues standing in a shallow pool. Beyond the fountain were swimming pools, wave simulators, diving platforms, sandy beaches and inflatables. Hundreds of people lay baking themselves on artificial beaches beneath a blue sim-sky and radiant emitters soaking them in tropical heat. I'd never seen so much open water on a ship before and shuddered to think what would happen if the starliner lost power. Without artificial gravity, thousands of metric tonnes of water would be free to float through the ship playing havoc with sensitive electrical systems – unless the entire chamber was engineered for such an eventuality? Sealing ships from radiation was one thing, that was essential for survival, but making them waterproof in case fountains and pools leaked was ridiculously extravagant.

I strolled casually through crowds of sim-sun worshippers while my DNA sniffer area-scanned them all. Surprisingly, I didn't get a single hit from my encyclopedia of mankind's most wanted. Either the starliner's wealthy clientele were remarkably law abiding – unusual in itself – or someone had gone to a lot of trouble to ensure only clean skins were aboard the *Aphrodite* for this cruise.

Once past the tropical beach, I followed a broad spiral walkway up through the ship, slowly circling a stand of giant photonic trees. Flocks of colorful lightbirds soared through the open air, occasionally vanishing as they flew out of the photonorama, only to appear at a different location as they 'dived' back into the enormous simulated aviary. The flawless imagery was perfectly complemented by directional sounds and a misty humidity that added a deceptive realism to the tropical forest.

The busy spiral walkway wound up through nine levels of shops, beauty salons, body sculptors, casinos, theme parks and restaurants, all overflowing with tourists unaware they were part of a lavish deception. The *Aphrodite* might have been one of the most extravagant starliners ever built, but it wasn't here for the view of a cosmic cataclysm in the making. It was hiding something else, something in plain sight even I couldn't see.

At the Aurora Level, I stepped off the spiral boulevard and headed past bars and cafes toward a stun barrier barring access to Constellation Hall. A wall of five glowing beams crossed the avenue through a series of silver bollards, broken only by an arch scanner in the center which verified every entrant's credentials. Four uniformed ship security men stood beside the arch ensuring only the anointed were allowed to enter.

Knowing my all-day Pleasure Pass would get me no further, I took a seat at an open air bar in sight of the checkpoint and ordered a non-intoxicating drink. Everyone who passed through the arch wore access chips pinned to their shirts identifying which areas they could enter. The security guards had the broadest clearance, but without a uniform, I wouldn't get far with one of their chips, so I waited for a media type, expecting they had the next best access. After twenty minutes, a tall man carrying a short data staff and wearing a media chip came out through the checkpoint.

I followed him to a bar overlooking the photonorama. He took a seat and ordered from the table top selector while I found a table from where I could watch him without being noticed. Once settled, he ran his fingers through the holographic image projected up from his staff, splicing together scenes for his datacast and occasionally recording a voice over. After two drinks, his report was stream-ready for couriers to distribute to audiences across Mapped Space. The reporter paid his tab and headed for the men's room. I followed a few seconds later. Inside the sparkling clean washroom, only one sanitation booth was sealed. When he stepped out, I struck him in the stomach, finished him with an elbow strike to the head as he doubled over, then dragged his limp body back into the booth.

"Only one occupant permitted at a time," a synthesized female voice informed me politely as I relieved the reporter of his access chip, then flushed his personal identification and room key down the toilet. By the time he came to, the ship's waste recycling system would have reconstituted them into useful byproducts making it impossible for him to verify his identity.

I stepped out of the booth, watched as the door sealed him in, then bumped into a drunk on the way out, slipping my all-day Pleasure Pass into his pocket. Satisfied the ship believed it still knew my movements, I headed for the security checkpoint with the reporter's data staff under my arm. It might have been an all-in-one holostudio, but its solid metal structure made it an effective close range weapon, one security scanners wouldn't challenge. At the checkpoint, the guards barely looked at me, then I strolled to Constellation Hall.

It was a circular edifice of refractive carbon and polysteel five levels high. On the podium, a well dressed bureaucrat droned on about the economic benefits to interstellar trade of viral self-propagating Society indemnified consignment contracts. I quickly realized that wasn't why I was here, so I headed back to the foyer where small groups of congress attendees chatted quietly. I took a seat, pretending to work with the data staff while I studied the people drifting in and out of the session.

Soon a pair of muscular, severe looking men appeared beyond the hall's towering wall-windows, walking slowly around the outside of the building. They looked like Orie Mercs in plain clothes with a harder bearing than the toy soldiers at the arch scanner. Both men carefully scrutinized everyone, occasionally whispering into their palms as they followed their patrol route, eventually moving off behind the hall, only to reappear at their starting position several minutes later. When they'd almost completed their third circuit of the building, Julkka Olen appeared. He spoke briefly with them, then moved on past the hall's entrance. I waited until he was almost out of sight, then shut down the data staff, slipped out through the main entrance and followed him at a distance. I hadn't forgotten Olen had cracked my head open on Krailo-Nis, but contrary to what I'd told Jase, revenge wasn't on my mind – what he was doing on the *Aphrodite* was.

I tracked him across a crowded plaza to a cluster of conference rooms opposite the media center. He passed three unguarded venues, each with glowing signs indicating when breakout sessions were due to be held there, then stopped at the entrance to the fourth, the Vega Room. It had a blank sign and two plain clothed Ories out front and according to my sniffer, both had boarded the *Merak Star* at Acheron Station with Trask. After exchanging a few words with them, Olen went inside, leaving me in no doubt, whatever the game was, it was being played out in the Vega Room.

I circled around the conference center, looking for a way in, but every entrance to the Vega Room was guarded. Not fancying my chances against Orie mercs with only a metal club for a weapon, I headed across to the media center. It was a rectangular structure with long rows of seats facing data screens crammed in side by side and surrounded by sonic nullifiers for privacy. The walls were filled with screens showing live feeds from Constellation Hall and empty conference rooms being prepped by bots for the afternoon sessions. Only the Vega Room was not shown.

I picked a workstation, then found the Vega Room feed was inexplicably out of service. The precinct floor plan confirmed there were only three ways into Vega, all of which I knew were guarded. That left technical services, the communications nerve center, as my next stop. It was only two doors away, occupied by a bored uniformed ship's cop and an overweight tech watching a multi-screen layout.

"No one's allowed in here," the company cop said, waving me half heartedly away without even bothering to rise. Beyond him, the fat tech didn't even glance over, but continued feeding an inedible slab of fried protein into his mouth as his eyes remained transfixed by his screens.

"The media center people told me you could help me," I said, closing the distance to the security officer before he even realized I'd ignored his instruction.

"This is a secure area," the guard said, finally starting to pay me some attention. "Get out now."

"The Procyon Room is dropping out. If it's not back up soon, my editor's going to have my head."

"Go through the help-bots," the tech said without turning toward me. "They'll lodge a service call if they can't fix it."

I struck the guard in the forehead with the data staff, relieved him of his stun gun as he crumpled to the floor, then aimed the weapon at the technician's round face. "But I don't want to lodge a service call." The tech's eyes widened in surprise. "Activate the Vega Room feed," I said, tapping the door's control panel, locking us inside.

He swallowed, glanced at a screen full of status indicators and said, "Vega's on a security lock out. I'm not supposed to access it."

"I'm not supposed to shoot you in the head, but I will if you don't give me access – now!"

He glanced anxiously at the gun, put his oily meal down and worked his console until the Vega room feeds appeared on four screens in front of him. "That's it. Anything else?"

"Yeah, you're in my seat." I stunned him in the

back, rolled his unconscious form onto the floor and sat in his place, resting the stunner on the console in front of me.

The four screens before me displayed different perspectives of a group of men and women gathered around a circular conference table. The only person talking was an enormously fat man wearing a loose fitting suit that couldn't hide the bulges of an exoskeleton hidden beneath his clothes. When he moved his arms, the exoskeleton appeared from beneath his sleeves or revealed supporting straps across his chest. Crowning his enormous body was a balding head with a thinning halo of silver hair and a chubby face above rolls of fat where his chin should have been. Most striking of all were his penetrating gray-green eyes, bristling with intelligence, and the unmistakable air of authority with which he spoke.

Listening to Fatman were six groups of three, each dressed in the styles of their respective cultures. Three groups were from the Union while the remainder represented East and South Asia and the Caliphate. I recognized only one man at the table, Governor Metzler from Hardfall, who sat with one of the Union delegations. All were listening attentively, sometimes exchanging grave looks or nodding supportively while a few tried to mask their feelings.

"I assure you ladies and gentleman," Fatman said in a silky tone, "they will be caught completely by surprise. We *will* have the advantage."

"We appreciate your optimism, Mr. Chairman," one of the East Asian men wearing a satin tunic said cautiously, "but how will our fleet penetrate the system defense perimeter?"

I set my listener to analyze every accent, to identify the worlds from which they came, but I didn't need my threading to tell the Chairman was a Union citizen and his East Asian colleague was from the PFA.

"Vice Chancellor Liang, let me assure you, the outer perimeter defenses will not be a problem," the Chairman said smoothly. "Our forces will never engage them."

"How is that possible?" a Hispanic woman with long dark hair asked. "We know their seeker drones are more than capable of destroying our long range weapons well before they could reach the target. Any attack must be launched from orbit."

The Chairman gave her a patient look. "We came to the same conclusion, Minister Delgado. The time to target for an extra-system attack would eliminate any possibility of surprise." He smiled wryly. "That is why we have developed an alternate strategy, one that gives us an advantage Earth Navy will not be expecting."

With the delegates hanging on his every word, he touched a control in the table, causing a holographic image of a long silver-gray ship to appear before them. She was bigger than a bulk carrier, had a row of cargo doors and docking ports along her sides and four large maneuvering engines astern, but she was no trade ship. She lacked offensive armament, yet bristled with point defenses and shield bubbles and was fitted with what looked like an oversized communications array amidships.

My threading tried silhouette matching the ship, but failed to identify her against any active classes. It was only when the search turned to ships no longer in service that her profile was projected into my mind's eye. She was an old Earth Navy depot ship, the last survivor of a decommissioned class no longer needed now that there were navy bases scattered across Mapped Space. She'd been designed to support fleet units far from home in the centuries following the Embargo, when Earth Navy had lacked bases outside the Solar System. More than two thousand meters in length, she'd once been a mobile naval base, one of the largest ships ever built for Earth Navy. The last of her kind had been sold for scrap years ago, yet somehow, she'd been saved from the wrecker's yard.

Behind her was an immense blue orb, a frozen world drifting at the edge of its system. Beyond the ice-giant was a red-orange river of super heated gas curving across the blackness of space toward a brilliant multicolored whirlpool. It was unmistakably the accretion disk swirling about Duranis-B, the white dwarf companion orbiting this system's red giant, a supernova in the making.

"This, ladies and gentleman, is our advantage," the Chairman informed them as my listener got a read on his accent. It was affected and pretentious, but he couldn't hide his colonial origins. He was from Ardenus, the same planet Governor Metzler came from, although his vocal tones suggested he'd spent much of his adult life on Earth.

"How's an old transport ship going to give us an advantage?" one of the Calies asked, clearly unconvinced.

"It's no mere transport ship, Doctor Sohrab," the Chairman said, zooming the image toward her topsides. From a distance, what I'd assumed was a communications array was, on closer inspection, the alien-tech tower that had been loaded aboard the *Merak Star*. "This structure utilizes an alien technology that will allow us to bypass the outer perimeter defenses entirely."

"We never agreed to use any alien technology," a man with a distantly North American accent said.

"What is it?"

"The technology is Hrane, Secretary Stilson," the Chairman replied.

"Did you steal it?" Stilson asked. "We don't want trouble with the Tau Cetins. Earth Navy will be a big enough problem." It was enough for my threading to conclude he was from New Liberty, a partially terraformed world thirty six light years from Earth. New Liberty was home to the single largest human population outside the Solar System and was only a thousand years away from becoming mankind's first fully engineered homeworld.

"We've stolen nothing," the Chairman assured him. "We merely salvaged an artifact that was abandoned thousands of years ago. The former owners, the Hrane, have no cause for complaint, not that they know or care. That is the beauty of our situation."

"I've never heard of the Hrane," a swarthy South Asian said. "Do we have diplomatic contact with them?"

"No," the Chairman replied. "According to our advisors, the Hrane last visited the Orion Arm centuries before we developed interstellar travel. They are mammals I believe, but that is the only similarity they have with us. I'm told we'd find their atmosphere rather toxic."

"If it's still working after all that time, they might want it back," Doctor Sohrab said warily. There was an eighty two percent chance he was from Qorveh, an agrarian colony in Core System space, one of the few Cali-founded worlds.

"Whatever they once were, they're now an inward looking, isolated species. A social transformation changed the focus of their culture, so much so that they rarely leave their homeworlds in the Carina Arm." The

Chairman shrugged indifferently. "Not every species are empire builders like us. What matters is they're long gone and our salvage operation was … almost legal."

"So you've salvaged this alien technology without our consent and installed it aboard one of our ships without our knowledge," the swarthy South Asian leader said. "Considering advanced alien technology is virtually unrecognizable to us, how do you propose to utilize this salvaged Hrane machine?"

"Installed aboard one of *my* ships, free of charge," the Chairman said sharply. From the look in his eyes, he'd always known it was going to come to this. Just as the ancient Greeks could never have repaired a thirty fifth century kaonic processor, we should never have been able to make use of Hrane technology, so steep was the slippery curve of advancing science. "And of course, we had help."

Mataron help!

"From who?" the South Asian delegate asked.

"Minister Shankar, there are some things I cannot discuss, even with this group," the Chairman replied slowly. "Suffice it to say, we have friends willing to aid us, providing their assistance remains confidential."

I silently cursed his arrogance. The Matarons weren't our friends and never would be. Any help they gave us would only ever be to their advantage, not ours!

"So what does this technology do?" Secretary Stilson asked with less unease than Minister Shankar had shown.

"It's a quantum tunneler," the Chairman said, clearly glad to get away from the subject of who was providing the technical expertise. "It tunnels through hyperspace."

"Hyperspace?" a quasi-Euro Union accented man sitting beside Governor Metzler spoke for the first time. "That's an unproven theory."

"Unproven to us, but a known physical dimension beyond spacetime long accessible to the Hrane," the Chairman explained. "You see, while the Hrane are far ahead of us, in galactic terms they are a mid level civilization. Their ships are slow compared to the Tau Cetins, but hyperspace gave them galactic reach."

The technician at my feet groaned and started to rise. I snatched the stunner off the console and shot him again, then gave the guard a second jolt for good measure.

"Galactic reach?" Vice Chancellor Liang mused, wondering at the possibilities. "And we can use this technology ourselves?" My threading decided he was from Xin Guizhou, a PFA Core System world ninety eight light years from Earth.

"We can use the salvaged technology," the Chairman corrected, "but synthesizing it for large scale exploitation is far beyond our industrial capability, at least for now."

"How does it work?" the quasi-Euro asked.

"It generates a micro-singularity, an extreme gravity point which pulls a sliver of our spacetime through hyperspace."

"Sounds like a black hole," Minister Shankar said.

"It's a point of infinite density and zero volume," the Chairman said, "which produces an effect similar to what a very small black hole would do."

"My dear Manning," the quasi-Euro said in a recognizably Ardenan accent, "wormholes are extremely unstable and quite unsuitable for interstellar travel. To my knowledge, not a single civilization in the Orion Arm employs such technology."

"That is true, Senator Proche," the Chairman conceded, "which is why we'll be injecting exotic matter into the sliver to inflate and stabilize it, creating a bidirectional wormhole large enough and safe enough for our ships to use."

"The energy requirements must be incredible," Shankar said thoughtfully.

"They are, but thanks to our friends, we have sufficient generating capacity."

That's what the Kesarn siphons were for, to power the Hrane quantum tunneler! It would make the depot ship undetectable, because she was running on dark energy – the first human ship ever to do so!

"And are our mysterious friends also providing us with exotic matter?" Minister Shankar asked. He was almost certainly from the Indian Republic world of Hindrati nearly two hundred light years from Earth.

The Chairman nodded. "Enough for several strike missions. We are negotiating for more, but it is a difficult material to procure. For now, our entire stockpile is aboard that ship, heading to its assigned position."

"It doesn't look underway," Minister Delgado said, puzzled.

"This is a live data stream from a camera drone, coming from the edge of the Duranis-B system. What you're seeing occurred almost two hours ago, the time it took for the signal to reach us. Our ship will arrive at its assigned position an hour from now, at which time it will begin deploying the tunneler. This signal is currently encrypted, but soon we'll open the feed to every news organization here."

"Is that wise?" Secretary Stilson asked, "considering the importance of security."

"Propaganda is also important, Mr. Secretary," the

Chairman replied. "I organized this trade congress specifically to lure every media organization in Mapped Space here. Soon, their ships will be racing each other back to the Core Systems, carrying news of our triumph to every human inhabited world." Realization spread across their faces, then he motioned to someone off screen. "General Trask will now deliver the tactical briefing."

Domar Trask appeared wearing a dark blue uniform with a gold star on each collar – not a uniform I'd ever seen before. He nodded crisply to the assemblage then the holographic image of the modified depot ship was replaced by a view of a ringed gas giant distinguished by bands of brown, orange and white and orbited by dozens of moons of various sizes. It could have been any one of a thousand such planets in Mapped Space.

"As you know, the outer defense perimeter has a gravity barrier preventing unauthorized superluminal flights into the system," Trask began, immediately causing my stomach to turn!

The dead EIS agent, Tiago Sorvino, suddenly screamed his warning at me from the grave: *aleph-null!* There was only one human controlled system in all of Mapped Space important enough for a system wide gravity barrier!

"Our fleet will commence its attack here," Trask continued, indicating a spherical marker to the left of the gas giant. "This is where the wormhole exit will appear, five million kilometers from Jupiter. This is how we will avoid the outer system defenses. We will never cross them. Four battle groups will simultaneously attack Earth Navy installations on the Galilean Moons – Io, Europa, Ganymede and Callisto." Four triangular indicators emerged in a line from the spherical wormhole marker, then diverged on separate courses toward their respective targets.

"Saboteurs will disable the Galilean Detection System before our fleet exits the wormhole. They'll never see us coming. The first Earth Navy will know of our presence is when we open fire from orbit. Without GDS targeting data, their surface and orbital defenses will be compromised while we will destroy Earth Navy's shipyards, maintenance docks and supply bases. At any one time, a third of all Earth Navy ships are at the Galilean Bases for refit and repair. Most will have skeleton crews and cold energy plants. None will be ready for battle, making destroying them on the ground a simple matter. The attack will last forty minutes by which time Earth Navy will be crippled. Our fleet will then withdraw back through the wormhole before other system defenses can be deployed."

Aleph-null! Aleph-null! Aleph-null! It rang like a clash of symbols in my mind.

"If we can send our fleet through a wormhole," Ambassador Delgado asked with a trace of irritation, "why did you make us spend months coming all the way out here?" She was from Inalis IV, a cold Union affiliated world settled from South America. She'd had the longest voyage to reach the conference and would have an even longer return trip as she'd have to steer well clear of the Solar System after the attack.

The Chairman nodded sympathetically, sending his voluminous jowls jiggling. "What better way to break the myth of Earth Navy invincibility than by destroying their main bases and a significant portion of their fleet from eight hundred light years away, watched by every news network in Mapped Space and by thousands of honest, law abiding citizens, all of whom will take what they see back to their respective homeworlds to spread fear and doubt. And in the Solar System, twenty four billion people will watch it live, the day it happens. I have seen to that." He paused, letting the breadth of his plan sink in. "In a few hours, the Mavia will be famous."

"Mavia?" Secretary Stilson asked.

"My penchant for ancient Earth history," the Chairman confessed. "I took the liberty of naming our secret weapon after Queen Mavia. She led a revolt in three seventy eight AD against the Romans in southern Syria, defeated them several times and eventually made peace on her terms. Rather apt, don't you think?"

"Only if we achieve a quick victory," Secretary Stilson said, "and freedom from Earth's interference."

I'd never considered Earth to be an interstellar Rome. Most colonies were self governing with little or no interference from Earth Council, except where Access Treaty matters were concerned and in those cases, opposition was not tolerated. Without Earth policing the worst of humanity, mankind would have suffered a setback by now far more damaging than the thousand year Embargo. Most human colonies would agree the arrangement worked well, but clearly not all.

"Our joint declaration will immediately follow our victory in the Jovian Moons," the Chairman said. "It will be issued here, by all of you, and will be carried across Mapped Space by the media, lighting a fire Earth will be unable to put out in a thousand years."

"It will take two years for news of this to spread to every colony," Minister Delgado said.

"By which time," the Chairman added confidently, "it will be all over."

"Don't be so sure of that," Vice Chancellor Liang warned. "An unprovoked attack will unite the four

Earth Collectives like nothing else could."

"And some of the colonial worlds," Doctor Sohrab added thoughtfully.

Trask stepped forward, breaking into the conversation. "While we have the Mavia, Earth Council will have to recall a large part of its operational fleet to protect the Solar System from more wormhole attacks. That will leave weak forces out here for our fleet to deal with on equal terms. Earth Navy will still outnumber us, but they'll be spread thin. They can't be everywhere and protect the Solar System at the same time, whereas we will concentrate our forces and pick our targets, fighting only when we have local superiority."

"We don't have to defeat them," the Chairman added, "just force Earth Council to negotiate."

"They won't negotiate on enforcing the Access Treaty," Vice Chancellor Liang said, "but Earth will retaliate. They will strike our bases, our shipyards and while they can rebuild theirs, we will be unable to do the same without Earth's help. It may take them years to recover, but they will recover. How long can our fleet survive without support?"

"Longer than you might think," the Chairman said, nodding to Trask who walked to the main doors.

Looks of shock appeared on the delegate's faces when the doors slid open and my brother walked into the room, fully armed and dressed as a Brotherhood Captain, watching them through his optronic eye.

"This is Captain Rix," the Chairman said. "He speaks for the Brotherhood."

Senator Stilson voiced what they were all thinking, "This man does not belong here!"

"On the contrary," the Chairman replied, "Captain Rix is an essential member of our group. The

Brotherhood has an extensive logistical network beyond the reach of Earth Navy, a network that will keep our fleet operational for as long as we need it. Isn't that right, Captain?"

Rix approached the conference table, sweeping the table with his cybernetic cyclops eye before speaking. "Seven Brotherhood Chapters have agreed to support your fleet. The remaining chapters will not attack your ships or raid your colonies … for now. They may even join later."

"If we win," Senator Proche said with a trace of cynicism.

"Certainly not if you lose," Rix said sharply. He started walking slowly around the table, gauging the strength of his audience. "Most of our bases are outside Core System space. All the large ones are, but we also have several smaller bases closer to Earth. Their locations will remain a secret, whether you win or lose. To preserve that secrecy, our navigators will pick up your ships from agreed locations, pilot them to our bases for repair and return them to you."

For the first time, Governor Metzler spoke. "Hardfall is one of these pick up points. It will also serve as our main base in Outer Draconis."

"We have a number of such bases prepared," the Chairman said, "all under the control of our people, all well defended. Martial law will be established to ensure Earth loyalists give us no trouble."

"Considering we already control all communications in and out of Hardfall and the other bases," Metzler said, "it could be a year or two before Earth Navy even realize where our bases are."

"How many ships is the Brotherhood providing?" Senator Proche asked.

"None!" Rix said. "We will not do any fighting for

you. We will not rescue survivors or conduct evacuations. We will not break Earth Navy blockades, carry supplies or aid your wounded. All we will do is repair battle damage. Any ship not flagged as a Separatist ship is a legitimate prize. If any of your ships fire on any of ours, the deal is off."

"And what does the Brotherhood receive in return for this generosity?" Minister Delgado asked.

"We will be paid in credits and equipment," Rix replied. "Terms have been agreed."

"Quite reasonable terms, I assure you," the Chairman added. "Even if Earth Navy blockades our worlds, which we know they will, this arrangement ensures we will continue fighting. Earth will have to agree to negotiate eventually. In the meantime, we are still discussing the possibility of Brotherhood ships acting as privateers on our behalf. Any Brotherhood privateer would be granted full immunity for past indiscretions and their Captains would be offered commissions in our fleet." The Chairman turned to my brother. "What would you think of commanding a Brotherhood squadron, *Admiral* Rix? Would that interest you?"

My brother gave the Chairman a sour look. "Not at all."

The door to the technical services center rattled as someone tried to force it open, then a fist banged on the door outside. "Hey Ardie, why's the door locked?"

I wanted to hear more, but I couldn't risk being caught now, not with what I knew. I disabled the console, killed the feeds from the Vega Room and stunned the technician and the guard again. Knowing I'd never get the stunner through the arch scanner, I left it on a shelf filled with spare parts, then slipped out through the rear exit, activating my communicator.

"Jase, you there?"

"Yeah, Skipper."

"Have Izin access the Aphrodite's passenger manifest. I want him to identify a passenger for me, name of Manning. Born on Ardenus, probably lives on Earth. They call him the Chairman."

* * * *

The Chairman's name was Manning Thurlow Ransford III. Izin discovered the *Aphrodite's* most expensive suite was permanently set aside for his personal use and a super yacht parked several clicks away was his private interstellar taxi. What he was chairman of, how he had the power to summon leaders from six major Core System worlds or why he would initiate an undeclared war on Earth with Mataron technical assistance was a mystery. He wasn't listed in my threading's catalogue of cosmic criminals and none of the public data services had any record of his existence. Wherever his talents lay, remaining out of the public gaze was high among them.

"Access to the Olympus Deck requires a restricted security pass," Izin informed me via communicator.

I'd found a vacant seat in a fast service diner. Serverbots hung from a network of slideways above the tables, dropping interactive menu screens in front of customers, lowering food from the kitchen onto the tables and scooping up empty plates with robotic efficiency. It was crowded, noisy and anonymous.

"Any way in?" I whispered into my hand.

"There's a formal dinner tonight for conference attendees, Captain," Izin replied. "Ransford's name is on the guest list."

"Too public."

"The ship's butler service is currently cleaning his dinner suit. It's due to be returned at four."

"Where's the butler service?"

* * * *

A short time later, I stepped from the service elevator onto the Olympus Deck wearing an ill fitting service uniform and an identification chip that told the ship's tracking system that I was a thirty two year old woman from Belize. The chip would open doors for me, but any scrutiny would reveal I bore no resemblance to the maid now bound and gagged in a cramped closet five levels below. At the far end of the corridor, a pair of guards at the main entry looked my way. I gave them a curt wave, which they acknowledged with a disinterested nod, then I carried Ransford's biowrapped suit to the Pantheon Suite's large white double doors.

"Suit for Mr. Ransford," I said to the door panel, hoping it was equipped with only a chip reader, not a DNA scanner.

"You are two minutes late, Miss Manzanero," the door panel informed me. "A performance decrement has been added to your efficiency profile. Your performance rating is now ninety three point four."

"Ninety three point four? That's good. Now open the door."

The double doors slid silently apart, giving me access to a long lounge area. A marble topped bar filled with a vast array of elaborately labeled and shaped drink dispensers ran off to my left, deeply padded lounge chairs occupied the center and an enormous curved table surrounded by transparent datapanes dominated the far side of the room. The rectangular thin sheets standing at the edge of the table scrolled with numbers, charts and news feeds, all playing to an enormous empty chair, the center from where the spider spun his cosmic web.

Opposite it all was a floor to ceiling holowall running the length of the room, providing a realistic vista of palm trees, pure white sand and an aquamarine sea reaching to the horizon. Muted sounds of the ocean and the aroma of tropical flowers filled the room. If I hadn't known I was aboard a starliner eight hundred light years from Sol, I might have believed I was at a luxury estate in Tahiti. It was an absurd use of space and energy on a starship, even a starliner, yet proof humans would pay exorbitant prices for a little bit of simulated Earth far from home.

I hiked across the sprawling entertainment area, past the Chairman's datapane encircled nerve center, to a door that slid aside as I approached. Inside was a dressing room with closets lining one wall, a wide entry to an immense bathing area opposite the wardrobes and access to a bedroom at the far end. Standing along the wall beyond the bathroom entry were ten recharging alcoves, each with its own full body exoskeleton, all identical in design except for their colors which ranged from black through the spectrum to white. The sound of running water came from the bathing area where a large circular shower rained upon a lavishly decorated spa pool. Strangely for a dressing area, there were no mirrors, perhaps a sign of the Chairman's dislike of his own appearance.

"Is that my suit?" Ransford called from the bubbling pool.

"Yes, sir," I replied with butlerish politeness.

"Do you want me to see to it, sir?" a female asked.

"No. Finish drying me."

The sound of absorbers wiping wet flesh came

from the bathroom, then a completely naked Ransford glided out on a pressure chair, his rolls of fat on full display. He was followed by a beautiful young woman. She was tall and lean with short golden hair and wore only a G-string. His pressure chair floated into the center of the room while she retrieved his undergarments from one of the closets. When she returned to his side, pressure fields lifted him into the air allowing her to dress him.

"Which color, sir?" she asked.

"It's a formal dinner, so … the black one, thank you, Dara."

"Of course, sir, an excellent choice."

Dara guided the pressure chair by hand toward the black exoskeleton while Ransford floated above it like a beached whale in white underwear, then he touched a control on the chair's arm and the black machine stepped from its alcove.

"That's far enough," I said, tossing the suit on the floor.

Ransford turned toward me, for the first time acknowledging my existence. He studied me curiously, gauging the threat, while his statuesque assistant moved to place herself protectively between him and me.

"You've crumpled my suit," he said without any sign of fear.

"Considering you're about to attack Earth for the Matarons, that's the least of your concerns."

A cold look spread across his face, then he nodded to the young woman. Dara immediately launched herself at me, kicking at my head with surprising speed. I barely evaded her attack, then she spun and kicked low and hard at my legs, sweeping my feet out from under me, sending me crashing back-first to the floor. Her speed and strength told me she was no mere plaything, but a gene-modded, combat trained dark angel. I'd heard of her kind, sex toy by night, body guard by day, born to kill and please with equal proficiency, but they were so rare and expensive, she was the first I'd ever encountered.

The moment I hit the floor she was in the air, kicking down at my throat. I rolled away as her heel slammed down with neck breaking force, then she kicked out at my head with her other foot as I came to my feet. I deflected with an elbow and kicked at her standing knee, but she somersaulted into the air and side footed me in the ribs, launching me through the bathroom entry. I struck the unbreakable ceramisteel tiles awkwardly as she landed with perfect balance.

"Bravo, my dear," Ransford said as if he was attending a sports event.

The dark angel leapt at me again as I started to get to my feet. I rolled beneath her, kicked up and caught her trailing foot, trying to knock her off balance, but she twisted in mid air like a cat and landed gracefully. Giving her no time, I charged. Dara tried gouging my eyes, but I deflected with one hand and caught her throat with the other, driving her back toward the spa-pool. She thrashed wildly, tried palm-striking my elbow, kicking my groin and clawing my face, but I deflected each attack before slipping on the wet tiles. We fell together, my weight on top as I drove her throat down hard. There was a sickening thud as her head struck the tiles at the edge of the pool then she went limp in my hands. I rolled off her, getting to my feet slowly as blood dripped from the back of her head into the pool and her glazed eyes stared blankly at the ceiling. Certain she was dead, I turned to Ransford who was watching from his pressure chair.

"Impressive," he said, showing no concern for his dead angel. "Dara would have killed most men."

"One look would be enough," I said walking into the dressing room as Ransford floated back in his chair, keeping his distance.

"I'll give you ten like her and a hundred million credits."

"You don't even know who I am or what I want."

"Does it matter? You just defeated one of the most highly trained, custom designed killing machines money can buy," he said, instructing his pressure chair to lower him down onto its cushions, "and you know things you shouldn't. I'm quite sure you're not here to help me dress."

"No," I agreed.

"Are you planning to kill me?"

"Would the attack on the Solar System stop if you were dead?"

"Nothing can stop it now."

"Why are you doing this?"

"Because I can," he replied coldly. "Because someone has to break Earth's control."

"What are the Matarons paying you?"

A superior smile appeared on his plump lips. "Paying me?" He chuckled incredulously. "They're not paying me anything. I'm paying one Mataron scientist a king's ransom to provide technical assistance and paying even more to the Brotherhood for a few alien-tech generators. If the Matarons discovered one of their people was working for a human, they'd kill him – and me!"

In a flash I realized Ransford, who thought he was pulling all the strings, had been tricked by the Matarons! "You don't know!"

"Know what?" he asked as a flicker of confusion

appeared on his face.

"The snakeheads are providing the energy siphons to the Brotherhood. Inok a'Rtor is their agent. They've been playing you from the start!"

Manning Thurlow Ransford III's eyes narrowed. "That's not possible."

"How'd you find out about the Hrane technology? Whose idea was it to use a wormhole to bypass the Solar System's defenses? Who has the most to gain if mankind tears itself apart?"

His expression hardened as he reconstructed events in his mind. "Inok a'Rtor offered me a way to speed up interstellar trade. How we are using that equipment was my idea."

"The snakeheads have the technology to listen in on any conversation you have. They knew you were looking for a way to break Earth Navy's power and they gave you exactly what you wanted. They used your greed for their own ends!"

"Why would they do that?" he asked suspiciously.

"Because the Tau Cetins will never let the Matarons attack us, but the Forum will sanction mankind if we try to destroy ourselves."

He stared at me with growing annoyance. "Who are you?"

"Sirius Kade."

His eyes widened in surprise. "The same Sirius Kade who was involved in the disappearance of the Soberano?"

There was only one way he could know about the *Soberano*, if he was the man responsible for sending her to the edges of Mapped Space a year ago. I realized he wasn't simply the chairman of a gang of traitors, he was *the* Chairman, head of the Consortium, the shadowy organization that used money as a weapon, that had the power to exploit planetary economies and control world governments. And worse, unbeknown to Manning Thurlow Ransford III, the Matarons had been pulling his strings since well before the *Soberano* incident.

"What did happen to the Soberano?" he asked.

"Ask the Matarons. I'm sure they're listening!" The details of her destruction were classified. She'd been listed as overdue and her crew lost for reasons unknown. The truth was, I destroyed her.

"A pity. Her Captain was quite useful to me. I suppose he's dead?" He took my lack of an answer as an affirmative. "Hmm. I took a hefty loss on that deal."

"Not as big a loss as you're going to take on this one!"

"That's where you're wrong. Even if the Matarons are getting what they want, so am I."

"You already have everything," I said. "Why risk it all by starting a war?"

"It's not about what I have, but what I don't have," he said simply. "More is always preferable to less." He pinched one of his rolls of fat absently as if his obesity was proof of his insatiable appetite.

"Attacking Earth Navy for the Matarons will make you the most hunted man in the galaxy, in all of human history."

He smiled coldly. "My dear, Sirius, I'm not attacking anyone. I'm merely enjoying a working vacation like thousands of other law abiding people, aboard this magnificent ship, which I own by the way." His expression hardened. "I also have an army of lawyers on a hundred planets ready to challenge any spurious accusations you might make against me."

"Your lawyers won't save you. Picking a fight with Earth Navy is only going to end one way."

"Earth and its fascist navy are an enormous obstacle to limitless free market opportunities. The Core Worlds are tired of Earth's interference every time some bureaucrat whispers Access Treaty. You're right. This is going to end one way, the only way it can, with an end to Earth's meddling in our affairs!"

"The Forum won't deal with us separately," I said. "Every species has one voice, one sole responsibility. It's a condition of entry."

"There's one thing I've learnt over the years, everything is negotiable. Everyone has a price. The Galactic Forum is no different." There was a smug confidence in his words that was entirely misguided. He was projecting his own self interest onto the Forum, derailing everything mankind had been working for since the Embargo had ended four and half centuries ago.

"If they won't negotiate with Earth Council, they certainly won't deal with you." Why should they? We had nothing to offer, while they had all the power and millions of years of peaceful coexistence behind them.

"They've been beating us over the head with that damned Treaty of theirs for twenty five hundred years," he snapped. "I think it's time we started using it against them. The Fourth Principle allows every civilization to develop in its own way. Well, this is our way! The Forum will have to sit on the sidelines and wait until we sort out our own affairs and then they will deal with whoever is left in charge." He gave me a knowing look. "I should know, my lawyers have gone over every line in the Treaty and its interminable guidelines, precedents, sub clauses and exemplars. We may not have the right to attack any other species, but we sure as hell can make war upon ourselves – as bloody and as brutal as we like. That is *our* right!"

"You do this and they'll see us as ungovernable primitives, incapable of cooperating with ourselves, let alone other civilizations. They'll think we're not ready."

"We'll convince them otherwise," he said confidently. "The Core Worlds will continue to honor the Access Treaty, but without Earth and its big stick looking over our shoulders!"

"You've got six Core Systems. You don't speak for them all."

"I don't need to. Once they see the Galilean Bases in ruins and a third of Earth's fleet destroyed, they'll waver, and a fractured humanity will be ripe for exploitation by the Consortium."

"In partnership with the Brotherhood?"

"I wouldn't call it a partnership, more a marriage of convenience, but that's your doing, not mine."

"My doing?"

"After the Soberano was lost, the navy cracked down on our ship building operations. Their constant surprise inspections made it impossible for us to arm our ships. Considering your involvement in the Soberano's disappearance, you bear the responsibility of forcing us to find other solutions, like dealing with the Brotherhood."

"Even if you turn the Core Systems against Earth, they can't win." Maybe in another ten thousand years when more people lived outside the Solar System than in, but not now, not with three quarters of mankind still living within sight of Sol.

He rubbed his chins amused. "The Consortium wins no matter what happens. We'll sell weapons and ships and everything else to both sides. Nothing drives up demand like a good war."

He was delusional about how the Forum, the Tau

Cetins and our neighbors would view us if we tore ourselves apart in another futile human civil war. No one would accept a collection of warring tribes into a pan-galactic community of peaceful civilizations. No wonder the Matarons were helping this maniac. He was doing their dirty work for them.

"You're guilty of high treason," I said, realizing this had gone beyond a mere interrogation. It was now a summary court and I was judge, jury and executioner.

"I have one alien technical advisor you can't link me to and a commercial arrangement with the Brotherhood you can never prove. That's not treason, Sirius, that's business."

"You're working for the Matarons, whether you know it or not."

"They're no better or worse than us," Ransford said dismissively. "They're certainly not my competitors."

"There's only one punishment for traitors," I said, my mind made up. Deep cover agents weren't assassins or executioners, but in Ransford's case I'd have to make an exception.

The Chairman's eyes widened in fear as he realized the change in me. I took a step toward him, then his flabby hand darted to the controls at his fingertips. His pressure chair tilted back and skimmed to the bedroom as his exoskeletons stepped from their recharging stations and turned as one to face me. The black exoskeleton nearby swung its pole-like arm at me, forcing me to retreat as the Chairman's pressure chair came to a halt inside the bedroom doorway.

"You didn't think I'd leave my safety in the hands of just one young woman, did you?" Ransford said as a smile appeared on his lips. "Goodbye Sirius. Try not to make a mess, my cleaning bill is already excessive."

The bedroom doors slid shut, sealing Ransford inside, then the black exoskeleton swung at me again, forcing me to duck under its arm. It struck the wall with a thunderous crash, leaving an imprint in the metal surface and convincing me it would crush my head like an egg if it landed a blow. Behind it, nine more polysteel automatons marched toward me like slow motion robots. They were articulated frameworks walking on jointed foot plates, lacking hands and heads and laced with motion sensors to detect the wearer's smallest movements. Without optics, they relied on room sensors to track my movements and a remote artificial intelligence to direct their attacks – all part of Ransford's personal security system.

I glanced at the sealed bedroom doors, certain the Chairman had escaped for now. "Another day," I declared, retreating toward the entertainment area followed by the mindless exoskeletons. They were built to carry the Chairman's enormous weight, not for speed, allowing me to easily outrun them.

At the main entrance, I spoke urgently to the door panel. "Open!"

"You have remained in the guest's quarters for seven minutes longer than required to complete your assigned task," the cybernetic doorman replied. "Three performance decrements have been added to your efficiency profile. Your performance rating is now ninety point four."

Behind me, the exoskeletons began bunching up as they followed the same simple pathing logic toward me.

"Open the damn door before I break it down!" I yelled as the robotic murder squad closed in on my position.

"Abuse of cybernetic service entities is a breach of

the employee code of conduct," the door panel informed me. "A formal reprimand has been added to your personal record. You are required to attend two hours of behavioral improvement counseling prior to your next performance review."

The black exoskeleton swung an arm at me, forcing me to darted away as its blow smashed the door panel, then all ten exoskeletons jostled each other as they tried to catch me.

I jumped onto the bar to escape, then circled around the lounge setting, activating my communicator. "Jase, can you hear me?"

The hissing static of a jamming field filled my ears. It might have prevented the Chairman's competitors from eavesdropping on his business, but Mataron spy-tech would have cut right through it.

I pocketed my communicator as the exoskeletons followed me around the lounge chairs. The last machine, painted bright red, was now the closest. It led the pack after me as I ran to Ransford's desk hoping to use its commlink, but quickly discovered it required a bioscan to activate.

The red exoskeleton swung at me, shattering several of the fragile datapanes, forcing me to retreat toward the Tahitian holographic wall. A bright yellow exoskeleton moved to cut me off as I ran through photonic palm trees. It tried jabbing me, but I dodged, leaping clear as the blow punched a hole through the crystalline wall, cracking the idyllic blue sky. White light flooded through from the other side, breaking the illusion as I raced back to the lounge suite and waited for the headless machines to come after me. They gave chase immediately, bunching up as I retreated behind the lounge chairs, then when the holographic beach was clear, I charged back toward the sea and hurled myself at the crystalline wall shoulder first. It shattered in a shower of supersiliconized shards, then I crashed through a second holowall on the other side and fell into the neighboring suite.

Surprised female screams filled the air as I rolled through a dense jungle, coming to rest in front of a white leopard which growled menacingly at me. I swept my hand through its holographic face, confirming it was an illusion, then jumped to my feet, watched by a room full of immaculately dressed socialites sipping cocktails, mostly older men and younger women. The suite was similar in size to the Chairman's, decorated with ice sculptures of exotic birds from a dozen worlds. Server trays floated between the guests offering drinks and hors-d'oeuvres while a twelve piece orchestra of Tau Cetin musicians played a late fortieth century symphony at one end of the room. It took me a moment to realize the orchestra was holographic, then the wall behind me exploded as ten exoskeletons came crashing through, setting off more startled cries from the party guests.

I ran through the crowd as the exoskeletons marched after me, scattering guests and floating server trays in their path. While screams filled the room, the holographic Tau Cetins played on obliviously, swaying in time to the music in a very non-TC way.

"Open," I yelled as I reached the entrance. This time, there was no argument. The double doors slid aside, then I darted through and turned to the exterior panel. "Close and lock, set password: no go."

"Confirmed. Password set," the panel replied.

There were no guards in the hall. The pair I'd seen outside the Pantheon Suite must have been exclusively for the Chairman's protection. Exoskeletons began hammering on the locked door as I headed for the guest elevator, peeling off my butler's coat and leaving it in the corridor.

"Jase, are you there?" I said into my communicator as the elevator arrived.

"Yes, Skipper."

"Get me out of here. Grab the first docking slot you can," I said, riding the elevator down one level.

"Will do."

I pocketed the communicator and stepped out onto the Upper Observation Deck. Alfresco cafes faced a floor to ceiling real time display of the river of super heated gas spiraling down onto the white dwarf's glowing accretion disk. Walking in front of the cafés were a pair of uniformed ship security men. They paid me no attention, so I mingled with passengers strolling along the boardwalk eyeballing the cosmic time bomb in the distance.

The fledgling supernova wasn't the only time bomb in the Duranis System. Somewhere out there was the *Mavia*, preparing to unleash its own catastrophe upon mankind – unless I could find a way to stop it.

* * * *

"We're heading in now," Jase's voice sounded in my ear as I took cover in the tropical garden beyond the hangar. I'd detoured several times to avoid the ship's uniformed security people who were now checking the identity of every man my height and build. Chairman Ransford had clearly ordered his toy soldiers to arrest me once he realized the exoskeletons had failed.

"On my way," I replied, starting toward the edge of the garden where I could see the infopanes outside the hangar entry. There were no uniforms in sight, then just as I was about to break cover, a small hand caught my shoulder. I spun around to find Anya Krol, the *Cyclops's* navigator, standing behind me dressed as if she'd just come from one of the swimming pools: minimal bathing suit, UV visor and wide brimmed hat over a scarf wrapped around her forehead like a bandanna hiding her commband. I almost didn't recognize her without her red armor and guns.

"You'll need this," she said, offering me a needler, small for my hand, just right for hers. "Twenty shots. Make them count."

"Thanks," I said uncertainly. "How'd you find me?"

"That airlock's the only one open for docking, the only way off the Aphrodite. Four of Trask's men are waiting for you in the hangar.

"No ship security?"

Anya shook her head. "They have orders to shoot you on sight, but not to enter the hangar." It was a kill zone and they'd been driving me toward it. She handed me a Pleasure Pass keyed to another identity. "This'll get you through the checkpoint without setting off alarms."

I pocketed the pass and the gun. "Why are you helping me?"

"Rix told me too," she said with a hint of irritation. "For some strange reason, he doesn't want you dead."

"Where's the Cyclops now?"

"Orbiting Duranis-B. They didn't want us spooking the tourists, so they made us park over there and use our launch. We'll be leaving as soon as I get back."

"Why didn't Rix come himself?"

She smiled sourly. "Because they're always watching him. They need us, but they don't trust us." She glanced down at her bathing suit. "I lost the two security men they had following me when I changed into this."

"Good disguise," I said trying not to stare at her near nakedness.

Her eyes narrowed suspiciously. "What are you to him?"

I realized my brother confided in no one, not even his most trusted lieutenant. "We crossed paths once, in another life."

"You're as big a liar as he is!" she said with simmering anger, not at me, but at Rix for not trusting her.

"Tell him Ransford's crazy if he thinks he can play the Matarons. Ransford's the one being manipulated."

She showed no surprise at the mention of the snakeheads. As navigator, she must have seen their ships when the *Cyclops* picked up the hijacked Kesarn-tech.

"They've done everything they said they would."

"Only because it's been in their interest. When this all falls apart, you don't want to be in the middle, because anyone helping the Matarons is going to end up dead."

"I'll tell him, but he won't listen," she said slowly, wondering what interest I had in Matarons. "You're not really a freighter captain, are you?"

"Sure I am. Ask anyone."

She gave me a dubious look, knowing it was another lie, then slipped away into the garden. I gave her a few seconds to get clear, then strode past the water nymph fountain into the passageway leading to the hangar deck.

At the transparent pressure door, a polite synthetic voice said, "The captain and crew of the Aphrodite hope you enjoyed your visit, madam. Please come again soon."

Most of the technicians and their multi-armed maintenance bots ignored me as my sniffer area-scanned the hangar. A red warning indicator flashed into my mind, pointing to the right, outside my peripheral vision. I turned, drawing the needle gun and aiming at a man with a red targeting reticule framing his head. He wore a technician's uniform, but was pulling a JAG-40 from beneath his coat. I didn't remember him, but my sniffer did, from the *Merak Star*. His assault gun was halfway up when I fired, sending his head snapping back as the needle struck his forehead dead center. The clatter of his gun hitting the deck as he crumpled caught everyone's attention, warning the other mercs that I'd arrived.

I ran to the side of the hangar, using one of *Aphrodite's* guest transports for cover as a shot whizzed past my head and struck the bulkhead behind me. The engineers, realizing they were in the middle of a gun fight, fled to the workshop, crouching to avoid stray slugs.

"Skipper," Jase's voice sounded in my ear, "we're alongside. I don't have docking permission, so … hurry!"

"I'm almost there," I whispered, dropping flat to the deck to look under the hulls of the parked craft. Multiple pairs of boots were running for safety while one pair moved quietly the other way. Returning to a crouch, I crept alongside the transport, periodically checking beneath its hull. At its thrust nozzles, I stopped to listen. The hangar was quieter now and the hunters had gone to ground, waiting for me to show myself. Knowing time was on their side, I edged around the engines, then crept alongside a cargo ferry toward the taxiway that ran down the center of the hangar to the space doors.

"You're not getting out of here alive, Kade," a familiar voice called out. It was Julkka Olen, Trask's lieutenant who'd shattered my skull and left me for dead on the muddy streets of Nisport. "Give it up and I'll make it quick!"

My listener analyzed sound reflection and distance, calculating Olen was near the hangar's inner space door. He'd hidden himself where he could ambush me as I went for the airlock, forcing me to go after him first.

Halfway along the cargo ferry, my listener detected the faintest click of a boot on deck plating behind me. I crouched and turned toward the sound as a woman stepped around the ferry's tail section holding an assault gun at eye height. My first shot took her in the shoulder, knocking her aim off as she sent a burst of heavy slugs whizzing past my ear. My second shot drilled her throat, severing her spine, then she folded like a rag doll, gurgling blood as she hit the deck.

"You shouldn't have done that, Kade," Olen yelled, his voice ringing hollowly through the hangar. "Now I'm going to do you slow."

He was a talker. Maybe he thought it was psychological warfare. Maybe he liked to taunt his victims. What he didn't know was every time he spoke, my listener improved the accuracy of its location fix.

Hoping he'd continue blabbing and while I said nothing in return, I crept toward the ferry's bow. The last of the engineers were gone now, leaving the maintenance bots to carry on unsupervised and make occasional mechanical sounds that broke the silence of the hangar. When I reached the taxiway running through the center of the hangar, I listened for any sign of the fourth merc, wondering where he was hiding.

They were playing a waiting game and I was out of time. The Nortin platforms might not fire on the *Silver Lining* while she was hugging the *Aphrodite*, but the more time they had, the more chance there was they'd find a way to cripple her without damaging the starliner.

The taxiway was wide enough for one craft to get to the space door. That made it risky to cross, but Olen was on the other side with the airlock in his sights, leaving me no choice. I took a breath and sprinted across. When I was almost halfway, a shot rang out narrowly missing my chest and giving my listener a clue to its source. I immediately dived into the gap between two cargo lighters as a second shot struck one of their hulls.

The clink of a grenade bouncing on deck plates sounded behind me, then I threw myself under one of the lighters and rolled behind a landing strut. When the grenade exploded, shrapnel peppered the small transport's hull while the landing gear shielded me from the blast. With my ears still ringing, heavy boots began pounding the deck as the merc charged toward me, spraying my hiding place with his JAG-40. It was standard assault tactics: disorient with a grenade and charge. It was what he'd been trained to do, what he was good at – and it was a mistake. He should have waited, gone for a sniper kill shot from cover, but that wasn't his way.

It was mine.

I aimed at his boots, fired and missed and fired again, catching him in the ankle. He stumbled and fell, continuing to shoot as he hit the deck. Heavy slugs drilled the lighter's hull and ricocheted off its landing struts, then I put two needles into him above his chest armor. He coughed blood, then his assault gun clicked empty. I stole a quick look past the landing strut to where the Orie merc lay face down, motionless.

"Not bad, Kade," Olen yelled. "Too bad twenty just like him are on the way. We're going to have a party and you're invited!"

He was trying to flush me out, to get me to run for the airlock so he could pick me off. Olen was more patient than the others, and smarter. That's why he was Trask's lieutenant. Too bad he was also a talker and my listener had his position triangulated.

Slipping out from under the cargo lighter, I crept between the workshop and the parked spacecraft. At each vessel, I checked the hiding spaces ahead, matching them to my threading's target finder. Now that it was just down to the two of us, Olen had gone quiet, knowing I was stalking him, that my only way out was through him.

At one of *Aphrodite's* white and gold passenger shuttles, I paused beneath its thrust cone to listen. There were only two craft left between me and the space door and according to my threading, Olen should have been in front of me, but he wasn't. I began to wonder if he'd moved, if he'd drawn me into a killing zone with his chatter, then silently relocated to target me when I approached his old position. The hairs on the back of my neck began to prickle as I anticipated a heavy slug coming from the shadows, then my listener detected the merest rustling sound, causing me to freeze.

Olen was above me!

Now that I knew where to look, I spotted the very tip of a JAG-40 barrel protruding above the shuttle's port engine housing. It was a good sniper position, on top of the transport with an elevated view of the airlock. If I went back, the shuttle's hull would block my shot and if I went forward, he'd see me.

"Skipper, Where are you? Aphrodite control is threatening to blast us if I don't undock immediately!" Jase yelled into my ear.

Olen was so close, I didn't dare respond, even with a whisper. Instead, I climbed into the port engine's cone-shaped thrust nozzle and pulled myself silently over the upper side of the cone with one hand. I saw Olen's boots first, then discovered him lying on his stomach, sighting on the airlock. I brought Anya's small gun up over the edge of the thrust cone, considered putting one into the back of his skull, then wondered if he could help me find the *Mavia*. I knew roughly where the old depot ship was, but she was running on dark energy and I had no way to track her if she'd moved.

"Drop the gun!" I said.

Olen froze, not even turning his head. Slowly, he pushed the JAG-40 away, letting it slide down the side of the shuttle to the deck, then I pulled myself up onto the top of the engine nozzle.

"You're a dead man, Kade," Olen growled, turning to face me.

"You had your chance." He frowned, confused, then I added, "On Krailo-Nis, right before you killed Tiago Sorvino."

Olen looked puzzled, then he studied my face with growing realization. "You're him! That spacer! But I killed you!"

"You didn't kill me enough."

Finally, he figured it out. "You were his contact?"

"Now you're going to help me find the Mavia."

"The hell I am!" he growled, snatching a grenade from his belt.

I shot him in the head. "That's for Sorvino," I said grimly as his lifeless fingers opened, revealing a grenade with its detonator flashing. The silver metal sphere rolled from his hand and over the side of the hull as I jumped down into the shuttle's thrust cone. The grenade struck the deck and exploded, blasting a hole through the shuttle's side and spraying the thrust cone with shrapnel.

"Skipper!" Jase yelled urgently. "If I don't undock in the next thirty seconds–."

"That's all I need," I said into the communicator as I jumped onto the deck and ran to the airlock. As soon as I'd cycled through into the *Silver Lining*, I yelled into the communicator, "I'm aboard. Go!"

"Releasing Aphrodite," Jase said with audible relief. "Go where?"

"Duranis-B," I said, "then straight to Earth!"

Chapter Eight : Duranis-B

Type 1A Supernova Progenitor
White Dwarf Star, Duranis Binary
Evacuation Zone, Outer Draco
16.2 billion kilometers from Duranis-A
Uninhabited

We unbubbled in the blue ice giant's orbital wake, quickly spotting the *Mavia* with optics alone. The old depot ship was parked well beyond the harshest effects of the giant planet's immense gravity, clearly visible in the light of the white dwarf's swirling accretion disk. Above the *Mavia's* reinforced hull, the Hrane tunneler's curved arms were unfolding like the petals of a flower while the trunk of the tower slowly lengthened, moving the arms away from the ship.

"They're not wasting any time, are they?" Jase said, impressed at how fast the tower had been installed. "What is it?"

"Our ticket to Earth," I replied.

Izin sat behind us, watching with interest. "The tower appears to be stretching elastically."

"Quantum weirdness," I said as the tower's arms locked into place, forming a hemisphere a thousand meters across.

When the tower's apex was nine thousand meters from the *Mavia*, it stopped extending, fixing the entire structure rigidly in place. Electrical energy began leaping from the tunneler's arms toward the center of the imaginary sphere they cradled. Where the streams of lightning met, a brilliant point of light appeared, small at first, but growing rapidly, dimming as it inflated. Once it had expanded to half the width of the arms, a thin beam of sparkling blue light shot from the tower's needle-like apex up into the heart of the sphere, pouring exotic matter into the darkening wormhole mouth.

Izin turned to his control console and scrolled through one engineering screen after another studying the nascent wormhole. "It's emitting powerful gravity waves."

"It's creating a micro-singularity," I said.

The sphere continued to expand, filling three quarters of the space between the arms and darkening to an inky blackness.

"Spacetime is collapsing sharply toward the center of the sphere," Izin reported.

"You seriously want to fly into that thing?" Jase asked anxiously.

"Do you know a faster way to Earth?" I replied as a pair of navigation beacons blinked on at either end of the *Mavia*, emitting red beams that crossed above the dark sphere. "That's our entry point."

"Theoretically, a wormhole sphere can be entered from any angle," Izin said.

"Except we don't want to fly through the tower's arms or the exotic matter," I said, deciding to play it safe.

"The gravity's increasing exponentially. Unless you want a long run in, Captain, we need to go now."

"Right!" Minimum safe distance for a bubble, even a sub-second one, was being pushed steadily away from the *Mavia* by the micro-singularity's gravity.

"The Cyclops is out there!" Jase exclaimed. "She's way over toward the edge of the system."

I glanced across at his sensor screen. The *Cyclops* was hiding on low power, waiting for her launch to return.

"She might come after us," Izin said, "once they see us approach the Mavia."

"No, she won't protect Separatist ships." My brother had made that abundantly clear during the meeting on the *Aphrodite*. "Ignore her, she's not interested in us and she won't fight for them."

I took one last look at the long range sensors, reassuring myself the Super Saracen fleet had not yet arrived, then we blinked to a point twenty thousand kilometers above the *Mavia*. The wormhole mouth lay in the center of our screen, flanked by the old depot ship's bow and stern beyond. She was protected by a military grade defense shield that extended several hundred meters from her hull while her sides appeared to curve and grow brighter amidships. It was an optical trick caused by the wormhole's gravity, bending and amplifying light coming off the *Mavia's* hull like a lens.

"We'll be a sitting duck if she starts shooting," Jase said apprehensively.

"She won't. The Mavia's unarmed. Big shield, no

guns," I said, diving the *Silver Lining* toward the intersecting beacons at full power.

"And an enormous acceleration field," Izin added, studying his console. "It's offsetting the singularity's gravity."

"Can our fields handle the singularity?" Jase asked.

"Once they finish tunneling, they'll shut it down." I turned back to Izin. "When we make our run, record everything, all the way to the Solar System."

"What for?"

So I could pass the data to Lena for the boffins on Earth to study until their heads exploded. "I know people who'd pay a fortune for that data."

"Very well, Captain."

The wormhole's black sphere was rapidly filling our wraparound screen, framed by lightning streaming from the Hrane tower's cradling arms, revealing a single blurry dot directly ahead.

"What's that light?" Jase asked.

Izin took a moment to answer. "The microsingularity's gravity is lensing light from the other side through the opening in the exotic matter. I can correct for the distortion." After a moment, the point of light expanded into a field of stars with a large golden orb at its center.

"Is that what I think it is?" I asked.

"Yes, Captain. That's Earth's sun."

"We've got company!" Jase declared. "It's a Super Saracen, no transponder, directly behind us. Make that two! Three!"

In the next few seconds, thirty two Super Saracens appeared with Earth Navy precision in line ahead formation, already on a trajectory aimed at the wormhole entrance. Aligning their entire fleet with the wormhole while in another system was some fancy navigation. It showed how well they'd mastered the kind of formation flying nav-tech Earth Navy used.

We'd seen some of the Super Saracens at Acheron, most we had not. As soon as they'd all arrived, they began accelerating toward the wormhole at a stately five g's, showing they preferred keeping formation to a fast transit. We had a minute's head start and were accelerating seven times faster, but I was planning to roll and decelerate down at the halfway point. Having no idea what was inside the wormhole, I couldn't risk diving into it at high velocity. I wanted to creep through slow enough to maneuver, if required.

"We'll reach the wormhole fourteen minutes ahead of them," Izin said, "assuming they start braking halfway."

"That'll keep us out of weapons range long enough to get off a warning to Earth Navy," I said.

"Suppose they don't believe us?" Jase said unconvinced. "You know how stubborn those navy types are."

"They've never seen a wormhole before. They'll listen." And I had a recognition code up my sleeve that would set alarm bells ringing all the way to Earth. "We'll have front row seats when Earth Navy blasts those Super Saracens to bits," followed by nearly eight months bubbled up to get back out here the old fashioned way.

"Perhaps not, Captain," Izin said slowly, transfixed by his console. "The gravity waves emanating from the wormhole are not diminishing. They're increasing."

We could see Earth's Sun, proving the tunneling was complete. "They should be shutting it down," I said, puzzled.

"The exotic matter has stabilized the wormhole, Captain, but the micro-singularity is blocking the exit mouth."

Damned tamphs, always spoiling the party.

"They're trying to stop us going through!" Jase declared.

"The Mavia shows no sign of even knowing we're here," Izin said. "We're a small target and interference from the tower is hiding us from them."

"Why is the gravity increasing?" I asked uneasily.

Izin's slender fingers ran over his console with lightning speed. Suddenly, he froze in an instinctive ambush predator response to danger. If he didn't move, his enemy couldn't see him.

"Izin?" I said, trying to snap him out of it. "What is it?"

He breathed again. "The stars on the other side, and the Sun, are not where they should be. The wormhole's in the wrong place!"

"Where is it?" I demanded.

Izin touched his console, throwing an astrographics overlay onto the main screen. "The exit mouth is here." The dark sphere was on one side of the screen and the blue-green orb of Earth was on the other.

"You calculated it wrong!"

"There's no error, Captain."

"They're attacking Earth?" Jase asked incredulously.

"Earth's defenses would blast those ships the moment they appeared," I said, confident Earth was safe from a fleet attack by a mere thirty two cruisers – even a surprise attack.

"Their fleet can't attack Earth," Izin said calmly. "The micro-singularity is blocking the exit mouth. Any ship attempting to use the wormhole will be destroyed. Us and them!"

That wasn't what Trask, the Chairman or the Separatist Leaders had in mind when they'd planned this little party. "How close to Earth is the wormhole?"

Izin studied his console a moment. "Twenty two thousand kilometers outside Earth's orbit."

I relaxed. "At least Earth's not going to hit it."

Izin ran a flood of calculations through his mind in the blink of his amphibian eyes. "It's not a collision, Captain, it's a slingshot. The micro-singularity's gravity is radiating from the wormhole mouth like a giant planet, close enough to perturb Earth's orbit."

Oh crap! "By how much?"

Izin's attention returned to his console as he directed the *Lining's* processing core to crunch the mechanics. "Earth's new orbit will be highly elliptical. Aphelion will be over three hundred million kilometers from the Sun, well beyond the orbit of Mars."

"Earth will freeze!" Jase exploded.

"That's the idea," I said ominously, for the first time seeing what was really happening. The Matarons weren't backing the Separatists, they were manipulating them, not to break away from Earth, but to destroy it!

They'd tricked everyone: the Consortium, the Brotherhood, the Core Worlds, even me. It would look like we stole technology we didn't understand and used it to accidentally destroy our own homeworld! No one would be able to blame the Matarons because everyone would believe we'd done it to ourselves. The Galactic Forum would have no choice but to rule against us, to isolate the survivors for their own protection, saving us from ourselves. It was clear cut. The Fourth Principle of the Access Treaty gave each species a right to develop in its own way except – second exception – when facing self inflicted extinction!

Forum intervention was not only permitted, it was *required!*

With the exit mouth blocked, we couldn't get through the wormhole, but that no longer mattered because there was nothing we could do on the other side. The real threat was this side, where the micro-singularity was being generated. Without waiting for the autonav to plot a new course, I immediately rolled the *Silver Lining* one eighty degrees, angling past the tower toward the *Mavia* as we began decelerating.

Jase gave me a surprised look. "We're not halfway yet."

"We have to brake now so our acceleration fields have something left to offset the singularity's gravity when we get there."

Jase's eyes widened, then he nodded. "Glad you thought of that!" he said with relief, realizing the alternative was to be crushed as we neared the wormhole.

"Scan the tower. Find out what it's made of."

Jase studied his console briefly. "Nothing our sensors can identify."

Considering the energies the tower was channeling, it was almost certainly impervious to our proton burster, which left only the *Mavia* herself. Like all navy ships, she was ruggedly built with reinforced double hulls and honeycomb bulkheads, as well as a heavy shield – and us with no drones.

"Two Super Saracens just powered up!" Jase said. "They're breaking formation, coming after us, pulling high-g's!"

"Izin, what do you know about wormholes?" I asked.

"Very little, Captain. If you'd wanted me to become an expert in wormhole dynamics, you should have told me – yesterday."

"I know one thing," I said. "They can't survive without exotic matter. So if we turn off the tap …"

"It'll collapse," Jase said. "Great idea, except that ship is crawling with guys from my home planet, guys with big guns and itchy fingers. They're not going to let you walk in there and flick a switch."

"I wasn't planning on walking. I prefer to ride." I turned to Izin. "Did you fix those battle suits you borrowed from General Trask?"

"I've restored pressurization and recharged their power cells, Captain, but I couldn't replenish their magazines."

"They have enough ammo for what I have in mind."

"They won't let us dock," Jase said. "You'll have to jump."

"We've had practice at that, haven't we Izin!" I said with a grin, glancing back at my tamph engineer. "We'll park alongside, then kick in the door."

Izin slipped off his acceleration couch. "I'll be in the cargo hold preparing the battle suits," he said as he hurried off the flight deck.

"He's excited," I said. "I don't let him off the leash very often."

"How can you tell?"

"It's the way his eyes scrunch up at the sides."

Jase gave me a doubtful look. "His eyes don't do that!"

I shrugged. "There must be some way to know what he's thinking."

Jase sobered. "Someone's signaling us."

"From where?" According to our sensors, there

were no ships close by.

"Seventy meters to starboard," Jase said surprised, then opened a channel.

The astrographic projection on the main screen was replaced by Gern Vrate's face. "My people are on that ship, Kade."

"I figured they were."

The only way the *Mavia* could be powering the Hrane tunneler was with the siphons and they needed to be close to their Kesarn symbiotes to function.

"I'm going aboard to get them," Vrate said simply.

"That wormhole's threatening my homeworld."

"I know."

"I'm going to do whatever it takes to shut it down."

"I would do the same."

"Just so we understand each other."

"I will protect my people," Vrate said, then his face vanished from the screen.

"Who's side is that guy on?" Jase demanded.

"His own." It was one thing we had in common.

Jase's attention was drawn back to his sensors. "Four more ships just arrived."

"How close?"

"They're a long way out, over a billion clicks. The transponders are faint, coming in now." When the call signs appeared on his personal screen, his eyes widened in surprise. "They're navy ships! The frigates Nassau and Delhi, the heavy destroyer Kirishima, and ... a battle cruiser! The Vigilant. What's she doing out here? What are any of them doing here?"

So, Gern Vrate wasn't quite the hardass he made out. I'd told Jase and Izin everything about my meeting with the Kesarn tracer, except my request that he give Lena Voss my destination. And from the looks of the navy squadron, Lena had told me only what I needed to know – keeping the fact she was joyriding in an Earth Navy battle cruiser a secret. Even so, her squadron was heavily outgunned by the Separatist fleet.

"Trust the navy to turn up when you need them most!" I said, converting their distance to light minutes.

The navy ships had taken up position between both Duranis stars, giving them room to study the two systems before committing to either one. My spirits sank when I realized they'd only just be receiving the *Silver Lining's* transponder signal from when we were alongside the *Aphrodite*, making Lena believe we were still in the red giant system. She wouldn't see us in our present position for at least another hour – the time it took our current emissions to reach her location!

By then, it would be all over.

* * * *

The flight deck screen was split into fore and aft perspectives, with the wormhole mouth on one side and the two Super Saracens racing to catch us on the other. The rest of the Separatist Fleet had rolled as one and were now decelerating, showing they were as cautious about flying through the wormhole as I was. Beyond the wormhole was the *Mavia*, its image greatly magnified by strong gravitational lensing from the singularity. Inside the *Silver Lining*, our internal acceleration fields were performing a delicate juggling act, counteracting the heavy gravity spilling from the wormhole while offsetting what little was left of our own deceleration.

"They're entering weapons range," Jase warned, "closing *real* fast!"

"Shield up," I said, bringing our battle shield online as the two converted merchant cruisers entered extreme range. Unlike us and the rest of the Separatist Fleet, they hadn't rolled to decelerate, but were bearing down toward us with engines straining at full power, following a course aiming to pass the wormhole rather than enter it. They were using their acceleration toward the wormhole to offset the pull of the micro-singularity's gravity, reducing the strain on their inertial fields and allowing them to accelerate at a rate far beyond what they would normally have been capable of. It was a clever move that would send them hurtling past us so fast they'd only have a moment to fire, followed by a long braking run once they were past the *Mavia*, but it would give them time enough to wreck the *Silver Lining*.

"Why aren't they shooting?" Jase asked. "It doesn't get any better than this."

"They're going to hit us as they fly by so there's no risk of damaging the Mavia," I said. No matter how good our shield was, it couldn't stand up to the combined firepower of two cruisers at point blank range.

"Charge up the burster," I said, certain our single cannon's expensive capacitor insulation would prevent the Super Saracens from seeing us prepare to fire. Unfortunately, its short range would force us to wait until we were on top of the tower – the same time they were on top of us. Our only hope was to maneuver, but fighting the pull of the wormhole, it would take everything we had just to keep the ship under control.

Or did control matter? I wondered, then ran a quick theoretical for an idea I had through the autonav.

"I know that look," Jase said warily. "What are you thinking?"

"Trust me," I said, ordering the autonav to plot the specifics.

"Now I'm really worried!"

We were heading for open space starboard of the *Mavia*, while the two Super Saracens were on a parallel course that would ensure they gave the tower's arms and the depot ship's big shield a wide berth. Hoping to put as much room between us and the cruisers as possible, I angled the *Silver Lining* in close to the tower's nearest arm, putting us on a collision course with the *Mavia's* upper works.

"Skipper," Jase said anxiously, "that's too close."

"No, it's just right," I replied as we plunged stern-first toward the tower arm and the separatist cruisers grew rapidly in size, their main weapons glowing hot.

"Plot a firing solution on the closest tower arm," I said, letting Jase handle weapons while I focused on flying. "Don't let the mount rotate until the last second." I didn't want to spook the Super Saracens and have them start shooting early.

"Ready," Jase said after he plugged in the targeting instructions.

The dark curve of the wormhole mouth now filled one side of the screen, fed by a stream of lightning pouring from the arm almost dead ahead.

"Skipper! More thrust!" Jase said as a collision warning sounded.

"Less is more," I said throttling down our main engines.

Jase eyes bulged when he saw what I was doing. "Skipper! We're too close! We're going to hit!"

We swept toward the tower arm, pulled in by the micro-singularity's gravity, then I said, "Rotate and fire."

Jase released the burster. Its turret mount swiveled

and unleashed a high intensity proton blast that would have punched a hole through most ship hulls. A ball of white energy momentarily enveloped the tower's arm then quickly faded harmlessly away.

"No damage!" Jase said.

When the tower arm filled our screen, I let the autonav take control. It immediately yawed the *Lining's* bow away from the wormhole, aiming our engine thrust at the singularity, fighting its gravity. We balanced on a tightrope, skating alongside the arm, following its curve down, pulled sideways by the wormhole's gravity as the Super Saracens swept up to us.

"They're firing!" Jase warned.

Rapid energy blasts flashed at us from the separatist cruisers, curving off course at the last moment toward the wormhole, grazing our shield and either striking the tower or flying on through to vanish into the dark sphere cradled in the tower's arms. Before the Super Saracens could adjust for their mistake, they hurtled past the *Mavia* while we were thrown sideways above her upper works. When we passed out over the depot ship's port side, the two Super Saracens were already out of range, rolling to decelerate, but it was all too late. I resumed piloting control from the autonav and fired the maneuvering engines, killing our velocity and sending us back toward the *Mavia* while Jase stared at the screen with an open mouth.

"A gravity assist?"

It was the oldest trick in the celestial mechanics handbook, I'd used the micro-singularity's gravity to perform a ninety degree course change, pulling us away from the Super Saracens just as they fired. The same effect that threatened to destroy Earth had saved us. "More than that," I said. "The curved space around the wormhole deflected their shots, like rolling cannon balls down a hill."

Jase looked at me incredulously. "The singularity screwed up their targeting!"

"Our burster only hit the arm because we were so close," I added.

The screen hissed with static briefly as we pushed through the *Mavia's* shield, then we leveled off and began gliding towards the Hrane tower emerging from the center of the depot ship.

"You could have warned me," Jase said.

"And missed that look of sheer terror on your face. Not a chance," I said, gratified by his scowl.

We skimmed the *Mavia's* upper works for a few more seconds, then nosed over her side and angled for the airlock nearest the Hrane tower. The closer we got to her hull, the more the old depot ship's oversized acceleration field enveloped us, nullifying the singularity's gravity, making flying easier.

When we stood barely fifty meters from the *Mavia's* port side, I said, "Blast that lock open."

There were ten airlocks on each side, each above a rectangular cargo door once used to resupply and repair docked navy ships. Depending on the pressure discipline inside the *Mavia*, ripping open an airlock might have no effect or it might cause ship wide explosive decompression. Before our burster had fully charged, all ten port side airlocks opened together.

"Are they surrendering?" Jase asked, surprised.

"Unlikely."

An incoming signal, audio only, forced its way onto the flight deck. "Hold your fire, Kade," Gern Vrate ordered, "or you'll kill my people."

I couldn't tell where the signal was coming from, but he had to be watching us from somewhere close,

close enough to override the Mavia's docking system.

"Power down the burster," I said, "and rotate it away from the Mavia."

Jase did as I asked, then Vrate's voice sounded again.

"Wise decision," he said in a way that left me in no doubt, his finger was on the trigger and we were in his sights.

"Now what?" Jase asked.

I slipped off my acceleration couch. "You take her. When we're suited up, open the belly door."

Jase nodded. "I'll keep you posted on the position of the Super Saracen fleet."

"You're not staying."

"I'm not?" Jase asked surprised.

"You're going to find those Earth Navy ships and bring them here."

It might take an hour for our neutrino emissions to reach Lena's squadron, but Jase could fly out there in a fraction of a second and tell her where the action was.

He glanced at his tracking console. The Earth Navy squadron was still there, or they had been, an hour ago. "What if they've moved?"

"They won't leave Duranis. If they're not there, bubble around until you find them. If the wormhole's still up when you get back, tell them to destroy the Mavia. Ignore the Super Saracens. Kill the wormhole."

Jase hesitated. "What about you and Izin?"

"Send us a warning, but don't wait for us."

He opened his mouth to protest.

"It's Earth," I said, cutting him off. "And every second counts!"

Jase nodded soberly. "OK, Skipper."

"We've got the battle suits. We'll make it, but if

we don't, the Lining's all yours." I gave him an encouraging wink. "Treat her like a lady."

* * * *

The battle suit sealed shut around me, this time without the hiss of escaping air, proof Izin had patched the hole behind my neck. The interior had been cleaned of blood spatters, the power cell fully charged and the suppressor still showed plenty of ammo.

"No holes this time," I said over the communicator. "At least my eyes won't pop."

"Being exposed to space is the least of your worries, Captain," Izin said as his suit came to life.

"Depressurizing the cargo hold," Jase informed us, then moments later, a rectangular section of deck hinged down into space revealing the gray hulled *Mavia* floating nearby. Each of her airlocks had large white numbers painted beside them, eleven to twenty.

"Jump for sixteen," I said.

"Do you want me to control both suits?" Izin asked.

"Not this time." I replied as we moved down the ramp on magnetized boots to the edge. "I was wondering, with all the gravity that micro-singularity's pumping out, are we being hit with time dilation?"

"That's a surprisingly insightful question, Captain, coming from you," Izin replied, ever the master of wrapping praise and insult together.

"I thought so," I said accepting the compliment, ignoring the tamph condescension.

"The acceleration fields, ours and the Mavia's, are offsetting the singularity's gravity. The only time dilation we're experiencing is what we'd get on Earth."

"Right, one gravity. OK! Glad we got that sorted,

now let's go shut this alien monstrosity down before it turns Earth into an ice cube."

Izin pushed off, gliding toward airlock sixteen with barely a flicker from his thruster. When he'd almost reached the *Mavia*, I demagnetized my boots and kicked off after him. I soon found flying one of these tin robots was harder than it looked as I feathered the thruster one way then another, overcorrecting each time. It was certainly nothing like bouncing around in zero-g in a low mass pressure suit.

Izin drifted into the airlock's dark circular cavity, while I prepared myself for a gentle collision with the hull close to the airlock entrance. Just as I struck, Izin's armored arm pinned my leg to the hull, preventing me from bouncing off, then I floated in beside him and was caught by the *Mavia's* artificial gravity. He then moved to the airlock controls while I glanced back to the *Silver Lining*. Her belly door was already closed and she was backing slowly away.

"Jase, we're in," I said. "Get going."

"Aye aye, Skipper. I'll be back with the cavalry in no time."

The *Silver Lining* turned on her length, then her engines glowed to life, pushing her into the *Mavia's* shield. An aura of static electricity sparkled around her as her shield interacted with the *Mavia's*, then as soon she was clear, she streaked away toward Lena's last known position.

Izin sealed the outer hatch, then when the inner door irised open, my battle suit was suddenly struck by multiple high velocity impacts, knocking me against the outer door. My headscreen's tactical overlay lit up with hostile contact markers, all crammed together in the blacked out corridor beyond the inner door. Points of blue light twinkled in the darkness, marking the electromagnetic muzzle flashes of the assault guns raking my suit. I rolled sideways, trying to regain my balance as a headscreen indicator began ticking down, warning that my suit armor was being shredded. In the cramped airlock, all I could do was turn my side armor to the incoming torrent of fire, spreading the damage, then a malfunction indicator flashed, warning that the suit's thruster pack had been destroyed.

Izin stood to the side of the inner hatch out of the line of fire. He raised his left arm, sent three fragmentation grenades on low trajectories into the corridor and immediately resealed the hatch. Three muffled explosions sounded a moment later, then he opened the inner door to smoke and silence and a corridor littered with shattered bodies.

"We appear to have lost the advantage of surprise," Izin observed dryly as he raised his suppressor and stepped into the corridor. His tamph instincts would have preferred to ambush our adversaries rather than go head to head.

"I guess you'll have to fight like a human this time," I said, following him into the corridor as my suit warned almost half its frontal armor had been ablated.

"I may not like frontal assaults, Captain, but you will not find me lacking," he replied, raising both weapon arms as he moved to the left.

I took the right side, stepping over bodies shredded by Izin's grenades, aiming my weapons down the corridor. Both suits were equipped with rapid fire, magnetically accelerated suppressors, each capable of delivering ten thousand rounds of hurt with computerized precision. Our secondary weapons were different. Izin had a thirty round grenade launcher, I had a laser cannon that drained my suit's power cell at a frightening rate. Being sensor linked, we each saw everything both suits detected, and while these armor coated widow makers could drop from orbit and deliver death and destruction wherever they landed, I was beginning to realize they were too large for fighting in confined spaces.

At the end of the corridor was a locked pressure door. My target finder quickly located its locking points, which my laser cannon sliced through like tin foil. Izin kicked the door, sending it flying into a large darkened compartment, then fired a salvo of grenades, evenly spaced, left to right. He waited for them to detonate, then stepped through and moved left, immediately coming under fire. I followed close on his metallic heels, going right, drawing ranged fire that sparkled like blue fire flies in the darkness.

The Orie mercs concentrated on our torsos, trying to ablate our chest armor for a kill shot. Our suits' thermal sensors detected their body heat while our optics tracked the flash of their weapons. Twenty six threat prioritized targets appeared in front of my eyes, half allocated to me, half to Izin. They wore heavier body armor than the troops that had greeted us at the airlock and had some cover, making Izin's grenades less effective. Our suits calculated who were more accurate and bumped the expert gunners to the top of the priority list. Izin ignored his suit's helpful advice, choosing instead to sweep the left side of the room with his suppressor, laying waste to everything in his path. I took the other route, firing short bursts at targets prioritized by the suit's combat system, conserving my ammo. I held back on the laser cannon, saving the juice in case we ran into something the suppressors couldn't handle.

Ten seconds after we entered, the only ones left standing were us. The room was now lit by burning equipment and strewn with bodies. The compartment had once been a machine shop for fabricating replacement parts for Earth Navy ships. Now it was a support facility for the *Mavia* in its new guise as a wormhole generator ship. A single vehicle door dominated the opposite bulkhead, showing signs it had been augmented with slab armor. Capital ships were built with armored citadels at their heart to protect critical sections, but I'd never heard of a repair ship being fitted with one. A small hand torch lay on the deck in front of the door, beneath thin black scars where someone had tried cutting through.

Izin fired a grenade at the armored door, which exploded on contact, doing no damage.

"I've got this," I said, clanking toward the armored door and switching my laser cannon from pulse to beam. I fired a pencil thin stream of white energy at the top of the door and began carving a horizontal line across it. Black smoke billowed into the air as molten metal flowed onto the deck and my suit's power level began dropping steadily.

Leaving me to my work, Izin marched to various open hatches and scanned for threats. When he'd finished his sweep, he said, "There's no one close, Captain, but I can hear movement."

"Maybe the crew's abandoning ship before we blow it up," I suggested.

Izin took up position beside me, aiming his weapons at the pressure door as I began cutting back up to my starting point. When I finished, with half my suit's power supply gone, he pushed the rectangular slab through to the other side. It crashed onto the deck with a horrendous clang, telling everyone where we were, but rather than inviting another hail of gunfire, we were met by an empty corridor, pitch black except for a distant flickering light.

Izin stepped through, weapons raised, then declared, "It's deserted, Captain."

I followed him through into a vehicle passageway immersed in darkness. It led to a blacked out intersection, then onto a large compartment at the center of the ship, the source of the flickering light. Izin moved quickly, almost recklessly, along the wide passageway, forcing me to hurry to keep up. The little tamph might not like frontal assaults, but when he had to, he preferred speed over caution. He paused at the intersection only long enough to scan both directions, then started across with me a few paces behind.

My headscreen suddenly flashed, then the visual feed broke into static and the tactical overlay began blinking erratically with meaningless symbols. No diagnostics popped up advising me whether it was a malfunction or jamming, but the suit's combat system was clearly scrambled. The only indicator that made any sense was the suit's power level and it was falling fast, threatening to trap me inside a metal coffin.

I slammed my chin onto the emergency release as my suit power flat lined, just in time for it to half open before freezing. The headscreen blacked out as unpowered pressure fields collapsed around my body, turning my suit into tonnes of scrap metal which toppled face first onto the deck with a thunderous crash. The unpowered suit was too heavy for me to open by hand, so I twisted my shoulders until I could squeeze my left arm across my chest to a small lever at my right shoulder. I started rocking the lever furiously, slowly cranking the clamshell torso open. When it was wide enough for me to squeeze through, I flopped out onto the deck, relieved to have escaped.

A glowing silver disk floated a meter above me,

humming and spinning as it bathed the suit in a narrow cone of light. I rolled away into the darkness, keeping the suit between me and the end of the corridor, determined to get my gun away from the disk before it too was drained of power.

DEVICE UNKNOWN, my threading informed me as I drew my P-50.

Izin's battle suit was still standing, a metallic statue beneath another disk the twin of the one that had knocked out my suit without firing a shot. Beyond the junction, my threading picked up a small thermal signature retreating toward the distant compartment. The red ghost was far too small for a Mataron or even a man. For a moment, I thought it was a child, then I caught a glimpse of its silhouette against the light coming from the compartment.

It was a *tamph*!

I shouldn't have been surprised the Consortium were recruiting tamphs. They were smarter than us and with the right training would make the best possible engineers for the Consortium's stolen alien-tech, once their Mataron instructor was gone. I could have tried for a shot, but I remembered how deadly Izin's aim was and ducked behind my fighting suit's torso as a streak of light flashed through the space my head had occupied a moment before. My threading then flashed another alert into my mind's eye:

WARNING! HIGH ENERGY PLASMA DISCHARGE, TECHNOLOGY UNKNOWN.

Another blast hit the suit as I made myself into as small a target as possible. I resisted the urge to return fire, certain the tamph was baiting me just as Izin would have done. More blasts hit the suit's legs, then the firing stopped. I brought my P-50 up, preparing to shoot in case the tamph was closing in for the kill, then

I noticed its power level was down a third. Even in the dark, the disk was draining it. Before my eyes, its charge dropped another tick, then I blasted the disk, shattering it with a single shot.

Now only the light from the disk above Izin's suit illuminated the junction, enough for an eagle eyed tamph to drill me the moment I left cover. Tamphs were infinitely patient, and this one had more time to spare than me. I raised my P-50 as if to fire blind, knowing if the tamph was waiting to ambush me, I'd lose my gun and probably my hand, but no shot came. Relieved to discover my hand was still attached to my arm, I stole a look up the corridor. There was no flash of a weapon, no silhouette, no ghostly infra red blur from my threading's optics. The tamph had retreated, perhaps summoned by his Mataron master.

I blasted the second disk, then darted across to Izin's suit, using it for cover. A hairline crack ran down its side, showing it had no more than unlocked before dying.

"Izin, can you hear me?"

"Yes, Captain. I can't open the suit."

"There's a lever beside your right shoulder. Twist and grab it with your left arm."

Soon I heard a rapid creaking sound, then the torso slowly opened. I could do nothing to help as the suit was too heavy and without power, the clamshell machinery was locked tight. When it was two thirds open, Izin climbed out and dropped to the deck beside me.

"Left the eject a little late, did we?" I asked.

"I was trying to block the power drain," Izin replied defensively.

"You were over thinking the problem."

"You, of course, ejected at the first sign of

trouble."

"Let's just chalk that one up to superior human survival instincts over excessive tamph tinkering."

"I do not tinker, Captain, and I'll let you know, my survival instincts are in no way inferior to yours."

"Then how come you were trapped like a sardine and I wasn't?" I asked with a grin. Before he could answer, I added, "Speaking of tamphs, there's one on this ship. He knocked out our suits."

Izin glanced at the two wrecked disks on the deck. "That's not Earth-tech."

"Neither's the gun he's using." I nodded to the shallow craters pockmarking my suit where the tamph's plasma weapon had vaporized the Union Army's finest ablation armor. "The Consortium are turning stealing alien-tech into an art form."

"It appears the Tau Cetins had more cause to interrogate me than we believed," Izin said soberly, ever able to focus on the truth, no matter how painful.

"Let's give them cause to trust you," I said, determined that the tamph traitor was not getting off the *Mavia* alive.

We started forward, creeping through the shadows toward the electrostatic hum coming from the enormous compartment at the end of the passage. It had once been the industrial center of the depot ship, a veritable mobile space dock that could be carried to the furthest reaches of Mapped Space. Now stripped of its human equipment, the circular base of the Hrane tower occupied the center of the cavernous chamber. Its trunk reached up through the *Mavia's* hull all the way to the wormhole mouth nine kilometers above.

Surrounding the quantum tunneler were four structures. Three were dark energy siphons surrounded by glowing white fields, each emitting a brilliant white energy beam into a receptor in the deck below, twins of the machine on Gern Vrate's ship. The hemispherical siphons floated off the deck, held in place by pressure fields, while a few meters from each siphon were rectangular cryochambers similar to the one I'd seen aboard the *Merak Star* on Novo Pantanal. Each held a Kesarn in hydrothermic suspension, alive enough to allow the Tau Cetin siphons to drain limitless energies from the universe. They stood at three corners of a square, with the fourth corner empty. The empty corner was where Gern Vrate's siphon had been meant to go, but clearly three were enough to operate the tunneler.

Standing in front of the tower and its three dark energy siphons was a bank of transparent chambers filled with exotic matter. The first chamber was two thirds full. Its glowing contents were being fed up through the center of the tower into the wormhole mouth, where it stabilized the hyperspace tunnel's fragile throat against the tremendous crushing forces pushing against it. Display screens lined the bulkheads on either side, filled with images of curved space, wormhole mouths, gravitational tides and a storm of chaotic forces fighting to collapse a perversion of celestial geometry that refused to buckle. One screen showed the micro-singularity itself, whose mere presence threatened the survival of all life on Earth.

Below the screens were consoles and human sized seats, all empty. Inok a'Rtor, the Mataron scientist from the *Merak Star*, stood in front of one console, busily making adjustments. He wore a Mataron energy weapon strapped to his chest and a loose fitting pressure suit, but showed no sign of a skin shield. The tamph traitor would have told him we were here, but with victory so close and with Earth about to be flung to a freezing death, he couldn't abandon his post – not

363

yet.

Not far from the consoles, three human technicians lay side by side, face down on the deck amid a converging pool of blood. They'd each been shot in the back of the head, execution style, gruesome proof the Matarons had double-crossed the Consortium. Once the human scientists had realized the wormhole exit mouth was in the wrong place and the singularity was not dissipating, the Mataron had eliminated them.

I realized the armored door I'd cut through hadn't been sealed against Izin and me, but to lock out the *Mavia's* human crew. It left the Mataron scientist and his tamph lackey free to do as they pleased, securely encased inside the ship's armored citadel. With all power coming from the dark energy siphons, they could control the *Mavia* from here. It was why the old depot ship's passageways had been immersed in darkness and why her crew had desperately tried cutting through the door with a feeble hand torch.

I pulled back into the shadows and whispered to Izin. "One Mataron. Three dead humans. No sign of the tamph."

"The tamph has moved."

"How do you know?"

"It's what I'd do."

I couldn't argue with that. "How long have we got?"

"He'll strike when he's ready, when he can win, not before."

"OK, we kill the Mataron, blow the ship and get out of here. We'll deal with the tamph when he shows himself."

"How do we get off the ship, Captain? The suits are dead."

"They must have lifeboats."

"This is a big ship and there are still crew aboard. Even if we find the lifeboats in time, the crew may not want to share."

"If you've got a better idea, I'm listening."

Izin hesitated. "Considering our homeworld is about to be destroyed, your plan will suffice."

Our homeworld! He really was a Terran, a Terran Amphibian. "Told you human survival instincts were superior to tamph's."

"If that were true, Captain, we wouldn't be in this situation. The Matarons would not have deceived my people the way they deceived yours."

It was probably true, but the Intruders had millions of years on *Homo sapiens*. "At least we're not at war with half the galaxy," I said, stealing another look into the siphon room, finding the Mataron was no longer visible. I pulled back quickly as a flash from his blast pistol almost took off my face.

"Earth's destruction's now on autopilot," I said. "He's just got to hold us off."

"Keep his attention, Captain. I'll find another way around," he said, vanishing into the darkness.

I fired blindly into the compartment, just to let the snakehead know I was still here, pulling back as another blast flashed past. After a few seconds, I dropped to one knee and let off another unaimed shot from close to the deck. It took the Mataron a moment to adjust before a blast scorched the deck plate in front of me. Black Sauria or not, this Mataron egghead could shoot.

Hoping to track the snakehead by sound, I cranked my listener's gain to full, but all I heard was the static hiss of the siphons – which gave me an idea. I fired once at the nearest siphon from waist height, but the stasis field surrounding it caught my slug harmlessly, then as I pulled back, a shot from the Mataron struck the bulkhead beside me.

"Worth a try," I muttered to myself, now certain a P-50 slug was no match for the universe's near-infinite supply of dark energy.

I considered running into the compartment, wondering if my ultra-reflexed speed would be enough to get me to cover before the Mataron shot me. There was a lot of open deck to cross, but fortunately, Izin's voice sounded in my earpiece, saving me from testing the reptilian's aim.

"Fire one shot, Captain,"

I let off a blind snap shot, narrowly avoiding a return blast, then I heard a single distant shot – Izin's shredder – followed by a guttural groan.

"Izin?"

"I have him, Captain."

I glanced into the compartment. The snakehead sat near the exotic matter chamber, holding his bleeding hand while his gun sparked on the deck a few meters away. Izin stood nearby covering him with his shredder, but there was no sign of the tamph traitor.

I hurried across to them, facing the Mataron. "Turn it off."

The snakehead glanced at me, opened his long snout and exhaled slightly, causing a synthetic word to sound from an implant in his throat. "No."

"You sure about that?" I said, switching out my standard ammo for hardtips. The snakehead didn't dignify me with a response, so I shot him in the ankle, shattering his dense reptilian bone with an armor piercing slug. He groaned, grabbed his ankle, then after giving him time to appreciate my resolve, I explained my position. "I'm morally opposed to torture, but we both know I don't have time for niceties. So … how do

I shut it off?"

Inok growled defiance in his own guttural language, so I shot his other ankle. He fixed his angled eyes on me with growing hatred, but refused to make any sound.

"Captain, I doubt this line of questioning will be effective."

"Give me a better idea."

Izin watched the Mataron bleeding on the deck, but said nothing.

"You snakeheads have more joints than we do," I said, aiming at his lower knee, "but I have plenty of ammo." I shot him in the left lower knee, waited a moment, then seeing Inok was ignoring me, shot the right one.

His legs slid out in front of him as his back slumped against the exotic matter chamber. The armor piercing slugs had shattered bone and caused a growing pool of dark fluid to form beneath his legs.

"Answer me, and I'll get you medical treatment," I said, aiming at his upper knee. "Otherwise, I'm going to let you bleed to death, after I run out of ammo."

Inok a'Rtor raised a hand as if fending off the next shot. "Wait!" I hesitated, then he added, "If you shut down the extraction field, the exotic matter will cease to flow and the wormhole will collapse."

I lifted my aim from his upper knee to the bank of exotic matter chambers and fired. The hardtip flashed harmlessly against a field surrounding it, then I returned my aim to the Mataron.

"Not like that," Inok said, nodding toward a control console in front of the containment chamber. "Drag the second vertical control all the way down … That will reduce the flow rate … to zero."

I stepped over to the console. It had a row of

vertical sliders. I reached for the control the snakehead had indicated, then a large Kesarn hand materialized out of thin air and grabbed my arm, pulling it back.

"No!" Gern Vrate declared as his stealth field dropped, causing him to appear beside me, a large weapon in his free hand.

"I have to!" I said, aiming at his face, knowing he cared more about three frozen Kesarn than billions of humans on Earth.

"That will collapse the wormhole," he said.

"That's the idea!"

Vrate released my hand and turned to watch the shadows, unconcerned by my gun. "Do you know what happens when a wormhole collapses?"

"What?"

"It forms a black hole." He looked me in the eyes. "Beside your homeworld!"

I turned to Inok a'Rtor who avoided my stare, confirming Vrate's warning. With controlled rage, I strode back to him and pressed my gun to his head. "Give me a reason not to kill you!"

The Mataron looked up at me and emitted a guttural coughing sound, what passed for reptilian laughter, challenging me to shoot him. It was what he wanted. If he were dead, I couldn't make him help me.

"You're Black Sauria!"

"Of course," he said, a fanatic in his own snakehead way.

"Vrate, do you know how to shut it off?"

"No," he said, drawing a small tracking device from his belt and studying it as he moved away from the exotic matter console.

"Izin, get over there!" I snapped, nodding toward the control panels on the far side of the compartment.

"Captain, I know nothing about this technology."

"You're a fast learner. Figure it out!"

He holstered his shredder and hurried between the siphons to the control consoles while Vrate glanced into one of the cryochambers, keeping his gun level and his eyes darting back to the tracker in his hand.

"Can you save them?" I asked.

"Yes, but they're very weak."

The *Mavia* suddenly shuddered, ringing hollowly as if struck by a giant hammer. A moment later, another resonant thunderclap reverberated through the ship. The three Kesarn energy siphons increased in brightness as they sucked in more power, feeding it into the ship's massive defense shield.

Jase's voice sounded from my earpiece through roaring static. "Skipper, we're here. Get out of there now!"

I glanced at Vrate, who heard it too. "If they destroy us, they'll collapse the wormhole!"

"Jase!" I yelled into my communicator, "cease fire. Do not destroy the Mavia! Tell the navy to stop firing!"

"Skipper, can you hear me?" Jase's barely audible voice came from far away. "The battlecruiser is here. She's blasting the Mavia!"

"No! Cease fire!"

"He can't hear you," Inok a'Rtor said, certain the siphons were causing too much interference.

I turned to Vrate, "Can you get a signal out?"

"Not through this," he said as the depot ship shuddered again, causing the siphon's energy stream to surge in brightness to compensate.

"Will the siphons overload?" I asked.

"No. They'll keep feeding energy into the shield until this ship melts from the inside out."

"And the wormhole will collapse!" I added.

"Yes."

The snakehead started his guttural laughing again, so I lashed out with the butt of my P-50, slamming it into his head, sending him slumping unconscious to the floor.

"You humans have a temper," Vrate said. "I like that."

A flash of light streaked out of the darkness and struck the Kesarn's chest, sending him flying back. He dropped his gun and tracker as he hit the deck, then groaned as wispy smoke wafted from a ragged hole in his body armor where mangled flesh and bone were visible. Within moments, fluorescence began spreading from his healsuit into the wound, trying desperately to seal it.

The surprise nature of the attack screamed tamph, so knowing I was next, I dived toward the nearest cryochamber as a blast flashed through where I'd been standing. Another blast grazed the cyrochamber, then my threading triangulated the tamph's position. He was at the vehicle passageway I'd entered from, having backtracked around behind me as Izin had predicted. I looked for Izin to warn him, but he was nowhere to be seen.

"I can get a shot from the other side, Captain," Izin's voice sounded calmly in my earpiece.

"No," I whispered. "You shut this thing down. I'll take care of the tamph."

"Remember Captain, he fights like me, not you."

The ship continued reverberating from the *Vigilant*'s bombardment as shockwaves carried through the shield into the hull every few seconds. Jase's voice was no longer audible above the static as the siphons pumped more and more power into the *Mavia*'s shield. Vrate was right, the battlecruiser might not be able to destroy the shield, but the old depot ship had never been designed to handle the kind of energies the siphons were feeding into her. It wouldn't be long before her interior began to melt.

I stole a glance around one side of the cryochamber, long enough to see a delicate hand holding a streamlined, silver weapon. I fired and pulled back behind cover as the tamph unleashed another blast from his plasma weapon, then I sprinted for the side entrance Izin had sniped the Mataron from. Halfway across, I let off an unaimed shot at the vehicle passageway, trying to keep the tamph pinned. When I reached the corridor, I threw my back to the bulkhead and aimed around the corner, waiting for the tamph to show himself, but he remained hidden.

While I waited, Izin's words echoed in my mind: *he fights like me, not you!*

The tamph's instincts would drive him to gain surprise, something he couldn't achieve if he stayed where he was. He hadn't shown himself because he was already circling around through blacked out corridors. With the light from the siphon chamber silhouetting me, I'd be an easy target once he got behind me.

I glanced over at Vrate who lay on his back, eyes closed, breathing shallow.

"Vrate, are you dead?" I whispered.

He coughed blood and wheezed, "No."

"The tamph's coming around behind me. I'm going after him."

The Kesarn turned his face toward me, opening his eyes. "Don't go to him ... Let him come to you."

I pumped my threading's thermal sensor to max, confirmed the tamph wasn't already waiting in the shadows, then crept along the corridor to the first junction. My instinct was to move toward the tamph, to hunt the hunter, but Vrate's words sent me down the opposite corridor away from the vehicle passageway. At the first open pressure door, I felt my way into a darkened compartment with a cold metal table, bench seats and food dispensers. After confirming there was only one way into the crew mess, I waited in the shadows inside the entrance, not daring to look out, relying solely on my listener to detect approaching footsteps.

Tamph eyesight was superior to human vision, especially in low light, and was augmented by their biosonar which doubled as sonic vision. If I stuck my head into the corridor too soon, the amphibian traitor would see me sonically and I would never know what hit me. I had to hide until he found his ambush position and was facing away from me, toward the wormhole control room.

Hearing the tamph approach was complicated by the shockwaves vibrating through the ship as the *Vigilant* continued to blast away. With my listener on high gain, every creak in the ship was a clash of symbols, every blast from the Earth Navy battlecruiser a pounding of drums. Nervous seconds passed with no sign of the tamph, making me wonder if he'd outsmarted me, if he'd gone into the siphon chamber and killed Vrate and Izin, leaving me hiding like a fool in the dark, squandering my last chance to avert a disaster mankind would never recover from.

Anxiety was driving me to move, then a threaded warning appeared in my mind:

INTERMITTENT, NON-MECHANICAL AUDIO CONTACT.

Amplify contact, I thought, *block other audio.*

Silence descended over me as my threading

suppressed every distracting sound except one. It wasn't footsteps or rustling clothes but shallow breathing, steady and slow, the way I'd seen Izin breathe when he turned to stone before firing his sniper rifle. It told me the tamph was close, waiting for me to show myself.

I leaned toward the open hatch and the sound of faint, rhythmic breathing, then I spotted a thermal apparition crouched close to the bulkhead outside. The tamph's weapon was aimed at the corridor intersection, perfectly positioned to ambush anyone circling around to the vehicle passage.

With painstaking slowness, I brought my P-50 up, knowing if the tamph heard me, he would attack with lightning speed. When my gun was aimed at the back of his head, I hesitated. If Izin couldn't figure out how to shut down the wormhole, this tamph traitor was our only hope. He'd been trained by Inok a'Rtor to operate the Hrane tunneler, and while the Black Sauria agent would never talk, Izin would know how to break one of his own kind.

I switched my aim to the tamph's weapon and fired. The P-50 sang as it magnetically accelerated an armor piercing slug past his head, through his hand, into the pistol. The energy weapon exploded in the tamph's hand, hurling him backwards, past the hatchway. I leapt forward, aiming my pistol at his head, ready to finish him if he resisted, but he lay on his back, badly burned with a rasping breath and a right hand missing its fingers.

"Any sudden movements and you're dead."

The tamph made no effort to resist, so I pulled him off the deck by his undamaged arm and half carried, half dragged him back to the control room. Vrate had crawled on his back to his gun and lay with one hand on it as phosphorescence glowed brightly across his chest, regenerating his body at an incredible rate.

"Thought it … killed you," Vrate wheezed as I threw the tamph onto the deck.

I aimed my P-50 at the amphibian's head while he pressed his finger stumps into his side to reduce the blood flow. "Tamphs are tough, not invincible,"

Vrate dragged his gun across his body to cover the prisoner. "Is that what you think it is? … A tamph? … Look again."

The diminutive amphibian wore a dark, skin tight jumpsuit with a metallic finish, a black belt covered with thin rectangular attachments and short black ankle-high boots. A thin metal strip laden with ultra-miniaturized technology ran from above the biosonar lobe on his forehead over the top of his bulging head halfway to the base of his long, streamlined skull.

"What are you talking about?"

"It's not a tamph…" Vrate said.

My prisoner turned toward me with a penetrating stare that sent a chill down my spine. Even though he was helpless and crippled, I felt a sudden pang of fear as I realized this creature was unlike any tamph I'd ever seen.

"It's an Intruder?"

"Take a good look, human," Vrate said. "Pray you never see its like again!"

"How'd you know?"

"I didn't, until it shot me," he said, never taking his eyes off the Intruder. "What didn't make sense was Matarons using Hrane technology. It's too advanced for them. They couldn't teach humans to use it any more than I could, not without help. When it shot me, when I saw that weapon, I knew."

"He was teaching the Mataron!" Not the other way

around. I looked down at the Intruder whose cold stare told me he understood our every word. There was no denial, no fear, only a quiet defiance. Before I could interrogate my prisoner, Izin approached from the consoles on the far side of the compartment.

"Captain, there's a–" He stopped suddenly as his eyes fell upon the blackened amphibian sitting helpless on the deck. The Intruder turned toward him, although its bulging right eye was so blackened and shriveled from plasma burns, he must have been half blind.

Vrate nodded toward Izin. "He knows."

"Izin?" I said, sensing something strange was happening to my tamph engineer, now transfixed by the diminutive figure at my feet. "Is this a tamph?"

"No. She's not … from Earth," Izin said slowly, having trouble speaking.

She?

There was a reason female tamphs weren't ever allowed off Earth. It wasn't just because the Forum insisted on it. It was because they couldn't be trusted. With one female for every hundred thousand males, the female's biological role was command. Their pheromones gave them the power to dominate the males. They were the queens, the Matriarchs, while the males were the obedient drones.

"Careful," Vrate warned. "They're communicating!"

"Izin!" I said, my finger hovering over my P-50's firing surface.

He ignored me, hypnotized by the female Intruder's pheromones as she used her biosonar to bombard him with ultrasonic commands.

"Snap out of it!" I yelled, flashing an order to my threading.

Expand auditory range to tamph ultrasonics.

My head filled with an incomprehensible melody, all going one way, from the Intruder Matriarch to Izin. He stood helpless before her, arms by his side listening to a siren song he could not resist. Suddenly I realized how dangerous she was to him, so dangerous I couldn't risk keeping her alive for the Tau Cetins to interrogate. I swung my gun toward her but she kicked up at my hand, sending my P-50 flying across the deck. Before I knew what was happening, she jumped to her feet, kicked me in the stomach with more strength than I would have thought possible considering her wounds and sent me reeling backwards. Vrate tried lifting his gun, but Izin trod on the barrel, pinning it to the deck as it discharged. Vrate was too weak to pull his gun free as the Intruder Matriarch projected her seductive song at Izin, who lifted his shredder, aiming at nothing. I expected him to turn and shoot her as she ran toward him, but he remained in a trancelike state.

She snatched the weapon out of his hand, aiming back as she ran. I rolled away anticipating a shot, but I wasn't her target. She fired once, putting a single shredder round into Inok a'Rtor's head, ensuring even the Tau Cetins couldn't extract what he knew, then I scooped my P-50 off the deck as she darted behind the exotic matter containment chamber. I started after her while Izin continued to stand on Vrate's gun, oblivious to what had just happened.

I'd expected her to head for the wormhole controls, knowing Izin's little shredder couldn't penetrate the siphon shielding, but instead, she ran to the nearest cryochamber. I thought she was going to use it for cover, but she leapt up onto it and aimed down through the transparent surface at the frozen Kesarn.

"No!" I roared as I realized what she was doing.

She fired once, then blood splattered up onto the inside of the transparent cover. The dark energy siphon nearby began to spark with flecks of orange and red lightning, slowly at first, then with growing strength. Now with its Kesarn symbiote dead, the siphon was doomed. Nothing could stop it cycling out of control, destroying the *Mavia* and collapsing the wormhole, ensuring Earth was flung from Sol's habitable zone.

"Why? Why are you helping the Matarons?" I demanded, aiming my gun at her. "What have we ever done to you?"

The Intruder Matriarch jumped down from the cryochamber, then touched the muzzle of Izin's gun to a control surface on her belt. "It's not about you," she replied in a flat, synthesized voice. "It's about us!"

She stepped toward the siphon, watching the brilliant yellow beam blasting down from the flat cylinder at its base into the dish shaped receptor in the deck. The beam's color continued to shift toward the red as the siphon destabilized.

"That's far enough!" I said, still hoping to extract a solution from her.

The Intruder Matriarch turned, studying me through her one good eye, then dropped Izin's shredder as if in surrender. "Now I know why the Matarons hate you."

"It doesn't have to be that way with us."

"You serve our enemy," the Intruder Matriarch said with chilling finality, then threw herself onto the deck and rolled beneath the stasis field into the siphon's energy stream. She was vaporized in a brilliant white flash, eliminating all trace of her existence. For a moment, I stared in disbelief at the energy stream, then turned back to the others. Izin was holding his head, eyes closed, while Vrate was struggling to his feet, using his gun as a crutch.

"I don't understand," I said. "We're not their enemy."

"You are, if they say you are," Vrate said, staring darkly at the blood splattered lid on the cryochamber where one of his people had just been murdered. "Especially now."

"Why now?"

He turned to me, hunched over in pain. "They're coming again, this time, not alone."

It took a moment for his words to sink in. My eyes fell on the dead Mataron, slumped on the deck with his brain shredded, then the pieces came together in a flash of realization. The Intruder Matriarch was gone and soon a massive dark energy explosion would rend space where we stood, annihilating the *Mavia* and her secrets, especially one secret the Intruder Matriarch had taken to her death.

"The Intruders and the Matarons are allies!" I exclaimed, shocked by the implications.

The Matriarch was here buying Mataron loyalty by helping the snakeheads destroy mankind, something they couldn't do by themselves, not with the Tau Cetins watching. They needed a partner, an ally with the power to match the might of the Tau Cetins. In return, the Matarons had betrayed the Alliance. It was how the Intruders had been able to sabotage the Alliance's sensor fields in the Minacious Cluster and how they'd known the location of the Forum Fleet prior to the attack. The five Mataron ships lost in the battle had been sacrificed to keep the snakehead treachery hidden from the Allies, and it had worked! Five ships was a small price to pay for our destruction and for the defeat of the Tau Cetins.

"The Matarons and the Intruders are very

different," Vrate said. "The only thing they have in common are their enemies and that makes them natural allies."

"The Tau Cetins will crush the Matarons when they find out!"

"They can't. No proof. The Matriarch saw to that."

"When the siphon explodes, the wormhole collapse will create a black hole. That's proof!"

"Only of human stupidity. The Forum will believe you used technology you didn't understand and paid a heavy price for it. No one will care."

"Their fear of the Intruders will make them care."

Vrate coughed blood and phosphorescence, then said, "The Alliance is weary. Every year, its fleet grows weaker. The Intruders know this. Last time, they destroyed all in their path, forcing many civilizations to unite against them. This time will be different. They will have allies and knowledge of their enemy. They will not give the Tau Cetins reason to convince other Observer races to fight. This time, the Intruders will win."

The dark energy siphon was beginning to emit high frequency sounds as lightning flecks flashed erratically through the transmission beam, while the other two siphons continued undisturbed.

"What about Earth?"

"It's too late."

"Captain," Izin said, slowly regaining his senses, "We don't … have to shut it off."

Vrate glanced at him confused. "Nothing can stop the siphon's destruction now."

I ran to Izin, holstering my gun, grabbing him by the shoulders. "How do we stop it?"

He blinked slowly, clearing his mind. "Retract it."

"Retract what?" I demanded. "What are you

talking about?"

He pointed to the consoles on the far wall. "The singularity guidance system."

I lifted him off the deck and carried him to the console. "Tell me what to do!"

"Pull the singularity back into hyperspace ... Break contact with the Solar System."

"Will that stop the black hole forming?"

"No," Izin said, "but it will be a one sided wormhole. Here only, not in the Solar System."

The control interface was a broad interactive panel, filled with touch sliders and colored control points, none of which meant anything to me. "Which one?"

Izin turned to the panel uncertainly. "I'm not sure, Captain."

"Guess!"

He reached toward an image of a three dimensional geodesic and dragged his finger across the curved surface. On the screen above, the image of a spherical wormhole mouth filled with a dead black sphere began to shrink. Closely bunched concentric rings around the wormhole mouth slowly began to expand as spacetime curvature in the Solar System began decreasing.

Behind us, Gern Vrate limped on his weapon-crutch to the second cryochamber and released the transparent cover with a hiss of misty air. He didn't wait to see the occupant revive, but continued on to the third chamber to free its frozen prisoner.

"How long?" I asked as the self destructing siphon's energy took on a dark red hue.

"I don't know, Captain."

Vrate opened the third cryochamber, yelling, "Kade, if you help me get my people out, you can come with me."

"Izin?" I said, following his gaze to the screen above the console. The tightly bunched concentric rings suddenly flowed like ripples on a pond after a stone had been dropped into it and began to fade away.

"The mouth has withdrawn, Captain. The singularity is back in hyperspace." Izin pointed to another screen showing an elongated shape resembling a sock with a heavy weight in it, slowly shrinking. "It's coming back this way."

I turned to Vrate. "We're coming!"

The Kesarn in the second chamber had his eyes open. He was cold and disoriented, but he didn't resist as I dragged him out of the chamber. He was heavier than a man, but I managed to sling him across my shoulders. Vrate was too weak to get the other one out, so Izin jumped onto the cryochamber and pulled the frozen Kesarn to a sitting position, then rolled him over the side, letting him fall onto the deck.

Vrate grunted unhappily at the roughness.

"Better bruised than dead," I said.

"Can your tamph carry him?" Vrate asked, ignoring Izin completely.

"I can drag him, Captain."

"I'll take his other hand," I said, turning to Vrate. "Where's your ship?"

"Near where you boarded," he said, limping on his weapon-crutch toward the vehicle entry.

I followed him, struggling under the weight of the half frozen Kesarn on my shoulders while helping Izin drag the other one by the arms. We struggled through dark corridors as the wail of the deteriorating dark energy siphon rose to a scream behind us and the lightning flashes grew brighter.

"You Kesarn need to slim down," I said.

"Harden up, human," Vrate growled, pressing his hand against the side of his chest, careful not to touch the fluorescence that was now lighting our path. Incredibly, it was healing him before my eyes.

The thunder of the *Vigilant's* bombardment continued unabated, almost drowned out by the shriek of the dying siphon. There was no sign of the crew, who may have been trapped in another part of the ship, but we couldn't help them.

"What's the siphon's blast radius?" I asked, feeling my shoulders turning to ice under the cold radiating from the Kesarn hulk I was carrying.

"Equivalent to a small nova."

"Will it reach the Aphrodite?"

"They have shields," Vrate said. "At that distance, they will survive."

We passed through an armored hatch, out of the *Mavia's* fortified citadel. In the corridor were a dozen dead Orie mercs, some were on fire, lighting our way.

"Your handiwork?" I asked.

"I took no pleasure in it. I am a tracer, not a killer. Survival is our burden."

"Your burden?"

"I find the lost that they may live," he said in a way that sounded almost ritualistic. "Failure means dcath."

"You couldn't stop the Matriarch," I said, thinking he was grieving the loss of the Kesarn the Intruder had killed in the siphon room.

"One life, one world, they are all our burden."

I glanced at his hard face, realizing he was talking as much about the dead Kesarn as the destruction of his homeworld. Having spied for the Tau Cetins during the Intruder War, his people had risked the ire of one galactic super power by helping another and it had cost them everything. No wonder he was bitter! More than that, I realized his entire race suffered survivor's guilt, making the loss of even one more Kesarn almost unbearable. It was why he was a survivor, why his people had invented healsuits and why he would scour the galaxy to save one life.

We moved on in silence to an open airlock, then Vrate helped Izin drag his Kesarn through while I struggled alone with mine. Once aboard, I released my Kesarn and followed Vrate as he hobbled to his flight deck.

"I need to warn the human ships!" I declared.

He limped up the ramp to his piloting position, dropped his weapon-crutch and placed his hands on the two command spheres, using them for support. Almost immediately, his ship moved away from the *Mavia* sending the navigational guides sliding across the inside of the spherical chamber.

The *Vigilant* was barely twenty clicks away, a rectangular armored slab with squat round turrets either side of a central superstructure. Her big guns were firing steady, controlled blasts, vainly trying to batter down the *Mavia*'s shield, while her secondary weapons poured rapid fire streams at the same point. Sheets of energy rolled across the *Mavia's* shield, illuminating its curved surface before fading away, showing no sign of buckling under the onslaught.

Far beyond the battlecruiser were three smaller Earth Navy ships exchanging fire with the Super Saracen fleet bearing down on them. None of the Separatist ships were heading for the wormhole mouth now. Either the arrival of the Earth Navy squadron had forced them to abandon their attack, or they'd detected the singularity blocking the exit mouth and had aborted the raid. Whatever the reason, the small Earth Navy force was suffering at the hands of its more powerful adversary.

The heavy destroyer *Kirishima* was adrift. Glowing plasma fires lit up her hull in a dozen places as her last surviving heavy gun continued to fire sporadically. With no shield or propulsion and the full weight of the Separatist fleet bearing down on her, she didn't have long to live, yet not a single escape pod had launched.

Retreating from the wreck of the *Kirishima* were the *Delhi* and the *Nassau*, firing as they fell back. The leading Super Saracens were already maneuvering to pass the *Kirishima* and refocus their attention on the surviving escorts. Their shields were still up, but a plasma fire had erupted from *Delhi's* starboard side and one of *Nassau's* turrets was already a jagged ruin.

Only the *Vigilant* was undamaged, having come in to destroy the *Mavia* while her escorts kept the Super Saracens away. Coming up from below the *Mavia* were the two converted cruisers that had detached to intercept the *Silver Lining*. They were still outside weapons range, but were decelerating on an intercept course with the *Vigilant*. Sheltering behind the *Vigilant* was the *Silver Lining*, carefully positioned not to obstruct the warship's guns, but close enough to swoop in and pick us up if we jumped clear in the battle suits.

"Speak," Vrate said as we passed outside the *Mavia's* defense shield.

I took a step up the ramp. "This is Sirius Kade to all Earth Navy ships and to the Silver Lining. The Mavia is about to become a nova. Evacuate the system immediately!"

Lena Voss's face appeared inside the sphere surrounding Vrate's flight deck. "ENS Vigilant to Sirius Kade, is Earth in danger?"

"No, but we are!"

Relief washed over her face. "Good work, Sirius. Vigilant out."

Lena's face vanished, then Vrate said. "Another message incoming."

Jase's face appeared. "Skipper, where are you?'

"On Vrate's ship. Get moving. Pick a direction, don't stop for a light year. We'll find you." I glanced at Gern Vrate. "Right?"

"If he goes now," he agreed, sending his ship hurtling past the *Vigilant*. In the blink of an eye, we were behind the *Silver Lining*, velocities perfectly matched.

"I'm out of here," Jase said, then bubbled away in a streak of light.

I looked at Vrate quizzically.

"Got it," he said, confirming how easily he could read our autonav.

A short distance away, the *Vigilant's* big guns fell silent. She turned slowly, thirty degrees, then bubbled, followed immediately by the two surviving navy frigates. Only the glowing wreck of the *Kirishima* remained of the Earth Navy ships, still being battered by the Super Saracens.

"Can you save her?" I asked, nodding toward the beleaguered *Kirishima*.

"There isn't time."

"Do the Separatist ships know what's coming?"

"I didn't include them," Vrate said, turning curiously. "Would you have preferred I did?"

"No, let them burn." At that range, even with their shields up, the Separatist fleet would not survive the explosion of the *Mavia*. "Are there any other ships in-system?" I asked, wondering if the *Cyclops* was still here.

"No."

"OK, let's go."

Vrate's ship turned after the *Silver Lining*, then his spear-like superluminal bubble formed, carrying us to safety. Several minutes later, a small nova bloomed at the edge of the Duranis-B system, consuming the *Mavia*, thirty two Super Saracen merchant cruisers and vaporizing the wreck of the *Kirishima*.

Fifteen hours later, the blast was captured by every major news service in Mapped Space, watched from the decadent comfort of the *Aphrodite* and dozens of smaller ships. The Separatist leaders were shocked to see their fleet repel an Earth Navy squadron only to vanish in a single annihilating flash. To most, it was a disaster, the ruin of years of planning and the expenditure of vast fortunes, made worse by the terrible retribution that would inevitably be inflicted upon them by Earth Navy.

To Manning Thurlow Ransford III, cradled in one of his colorful exoskeletons, the bright light in the sky marked a huge increase in demand for ships and weapons of all kinds, from both sides. The loss of this fleet was a setback to the Separatist cause, but he knew there were other squadrons that were even now launching surprise attacks upon isolated Earth Navy outposts across Mapped Space. Considering the distances involved, it would be many months before news of the Duranis-B disaster reached them, by which time Human Civilization would be ablaze.

In the secluded comfort of his super yacht in its private berth alongside the *Aphrodite*, he watched the distant nova slowly fade, not with trepidation but with delight, certain that business would be booming for years to come.

* * * *

Vrate's ship unbubbled a light year from the Duranis binary after a few seconds of flight. By the time the *Silver Lining* arrived seven hours later, the two kidnapped Kesarn had recovered their strength enough to eat and drink, but do little else.

Vrate locked onto the *Lining's* port side airlock, eager to get rid of us and take his two companions home – wherever that was. The Kesarn were an obstinately solitary people, suggesting much about their origins. I could imagine lone hunters prowling the plains of a long lost world during a time predating technology. Now they prowled the galaxy, alone and remorseful, tortured by survivor's guilt, longing for a world that no longer existed.

At the airlock, Vrate gave me an appraising look. Incredibly, his chest wound was showing remarkable progress while his suit was already beginning to repair itself. For loners wandering the galaxy, isolated from mainstream civilization, the Kesarn healsuit was the ultimate achievement in self reliance. I wanted one.

"You kept your word," Vrate said. "You found my people."

"You kept yours. Thanks for trusting me."

"Are you typical of humans?"

"Some of them."

He fell silent, deep in thought. Finally he said, "The Kesarn have few friends."

"I find that hard to believe, you're such a bundle of laughs."

The Kesarn's granite face didn't budge. He was as tough as a Gesion razorback, and about as affable.

"I will recommend we establish contact with Earth."

That was a surprise. "I thought we were primitive barbarians?"

"You are, but so were we – once. Even more than you." He hesitated. "In time, we may come to an understanding."

"Any Kesarn ambassador will be welcome on Earth."

In fact, Earth Council would fall over themselves to build a friendship – perhaps even an alliance – with the Kesarn, a people hundreds of thousands of years ahead of us who were beholding to no one, who feared nothing and now had a reason to hate the Matarons.

Vrate held out both hands palms up and nodded his head slightly forward. I wasn't quite sure of the meaning of the gesture, but I guessed it had something to do with trusting me enough to show he held no weapons. I mirrored the gesture back to him. His dark stony face gave no hint as to whether it was the right response, but he didn't insult me so I figured he'd taken it as a good attempt at respecting his customs.

I followed Izin into the airlock and turned back to the Kesarn tracer. "If you're ever back this way –" Vrate touched the wall panel, sealing the airlock shut. "– look me up," I said to the dull metallic hatch.

"I don't think he likes me," Izin said.

"He doesn't know you like I do."

Izin turned toward the outer hatch as it opened into the *Lining's* airlock. "I'm sorry the Intruder Matriarch overpowered me, Captain."

I patted him on the shoulder reassuringly. "Don't worry, Izin, we all have women trouble. It almost makes you human."

"No need to insult me, Captain," he said as the *Lining's* airlock sealed shut behind us.

Chapter Nine : Uralo IV

Earth Navy Supply Base
Uralo System, Outer Ursa Minor
0.78 Earth Normal Gravity
746 light years from Sol
1,256 Enlisted Personnel

Lena summoned me to a debrief after the destruction of the *Mavia*. The *Vigilant* and her two damaged escorts had retreated to the nearest Earth Navy facility, a small supply base between Middle and Outer Ursa Minor. *Nassau* and *Delhi* were on the ground when I arrived, undergoing what repairs a base with no maintenance dock could offer. The *Vigilant* remained in parking orbit above, carefully stationed inside the firing envelopes of the base's aging surface batteries. Because the summons came as an Earth Navy directive, not a request from my EIS controller, there was no need of a cover story for Jase and Izin. After we landed, they remained on board while I tramped across the cold landing field, past a row of rectangular warehouses and pressurized utility buildings to the *Nassau*.

The frigate was surrounded by a cluster of mobile cranes working to patch damaged hull segments and remove her forward turret. The turret's heavy plate armor had been peeled open like tin foil, although her remaining armament looked intact. It would take months to get a replacement turret shipped out from Earth and a proper dock to install it. Until then, the best Uralo IV's minimal facilities could do was ensure the *Nassau* was airtight, if not battle ready.

The *Delhi* was another matter. She was parked two clicks away, a blackened hulk with flash scoring along most of her hull. Her main armament was in ruins and one of her maneuvering engines had been holed. Only the redundancy built into her spacetime distorters had saved the crew from being trapped in the Duranis-B system with the *Kirishima*. Now she lay like a charred corpse on the landing field, with only one crane and a few ground vehicles alongside, a sure sign that the navy had decided to focus their efforts on getting her sister ship operational.

At the base of *Nassau's* aft access ramp, a pair of armed URA troopers glanced at my ID and subjected me to a cursory DNA scan, confirming my identify.

"They're waiting for you, sir, frame D forty six, port side," one of the troopers replied. "Do you need a guide?"

"I know the way," I said then strode up the ramp.

I followed the port passageway forward, through corridors crowded with crew and base personnel hurriedly conducting repairs under the watchful eyes of overworked engineering officers. Melted panels, cables and tools littered the decks while maintenance bots cut away twisted bulkheads and crewmen installed what replacement parts were available. It was organized chaos, driven by an urgent need to get the *Nassau* back into space as soon as possible.

When I reached frame D forty six, I was met by another armed URA trooper who led me through to the chief petty officer's mess. It was now lined with screens displaying sensor feeds of the Uralo System beamed down from the *Vigilant* and watched by tactical officers sitting at hastily assembled operations terminals. The far end of the compartment was screened off from the makeshift command center by a dark curtain strung across the room. As soon as I passed through it, the sounds of the ship under repair and the muted chatter from the command center died, telling me there was a sonic nullifier in place around the area.

Lena Voss, wearing a dark jumpsuit showing no rank, stood beside two senior officers. One was portly with graying hair and four stripes. The other was younger and taller with a full beard. Beside them was a small figure wrapped in a loose fitting, hooded Earth Navy jacket. All four stood in front of a holo display showing our little corner of the Orion Arm.

Lena greeted me with a sober nod. "Sirius, good to see you." She motioned to the two officers. "This is Captain Reynar of the Vigilant and Commander Desouza of the Nassau." The two officers nodded curtly. The smaller figure turned, revealing a Tau Cetin face as Lena added, "I believe you've met Observer Siyarn."

"Yes," I said, barely masking my surprise. "I thought you were in the Minacious Cluster."

"I was," Siyarn replied without moving his lips. Somewhere inside that Earth Navy jacket, a translation device spoke for him. "In light of events in the Duranis System, my return was required."

I gave Lena a questioning look, wondering how the Tau Cetins had gotten the news so fast. It would be months before couriers could report to Earth and up to two years before every navy ship and base received an update on what had happened at Duranis-B.

"Siyarn approached me," Lena explained. "Apparently the Kesarn briefed the Tau Cetins."

"Did they?" The Kesarn might not entirely trust the Tau Cetins, but they hated the Intruders whom they were no match for. If the Intruders were coming out again, the Kesarn had no choice but to turn to the Tau Cetins.

"We detected a particularly destructive explosion," Siyarn said, "of a type that could only have come from a Kesarn ship. We were naturally curious."

"Yeah, those dark energy siphons make a hell of a bang. It was the Intruder Matriarch's fault, she blew it up, although the Matarons stole it."

"So the Kesarn say," Siyarn said.

Lena gave me a curious look, signaling Siyarn had not told her everything. "The Tau Cetins have agreed to deliver a report on the current situation to Earth for us, and to our bases across Mapped Space."

"How very helpful of them," I said, surprised the Tau Cetins were doing us any favors.

"We have observed fighting on a number of human worlds," Siyarn said, "and detected attacks on Earth Navy ships throughout human space."

"Surprise attacks," Captain Reynar added. "They're catching our ships with their shields down. Some on the ground, some in parking orbit."

Lena motioned to the holo display. It depicted a sphere approximately two thousand four hundred light years across with Earth at its center. Red contact markers were sprinkled throughout, mostly beyond the Core Worlds. "As you can see, the attacks are widespread."

"How fast can the Tau Cetins warn them?" I asked.

"Within a week all of your bases will be advised," Siyarn said.

"Are you allowed to do that, Fourth Principle and all?"

"The Development Principle ensures each civilization develops in its own way, Captain Kade. While it precludes advanced civilizations accelerating less developed societies, passing on information you already possess does not contravene the basic principle. In any event, the collective security exception provides an arguable rationale for our assistance."

It was space lawyer talk, but he was undoubtedly right. In all the volumes of Access Treaty legalese they'd given us there were endless exceptions and qualifications which the Tau Cetins had proven time and again they knew better than anyone else in the galaxy – probably because they wrote half of them!

"How do humans blowing each other's brains out affect the galaxy's collective security?" I asked.

"Any action involving the Intruders affects our collective security," Siyarn replied. "Your species has been unlawfully destabilized by the Matarons and the Intruders. We are merely mitigating the effect of that interference, although we would not reveal that unless challenged."

"You know the Matarons started this?" I said relieved. "And you're going to drop the hammer on them, right?"

"What we know," Siyarn said carefully, "and what

we can prove to the Forum Membership are not the same."

"But the snakeheads betrayed your fleet!"

"So it is claimed, by you and the Kesarn," he said cautiously. "Even if we believe you, many of our distant partners will not. They require a high burden of proof."

"Because they're tired of blockading the Intruders," I said, remembering Vrate's warning that the Alliance was weakening, "and they want out."

"They are weary, but they also doubt that a species at your level of development would warrant this kind of attention from the Intruders. They don't understand Mataron psychology, trading your destruction for their allegiance. And while the Forum Powers have contained the Intruders for over two thousand years, many believe that is long enough. They think it is time to negotiate."

"But not you?" Lena asked.

"The Intruders are an ever present threat. It is their nature. However, we cannot act alone, which is why any unauthorized assistance we offer you must be discreet."

"I've seen you analyze stuff," I said. "Can't you do that in the Duranis System, find proof that'll hang the snakeheads out to dry?"

"There is now a black hole orbiting Duranis-B," Siyarn replied. "Whatever evidence may have existed has been consumed by that black hole. Nothing useful remains."

"You can't let the Matarons get away with betraying your fleet!"

"There are advantages to not letting the Intruders or the Matarons know we have become aware of their alliance. In terms of the Matarons, we will ensure that any reinforcements they send to the Alliance Fleet are assigned to noncritical sectors."

"What about the Intruders? Gern Vrate thinks they're coming out again."

"We are currently blind to their intentions. It remains to be seen if we can assemble sufficient strength to reinstate a close blockade of the Minacious Cluster."

"You have your masking technology."

"Unfortunately, it is not as effective against the Intruders as it once was."

"So the snakeheads win," I said. "You sit around doing nothing, while we tear ourselves apart and they get help from the Intruders." The odds against us suddenly took a terrible turn for the worse.

"In matters of galactic security, we are never idle," Siyarn said. "In relation to your present internal conflict, the Forum will not allow us to intervene unless you attempt to annihilate yourselves, in which case the only action we could take would be to impose an embargo, to ensure your species' survival."

"And that would be ten thousand years without interstellar access rights," Lena said soberly.

"To give you time to mature," Siyarn said. "Unfortunately, the Matarons have played upon the fact that the only peer-to-peer conflict possible for mankind is a civil war. All of your neighbors are far too advanced for you to fight, not that the Forum would permit such a one sided conflict. A civil war gives you an adversary with equivalent technology, who is also close enough in the galaxy for you to engage. Technological equivalence and spatial proximity are the limiting factors, the reasons why war between early interstellar civilizations rarely, if ever, occurs. In a galaxy such as ours, it is a virtual impossibility."

"Really?" Commander Desouza asked incredulously.

"No two civilizations ever emerge at precisely the same time, in exactly the same part of the galaxy. Peer-to-peer conflicts are far less likely to occur in space than they are on a single planet, where societies appear and develop together. Of course, the preferred solution to your present crisis lies in your hands, not ours. Learn to make peace with yourselves, then you can join the Forum and live in peace with all its members."

"There's nothing I'd like more," Lena said to the silent nods of the two naval officers.

"You talk of galactic peace," I said, "but you've been at war with the Intruders for thousands of years."

"That is true," Siyarn conceded. "It is the only kind of interstellar conflict possible between equals, a war between ultra-advanced civilizations with approximate technological parity and the means to travel the vast distances needed to engage each other. It is not a situation of our choosing. Normally, civilizations at such advanced levels have learned to avoid conflict, however, the Intruders are an aberration, an exception. That is what makes them so dangerous."

For the first time, I sensed uncertainty in Siyarn's words. "You don't think the Intruders have a chance of winning, do you?"

"They have had more than two thousand years to prepare, to study us, to understand our strengths and weaknesses … and to find allies. If what you and the Kesarn say is true, the Matarons now give the Intruders eyes and ears across the galaxy, something they never had before."

"Sounds like a good reason to shut the Matarons down," I said.

"When we have evidence, we will present it to the Forum membership and a collective decision will be made. Until then, we must watch and wait for them to make a mistake. There are too many Forum members ready to accept unwise compromises with the Intruders, members who would oppose us if we acted hastily. They want peace even if it leaves us with a much heavier burden later."

"And we're on our own, again," I said bitterly.

"Not exactly," Lena said slowly. "We've come to an understanding, Sirius," she glanced meaningfully at Siyarn, "with the Tau Cetins."

"What kind of understanding?"

"As Observers," she said, "they must be impartial in their dealings with all civilizations. They can't give the Matarons or us special treatment."

"Kind of tough considering the Matarons are working for their enemy, isn't it?"

"Galactic diplomacy," Siyarn said, "is a very complex affair, Captain Kade, one we have successfully manipulated for millions of years."

It was perhaps the truest thing the Tau Cetin Observer had ever said. They were master manipulators on a galactic scale. It was their greatest skill.

"For the Tau Cetins to retain the trust of the Forum, they must be *seen* to be impartial," Lena said. "That doesn't mean they're neutral."

I knew from her tone, from the look in her eyes and from the two naval officers' demeanor that this was important. "What's the difference?"

"Though we cannot prove it to the Forum membership," Siyarn said, "we believe the Matarons are working for the Intruders, hoping to break the power of the Alliance. To do that, they must defeat us."

"You are the big target," I agreed.

"Because the Matarons are spying for the Intruders," Lena added, "We have agreed to work more closely with the Tau Cetins, in secret of course."

"Have we?" I said warily.

From the eagerness in her eyes, it was clear she was delighted the Tau Cetins were taking us in close, showing us a level of trust we could never have hoped to achieve if they weren't themselves under threat.

"We will continue to take a serious interest in what the Matarons are doing," Lena said, "and share our findings with the Tau Cetins. If we're caught, we'll be censured, but the Forum knows there's tension between us and the Matarons. We can take risks the Tau Cetins can't, because we don't have to be neutral. No one cares if we stick our noses where they're not supposed to be."

"Except the Matarons, who will cut our noses off."

"Then you better not get caught." She smiled. "And if other problems crop up, like Intruders in Mapped Space, we might look into that as well."

"Just so long as no one can blame the impartial Tau Cetins for what a bunch of primitive humans do?"

"Exactly. And in return for our help, the Tau Cetins will actively sponsor our membership to the Galactic Forum."

"That's forty nine years away."

"In cosmic terms, it is the blink of eye," Siyarn said. "In the meantime, we will assist you in other ways. The Fourth Principle prevents us openly accelerating your civilization, however, where you encounter obstacles, we will provide solutions. Nothing far beyond your reach, but solutions you might plausibly have achieved on your own – eventually."

It sounded like a cut down version of the deal

they'd offered the Kesarn, a deal that had cost Gern Vrate's ancestors their homeworld. There were huge benefits trouble shooting for the Tau Cetins, but I wondered if Lena realized how great were the risks. Human Civilization might be young and full of energy, but in raw power terms we were insignificantly small, a minnow about to be drawn into a cosmic power struggle between ancient galactic superpowers. It was an incredibly dangerous game, one we couldn't control or predict the outcome of, a game with catastrophic consequences if we backed the wrong side.

"Does that mean we're getting dark energy siphons and trans galactic drives?" I asked.

"No," Siyarn replied. "We could not hide such a gift."

"You gave them to the Kesarn."

"They were Forum members of long standing, their homeworld was being invaded and many others were under attack at the time. It was a clear Fourth Principle exception. Collective security was threatened on a galactic scale and such a transfer benefited many civilizations. These circumstances are not the same."

"That deal cost the Kesarn everything," I said. "Why should we take the same risk?"

Lena gave me a sharp look. "Because Earth Council wants this."

"I understand your concern, Captain Kade," Siyarn said. "Know that we could not help the Kesarn at the time. We were fighting for our own survival. After the war, we engineered a new homeworld for them, ideal in every respect."

"Except they were dead."

"Sirius!" Lena snapped.

"No," Siyarn said, "he is right. We have a debt to the Kesarn we can never repay. We assisted them knowing they would resist and the Intruders would not tolerate that resistance. The Kesarn were always going to be crushed. The truth is, our help saved them from extinction."

An awkward silence fell over the room.

Finally, I said, "So we risk everything to help you. What do you risk?"

Lena fixed a cold stare upon me, but said nothing.

"Your homeworld is less than twelve light years from ours," Siyarn said. "If we are destroyed, what chance is there for you?"

Siyarn was as slippery as a Silurian slime-eel, but he was right. Whether we liked it or not, we were in it together because Earth was in their sphere of influence. Maybe that's what the Intruder Matriarch had meant when she'd said we served her enemy. She knew we were in the Tau Cetin sphere and we had no say in it, we couldn't opt out, but we could have done worse. We could have been close to the Matarons with no Forum ruling the galaxy, or stuck in the Minacious Cluster, subjugated by the Intruders.

"I get it. So, what are these helpful solutions you're going to give us?"

"This for one," Lena said, holding up a small data disk. "A way to penetrate Mataron skin shields. In a few months, we'll have new ammunition for your P-50, ammo that'll cut through their skin shields like paper."

I liked the sound of that, but a few micro-contour shield busting slugs was hardly enough for us to risk our entire civilization. "Is that it?"

"There are other aspects to the agreement," Lena said meaningfully without telling me anything above my security clearance, "but secrecy is paramount."

From her tone, I knew the decision had already been made and I'd only discover what those other arrangements were when I had a need to know, if ever. "What now?"

"Tell us everything," Lena said.

"I'm particularly interested in the Matriarch," Siyarn said.

Izin could have told him more, but after the way the Tau Cetins had vacuumed his brain, I doubted he'd be in a mood to help. "The Matriarch is the end of the story."

"Of course," Siyarn said, restraining his curiosity. "Begin at the beginning."

"That'd be Krailo-Nis," I said, "a filthy, fungus covered rock with lousy weather and infested with giant bugs ..."

Visit the author's webpage at:

www.StephenRenneberg.com

If you enjoyed this book, please post a recommendation and rating on the site where you purchased your copy.

The Mothership
by
Stephen Renneberg

A compelling, visionary must-read
for literary sci-fi fans.
– Kirkus Reviews

A massive alien ship crashes into one of the most remote places on Earth – cutting all contact with the region.

Within hours, Major Robert Beckman and his specially equipped Contact Team are hurriedly dispatched from Area 51 to investigate. Is it a forced landing, or the beginning of an invasion - a technological treasure trove, or an extraterrestrial Pandora's box that spells disaster for life on Earth?

Infiltrating the vast tropical wilderness of northern Australia, Beckman's team encounter strange machines, alien structures and a handful of human survivors struggling to evade capture.

When Beckman's team penetrates to the heart of the Mothership, they discover an answer they never expected and a universe far larger than they had ever imagined.

Paperback Length 465 pages
ISBN: 978-0-9874347-3-9

The Mothership
by
Stephen Renneberg

A blockbuster science fiction thriller.
– Kirkus Reviews

A massive alien ship crashes into one of the most remote places on Earth – cutting all contact with the region.

Within hours, Major Robert Beckman and his specially equipped Contact Team are hurriedly dispatched from Area 51 to investigate. Is it a forced landing, or the beginning of an invasion - a technological treasure trove, or an extraterrestrial Pandora's box that spells disaster for life on Earth?

Infiltrating the vast tropical wilderness of northern Australia, Beckman's team encounter strange machines, alien structures and a handful of human survivors struggling to evade capture.

When Beckman's team penetrates to the heart of the Mothership, they discover an answer they never expected and a universe far larger than they had ever imagined.

ISBN: 978-0-9874347-3-9

The Antaran Codex
by
Stephen Renneberg

This high-octane sci-fi novel is powered by grand-scale action and adventure, larger-than-life characters, a richly described backdrop and, above all else, relentless pacing ... Fast and furious fun in humankind's distant future.
- Kirkus Reviews

Two and half thousand years after *The Mothership*, mankind nears its goal of Galactic Citizenship.

Sirius Kade, trader and Earth Intelligence Service deep cover agent, learns that wealthy and powerful leaders from across Mapped Space are vying for control of an alien relic they believe is the key to untold riches – unaware they are being deceived.

Sirius soon finds himself entangled in an interstellar plot to make humanity a cosmic outcast, denying it its place as the newest member of the vast and ancient community that has governed the galaxy for eons.

With mankind's fate in the balance, Sirius must overcome ruthless alien adversaries and deadly human rivals as he seeks to discover the secret of *The Antaran Codex* and safeguard man's future among the stars.

ISBN: 978-0-9874347-9-1

The Riven Stars
by
Stephen Renneberg

**Blistering action. Arresting characters.
A densely plotted epic.
Renneberg aptly portrays strikingly different
worlds ... (in) an exhilarating espionage tale
involving the threat of galactic war.**
– Kirkus Reviews

Earth Intelligence Service agent Sirius Kade is sent to
intercept a mysterious visitor to the Orion Arm from
the remote Cygnus Rim. He must discover why an
alien race humanity has never before encountered
conspires against Earth and its far flung colonies.

While civil war ravages mankind, Sirius discovers old
and new enemies entwined in a sinister scheme of
cosmic proportions. His mission takes him to barbaric
human and oppressive alien worlds before a final
reckoning in the ancient halls of galactic power.

Deceived and betrayed, Sirius is forced to choose
between love and duty as the fate of galactic
civilization is decided.

ISBN: 978-0-9941840-5-4

Made in the USA
San Bernardino, CA
11 August 2019